ONE MORE MESS

ONE MORE MESS

A Novel

04/20/2002

The Siebert Family,
Welcome to my Mess!
I hope you enjoy reading it as much as I enjoyed writing it for you.
Les Stevens

Les E. Stevens

Library of Congress Number: 2001118654
ISBN #: Softcover 1-4010-2957-4

This book was printed in the United States of America.

To order additional copies of this book, contact:
Xlibris Corporation
1-888-7-XLIBRIS
www.Xlibris.com
Orders@Xlibris.com

The author wishes to acknowledge Edward O. Uthman, M.D., for sharing his keen insight into the autopsy process. The author also conveys his indebtedness to his wife, Becky, without whom this book could not have been completed. The novel is dedicated to those who teach and pass along to us a love of learning, to those who work to serve and protect, and to those in the print media who endeavor to keep us informed.

ONE

Each had heard her body and the chair to which they had tied her hit the floor. Now, as they struggled to get past the door they had locked so securely, Luke and Marcus knew that something was horribly wrong. When the door was finally open, it was apparent to them both just how wrong things could be.

"Oh, shit!" Marcus said, as Luke checked her wrist for a pulse.

Neither Luke nor Marcus could possibly know how the girl had died or to what end her death might lead. But they knew trouble when they saw it. And panic set in quickly.

This—this heap on the floor in front of them—this was not part of the plan. Nobody had said anything like this could happen. Murder had never been discussed and this, Luke feared, looked like murder. Their captive was dead. Luke and his partner were deeply involved in something beyond their comprehension.

Since kidnapping was a new trade for them, Luke and Marcus were unacquainted with prescribed and proscribed kidnapping procedures. But they had been smart enough to ask no questions and blindly follow their employer's orders. It paid well to follow orders when they sprang from someone like him.

They had done as they were instructed. They had taken the seventeen-year-old that morning while she was on her way to school. Understandably, she had resisted, kicking and screaming, violently writhing, as they stuffed her into the rear of a stolen van. She was strong, not necessarily athletic. But she had put up a good fight.

She had even bitten Luke, as he pinned her down to the floor of the van. He was trying to quiet her while Marcus jumped behind the wheel and drove away. Luke cursed her and told her he'd kill her. His finger bled badly for a time. But he hadn't meant the threats. He couldn't harm her, or anyone else for that matter. Besides, he had instructions not to. He and Marcus were to nab her, keep her hidden, and wait, perhaps for days, for further instructions.

They had done all these things, first traveling east out of town, before switching to their own vehicle and ditching the stolen van, then doubling back around town to the north. Now they waited with their prize in a solidly built, but rustic cabin near a secluded pond twenty miles west of Jacksonville, Illinois.

No contact with their employer would be coming soon. He had been exact in telling them that. They were never to contact him. He would contact them. The only thing to do was to wait. Trey Cederquist would not be happy.

Since arriving from Kentucky and making the acquaintance of Cederquist, Luke and Marcus had always been generously rewarded with money and alcohol. Up to that point, this had more than made up for the ridicule to which their boss had often subjected them.

But never before had they screwed up this badly and they desperately needed direction from Cederquist. Luke was torn between wanting to hear from him soon, so they could tell him of the girl's death, and wanting to postpone his hearing of it till the last possible moment. Cederquist had always been quick to kill the messenger. Luke had seen this side of him often and did not wish to be the target of his anger again.

Thoughts of a murder charge stuck in Luke's mind. Manslaughter, at the least, he thought. They could not be held responsible for the girl's death, could they? How could this be happening? They had done nothing to cause her anything but some discomfort. Her hands were tied. Her mouth was gagged. A pillowcase had been placed loosely over her head, and for only a short time. She had been placed in a chair, tied about her waist, tied also by her hands and legs to the chair, and left in a small, dark room behind a locked door. People don't die from this.

Luke felt again for a pulse, this time at her neck. She was hot to the touch. So much so that he instinctively pulled his hand away.

"What'd you do to her, Luke?" the other asked.

"What do you mean, 'What'd I do to her?' I didn't do anything to her, you idiot."

"You did something, Luke. She's dead. You said you'd kill her. I heard you."

Luke was yelling now.

"I told you I didn't do anything to her, Marcus. When did I have time to do anything to her? You been here all the time. I been in the other room with you or outside the whole damn time we been here."

Marcus was crying uncontrollably. He lunged at Luke and tried to push him, his hand reaching for Luke's chest.

"You killed her, Luke!" he screamed.

Luke countered Marcus' movement by stepping quickly to his left and unloading with a powerful punch to Marcus' head. Marcus lay motionless on the floor beside the girl. He wasn't dead, but Luke was confident that Marcus would not stir for several minutes.

"Great! That's all I need," Luke said, rocking back against the wall and sliding to the floor.

Dinner for four in Springfield. They had done this often. Gary McLean, his wife, Lisa, her sister and brother-in-law drove the very familiar and not-particularly-interesting thirty-five miles to the state's capital to shop or eat. The trip had long before become boring for Gary, but he loved his wife and did not hate her sister. Lisa's brother-in-law was a nice guy, but not enough of a conversationalist to make Interstate 72 any more than a painfully flat, long stretch of pavement. Gary had suggested, as he almost always did, that the foursome take the old, two-lane blacktop to Springfield.

4-STEV

"More turns, more hills, more to see, more character," he argued.

As usual, he was outnumbered. The group moved smoothly along I-72. As the two couples moved eastward toward the city Lincoln called home, the events of his day replayed in Gary's mind.

Gary decided to tell the others about his day at school. It had been a typical school day in many ways. The students entered his classroom, not particularly interested in what Gary had to offer. Most, however, were willing to give him their token attention for at least part of their allotted class time, but only that, for it was Friday and late in the term, after all. He had tried, as he did everyday, to give them their parents' money's worth, entertaining them, cajoling them, begging them to care half as much as he did about Shakespeare, Twain, or Hemingway.

One class, in particular, had been somewhat open to his efforts. There had been some lively discussion about Tom Joad and his "I'll be there" speech, near the end of *The Grapes of Wrath*. But the most enlightening event of the session had come very nearly to the end, when he asked the class about a student who was not there.

"Where is Amanda today?" he had asked. "She usually has something interesting to say when we get into these discussions. Too bad she's not here today."

"Who cares?" one boy asked.

"Don't be such a jerk, Mark," was Melissa's comeback. Melissa was Amanda's best friend.

"I haven't seen her all day, Mr. McLean," another girl remarked.

"That's unusual. She's hardly ever absent," Gary said.

McLean was, however, less curious about Amanda's absence than he was about the next question from Mark Bolen. "What do you care?"

"What do you mean, Mark?" Gary responded. "I care about all you guys. Does that surprise you?"

Apparently it did. Mark was convinced, as were so many of his peers, that teachers did not care about the students they taught.

Gary had run into this before. Thirteen years of teaching had prepared him for the discussion that followed. It frustrated him. He heard the students complain about how their parents did not care. Their teachers did not care. Nobody cared. Gary was convinced that this was, of course, totally untrue. He knew of teachers, most teachers, practically all teachers, who cared and tried very hard to show their concern for their students. But, for whatever reason, the message was not getting through.

"Why do you care?" Lisa's sister, Kim, asked, when Gary recalled these events, his attempt to inject some life into their trek to Springfield.

Lisa was glad to hear some conversation, finally. She had been in the house all week with Maddie and Steve, the couple's four-year-old twins. She had looked forward to hearing adults speak. It was finally here and, although she and her husband of eleven years had discussed these issues before, dozens of times, she was not going to let the chance to hear articulate, adult conversation slip away.

"Yes, Gary, why do you care?" she echoed, giving her husband his cue.

Gary looked at Kim's husband, Stan, as if to say, "Your turn." Stan was too busy surveying the nondescript landscape and missed his turn. Too bad, Gary thought.

"I guess I'll just have to get on my soapbox again. Whew! Twice in one day," Gary exaggerated. Actually, Gary relished these opportunities to witness for himself and his fellow educators, even if it was to his own wife and her simple-minded sister.

"You can't work with these kids and not care, Kim," he began again. "I am sure there are teachers who have temporarily lost track of what got them into teaching, but we all care. When I'm home with Lisa and the twins and we hear a siren, my first thoughts are of my students. 'I hope they're okay,' I think." He paused. "The sad thing is that they find that so hard to believe."

Lisa yawned. She had heard this speech so many times before. At least it was coming from an adult's mouth.

Kim thought about what her brother-in-law had just said. Not that many years out of school herself, she had not bothered to think much about this previously. She understood, she guessed.

Stan gazed out the window, still oblivious to the whole conversation. He had heard it, but had not listened, had not cared.

Gary drove on and was happy he heard no sirens.

Amanda Hayes's mother paced the floor of her kitchen worriedly. The school had called that morning, asking about her daughter's absence. She had learned of this only when she had arrived home from work and checked the answering machine. The school attendance monitor had explained on the taped message that they had no work number for her and that her husband could not be reached at Cederquist Industries. Margot Hayes immediately checked Amanda's room. She was not there. Perhaps she had become ill after her mother left for work this morning, Margot thought. It was five forty-five now. Where could she be?

She would not skip school. Margot was sure of this, despite the fact that Amanda had a new boyfriend. Margot and her husband, Ben, knew little of this young man and Amanda had been more secretive than usual. Perhaps she was getting more serious this time. This had concerned Margot and her husband. But Margot was sure that Keith had nothing to do with her absence from school.

At least Amanda had not been in the funk she had experienced for several months the previous year. No, it would not be in character for Amanda to ditch class. She was a good student with a love for learning, although she was impatient for high school to end, so she could study at the University of Illinois two falls hence.

Ben would arrive home shortly and Margot was hoping that Amanda would precede him with an explanation for her absence. Her husband had seemed to have a lot on his mind lately and she did not want to concern him with whatever Amanda was up to if it were not necessary. Business was a priority with Ben and he expected Margot to handle the home, including their daughter's upbringing.

Supper was not going to prepare itself, so Margot got to work quickly, trying hard not to worry. Amanda would be home soon, Margot hoped, eager to help set the table but careful not to tell her mother too much about the new boy in her life.

Max Jansen gulped his coffee, propped his feet up on the desk next to his computer terminal, and settled in for a long night in the newsroom of the *Capital City Times*. This job was getting him nowhere.

Not much was going on in Springfield or the surrounding area that was newsworthy, at least not in Max's judgment. The governor was doing a reasonable job of keeping his nose clean and out of the public's watchful eye.

The legislature had never been of much interest to Max and Springfield's municipal government was carefully walking the line between serving the people of Springfield and upsetting any large block of the voting public. Crime was always a favorite of Max's, but his editors would rarely assign him to any story concerning a major fracture of the Springfield or Illinois criminal codes. Violent crime was never assigned to Max, to his chagrin. Anyway, Max often rationalized, the perps in Central Illinois lacked imagination.

His uninspired journalistic skills and jaded outlook had conspired to impede his escape from his current position with the newspaper, which called for him to sit nightly, listening to the police scanner. He monitored the ten o'clock television news, and half-wished he had taken the position with a Chicago weekly newspaper a few years back.

Now, however, he had, himself, begun to doubt his abilities. His graying temples betrayed his age. Slightly overweight, he wondered, first, if he still had the physical stamina required for the necessary legwork to cover a major story and, secondly, if he had the investigatory skills to uncover the truth in a headline maker.

His professional juices, all but dried up years earlier, he had long ago stopped hoping for that prize-winning story that, for some, defines a newspaperman's career. Actually, he had not stopped hoping, so much as he had stopped believing such a story would ever come along. Max was putting in his time, waiting for retirement. The sad fact was that he was only forty-eight, too young, it seemed, to be thinking about selling the house and moving to Florida.

And it did not really matter what Max thought. The editors of the *Times* were convinced someone else, someone on the way up the journalistic ladder, could better handle these hot stories. Max would have to chase the occasional ambulance and settle for the tamer, more pedestrian fare that came across his scanner. Max Jansen was not a shining star and he knew it. Investigative reporting had once been a romantic aspiration of a younger, hungrier Max Jansen.

Max longed for the chance to prove he had it, but also feared he might fail miserably if given the chance. Perhaps it was better to leave the question unasked, protecting his right to speculation and uncertainty. Perhaps this fear of failure was also at the heart of the problems that he seemed to be having with Meg, as well. He'd have to think about that.

"I'm outta here," L.J. Stiles, Chief of Detectives for the Jacksonville Police Department, said to the dispatcher.

"Goodnight, Lieutenant," came the dispatcher's response.

"Don't let 'em rouse any bad guys tonight, Chuck. I need some rest this weekend."

Chuck smiled back, admiringly. Lieutenant L.J. Stiles was an admirable man. Six-feet-three, two hundred pounds, and sharply dressed, he looked to be the prototype lead investigator. Jacksonville was lucky to have had him in their employ for so long, luckier still to have hung on to him in the midst of a barrage of offers from Springfield, Bloomington, Peoria, the Secretary of State's police, even an inquiry some years earlier from the FBI. But Stiles had stayed put and would, most likely, continue to do so.

If ever there were a time when Stiles might be wooed away from Jacksonville, however, it was now. Months of investigation had culminated recently in a lengthy trial and conviction in a racially charged case, which had divided the city and taken its toll on Stiles. His work on the case had, as always, been exemplary. But Stiles had, for the first time in his career with the JPD, taken some heavy criticism from factions within the community.

Compounding his troubles was the fact that the city's illegal drug problems would not go away. The department had taken heat for its inability to stop the flow of cannabis and there was an increased presence of methamphetamines in the area, which soured the public on law enforcement, in general, and haunted Stiles as Chief of Detectives, in particular.

Were it not for the loyalty he felt for his fellow officers and to Stella Grimes, he might consider a change. Stella was not Stiles' secretary. But he and Stella both acted as though she were. She was a great assistant, at any rate, and he missed her while she was away for an extended stay with her daughter's family following a grandson's graduation.

As he exited the station and approached his unmarked car at the end of the parking lot, Stiles recalled the long hours he had put into the recent case. The media circus that came with such cases and the tension the town had experienced for over a year were hard to forget. At least, there had been a conviction, he thought. Perhaps, now, life would return to normal.

Almost immediately another thought came to mind. What's so great about "normal?" Stiles lived alone, had done so since his wife took their two daughters and left him three years ago. While Stiles was happy to be leaving the station, he was in no hurry to return home. He was tired, but would once again put off opening the door to a small, empty apartment for a while longer.

He decided he was hungry, having only moments earlier convinced himself at the station that he was not. He picked one of many fast food restaurants on Morton Avenue, opting to drive through. As instructed by a youthful, squeaking voice, over the drive-through intercom, Stiles pulled up to the pick-up window and paid for his meal. He proceeded to park at the end of the restaurant's lot, turned on the re-broadcast of the Jacksonville High School baseball team's game on one of the local radio stations, and tried to enjoy his supper.

A former classmate of his older daughter struck out on a called third strike to end the team's half of the sixth inning and Stiles found himself where he had so often, thinking of his children, remembering, regretting.

One has only so much of oneself to give, Stiles had discovered. If he gives all that is required to successfully perform the duties of Chief of Detectives, even in a community of twenty thousand, little is left over for himself or for family. The demands of his job and his desire to do it right had cost him his family. Stiles could resign himself to the realities of that situation. But the hurt still lingered and a tear still found its way to the surface and slowly ran down the length of his taut cheek.

"I'll have another," Ben Hayes said to the attractive, leggy barmaid.

She was dressed in black stockings, a short black skirt, and a white half-shirt, tied in a bow, exposing her tiny waistline. She responded with a wink and a smile. The bar was about half filled with a diverse clientele, part professional, part blue collar. The group had a common goal, unwind, get numb, put work aside for forty-eight hours. The crowd would swell and grow noticeably younger very soon and Ben was not interested in staying much longer. He had often stopped at the motel lounge on his way home from work, but with greater frequency in the past year, it seemed.

A strong hand on his left shoulder snapped Ben to attention, as Marshall Cederquist, Jr. slid into the seat next to Ben.

"How you doing, Ben? Mind if I join you?" Cederquist asked.

"Be my guest, Marshall," Ben responded.

Cederquist offered to buy a drink, but the barmaid was just getting around to serving Ben his beer. After thanking Cederquist for his offer, Ben shoved a ten-dollar bill at the barmaid and added what he knew Cederquist would have ordered for himself.

"Give Mr. Cederquist a bourbon and ginger ale, Trina. And don't bring me any change."

"Thanks, Ben," she said.

"Thanks, Ben. I'll get the next one," Cederquist said.

Employer and long-time employee, sharing a drink after a hard week at work. It looked, on the surface, like a harmonious pairing. The two men, who had known each other for over twenty years, shared the next twenty minutes, smiling, making small talk, each as uncomfortable as he had been in recent memory.

"Well, Ben," Cederquist said finally, "how's that boy of mine treating you these days?"

"Just fine," Ben replied, reluctant to alarm Cederquist of the feelings Ben had about the younger Cederquist. He went on, too much so Ben worried, about monthly sales figures and quotas his department had met, in the hopes of satisfying Cederquist.

"Has he gotten over my putting you in charge of international sales, yet?"

Hayes winced slightly, not wanting to appear ungrateful for the recent promotion. Still, Ben shook his head.

"You had to know that would piss him off, Marshall."

"Yeah, but he's got to get used to it sooner or later, Ben. You deserve to head that division."

Ben thought of so many things that he couldn't tell Cederquist. "It'll be okay," he said, finally.

"Well, has he given you any particular grief lately, Ben?"

"Nah," Ben replied, trying to sound convincing.

In fact, Trey Cederquist had given him plenty of trouble over the years and especially so lately.

"Ben," Cederquist said, pausing, "you'd tell me if Trey were up to something he ought not be doing; wouldn't you? I mean something that might hurt the company?"

Before Ben could answer, Cederquist interrupted.

"I don't mean the kind of things Trey has always brought upon himself, or his family, or the company in the past. I know he's no angel. Lord knows, I've cleaned up more than my share of Trey's messes. I mean 'real' trouble."

Ben looked Cederquist squarely in the eye and he lied.

"Sure I would, Marshall."

"Good," Cederquist said, reassured. "Now, let me buy you that drink I owe you."

"No, thanks. I've got to get home. Margot and Amanda are waiting with supper." And with that, Ben Hayes turned quickly and headed for the door.

Good man, Cederquist thought, guiltily.

Keith Utterback exited Interstate 72 and drove west past the Jacksonville Correctional Center and into the town of Jacksonville. About to complete his first year at the community college in Springfield, he was anxious for summer to arrive. He was hopeful of earning some money at the job he had secured for himself at the Nestle factory in the northwest corner of town and of spending lots of time with his new girlfriend, Amanda Hayes.

He pulled his pickup truck into the lot at Huck's, a gas station and convenience store on Morton Avenue. He quickly dialed the number. The phone rang only once before Margot Hayes picked up.

"Mrs. Hayes?"

"Yes. Who is this?"

"Keith Utterback, Mrs. Hayes. I'm calling for Amanda."

"She's not here, Keith. I was hoping to hear from her. Have you seen her today?"

"No, ma'am. I've been in Springfield at classes all day. Besides, Amanda had school today, too."

"But she wasn't at school today, Keith. I was hoping you had seen her. I know she's been seeing someone lately and I'm assuming that's you."

Keith was alarmed now.

"She wasn't at school at all today?" he asked.

"No. Are you sure you haven't seen her?"

"Yes," Keith said, trying not to sound resentful. "I haven't seen her since late last night. I dropped her off after she got off work, around eleven fifteen."

Cautiously Keith continued, "Mrs. Hayes, you're saying that Amanda didn't go to school today and she hasn't been home either?"

"Yes, that's right. She was showering this morning when I left for work. Do you have any idea where she could be, Keith? I've called all her friends that I know of. I couldn't call you because she hadn't given us your name."

"No, Mrs. Hayes. I haven't seen her. But I'll look around," he told her, hanging up.

He had never met Margot Hayes. But he heard the concern in her voice. It was unmistakable and he grew more concerned as he called Melissa Schumacher's home, only to learn that Melissa was out looking for Amanda herself. He had hoped that the two were together somewhere. Melissa's mother promised to have Melissa or Amanda call when they turned up, contacting either Amanda's mother or Keith. His parents had insisted on his having a cellular phone in his truck, as he was on the road a lot, traveling the distance from home to the Springfield campus of Lincoln Land Community College, sometimes during inclement weather throughout the school year. He dictated the number to Mrs. Schumacher one more time and hung up quickly, running to the truck.

It took Keith only a few short minutes to locate Melissa at the McDonald's just up the street. She saw his pick-up and came running, climbing into the seat next to him as she pulled her long, blond hair back from her face.

"I can't find Amanda anywhere, Keith. No one has seen her all day. Do you have any idea where she could be? I'm worried."

"No." He didn't have a clue about where Amanda might be and was worried, too.

Keith went on to explain all he had told Amanda's mother. Keith and Melissa, not the best of friends and connected previously only by their common affection for Amanda Hayes, were suddenly a team.

Marshall Cederquist III, Trey, entered Springfield at around eleven o'clock on the Sixth Street exit at the junction of Routes 72 and 55. A right on Stevenson Drive put him in proximity of his first destination of the evening, Deja Vu, a gentleman's club featuring topless dancers working hard at being eye candy for their clientele. Trey Cederquist was on the prowl.

Lately, Jacksonville had held little interest for Cederquist. From his narrow perspective, Trey had long ago conquered all of the available, desirable women of Jacksonville. A more objective view, however, suggested that the women of Jacksonville had communicated to one another the dangers of becoming involved with Trey Cederquist. The smart ones stayed away.

Trey parked his BMW diagonally in two adjacent parking spaces, as was his habit. Best car on the lot, he thought. Trey saw the Beamer, and the Lexus parked at home, as reflections of himself, a cut above all others. No one else quite stood up to the Trey standard.

"How ya doin', my man?" Cederquist asked a beefy man at the door of the establishment. The man's job skills and duties were obvious, but Trey treated him like a servant, pushing a five-dollar bill into the man's hand. There was no reason to tip him, but it made Trey feel important.

The man at the door pocketed the five and shook his head in disgust.

Happens every time the jerk comes in here, he thought. If it makes him feel like a big shot, so be it.

Men like Trey are seldom kind without motive. The man, however, had no favors to give anybody, a fact that Trey might or might not discover at some point in the future. It mattered not to the man at the door.

Once inside, Trey dove into the crowd, one subtle difference between him and the rest of the male patrons. While every other man there was all eyes, taking in all they could of the visual feast Deja Vu had to offer, Trey went about the business of being seen. He smiled and winked his way across the room, waving to an acquaintance, placing his hand on the bare shoulder of one of the dancers he knew.

Trey was dressed casually, but richly, a crested sweater shirt over khaki's and expensive loafers. His gold watch was hard to miss. He liked to be seen and dressed in such a way that it was hard not to notice, at the very least, that he had money. Money translates into power, a tool that Trey simultaneously displayed and craved. "Show them you have it, and it grows," his thinking went.

"Usual, Mikey," Trey said to the man behind a bar where no alcohol was served.

Mike Lansing pushed aside his dislike, poured a glass of orange juice, and greeted Cederquist.

"There you go, Mr. Cederquist."

Trey liked Lansing, who always showed Trey the proper respect. Not enough people did that. Certainly not the Ben Hayes's of the world.

The sonofabitch, Cederquist thought.

Trey tried to shake himself off a sore subject and convinced himself once again that he would enjoy himself tonight. Ben Hayes would find out soon enough who the better man was. Trey would see to that.

"Where's Cheryl, Mikey?" as Mike began to look around, not wishing to find the dancer to whom Cederquist had referred.

God, I hate it when he calls me 'Mikey,' Lansing thought.

"Don't know, sir. I haven't seen her for about an hour or so. She must be busy."

"Bitch still love me, Mikey?" Trey asked, winking.

"They're all in love with you, Mr. Cederquist," Lansing said, as he rearranged coasters, which did not need rearranging.

Cederquist was up and out of his chair, moving toward the stage, finally aware of the on-going show.

"Gotta go, Mikey. Things to see, people to do," Cederquist said smugly and laughed as he left a five on the bar.

"Boy, I hate that guy," Lansing said to himself, once the man was out of earshot.

As the music grew more intense, Cederquist seated himself where he could be seen.

By 12:40 a.m. Cederquist was quickly out of Springfield and doing eighty miles an hour on the road back to Jacksonville, a hometown which had come to mean little to him. It never had, he felt, had much to offer, aside from what Cederquist Industries brought his way and what being the son of one of its major players afforded him.

His mind suddenly drifted back to Ben Hayes and the recent exchanges the two men had been having. The nerve of this old man, suggesting that what he thought he knew somehow gave Hayes leverage in their old and bitter feud.

When Ben had stumbled upon Trey's extracurricular activities over a year earlier, Trey had been forced to threaten Ben. And Trey had played his Amanda card. He had threatened the girl and knew he could make use of her at any time. She'd be his handle on Ben.

Matters at home, concerns about his daughter, Trey surmised, had kept Hayes quiet and compliant for several months. Ben, at any rate, had been consumed with something away from work. Perhaps the daughter had done nothing to keep her father away from Trey and his affairs. But things had worked out somehow. And Trey was sure the girl had kept her mouth shut.

Recently, however, Ben was at it again. Ben had, it seemed to Trey, some new confidence and was balking at nearly every command Trey sent Hayes's way.

Then there was the promotion. Trey's father had bypassed Trey and given Hayes new powers at Cederquist Industries. Powers that meant Hayes, on certain projects, no longer had to confer with Trey before acting. This infuriated Trey and probably explained the bravado Hayes occasionally displayed. Hayes had even been so bold, a week or so ago, as to threaten Trey with telling the elder Cederquist what Ben had seen a year earlier if Trey did not "back off."

"That son of a bitch will think twice before he threatens me again," Trey said to the empty passenger seat. He laughed aloud and jammed the accelerator to the floor.

Trey had planned on leaving Luke and Marcus on their own until Sunday morning. But he was anxious to know that all had gone well and to see Amanda. He intended to frighten her, regain a measure of control over her, and then send her on her way with instructions to keep her mouth shut. He trusted her to hold her tongue, for she had done so previously where Trey Cederquist was concerned. In the future, if Trey deemed it necessary, he merely had to pull her string and she could be used to pressure her father into laying off of Trey. At least, that was the way it was supposed to work. He was finding Ben Hayes more troublesome lately and wanted some insurance against Hayes's meddling.

Now Trey decided he would pay a visit to the cabin to check on the boys and their prize. He knew that they had been successful in their captive-taking the previous morning. He had called the school asking for Amanda, allowing the call-taker to think he was her father. When he was told she was absent, he quickly hung up. He was assuming that all had gone as he had planned it and smiled at the thought of Ben Hayes, looking frantically for his daughter.

Hell, Trey thought, maybe Amanda and I can revive some old memories tonight. He had enjoyed their first encounter, almost a year earlier. Trey always enjoyed it more when they resisted.

"Yes, sir," Cederquist howled. "We may just have us some fun yet tonight."

Dinner had been uneventful. Once Gary had become convinced he had made his case, proving once and for all that teachers cared more about their students than the students could possibly imagine, he had managed to behave himself. Not once had he made fun of his wife's sister or her husband. And he had even engaged Stan in conversation about Stan's job. This was not an easy thing to do, Gary had long ago concluded.

Kim and her husband were leaving in the morning for a week's vacation, just in time for the girls' parents to arrive for a few days. Gary looked forward to having Lisa and her parents to himself. Sharing them with Kim complicated matters somehow and Gary often resented that.

He sat now on the edge of their bed, eagerly awaiting his wife's emergence from the bathroom. As she had each night since they had married, Lisa McLean came out of the bathroom, wearing only her panties. She tiptoed across the carpeted floor toward their bed, her hair pulled to one side, held by an elastic band.

"You were nice tonight," Lisa said as she crawled into bed opposite Gary. She pulled the covers up around her ears and added, "I guess."

"So, this is the thanks I get?" Gary asked, tugging playfully at the comforter, which hid Lisa's ample, but lithe body from his view.

"You weren't that nice, Gary," she responded, clutching the edge of the blanket with both hands. She was being somewhat playful herself, but there would be no lovemaking at the McLean home tonight. She was tired, had said so earlier, and Gary knew the signals all too well.

Nevertheless, he moved closer, leaning on his elbow, cradling his chin in her neck, her back turned away from him as she lay on her side. His hand moved over her hip and down her thigh as he whispered in her ear.

"Lisa," he said playfully, his lips touching her ear, "it's been four days."

"Gary, it's been four days for me, too. What's your point?" Lisa asked over her shoulder, the smile on her face detectable in the moonlight.

How could he respond to such logic? No words came to mind for one who so infrequently found himself at a loss for words. He tried not to be hurt.

"Lisa," he said now, lying flat on his back, staring at the ceiling. "Do you—"

"Of course, I love you, Gary," she interrupted. "I'm just too tired to be horny tonight."

Victory and defeat. In one sleepy sentence, Lisa had been able to do what few other women could do, lift a man to new heights and slam him to the ground—all with one sentence.

Yes, Gary thought. This is a remarkable woman.

He'd be content, he told himself, to lay beside this special woman and count his blessings.

"Good night, Lisa."

"Good night, John-Boy," she quipped. "Now, get some sleep. The twins will be up before they need to be and Mom and Dad get here around noon."

She rolled over quickly and kissed him lightly on the cheek.

Luke paced the floor, as he had since he and Marcus had discovered that they had a huge problem, which was not going to go away. Marcus lay on an old couch, shifting his weight and trying in vain to forget that the body of seventeen-year-old Amanda Hayes lay just down the hall on the floor where she had fallen. Marcus' head still throbbed from the blow given him by Luke. They were both sickened by the thought of her body and of arrest and imprisonment.

"Your held still hurtin', Marcus?"

"Of course, it is, Luke. What'd you go an' hit me for, anyway?"

"Why'd you come chargin' at me, you dipstick? Sayin' all those things about me? Like I had somethin' to do with her dyin'."

"Well, what happened to her, then? If you didn't do nothin', how'd she die? Tell me that, will ya?"

"Shut up, Marcus. You don't know what you're talkin' 'bout."

"Well, I know this, Luke. Trey is gonna shit nails when he finds out. I don't wanna think about what he's gonna do to us," Marcus said, shaking his head.

"Yeah, I know, Marcus. Been thinking about that."

He hesitated.

"Think maybe we oughta get outta here 'fore he comes. Hit the road. Whatcha think?"

It took awhile for Marcus to comprehend, until he finally asked, "Where would we go, Luke?"

Marcus now was sitting upright on the edge of the couch.

"Montana," Luke said wistfully. "I always wanted to go there."

He grew quiet and stared blankly at the darkness outside the single window of the cabin's front room. Both men were tired. It had been a long day and there was no end in sight.

Suddenly, headlights bounced along the dirt road, which wound its way around a small lake and led to the cabin. The lights came to a halt, fifty paces from the front door, and dimmed before they burned out all together.

"Get up, Marcus," Luke said. "It's Trey."

Two a.m. and Gary still lay awake, perhaps too tired to sleep.

"Relax," he told himself out loud, but not so loud as to awaken Lisa. She had worked hard all week and was looking forward to her parents' visit. He was sure she had spent most of the previous day cleaning and preparing the guestroom for their stay.

He, too, had worked hard. While he was convinced that Lisa would never fully appreciate how hard he worked at his teaching, he reminded himself that he was doing what he loved, what he had always wanted to do. Meanwhile, Lisa had put her career on hold until the twins would start school. She loved her family, but Gary knew she looked forward to returning to her career, too. Soon she would begin a search for work in one of the area's many banks, preferably in Jacksonville.

Gary lay in bed thinking of the career choices they had made for themselves. While Gary had become used to having Lisa at home, he understood her desire to jump-start her career, even if hers didn't involve teenagers.

Suddenly, Gary was aware of a siren's wail in the distance.

TWO

Gary awoke around seven-thirty, Saturday morning from a relatively restful five hours of sleep, which had followed much tossing and turning. The sun was up and the sky was clear. The fresh air he forced through his lungs would serve him well and Gary ambled into his front yard expectantly.

April 26 promised to be a beautiful day. The two-story home he and his wife had purchased three years earlier looked magnificent to Gary. He liked the line of it, the way the home was framed by the spectacular trees surrounding it, and the way in which the two-car garage was halfway tucked in behind the right side of the house.

Gary wanted to get the house and yard in order before his in-laws arrived. So he planned to get right to work on the dozen-or-so odd jobs he had listed for himself earlier that week. The first of these jobs involved backing the car out of the garage, so he could get to some of the lawn and garden tools he planned to use that morning. He got into the family's Dodge Caravan and immediately decided that he should add cleaning the car's interior to his list. The twins had really made a mess of the back of the vehicle and he told himself he would have to have a serious talk with them. He smiled at the prospect of lecturing the two four-year-olds on the condition of the van's interior.

Once he had the car's carpet vacuumed and the windows cleaned, Gary set about wiping the dash and decided to turn on the radio. No news of the siren he thought he'd heard in the early hours of the morning. The local radio station to which he listened regularly was broadcasting the news. But there was no mention of activities warranting a siren in the middle of the night. Perhaps he had only dreamed of hearing one.

As he completed his work in the car, he turned the radio off and began again to gather the lawn and garden tools. He would need them to have an excuse to be outside and, hence, avoid being drawn into Lisa's web. If she saw him dawdling about in the yard, she would have him helping her straighten the house's interior, as she perfected their home for her parents' arrival.

"How you doing today, Gary," a neighbor hollered across the fence that separated the McLean's yard from the Welch's next door.

"Fine, John. How are you?'

"Just fine. Finishing my walk. Looks like you're a busy man this morning. What could you possibly be doing with all those tools? Your lawn already looks great, as always."

"Oh, I've got a little work to do around these shrubs and Lisa bought some plants I'm going to set out later this morning."

Gary leaned over slightly, cupping his hand to one side of his mouth.

"I also have to stay busy out here for a couple of hours. Lisa's folks are coming in today around noon and I've learned it's best to stay out of her way when she's getting the house ready for her mother's white glove test."

"How thoughtful of you, Gary," his smiling neighbor said.

John Welch was much older than Gary, having recently retired; but he remembered well his own efforts to stay busy outside while his wife worked inside on many a Saturday morning. Nowadays, he contented himself with the notion that their children worked tirelessly in anticipation of their visits to see their grandchildren. Age had at least one advantage, he had concluded. Still, John envied Gary and Lisa.

"Well, Gary, if you run out of things to do this morning and still want to stay out of Lisa's way, you just holler. I'll see if there is anything over here we could have you do."

The two neighbors laughed, as they often had since Gary and

Lisa had moved into the neighborhood. Gary looked forward to growing old with Lisa as the Welch's had done, so happily.

Gary went back to work as John went into his home, leaving Gary to his thoughts. As he raked around the base of the shrubs in front of their home, Gary thought about the up-coming final exams and planned a new English course in his head. He was trying to organize his presentation to his principal, which he planned to make the following week.

Soon Gary was busy at the side of the garage nearest the rear of the home. An hour had passed since he had left Lisa inside. She had been trying to help the twins clean their room when he left them. He wondered how much further she had gone in her preparations for her parents' two-day stay. He was confident that she had all the help she needed in the two children. He smiled as he envisioned Maddie and Steve trying to help their mother put the house in order. One day soon, Steve would be joining him in the yard. The thought broadened the smile on Gary's face.

"Gary, you have a phone call," Lisa interrupted from the back porch.

"Who is it?"

Lisa responded with an exaggerated shrug, suggesting that she had no idea who was calling. "It's a girl," she whispered, as he neared the back steps.

She paused for effect, raising her chin to look down her nose at him as he ascended the steps.

"Anything you need to tell me, dear?" she said, obviously enjoying the tease.

Gary was quick to pick up the game. "Gee, Lisa. I don't know. I told Scarlet not to call me at home."

Gary wiped his feet on the worn welcome mat outside the back door. He brushed past Lisa as the screen door swung shut behind him. The phone lay on its side next to the microwave. Gary picked it up and greeted the caller.

Melissa was obviously upset.

"Mr. McLean? This is Melissa Schumacher. I'm sorry to bother you, but I didn't know who else to call."

"What's wrong, Melissa? I can tell something's bothering you."

"It's Amanda."

Goddamn siren, Gary thought.

"What's happened, Melissa. Did something happen to Amanda?"

"I don't know," Melissa said, obviously fighting back tears.

Gary was confused momentarily.

"She's gone, Mr. McLean. No one has seen her. Her parents are worried. I looked everywhere for her last night. Me and her boyfriend talked to all our friends last night. I've made I don't know how many calls. No one knows anything."

"Has anyone called the police?"

"Mrs. Hayes just told me she was going up to the police station to report her missing. I think she had called them last night, when she realized Amanda hadn't been to school or reported to work at the bagel shop."

"Well, I don't know what I can do to help, Melissa. If you think of something, call me back. I'll call her parents in a little while to see if there's been any news. If you hear anything, please, call me back."

With that, Gary hung up. Lisa had just begun to tune into her husband's end of the conversation when she noticed the concern on his face. "What's wrong, hon?"

"One of my students is missing. She wasn't in school yesterday and no one's seen her."

After some consideration Lisa decided to point out what had just occurred to her. "Well, you must feel pretty good, Gary," she said with a half-smile.

"Huh?" a confused Gary responded.

"Now you know that at least some of your students know you care. That's gotta make you feel good."

He was too worried to enjoy the revelation.

Startled by sunlight through a torn curtain, Trey Cederquist awoke suddenly. He reoriented himself, but was disappointed that the nightmare Luke and Marcus had presented him the previous evening had not been a dream.

With reluctance, he replayed the events following his arrival at the cabin several hours before.

"What's happenin', boys?" he asked as he pushed the door open and banged a quart of beer down on the table, causing the bottle to overflow slightly.

Neither Luke nor Marcus answered.

"I said, 'What's goin' on?'" Trey repeated, obviously annoyed.

Again, neither responded for several seconds, until Luke spoke, haltingly.

"Trey, we got a problem."

"Problem?" Trey said, looking around the room for some further indication of trouble. "What problem? You got my girl, right?"

"We got her, Trey," Marcus said. He repeated the words, annoying Luke.

"So, if you got the girl, what's the problem?"

Luke and Marcus each gave the other a predictable well-you-tell-him look. Then Luke decided to get it over with.

"She's dead, Trey. I don't know what happened. We was just sittin' here, Trey, and we heard this thump and we went down the hall and unlocked the door. She was dead."

Trey had been drinking on his way back from Springfield, but he wasn't drunk. Perhaps fatigue played a role in Trey's inability to recognize the true import of Luke's words. At any rate, Trey did not respond in the predictable way, at least not immediately.

"Dead?" Trey said, almost in a whisper, as he finally looked up to meet Luke's gaze. Marcus has staring first at the floor and then the ceiling. "You're tellin' me she's dead?"

"That's right, boss. She's dead an' we ain't got no clue about what caused it," Luke volunteered.

"How the hell can she be dead?" Trey shouted, now growing angry, as the pair feared and knew he would. "I wanna know what the fuck happened, Luke. Now tell me what happened. Are you sure? Did you check for a pulse? If you're wrong about this, goddamn it, I'll kill you," Trey rambled, recognizing the enormity of the problem he was facing.

"How long ago'd this happen, Luke?" firing questions now faster than Luke could respond even had he known the answers. "Where is she?" Trey asked before finally waiting for a response.

"Back there, Trey, in the bedroom on the right," Luke said.

They followed Cederquist down the short hallway and into the room where the body of Amanda Hayes lay, still tied to the chair at her feet and one of her hands. Luke had untied the other hand in the hopes that it might reveal a pulse.

"We picked her up, just like you said, Trey," Marcus began. "It went just like you said it would. Weren't nobody around at that intersection. I pulled up close to her and Luke, he jumped out the van and grabbed her 'fore she knew what hit her."

Trey was only half-listening, while Marcus rambled on.

"Luke threw her in the back of the van and jumped on her. She was kicking and screaming an' she bit him. Made him bleed. Show him, Luke. Show him your finger."

Luke's response was a look in Marcus' direction, which said, "Shut up."

Marcus, however, was just warming up.

"She bit him good, Trey. And he told her he'd kill her. Luke musta done somethin', Trey," Marcus said, moving to the other side of Trey Cederquist, keeping him between his partner and himself.

"Goddamn you, Marcus, I told you I didn't do nothin' to her," was all Luke could muster.

Trey was in Luke's face now.

"Did you kill 'er, Luke?" Cederquist asked, his voice breaking.

"No, Trey; I didn't lay a hand on her. I swear."

"Then what the hell happened? 'Cause, she's dead, goddamnit," Trey screamed.

He continued, "What the hell am I supposed to do now, boys? Clean up your mess?" He massaged his aching head with both hands. "Goddamnit, I thought I could trust you morons to get this done right."

Trey shook his head. "Why the hell did I trust these guys?" he asked himself out loud.

During the next few minutes, Trey began to think more rationally, attempting to assess the damage. Had anyone seen them take her? Were they sure no one had noticed? Nothing had been reported over the radio or TV? What time had they picked her up? Had they wiped the stolen vehicle clean? No prints from the two of them or from the girl? Were they sure? They had to be sure.

The pair assured him that they had looked carefully. No cars were in the vicinity. There were no passers-by; the view from the homes across the street was obstructed by the stolen van, a full-size customized Ford, but older and not flashy, so as not to attract too much attention.

They were sure they had not been seen and complimented Trey on the development of a successful plan, trying to forget that it really didn't matter anymore.

"Listen, you guys," Trey said. "You're the one's with your butts hangin' out on this. You gotta get rid of her."

Trey was not thinking clearly and was, at first, perfectly happy to allow these bunglers to dump the girl's body without discussion or reminders of what not to do, lest they arouse suspicion. He was quick to re-think the problem, however, and knew that these two could not be left to their own devices on such an important task.

He would have to come up with a plan. He told himself he was regaining his equilibrium steadily, for he knew he would come up with one that would work. He didn't know what he would have the boys do. But he knew that it must be, would be them, and not him, who would dump the girl's body. They would take the hit on this if it ever came to light. He hadn't done anything wrong, he convinced himself, and was not going down for this or any other crime he and the boys had committed.

"Leave me alone, you two. I gotta think. I'm gonna try to save your asses, boys, 'cause I like you. But you gotta promise me you'll follow my orders to the T. You understand?"

This made each of them feel better, momentarily.

"What's the plan, Trey," Marcus asked, anxious to learn how he was going to be saved by Trey's superior mind.

"I don't know yet, shit-for-brains," Cederquist snapped. "I gotta come up with a plan first and you're hanging around me is only gonna make things worse, if that's even possible. Now, leave me alone."

With that, he shoved Marcus and a retreating Luke from the room.

The next hour or so went by slowly for them. Trey was the first to fall asleep, but only after thinking and re-thinking the predicament in which he found himself. All he knew at this point was that he would do anything to avoid dirtying himself in this mess. That anything included sacrificing Luke and Marcus, if necessary or convenient.

Margot Hayes waited impatiently for the desk sergeant to return with news of what he was going to do about her missing daughter. He had taken down all the vital information and shared it with a higher-up, but, so far, had done nothing to allay Margot's fear or apprehension.

By the time the desk sergeant returned, with no further information about how the disappearance of Amanda would be investigated or when the police would begin searching for her daughter, Mrs. Hayes had tried to tell her story to every person who entered the station, police or civilian. She hoped that she would soon run across someone who could help her find Amanda.

Ben Hayes was exhausted. He had been out all night, looking desperately for Amanda, fearing the worst, recalling the odds he had read about in some magazine, odds which stated that the likelihood of Amanda's return diminished with each passing hour. He had checked in with Margot every half-hour throughout the night. He was still out and he was afraid of what he might find as he moved through certain sections of town.

There were parts of town with which he was unfamiliar, that he knew only by reputation. This despite the fact that he was a native Jacksonvillian. He was ashamed of himself for thinking of these things along racial lines. But he was too consumed with worry about Amanda to chastise himself for very long.

Ben had driven almost a hundred miles since he had arrived home the night before and had not left Jacksonville. He did not know enough of her friends. Nor did he know enough about his daughter to guess where her friends might be. He had long ago lost touch with a moody adolescent, about the time she had entered junior high school, he guessed.

In recent months, it had been reported by her mother, Amanda was turning a corner and growing into a well-adjusted, mature young woman. Although Amanda had obviously gone through something the previous year, she had bounced back from whatever had troubled her and was blossoming into womanhood. Ben had noticed her improved attitude and cheery disposition himself. And there was no mistaking how beautiful she had grown. The father-daughter relationship, however, had not been close since those junior high days, a fact that Ben had chosen not to dwell on until now. Regret had been his companion during a lonely search for his baby.

He drove aimlessly at times, wanting desperately to see something that might lead him to his daughter. Why he found himself driving past the Jacksonville Country Club was a mystery to him and when he realized, once again, the futility of his random searching, he turned around, returning to the house and hoping that Margot had heard from their only child.

The drive Marshall Cederquist hit from the third tee was a welcome improvement on his previous tee shots. He smiled with satisfaction as the ball landed in the middle of the fairway.

"Nice shot, Marshall."

"Thanks, Stu. But I'm still twenty yards short of you."

The two bagged their clubs and climbed into Stu's cart. They had been a regular Saturday-morning twosome for many years and looked forward to another season together, searching both for that magic round of golf that proved so illusive and for a weekly escape from their respective offices and the problems they held.

Marshall Cederquist had been a good friend when Stu had needed one. Stu's wife had passed away in December and it was good for him to be outside, occupying himself rather than retreating to a lonely house he no longer thought of as a home. And Marshall's lawyer, Stu Murphy, had often been there, too, for Cederquist. Stu did not feel he could ever repay Cederquist for having seen him through the personal hell of the past few months. But he would try.

South of town L.J. Stiles was enjoying the peace and quiet of Lake Jacksonville. He had put in at daybreak, a cooler filled with lunch and tackle box at his side. Stiles lay back in his johnboat, baseball cap pulled down over his eyes. He cared not that the fish were not biting. He struggled, but not too much, to recall whether he had even baited the hook. He would be content to sit, enjoy the quiet, and not have duty call.

Soon the temperatures would rise, bringing the boating crowd and their faster, wake-producing boats, forcing Stiles to retreat to quieter recesses of the lake in search of calm waters and more of the solitude he had been enjoying. But so far he shared the lake with only a few dedicated fishermen and, perhaps, a fellow lost soul who just wanted to slip the bonds of responsibility for a time.

When suddenly the beeper on his belt interrupted his solace, Lieutenant Stiles was quick to respond. He grabbed the pager, pressed the button revealing his message, and shook his head in disgust.

"I knew it couldn't last."

Stiles reeled in his line, quickly arranged his belongings, and started the engine. He had to get to a phone, as he had chosen not to bring the cell phone along. He would dock his boat at the marina, walk the short distance to the pay phone there and, with any luck, learn that the problem prompting his page was no longer a problem.

Jimmy Larkin picked up immediately when the phone rang.

"Stiles here."

Larkin did most of the talking.

Still, Stiles controlled the conversation, as usual.

"How old? When was she last seen? Who saw her last? Where? This guy her boyfriend? Do we know where he is? What's the mayor doing there? Yeah, I guess I'd better."

Stiles thought hard. Pressure, already.

"I'll be in right away. While I'm on my way, you can be doing the following, Jimmy. BOLO all patrolmen and get one of our people over to the Hayes home to pick up a picture. Then have Stinson contact both LEADS and NCIC."

His orders to alert all Jacksonville policemen on patrol to "be on the lookout" for Amanda Hayes and for contacts to be made with crime databases were routine. The Law Enforcement Agency Data Systems and the National Crime Information Center would post Amanda Hayes's description in a thousand places and pictures would soon follow that. There would be nothing routine, however, about this investigation, Stiles feared.

Helluva time for Stella Grimes to be out of town on vacation, Stiles thought.

"Shit!" he said beneath his breath, as he marched back to his boat. "Here we go, again."

Trey Cederquist was finding it hard to concentrate. He could not believe what had happened. He tried continually to snap himself to attention and come up with a solution to a problem he had never anticipated but could not escape. The drugs he had recently ingested would soon come to his aid, he hoped.

"You boys done yet?" Trey asked, as he neared Luke and Marcus. Marcus looked around the open pick-up truck bed and nodded. Luke stood with his left arm extended and resting on the truck's side, which cast a shadow on the body of Amanda Hayes. He was obviously shaken, fighting back tears and shaking his head. Trey tried to sound confident in front of the two, doubting that he could depend on them much longer. But he was in need of their assistance for awhile.

They had followed Trey's instructions, untying Amanda's legs and arms from the chair then carrying her out to the truck, wrapping her stiffening body in a tarp, and lifting her into the truck bed. Next they were to do a search of the cabin, removing anything that hinted of Amanda's having been there. He would do a search himself for anything they might have missed. It was as logical and methodical a plan as he could come up with, thus far. He was actually only able to extend his thinking to the next step or two, developing his plan as he went along. He did not, however, want his two companions to sense doubt or weakness.

"Don't worry, boys. Ol' Trey's got a plan. There's nothing to worry about."

"What is the plan, Trey?" Marcus asked, impatient and in need of reassurance.

Even now, Trey could not resist his own sense of playfulness.

"Well, I can't tell you everything, Marcus, ol' buddy. 'Cause then I'd have to kill ya," Trey responded, laughing, as he slapped Marcus on the back.

Marcus, dull as he was, was smart enough to realize that Trey was only kidding. At the same time, Luke, far from being a Rhodes scholar, was smart enough to fear that, very possibly, Trey might not be joking.

Trey slammed the truck's tailgate closed and told the others to search the cabin as he had instructed. They would get more orders shortly.

When they were inside the cabin, Trey donned latex gloves and removed a watch from the left hand of Amanda's corpse.

Max Jansen searched the apartment for his keys, anxious to begin his hiatus from Springfield and the *Capital City Times*. He had already checked the pockets of the pants he had worn the night before. He had worn no jacket, as the weather had been pleasant. They could not be there. He could not imagine where they might be.

It was common for Max to misplace such things, for he was not very organized, except where his writing was concerned. He took pride in tying up loose ends in all his reporting, but his personal affairs and personality traits were another story.

On this particular day, Max felt rushed to locate the missing keys. Meg Watkins would arrive any minute to accompany him on his getaway which, like much of Max's life, was totally unplanned. The two had gone on similar sojourns before. During the three years they had been dating, Meg had logged plenty of travel time, almost constantly on a bearing for unknown destinations.

Max loved to just get in the car and drive. Like a news story that had an unknown ending, such trips were an adventure for him. This go-where-the-story- takes-you attitude had served him well in his career, such that it was, and it made for a great vacation too, he had concluded. Meg was not so sure.

A knock at the door turned Max's attention to the front door of his apartment through which waltzed Meg Watkins, ten years his junior, fit, and with a constant smile fixed on an attractive face. She would be pleasant company on his weeklong adventure.

"What are you doing, Max?"

"Can't find my damn keys again, Meg."

"Try looking under the chair."

Max followed her gaze. There they were. How she did this, time after time, he would never understand. It was as if Meg were able to see things Max would continually miss. It was a perfect analogy for their relationship. She had told him on many occasions of this basic truth, which, she had reasoned, ruled their existence. He figured it was too complex for him to fathom; so he did not think of it.

"You are amazing, dear," Max told her with genuine affection. But he dared not go further. Something very deep and very masculine told him not to venture forth in declaring his love for her, if that was what he felt. He had not actually decided. Too introspective, too complex, too damn scary.

"Are you all packed, Max? I don't want you to forget your shaving kit this time. Listening to you gripe about it last time was all I could handle."

She lifted her chin and looked down her nose at him, her smile present, as always. Meg loved to feign disappointment in Max. She had, perhaps, more than enough reason to actually feel disappointment in him, but she loved him dearly. She had told him so many times.

He kissed her gently and squeezed her buttocks with his left hand, as he held a suitcase in his right.

"Got it all right here, Meggy. Your stuff out in your car?"

"I tossed it in your back seat on my way in. Can I use your bathroom?"

"Sure. I'll take this down to the car and come back up to get my scanner and the adapter. I wanna keep my ear to the ground while we're on the road."

She had known this would be the case. If she wished to listen to music on the radio, she would be doing so with her WalkMan and headphones, for Max Jansen would be listening to the police scanner, listening in on the world around him.

Once they had double checked their belongings and driven

the few blocks to gas up Max's Impala, they drove through at the nearest fast food restaurant and headed west on Interstate 72. Before Max was done with his second burger, the scanner came to life and, for the first time in his life, he heard the name of Amanda Hayes.

THREE

Lieutenant L. J. Stiles had wasted no time in organizing the department's search for Amanda Hayes. He had his staff contacting everyone on a list of names provided by her parents. He had contacted first the principal at Jacksonville High and then the attendance monitor himself. He had secured a list of Amanda's teachers and was about to call the name at the top of that list when the Chief of Police interrupted him.

"Any sign of her, L.J.?"

"No, Chief. But we'll find her."

"Word's got out that we got us a missing child, L.J. Folks'll be ready to panic 'fore long. Let's pull in all we got on this one. I don't want the city to go through this again."

Chief of Police Maurice Chappel was reflecting on the disappearance of a local girl five years earlier. Panic had set in overnight. While the girl had turned up as a runaway three days later, alive and well, Chappel did not want a repeat of the chaos the incident had brought about. Stiles knew the chief well enough to know that this was important to him.

"The Mayor has already called me, L.J. Get the fat outta the fire if you can."

"I read you loud and clear, Chief."

Turning to one of the uniformed policemen in the squad room, Stiles asked, "Any news on that stolen van County reported yesterday afternoon?"

"Not that I'm aware of, Lieutenant. But I can call County and check."

"Do that, Gardner. And ask for more than just the identity of the van's owner. I want to rule out any connection with the Hayes girl's disappearance. If we can't do that, I want to find that van."

"Yes, sir."

"Sexton, you getting anywhere with the girl's friends?"

"Nothing hard, Lieutenant. None of her friends report having seen her yesterday at all. And I'm having a tough time getting hold of the boyfriend."

"He's not missing, now. Is he?" he asked with alarm.

"No, sir. He checks in with his folks every so often. They haven't been able to convince him to stop looking for her long enough to talk to us."

"Sexton, have one of our uniforms bring the boy in ASAP. If he's really interested in finding her, he's gonna have to leave the looking to us. He might have information we need and know how to use." He paused. "Any chance he's just trying to avoid us?"

"I don't think so, Lieutenant. I was the kid's D.A.R.E. officer. He's a good kid."

"I hope you're right, Sexton," Stiles said, stroking the stubble on his chin. "I hope you're right."

"You sound like you've got a bad feeling on this one, Lieutenant. Am I right?"

"I always think the worst, Sexton. Hope for the best, but –"

He shrugged, plaintively. "Well, back to the phones. I've got some teachers to call."

Stiles returned to his desk, located the list of phone numbers of Amanda's teachers and dialed the one listed first. Three rings later, Lisa McLean picked up.

"Hello. McLean residence."

"Mrs. McLean? May I speak with your husband, please? This is Lieutenant Stiles of the Jacksonville Police Department."

"Sure, Lieutenant. Let me get him for you."

Gary was standing in the driveway when he noticed the Olson's Nissan turn in and pull up to where the sidewalk extending from the front door met the drive. He lay his rake down atop the wheelbarrow and walked around to the driver's side, where Lisa's father was out of the car, quickly extending a hand to his favorite son-in-law.

The two shook hands and met Lisa's mother at the rear of the vehicle. She extended both arms, embraced Gary warmly, kissed him lightly on the cheek, and whispered, "Where are my grandchildren?"

"They're in the house, playing. They're anxious to see you."

The three turned toward the house to see Lisa. She stepped out the front door, extended her thumb and pinky, and raised the sign to her cheek. She looked as though she had been rattled by something and Gary stepped out ahead of his mother and father-in-law in response to her signal.

As he ascended the three steps onto the front porch, Lisa reached out and placed the palm of her hand on his forearm saying only, "The police." With that, she turned toward her parents, smiling warmly and hugged them both.

"Come on inside. The twins are playing. You both look great. Dad, have you lost more weight?"

"What exactly do you hope to accomplish, Max?"

"Are you kidding, Meg? I'm a reporter. I want to find out what happened to this girl and report on it."

As the pair drove west on Morton Avenue for the third time, Meg Watkins continued to mourn Vacation Lost and attempted to do the impossible, get Max Jansen to change his mind.

"You just got off the phone with your editor, Max. And he told you go ahead with your vacation. He's putting someone else on the story."

"Yeah?"

"So, go on with your vacation, Max. Our vacation."

"Look. I'm sorry. Okay? I know you were planning on getting away for a few days. Maybe we could just hang out here in Jacksonville. I can cover the story while you kick back at the pool at the Ramada Inn."

"Well, I was planning on getting a little further away than Jacksonville. What is it? Thirty-five miles from Springfield? I used to drive over here to teach a night class."

"I know. I know."

"That's no vacation. Besides, I was wanting to spend time with you, Max."

"I know, Meg. But this could be the area's story of the year."

Meg reflected on their relationship, on its pluses and minuses.

"Look, Max. I know what it's like to commit to your work and I know we make sacrifices to accomplish what we want in our careers. But you need a break from time to time. You're on vacation. You can't cover every story in west-central Illinois."

"Well, I'm going to cover this story, Meg. I got a feeling this is going to be a big story and I'm going to be there when it breaks. Even if I've got to quit the *Times* and freelance it."

Now, Max reflected. He did not want to lose Meg. For this reason, he chose his words carefully. But he knew that he would have to say them.

"But if you don't want to do this with me, I can rent a car and you can take this one back to Springfield."

With some trepidation Gary picked up the receiver and acknowledged his caller.

"Gary McLean? Do you teach at Jacksonville High, sir?"

"Yes, that's right."

"Mr. McLean, I am Lieutenant Stiles from the Jacksonville Police Department. Sorry to bother you today, sir, but I have some questions about one of your students that I must ask you. I got your name from Mr. Singletary, your principal. I hope you don't mind my calling you at your home."

"No, not at all. This is about Amanda, I assume."

"Amanda Hayes. That's right, Mr. McLean."

"I heard from one of her classmates earlier today, Lieutenant." He swallowed hard. "Is she okay?"

"We don't know that, Mr. McLean. Amanda has not been located yet. We are trying very hard to find her, though. If you don't mind my asking, Mr. McLean, what other student did you hear from earlier today?"

"Melissa Schumacher. She is in my English III class with Amanda. Melissa was very upset. I told her not to worry. But, I must confess, I've been a little worried myself since she called."

Stiles apologized. "I'm sorry, Mr. McLean, that I'm taking so long between questions. I'm taking some notes here. I'm sure you understand. What time did she call, Mr. McLean?"

"Around nine."

"Why would she have called you, Mr. McLean?"

"I don't know exactly, except that she knows that Amanda and I talk a lot. Amanda's a good student, eager to learn. I try to encourage that."

"Did Melissa have any reason to believe you might know where Amanda would be last night or this morning?"

Gary was not sure he liked the question or what Stiles might be implying.

"Not that I can imagine, Lieutenant."

"I'm assuming that you don't know where Amanda Hayes is, Mr. McLean. Or you would have said so, right away. Correct?"

"Absolutely not, Lieutenant. I mean, absolutely. No, I don't know where she is. If I did, I'd have said so, yes." Gary was, by now, quite nervous.

"Could you guess where Amanda might be, Mr. McLean?"

"No."

"When was the last time you saw Amanda?"

"After school on Thursday afternoon, I guess. She waved to me as I walked to my car in the parking lot."

"And do you recall anything out of the ordinary then or in your class on Thursday morning? Was she acting differently from normal?"

"Not that I can recall."

"Was she dressed in her usual fashion, Mr. McLean?"

"I don't recall what she was wearing, Lieutenant." He paused. "I guess that would mean she was dressed as she usually dresses, since I didn't notice anything out of the ordinary."

"Did Amanda say or do anything unusual?"

"Not that I can recall."

"You said that Amanda was a good student, Mr. McLean. Does that mean she was an A student in your class?"

"A-minus, B-plus. I'd have to check her scores in my grade book to give you an accurate grade right now."

"You said earlier that you talk a lot with Amanda. Is she especially close to you, Mr. McLean?"

"I don't know, Lieutenant. We talk a lot, about her school work, about her plans for the future, about college."

"And you haven't seen Amanda since Thursday?"

"That's correct, Lieutenant."

"Mr. McLean, I want to thank you for your time. I may need to call on you again, but that's all for right now. Again, I am sorry for any inconvenience."

"That's okay, Lieutenant. I'm glad to help. I mean, I hope I've helped. Please, call me again if you have more questions."

"And you call me, please, if you think of anything we haven't touched on just now. If you recall anything else about Amanda you think might help us, and that could be any small piece of information, just get hold of me here at the station. Thanks, again."

The two men hung up, each looking at the telephone in front of him. Stiles wrote one last note on the page headed with Gary's name deciding he wanted to have a face-to-face with Gary before he began to dial the second number on his list of Amanda's teachers. Gary McLean turned toward the living room, where Lisa and her parents were all on the floor, playing with Maddie and Steve.

"Everything okay, hon?" Lisa asked.

"Yeah."

He hesitated. "I mean, no. She's missing." He turned toward

Lisa's parents. "Amanda Hayes, that's one of my students. She's missing. She wasn't in school yesterday and they can't find her. That was the police on the phone."

Lisa rose to move nearer her husband, who had fallen into the recliner, one leg wrapped over the arm of the chair. She brushed his hair and began to reassure him that Amanda was just fine and that she would turn up soon. She was not very convincing, she was afraid. Gary would have had to agree with her appraisal.

"Sir?"

L.J. Stiles rose from reading the report, which lay upon his desk to find a young man standing in his doorway. The young man's escort, the newest member of the JPD and not much older than the civilian he had led to Stiles' office, stood just behind the younger's left shoulder. Stiles was not sure which young man had spoken to him.

"Yes?" Stiles inquired, who was guessing that Amanda's boyfriend was making an appearance, finally.

"My name's Keith. Keith Utterback, sir. They told me you wanted to see me," clutching the bill of a baseball cap in both hands and nodding in the direction of the young officer.

"Yes. Yes, that's right. Come on in, Keith. Have a seat." Stiles moved quickly to his left around his desk and smiled, as he gestured to show the lad a lone chair in front of the desk. The young officer continued to stand in the doorway, witness to an interrogation he was sure was about to begin.

Utterback sat in the chair as instructed and looked nervously around the room. A small office, its door and front wall almost all of glass. Its other three walls provided a backdrop for every imaginable certificate, plaque, or framed mounting a policeman might receive for meritorious service. The single, most impressive decoration was the gold shield framed on purple velvet by a five-by-seven inch oak frame.

Stiles smiled as he watched the lad take notice of the office decor. "I understand you have been out looking for Amanda," he began.

"That's right, sir."

"You had any luck, son?"

"No, sir. I haven't."

Stiles wondered if the lad's quivering lip meant he was simply nervous at being questioned by the chief of detectives or if he were sorely wanting to turn the tables and ask Stiles if he had had any luck in locating Amanda Hayes.

Contrary to the younger officer's expectations, Stiles was not ready to interrogate Utterback at this point. First, there was a point to be made. Stiles was genuinely upset with Utterback for not having made himself available for questioning earlier in the day. And, it was way too early in the investigation to rule the kid out as a suspect in possible foul play. Yet Stiles was finding it difficult to picture Utterback as a guilty party. The kid looked so innocent. Fashionable clothes, although a bit unkempt; neatly trimmed hair, a bit mussed; an honest, worried face.

"Keith." He hesitated. "Can I call you 'Keith'?"

Utterback nodded.

"Keith, I am doing everything I can possibly do to find your friend."

Stiles was measuring his words carefully, allowing them their full effect. He bent in close to Keith and placed his hands on the armrests at either side of the chair. In a low voice, he continued. "But I have had to start our search for her without the benefit of some very important information that I could only get from you, first-hand." He allowed a brief hint of a smile. "I understand your concern and your desire to just go find her." Then he growled, "But I needed your butt in here earlier this morning."

Utterback sat up straighter in the chair and began to respond, but it was too late.

"I understand that my officers have been trying to reach you through your parents all morning. I've been told that your parents have relayed our messages for you to come in here several times and you're finally finding your way in here now," raising his voice, as he checked the clock hanging over Keith's shoulder, "at four o'clock in the goddamn afternoon."

Again, Utterback tried to speak. Out of habit, Stiles used a flip of his open hand, American Sign Language for "Stop it." Jacksonville is home to the state's residential school for the deaf and Stiles had learned a great deal of sign language over the years. He was no stranger to the school's campus or, for that matter, to the campus of the state's blind school at the opposite end of town. As a result, Stiles often responded to crisis with sign language. Stiles heeded his own stop sign and regained control of his demeanor, if not his emotions.

"I didn't need to have officers out chasing you down this morning, Keith. I needed them out looking for Amanda. And we all could have done a better job, perhaps, if you had come in and provided us with answers to some of our questions."

Stiles paused, but there was no response. He continued, "Are you getting the impression that I am not too happy with you, Keith?"

"I'm sorry, sir."

Neither spoke again for several moments, until Stiles got to the point.

"Do you know where Amanda Hayes is, Keith?" Stiles asked. No sense beating around the bush any longer, he thought.

Keith raised his head to look Stiles eye-to-eye.

"No," Utterback answered, having looked neither right nor left, up or down.

Stiles was reasonably sure he was hearing the truth. Utterback answered the questions without hesitation or preface. No "to tell ya the truths." No "swear to Gods." Stiles wasn't so sure of his skills in reading people that he would strike Keith Utterback completely from his yet-unwritten list of possible suspects. But Stiles told himself that he would have to be shown some hard evidence before he would move the kid to the top of such a list.

"Do you have any idea where she could be, son?"

He did not.

The questions continued for almost another hour. Stiles wrote nothing, but asked the questions and listened intently. Stiles noted mentally that Keith was left-handed and saw that whenever the lad had answered a question that called for him to remember the events of Thursday evening, his eyes darted left. This Stiles took as an indication that he was, indeed, recalling information, rather than making up a story.

Keith recounted the brief meeting with Amanda on Thursday evening. He had picked her up at her place of work, a bagel shop on a strip mall on Morton Avenue. He gave the time as ten o'clock. He told the detective that he had wanted to stop somewhere and have a Coke before he took Amanda home. She was not feeling well, though, she had told him. He thought she had placed her hand on her stomach when she told him this, but he could not be sure. He was driving while they talked. He did say, however, that she felt warm when he kissed her goodnight at front door of her parents' home. He had noticed nothing unusual at the house and he had watched her go into the house before he left.

Several times during the session, Utterback referred to Amanda, always in the present tense, a fact not lost on Stiles. The youth told the detective he was worried about Amanda and that he didn't think there was any possibility that she was a runaway, and that he feared she had been abducted. When Stiles asked him how he had reached such a conclusion, the youth told him that, through a process of elimination, he could come to no other.

After they had exhausted the subject, Stiles began asking the same questions, this time asking Keith to record his own answers in his own hand. Later, he would be asked to sign this statement in front of Stiles and another officer.

When Stiles was finally sure that he had all the information he might need for the time being, he waved the young officer back into the room to act as a witness. Utterback signed his statement and the session was finally over. Stiles rose and moved toward the door. With his back to Keith, he asked the youth if he would mind taking a polygraph test in the future. He gauged the youth's reaction in the reflected glass in the open office door.

"Sure."

"Good. We'll let you know if we decide to pursue that avenue," and Stiles was gone.

The youth looked up at the young officer who stepped back into the doorway after allowing Lieutenant Stiles to brush past him. The uniformed youth motioned the other to follow him and the two walked the long corridor to the end of the building.

As Keith Utterback stepped into his vehicle, L.J. Stiles watched from the office of a colleague. He wanted to get a sense of what Keith was feeling now that the questioning had taken place. Relief? Agitation? Anxiety? Stiles saw nothing to indicate the youth was anything but a very worried boyfriend.

If he's acting, Stiles thought, he's damn good.

"Are you sure you want to do this, Max?"

"Yes, Meg, for crying-out-loud. How many times do I have to tell you?"

The two stood on the front lawn of a Jacksonville couple Meg knew from college. Over the years, Meg and the couple, along with some other Eastern Illinois University alums, who now lived in West-Central Illinois had gathered on occasion to catch up with one another. She had not caught up to visit with the Fletchers during the past two years. But they had been gracious. Upon Meg's recommendation, they would allow a stranger, and no one was stranger than Max Jansen, to stay with them indefinitely, while he investigated the disappearance of one of the town's young girls. Meg, embarrassed to do so, but wanting to help Max if she possibly could, had imposed upon the Fletchers and was intent on making Max pay dearly, in one way or another, and very soon.

"I can't believe you talked me into this, Max. These people are my friends, Max. If you cause them any trouble—"

"I can believe you did this, Meg, 'cause you're the greatest.

And it's a good thing these people are your friends, dear, 'cause only friends would say yes to us, right? Hey, these folks are great, Meg. They don't mind at all. Barney even took me uptown to rent a car, didn't he?"

"Yes, Max, he did; but, his name is Arney. Do you see how you are, Max? This man takes you into his home and you can't even remember the guy's name. I don't believe you."

The Fletchers, perhaps wondering what they had got themselves into, stood on the front porch of their home and watched as Max ushered Meg to Max's car.

"You can stay at my place if you want, Meggy. You know you like it there. It'll be a mini-vacation, huh?"

"Vacation? Are you for real, Max? Staying at your place, while you're over here, playing Supersleuth, is hardly a vacation."

"Okay, Meg. Have it your way," Max said, keenly aware that, as usual, he was having it his way. "Enjoy yourself, wherever you decide to stay."

"I'll be staying at my place, Max. And you'd better call, too. And don't you dare impose on these people any more than you already have. Hear?"

"Sure, Meg." And he closed the car door. She started the engine and moved slowly away.

Max moved quickly up the sidewalk.

"Well, she's gone. What's for supper?"

Disposing of Amanda's body would be easy work, according to Trey Cederquist, who, interestingly enough, was nowhere near her body. This fact was not lost on Luke. Still, he had become convinced, after awhile, that Trey was correct. Even though the girl's death could not be attributed to them, Luke was afraid that he and Marcus would be held responsible, at least in part, for her death. There would be arrests made, trials tried, innocence or guilt decided upon, and judgment carried out. It scared him.

After crossing the Illinois River at Meredosia, Luke and Marcus headed south on Route 100, through the small town of Bluffs, east briefly on Interstate 72 and south to Winchester. Back west, then crossing the Illinois again, at Florence. Through Milton, Pearl, and Kampsville, they sped until they got to Hardin, where they crossed the Illinois River a third time. South, farther still, until they passed through Marquette State Park and the river town of Grafton. Soon they would make their way through the city of Alton, just north of St. Louis. Where the Illinois River meets the Mississippi, they would connect with Route 3 and bend with the rivers around St. Louis.

The body of a beautiful, seventeen-year-old girl lay in the bed of Luke's pick-up truck, covered with a jumble of blue plastic tarp, held down in the truck bed by four tires. As Luke and Marcus and Amanda neared their destination, the two living travelers became anxious once more at the prospect of handling the dead one again. Aside from sporadic duty as pallbearers for a dead uncle or aunt, neither had handled so directly the corpse of another human being.

Trey's plan called for Luke and Marcus to dispose of the body far from Jacksonville and in an urban area, preferably a high crime neighborhood, so that it might appear that Amanda's captors had been from outside the Jacksonville vicinity, drifters perhaps, passing through.

There was a certain logic to Trey's plan, which included traveling in the late afternoon, dumping the body in the cover of darkness, and getting back into Jacksonville to establish an alibi. First, don't be seen; then, become visible in another locale was how Trey had put it. Luke would have felt better had Trey Cederquist accompanied them and shared in the risk involved in his plan. This, however, was not the case and Luke was all alone, except for Marcus, and this was small consolation, even Luke would have to admit.

Perhaps it was Luke's thinking about getting back to Jacksonville quickly that caused his foot to depress the accelerator so. His truck approached seventy miles per hour on the two-lane blacktop, which ran along the shoreline of the Illinois River. The view, too, may have distracted Luke, for the bluffs at the approaching confluence of the Illinois and Mississippi Rivers was breathtaking. Just as breathtaking was what Luke suddenly saw in his rear-view mirror, the flashing lights of a Jersey County Sheriff's cruiser.

The blood rushed from Luke's face, for he had not yet made his delivery. A girl lay dead in the bed of his truck, covered only by the blue tarp. A sheriff's deputy was getting out of his car, donning his hat and preparing to approach Luke and Marcus, passing within a few feet of the body of Amanda Hayes.

"Afternoon, boys." The deputy looked the vehicle and the occupants of its cab over slowly. "May I see your driver's license and registration, please?"

Luke fumbled for his license, trying to keep an eye on the deputy and hoping the deputy would not grow curious about the contents of the truck bed.

"Here you go, Officer."

"Take the license out of the wallet, please."

"Here you go," Luke repeated.

The sheriff's deputy excused himself and returned to his cruiser with Luke's license, giving Marcus a chance to speak for the first time. "We gotta go, Luke. Now."

"Just sit still and let me handle this, Marcus. We'll be okay, so long as our friend here don't look in the back." Luke watched the policeman in his side mirror and hoped there would be nothing to handle. Beneath his right buttock lay the gun Trey had given Luke just before the departure from the Cederquist cabin.

A short time later, the deputy was again at Luke's window. "You boys were going a little fast back there. You in a hurry?"

"No, sir."

"Well, I'm gonna let you fellas off with a warning today. But, you slow it down. Ya' hear?"

"Yes, sir," came the response from both men.

With that, the deputy returned to his car without bothering the contents of Luke's truck bed and without forcing Luke to make a decision, which could have been disastrous for all. The deputy made a U-turn and disappeared. Luke and Marcus remained silent and only looked at one another in disbelief at their good fortune.

Twenty minutes later the men were outside Granite City, where they found a deserted warehouse in a remote part of the city's industrial park. Their activities could not be seen from the roadway passing by, once they had used bolt cutters to rid the gate of its padlock. Marcus walked around the building, inspecting the inside through the broken windows, as Luke had ordered him to do. He saw no one and saw no way anyone could see him or them. He returned to the truck to find Luke, having his own look with a set of binoculars that Trey had given them earlier.

When Luke was satisfied that no one was around and that there was no way someone could observe them from afar, he and Marcus uncovered Amanda's body. They dragged her by her arms to the end gate and lifted her corpse for the short walk to the door at the south end of the building. They set her gently among the many discarded pieces of machinery inside the building and returned to the truck. One last look assured them that they had not been observed and they were in the truck and gone.

Ben and Margot Hayes closed their front door, as the Jacksonville police chief and a counselor from the county health department descended from the front porch and disappeared into the night. No news had not been good news for two very worried parents. They had asked all the questions they thought were possible of the police chief and still had no idea where their daughter was. For their part, the police had asked lots of questions, too. Of Amanda's parents, of the neighbors, of the girl's friends, teachers, and boyfriend. No one knew the whereabouts of Amanda Hayes and, while no one wanted to admit it, all were beginning to wonder if they would ever see Amanda again.

FOUR

Sunday morning brought with it a realization for those close to Amanda that she could conceivably be the victim of foul play. No rational hypothesis could be purported which did not include a person or persons somehow detaining Amanda, at the very least. The other end of the spectrum of possibility was too ghastly to even think about.

Her family and friends chose, instead, to concentrate on the facts as they saw them. She was no runaway. Her clothes, except for what she had on her back, were apparently all accounted for, either in her closet or in the wash. Although it seemed so, she had not simply vanished. Aside from an alien abduction, which few would give credence to, no other theory could account for such a scarcity of evidence in her disappearance. It was becoming more obvious to friends, family and classmates that someone was behind her disappearance.

The rest of the city awoke to find headlines in the local paper that riveted their attention and alarmed their sensibilities. "Local High School Student Missing," read the banner headline on page one. Parents searched for details that would relieve their fears. Children wondered if their parents' concern was something they, too, should be alarmed about. They also wondered if it were going to affect their personal freedom. School administrators met at the home of the superintendent of schools to discuss measures that might be taken to assure parents that children would be safe going to and from school the next day. Jacksonville was in shock.

Things were getting scary out there and there was no sand into which the population could collectively bury its head. They feared the worst, hoped for the best, and silently mouthed a prayer of thanks that it wasn't their kid that was missing.

The police followed long ago-established procedure at the direction of Lieutenant L.J. Stiles. All Jacksonville PD and Morgan County patrol cars had been "BOLO'ed." Neighboring communities who had police forces, most notably South Jacksonville, were informed. State and national crime information centers had Amanda's description, as well as the latest photograph of her. IWIN computers in squad cars across the state were flashing Amanda's digital image on laptop screens. Illinois' wireless information network was at work.

At Stiles' direction, her parents had contacted, through its 800 number, Child-Find, an organization that assists parents in locating their missing children. Information about Amanda was even posted on the city's Internet web page.

The print and broadcast media of central Illinois swarmed on Jacksonville, filling hotel rooms and parking spaces with cars, vans, and trucks proclaiming their affiliation with huge lettering and logos. While peanuts and cotton candy were not being hawked outside the Ramada Inn, the circus, nevertheless, had come to town.

Marshall Cederquist, Jr. read the story of Amanda's disappearance with more than the interest of a casual observer. He was acquainted, of course, with Amanda's father, Ben, a long-time employee he had encountered only thirty-six hours earlier at the Jacksonville Ramada Inn. Cederquist's thoughts were on Mrs. Hayes, however. He had known her quite well, many years ago, and was heartsick at the thought of Margot's anguish at this moment. What a lovely girl, thought Cederquist as he stared at the picture in the newspaper. A beautiful girl with coal-black hair, a winning smile, and lustrous eyes, she greatly resembled her mother.

Cederquist convinced himself that he would use whatever resources he had to aid in the search for Amanda Hayes, a girl he had occasion to see only a very few times over the past ten years or so, but whom Cederquist had never had the pleasure of meeting.

Memories cascaded over Cederquist like they had not for some time. The feelings he had for this poor girl's mother had been so very intense at one time that he had thought it impossible to live without her. He had told her he would do anything, leave his wife and son, give up or move the business if she insisted on leaving Jacksonville, even setting Ben up in a business of his own, if such a thing could be done without further subjecting him to indignity.

Margot had dismissed it all as folly. She was convinced that Cederquist would never follow through with his half-baked plans. He was too committed to the growth and expansion of Cederquist Industries. She had, after all, witnessed his rise in business as a secretary to one of Cederquist' assistant managers and knew that business and making money were his prime motivators.

Now, Cederquist was alone with his money. His wife had succumbed to cancer six years earlier. He had been with her through very rough times, in love for a time before that with another. But he was trying always to convince himself that he had done the right thing, and recognizing, finally, that Margot had, after all, been correct where it concerned his promises to her. Nevertheless, he knew that he would never love again like he had so many years ago.

Ben never knew. Margot and Marshall always kept an appropriate social distance at company gatherings until Margot quit attending such events altogether. Both she and Marshall were sure that Ben had not the slightest inkling of their indiscretions, which had ceased when Margot became pregnant and left the employ of Cederquist Industries to raise her family.

There were, of course, some anxious months on both their parts when it was learned that Margot was expecting a child. Cederquist was convinced that there was, at the very least, a possibility that the baby could be his. Margot assured him that this was not the case, even providing the results of blood tests that discounted the possibility of Marshall's paternity shortly after Amanda had been born.

It had hurt Cederquist to think that, while Margot and he

had been sexually involved, she apparently had been active with Ben also. He was, after all, her husband, she had explained at the time. But what really hurt Marshall was the loss of one so lovely, both in body and spirit. She had made him feel more alive than any woman, including the woman who had borne him a son.

Cederquist lay the paper down on the desk, buried his face in his hands for nearly a minute, wiped away the germ of a tear, and picked up the phone to call the mayor. Perhaps he would put some of the money at his disposal to help in the search for Amanda, covertly, of course. The mayor might know how this could be done. Or perhaps Stu Murphy would know. He paused.

More memories, more reminders of a life he had not intended for himself, flooded over him. Dutifully, Cederquist had stood pat with his family, such as it was, playing the part of devoted father. That is, a father devoted to making money, and lots of it. He rationalized that it was for the family that he worked so hard. He had to have something to give his son when the time came. Never mind that the time he spent building the company robbed his son of the time it might have taken to help that son grow into the kind of man who could handle such a company.

Now, he thought of Trey and wondered where he had gone so wrong, so horribly wrong. The boy, in his thirties but still a boy, just had not come around as his father had hoped. He seemed intent on taking shortcuts, gambling in business, probably in his personal life, too, the elder Cederquist thought. Actually Marshall knew little of his son's personal life. An estranged wife, a granddaughter he checked up on too infrequently. That was about it. He wasn't even sure if he knew where Trey was living now. Somewhere on the west side of Jacksonville, he knew. But he could not come up with an address readily.

Thoughts of offering a reward were no longer a priority, as he scored an imaginary ledger on which his success as a father could be measured. Perhaps he would return to the idea later.

Lieutenant L.J. Stiles sat comfortably enough in his recliner, scanning the local newspaper for something newsworthy that did not have his name in it. He did not want to think about Amanda Hayes or her disappearance, if for only a few minutes. Stiles knew that the front page would be full of news on her disappearance and sought to avoid it.

Page two carried more bad news. A growing problem plaguing so many Mid-western cities was, again, a big story. Methamphetamines was the drug of choice, immensely cheaper than cocaine, and easily manufactured from ingredients readily available in many Jacksonville stores. The problem had been growing steadily for sometime now, an increase in crime rate the constant companion wherever methamphetamines could be found.

The latest evidence of a methamphetamine presence in Jacksonville involved the arrest of several young people for possession. None of them were talking about where they were getting the drug and no leads existed which might identify the producer, who Stiles felt had to be located in the Jacksonville area. There were also numerous reports from area farmers of stolen or missing anhydrous tanks. And calls from retailers all around town were steady, reporting large purchases of lithium batteries and sinus medicines.

Stiles decided to concentrate on the sports page, reminding himself, in his solitude, that he had long ago ceased making a name for himself in those pages. A pretty good athlete, but nothing really to brag about, he thought. How many others could, or should, say the same? He had never kidded himself, as people often do, about his own athletic accomplishments. He had made his starting high school football team in Mattoon, Illinois, but barely. No college recruiters, pen in hand, had come calling at his home. Only the Army had shown an interest in him and it had not been West Point that had beckoned.

A six-year stint in service to his country saw Stiles move steadily through the ranks as a military policeman. Upon his discharge Sergeant Stiles attended a police academy at the University of Illinois and went to work immediately afterward in Jacksonville. He attended every in-service opportunity that he could, hungry for knowledge and intent on advancement.

In his second year on the force, he married a girl he had met while in the service and became a father the following year. Two years later, a second child was born. His advancement did not come quickly enough for his wife, who had never seen Jacksonville as the place for her or her children. The fifteen years that followed were unhappy ones and, while he loved his two beautiful daughters more than anything in the world, he could not respond affirmatively when his wife said she was moving with the girls to the town where she had been born. He felt abandoned, yet understood her desire to be nearer her family. The anguish he felt at the loss of his daughters' companionship was still very real.

As usual, thoughts that began with Stiles attempting to get work off his mind were successful for only a brief time. If his mind did not wander back to work, family crept into his thoughts and he was instantly depressed. He hoped that, in time, things would get better. It had not happened yet and it had been three years. Sheila had kept the door open for him for almost a year, but had filed for divorce when it became apparent that Stiles was not going to follow her back to West Virginia. She had remarried six months ago and the girls seemed happy enough. Let it go, Stiles thought. Let it go.

Once Stiles decided to look at the front page of the paper, he was surprised that more non-information did not appear there. There had not been much to tell the paper's reporter the previous evening when he had called him at home. This had not prevented the press from guessing about possible scenarios when covering other important stories in the past. But he had been careful not to fan the flames of speculation that were wrapped in every question the reporter had asked of Stiles.

Enough of this sitting around, doing nothing, Stiles thought. I have had my rest. Time to go to work. He reached for the telephone on the end table beside his chair and dialed the number he had written on an index card and stuffed into his pocket earlier.

"Mrs. McLean?"

"Yes, who is this?"

"Lieutenant Stiles, ma'am. Jacksonville Police Department. Good morning. Is your husband at home?"

"No, Lieutenant. Gary's out walking. He just left about five minutes ago. He usually walks for about an hour on Sunday mornings. Is there a message?"

"No, ma'am. I'm just trying to figure out where this missing Hayes girl could be and I thought your husband might have some insight into what kind of girl she is, who she hangs around with, that kind of thing. Just tell him I called, please."

Stiles could tell he had made Mrs. McLean uneasy. This was the case with most of the people with whom he talked. A hazard of his profession, he had long ago concluded. At times, he enjoyed it. But this was not the case today.

He decided that he had nothing better to do than to see if he could locate McLean on his walk and have a little chat about Amanda Hayes. He hoped, in part, that he would find the man, so that he did not have to bother Lisa McLean again.

Trey Cederquist banged loudly on the door three times and finally let himself in. Vicki Cederquist, his estranged wife, was about to turn the knob when Trey bolted in. She jumped as the door flew open and immediately backpedaled until she found herself behind the island in the middle of the kitchen. It was not uncommon to find herself with something between her husband and herself. All too often, however, such obstacles proved only to be delays for the inevitable.

"Good morning, Vic. What's shakin'?"

"Good morning, Trey. How are you?"

She was nervous.

"Fine, just fine, Vicki." He scouted the apartment, looking first in the living room area and down the hall toward the three bedrooms. "You alone, Vic?"

"Yes, of course, Trey. I mean, no, your daughter's in her room, taking a nap. I don't think she's feeling well. But that's all. There's no one else here. Who would be here?"

She sounded defensive.

"Good. You been here all night? I mean, did you go out last night?"

"Yes. No. We went out for supper and came home, Trey. Why?"

"Well, which is it, Vicki? Did you go out last night or not?" He moved closer to the island.

"We went to Burger King around seven and then came home. Melinda watched a videotape we had rented earlier and she went to bed around nine. Why, Trey? I didn't do anything wrong."

"Good, Vicki. That's good." Trey seemed on edge, but it was difficult for Vicki to tell. She had not felt like she knew Trey or his moods very well since they had separated shortly after Melinda's birth. Trey continued. "You see, Vicki. I've been here with you. All night."

"What are you saying, Trey?"

"I'm saying, 'I've been here all night, with you, and Melinda.' If anybody asks where I was last night, I was here, with you and my little girl. You understand?"

Trey had a pointed finger just an inch from her nose and she was getting Trey's point clearly now.

"Sure, Trey. I understand."

What Vicki Cederquist understood was that it was never a good idea to argue with Trey when he was insistent, which was usually the case.

Now, Cederquist was around the island and grasping her arms. His hands were strong on her forearms. She knew what would come next. He pulled her arms apart and wrapped his around her waist. As he drew her close to him, she shuddered. Burying his face in her hair, he breathed deeply and cupped her right breast in his left hand, squeezing it harder than she would have preferred had she been open to his advances in the first place. She resisted when he moved to kiss her, but the effort was futile and short-lived.

"Since I been here all night, Vic, we might as well enjoy our time together," he whispered and then he laughed out loud, his breath hot against her neck.

Vicki's eyes moistened as he directed her down the hall to the largest of the three bedrooms. He pulled the door of his daughter's bedroom shut as he passed by, not bothering to look inside the room.

Ten o'clock Mass at Our Savior's Catholic Church had been well attended, as usual. Many of Ben and Margot Hayes' fellow parishioners had stopped by to offer encouragement to them after the Mass had ended. Father Schmidt had mentioned Amanda's disappearance in only general terms, saying that the parish needed to pray for one of its own, a lost lamb who, he hoped, would soon be found. Following the ride home, the couple discovered that some of their neighbors had prepared brunch for them. Food came from all directions on the block where Amanda had learned to ride her bike and on which not a single tree that was worth climbing had not been climbed by a younger Amanda.

It was mid-afternoon when Father Schmidt walked up their driveway with prayer book in hand. He was invited inside where he spoke of Amanda in the present tense and tried, as so many had before him, to comfort two very worried and weary parents. He complimented them both for their outward composure, although the priest was keenly aware that Ben was very near emotional collapse. Margot, it seemed, had her wits about her. But she, too, was scared. Father Schmidt lay his hand on his heart and looked deeply into both sets of eyes, bidding them good day and reminding them that God was on their side and would be a source of comfort in trying times.

"'Source of comfort,' my ass," Ben said, when the priest was far enough down the driveway and out of earshot.

"Ben!" Margot scolded.

"Oh, I know; he's trying to help, Margot. But, honestly, I don't see how God could ever allow something like this to happen to us," he paused, "to Mandy."

Margot's eyes widened. "Nothing's happened to her, Ben. She's all right. She's got to be."

"Sure, she is," Ben responded, holding her now in his arms. He tried hard not to think the worst and even harder not to let Margot know that he was.

Max Jansen sped east on College Avenue, passing Koskciusko, then Fayette, when he saw a squad car parked in a driveway near the Masonic Lodge a block ahead. Max did not need another speeding ticket. He slowed his vehicle, partly to avoid a summons and partly to learn the identity of the man with whom Lieutenant L.J. Stiles was engaged in conversation.

Max was quite familiar with Chief of Detectives Stiles. Over the years they had encountered each other, each snooping for the truth in differing ways and with varying purpose.

Now, a young man, dressed in sweats and cross-training shoes stood with his hands on his hips as he spoke with Stiles. The young man appeared to be perturbed, shrugging his shoulders. Then, his arms opened wide, his palms to the cloudless sky. Max surmised that the young man must be telling Stiles something for about the tenth time.

Jansen moved through the next intersection at Church Street and past the pair, before quickly turning left at Dunlap Court. Two more lefts brought him, once again, to the lighted intersection at Church and College, this time heading south. The light changed as the two men ended their conversation, Stiles moving toward his squad car, the other finding his pace once again as he approached Church Street, where he waited for Max Jansen, in the fourth of several cars to move along, so that he could continue his walk.

4-STEV

Max's right on Beecher, followed by another right, brought him back to College, but the man with whom Stiles had spoken was nowhere to be seen. Max wondered what, if anything, this mystery man had to do with Amanda Hayes. Perhaps nothing. Perhaps, a great deal. Reporter's job to find out, Max thought.

Margot had already checked the laundry and found nothing notable there. She had busied herself by doing the laundry late Sunday afternoon. On Sunday evening Margot Hayes straightened Amanda's room. The police had been through the room twice on Saturday afternoon and evening, finding nothing in the way of a clue to her daughter's whereabouts.

Perhaps, she thought, I can find something the police have missed. They had taken nothing, she had been told. They had opted, instead, to take pictures of just about everything. They had asked her to check Amanda's closet and her chest of drawers to see if anything were missing.

From what she could tell, nothing had turned up missing, except the jeans and sweater she had apparently worn on Friday. Amanda, apparently, had also worn a new watch her mother had given her for her seventeenth birthday. It had Amanda's initials engraved on its backside. AMH –Amanda Madeline Hayes.

Nothing unusual about her desk, Margot thought. Her daughter was a neat-freak when compared to some other teenage girls. Her room was usually well kept, vacuumed weekly, dusted even more frequently, and everything in the room had its place. Amanda's father had often teased her about carrying over her tidiness to the rest of the home, for Amanda was noticeably less particular about the rest of the house. Margot had not minded doing the bulk of the cleaning around the rest of the home, but had to admit, she was curious about her daughter's willingness to let the rest of the house go, while insisting upon perfection in her own quarters.

Thinking about it brought a smile to her face. A tear, as well, found its way down the length of Margot's cheek. Nothing compared to a mother's grief. Her great fear was that grief was about to visit her home. How would she bear the loss of her daughter?

Trey Cederquist had finished eating supper and watched as Vicki washed the dishes, while Melinda played on the floor in the living room. He had satisfied himself at his wife's table as well as in her bed. Now, it was time to go. He rose from the table and stretched his shoulders, turning his torso left and right. He moved toward the door, offering a hollow good-bye to his daughter. She smiled back at him briefly.

As he reached for the doorknob, Vicki quietly spoke to him. "Trey, you got a minute before you go?"

"What is it, now, Vicki?" he snapped back.

She was cautious, choosing her words carefully. "Trey, I have to take Melinda in to the dentist again. She's gonna have to have some work done." She hesitated. "He's gonna want some money, Trey."

"Money? It's always money with you, isn't it? I give you money, Vicki. I pay for this goddamn apartment, Vicki. What more do you want?"

"Not much, Trey. Not much."

Melinda was aware that Trey's voice was growing louder. She could not see him any longer, for he had moved away from her and toward her mother. She heard the back of her father's hand strike her mother's cheek first, then the sound of a breaking dish, knocked off the kitchen counter as Vicki scrambled away from Trey. Vicki fell to the floor, Trey standing over her.

"Don't you be asking for any more money now, Vicki. I take good care of you." His voice grew strangely malevolent. He laughed an evil laugh. "I took good care of you this morning, now didn't I, Vic?" he said, bending over and stroking her hair with his left hand.

Suddenly, he had her face in his right hand, squeezing hard and directing her eyes toward his.

"You bitch! You don't ever ask for money from me again, you hear? I'll give you what I want to give you. Understand?"

Vicki tried to shake her head. He knew she understood and he let her collapse onto herself.

Trey moved around the kitchen's island and heard Melinda scurry around the other side toward her mother. She held her mother in her arms and cried with her, as her father left the apartment.

"Who'd this van belong to, again?" Lieutenant Stiles asked of Patrolman Doug Hurst as the two men moved cautiously up the hill, flashlights cutting the darkness before them.

"Tim McMichael, sir," came Hurst's response as he stepped sideways to avoid another puddle in the muddy lane leading toward the van. His whole body seemed to creak, the leather about his waist and at his side twisting, as he shifted his weight from one foot to the other and constantly adjusted the Kevlar vest beneath his uniform shirt.

"And what do we know about Mr. McMichael, Doug?"

"'Twenty-five, not married. He's a self-employed carpenter. He reported the van stolen late Friday afternoon. Says he's been out of town since Tuesday. He and a buddy were camping at Mark Twain Lake all week. Got home around noon and figured his brother might have borrowed the van. When he got hold of his brother, he learned that the brother hadn't touched the thing; so, he figured someone else must have borrowed it. Without asking, of course."

"You got the name of this buddy he was camping with?"

"Yes, sir."

"Good, Doug. Check his story out when we get done here."

The two joined a Morgan County Sheriff's Deputy and the farmer who had discovered the stolen van an hour earlier at the top of the hill. The van was parked behind a grove of trees and would be visible from the road only if one were looking for it. When the farmer found it parked on his land, he had looked inside, finding no occupants, then called the police.

"Hi there, Deputy Riley. How are you today?"

The two shook hands, Riley acknowledging the presence of Patrolman Hurst with a nod in his direction.

"Just fine, Lieutenant Stiles. And how are you?"

"Oh, we could be better, Deputy. I guess you heard that we have been looking for a missing girl."

"Yes, sir. I know her father. Any luck yet?"

"No," Stiles said, as he moved closer to the van. "I thought we might come out and take a look at this van. See if it might be connected to our missing person."

"Be my guest, Lieutenant."

Stiles directed Patrolman Hurst to return to the cruiser to get a camera.

"I've just finished taking Mr. Williamson's statement here, Riley continued. "This is his land and he found the van just a little while ago, before sunset. No one's touched it since I got here, twenty-six minutes ago," Riley said, checking his watch.

Stiles greeted Williamson with a handshake and a smile, yet never took his attention away from the van.

"Did you touch the van, Mr. Williamson?"

"Yes, sir. I did. I didn't know what to think when I seen the thing here. I yelled, first. Didn't know if someone had pulled in here and fell asleep, or what. Didn't no one answer, so I come up here on this side," indicating the passenger side of the vehicle, "and looked in the window. When I didn't see anyone, I moved up to the window there and leaned in. I didn't get in or anything, but I touched the door there when I looked in. Sorry if I did somethin' I wasn't supposed to, Officer."

"Oh, no. That's okay, Mr. Williamson. I just need to know if anything was disturbed. I expect that Deputy Riley's gonna want to fingerprint the vehicle, but I would have expected to find your prints. You didn't do anything wrong. Don't worry."

Stiles wished the farmer hadn't touched the vehicle. But it

would do no one any good to make the gentleman feel bad about it.

All the while Stiles had listened to Williamson, Stiles had been looking the van over, top to bottom, front to back. He tried to notice footprints around the vehicle, looked briefly to see what kind of footwear the farmer had on and, then, to see if the tall grass around the vehicle had been trampled down or if trash had been discarded in the near vicinity. Now, he moved toward the front door on the passenger side, much as Williamson must have done two hours previous to Stiles' and Hurst's arrival.

Careful not to touch anything himself, Stiles used his greater height to lean in through the open window, direct the flashlight's beam inside, and look toward the back of the van's interior. He saw a two-seated van, the back end of which was obviously converted to accommodate carpenter's work. More than what he saw, however, he quickly became aware of what he smelled.

"Whew," Stiles said, as he pulled his head from inside the window.

"Pretty ripe, isn't it, Officer?" the farmer volunteered.

"I should say so, Mr. Williamson."

"Yeah, I noticed it, too, Lieutenant," Riley offered. "Smells like someone got sick in the back end."

"Let's see if we can take a closer look," Stiles said, as he moved toward the rear of the van.

Patrolman Hurst removed a handkerchief from his pocket and looked to Stiles for a nod of approval which came immediately. Hurst proceeded to carefully trip the door handle and, using a pen from another pocket, pulled the door open.

Hurst snapped a few pictures. Tools were neatly secured on the walls and in mounted bins along the right hand wall of the van's rear section. A few scraps of lumber were strewn about the back end atop a piece of carpet, which had been cut roughly to fit the floor of the van. To the left side of the van stood two saw horses, one straddling the other. On the carpet, near the middle of the floor, was a mass of what appeared to be vomit, staining the carpet and filling the air with the stench the men had smelled from the other end of the vehicle.

Stiles spoke succinctly and with authority. "Deputy Riley, let's get a crime scene unit from Springfield out here, right away. We need prints, pictures, the whole works, even a forensic pathologist, Deputy." He paused. "I wanna know if that vomit came from Amanda Hayes."

Deputy Riley had no problems with taking such suggestions from a city police officer, at least not from this one, for he had great respect for Stiles. And while they were in the county, clearly in his jurisdiction, he knew that his boss, County Sheriff Lloyd Finney, would want full cooperation between county and city on a case like this. He was on the radio immediately, asking for the Illinois State Police to send a crime scene unit.

FIVE

When Gary entered his classroom on Monday morning, he did so without his characteristic enthusiasm. How he would get through the day was a mystery to him and, yet, he knew that he must, somehow. If he was struggling with Amanda's disappearance, how must it be affecting his other students, he reasoned. He would have to find a way to answer their questions, perhaps give them a chance to vent their fears, and carry on.

His arrival at school had been followed, as usual, by a stop at his mailbox and greetings with other faculty members. As he had expected, the talk was about Amanda. Had anyone heard anything that morning? Was there really a chance that she had run away? Did anyone know anything? He stuck his head into an assistant principal's office and asked him if the police had made any suggestions about how to answer questions that students might have about the disappearance.

"Memo to all the faculty members is being copied now. You'll probably have it before first hour begins, Gary."

"Good. Thanks, Steve."

"You doin' okay? I know Amanda was in your class."

"She 'is' in my class, Steve. She is in my class."

"Right. She's in your class."

"I'm sorry, Steve. I haven't had much sleep and I'm kinda grumpy this morning. I'm doing okay, though. Thanks for asking."

The faculty lounge, too, was abuzz with conversation about the disappearance. Very little else seemed important to anyone at Jacksonville High School at the time. Gary poured a cup of coffee, exchanged "good mornings" with several teachers and ran into Sue MacFarlane as she entered and he was about to exit the room.

They had known each other for a long time. She had taught him English during his senior year seventeen years ago. Now they taught on the same English department faculty and were close. Sue knew that Gary would be taking this whole mess very hard and this was her first chance to see him, since she had been out of town with her husband for the weekend. But she had read the papers upon their return home late the evening before. Gary had been on her mind, almost as much as Amanda, ever since.

"You okay?"

"Fine," he said, giving her a one-arm hug, his notebook under the other arm and coffee cup in hand.

They looked at each other in much the same way they had almost six months earlier, when Mike Mitchell, a gifted athlete at JHS, was robbed of his life in a tragic, and senseless, automobile accident. They shook their heads and moved on, she to the coffee maker in the lounge and he toward his classroom.

Now, Gary sat at his desk, awaiting the arrival of the first few students for his first hour, freshman English class. He wondered what to expect from them. Being freshmen, they were, by nature, a self-absorbed lot, often acting as though they were unaffected by events around them. Would they recognize another's pain? Would they recognize their parents' fears? Would they even be in touch with their own?

Soon students began to trickle in, pairs and groups of four or five. Traveling in packs, as usual. Did no freshman walk alone, Gary laughed to himself. He shook his head, marveling at the wonder of youth. He reminded himself that he truly was doing what he loved, what he had always wanted to do.

Gary loved teaching. Recently, however, he had seriously considered looking elsewhere for a job where he could make some more money, have a better insurance plan, perhaps put an extra three-months salary each year away for the twins. During the Christmas holiday he had actually contacted an old friend who worked at Horace Mann in Springfield and who had persistently worked on Gary over the years, urging him to consider the advantages of coming to work for the insurance company. Gary had politely listened and dismissed the notion each time Samuel had brought it up.

Now, when Gary initiated contact at Christmas and had told Samuel that he might be interested, Samuel was eager to talk with Gary and to his contacts at Horace Mann about any openings in the Mann corporate offices. It was right up Gary's alley, Samuel had said repeatedly.

I cannot quit teaching, Gary had thought to himself. He did not have his heart in the effort, he admitted to himself alone.

There just hadn't been enough money. Not enough to provide Lisa and the kids with all he wanted to give them. Extras, he told himself, trying to justify his desire to remain a teacher. Things they'd all just do fine without. Like vacations. There hadn't been one since he and Lisa had married. Not a real vacation. Two whole weeks. Somewhere outside the immediate Jacksonville area. A weekend in Chicago or St. Louis hardly seemed like a vacation.

And there was college to plan for. The twins inched their way toward inevitable tuition bills with each developmental milestone and Gary had been unable to chart a course that would enable him to adequately save for this certainty as of yet. It did not appear that circumstances were going to change, unless Gary made the leap.

Still, there were the students. How could he even think about leaving the profession? Especially now, with a roster full of bright, energetic kids filing into his classroom.

All seemed normal until Sara Jamison entered the room. She had obviously been crying. At last, Gary thought, we have one student showing empathy for another. It wasn't that Gary hoped the day would just be one huge series of depressing class sessions. He realized that life, and education, must go on, despite the disappearance of one of his students. It was just that somewhere along the line, these kids needed to start caring about each other in more than a superficial way.

Gary's realization that Sara was upset, not because of Amanda's disappearance, but because her mother had insisted on driving her to school, and that her mother would be picking her up after school, came quickly.

"Can you believe the woman?" Sara asked her friends. "Just because Amanda Hayes doesn't come home for the weekend, I have to be chauffeured around by my mommy."

"She doesn't want the boogie man to get you, Sara," a friend laughed.

"Oh, right. Like that's reality. I don't know what I'm gonna do; my mom's nuts over this thing."

Gary was not surprised. Once again, he shook his head and called the class to attention. English I was, again, underway.

Stiles entered a small room inside Jacksonville Police headquarters, housed within the confines of City Hall, along with fire station, mayor's office, and city council chambers. Awaiting him was a very nervous Keith Utterback. A third interview with Jacksonville police in as many days. They don't believe me, Keith thought to himself.

"Hi, Keith. I know we have already spoken about Amanda's disappearance. But we need some more information and, to be honest with you, Keith, we need to know if you're telling us the truth."

"I am, Lieutenant. I am telling you the truth. I don't know where Amanda is and I want to help you, but I don't know how I can."

Keith ran his hand through his hair.

"Now, you tell me you don't even believe me."

"Keith," Stiles interrupted, "I didn't say we didn't believe you. We just want to be able to reassure ourselves that you are telling us the truth, so we don't go down the wrong road in trying to find your girlfriend." He paused. "We have your parents outside, Keith. And they have talked to your family's lawyer. He's on his way, right now, to talk with you."

"Talk with me? What about? I didn't do anything wrong. What do I need a lawyer for?" He was upset, as Stiles had expected.

"I am asking you to submit to a polygraph test, Keith. When your lawyer gets here, he's going to visit with you and your folks. Then I'm going to come in again and ask you to take the test. Again, it's so we can move ahead, sort of eliminate you from any wrong-doing and move ahead with our investigation into other areas of Amanda's disappearance."

Stiles wanted desperately to believe the young man, and knew that the poor guy was scared witless, but he also knew that the polygraph test was the only way he could quickly eliminate Keith Utterback as a suspect and move on to other, as yet unidentified, suspects. He planned on asking the Hayes couple to submit to testing, as well. That would come later, however.

Gary's second period class was very different from the previous group. Juniors, juniors who were used to moving from class to class with Amanda Hayes, who were used to sitting next to her once in those classes, some of whom had known Amanda since kindergarten, were arriving en mass to Gary's classroom in a somber mood. They took their seats in the usual configuration. When all were seated, almost everyone's eyes were on the empty desk, usually occupied by their missing classmate.

"Okay, close those books," Gary said quietly. "Let's talk about it."

Since Keith Utterback's lawyer had, at least for the present, nixed the idea of a polygraph, Stiles had been forced to move on to other things. He wanted to confer with Keith some more. But he understood the lawyer's hesitance and knew that there was nothing he could do to force the issue for now. Stiles decided to investigate more closely the stolen van.

Tim McMichael sat on the top step of his front porch, waiting for the squad car to arrive. Someone from the Jacksonville Police Department had called a half-hour earlier to tell him that his van had been recovered and that a detective would be arriving shortly to talk with him. McMichael was anxious to get his van back, as his livelihood depended on it.

Stiles pulled up to the curb in front of McMichael's small home on the city's northeast side just in time to see Lieutenant John Odgen arrive.

McMichael rose to meet the officers, Ogden in his uniform and Stiles in plain clothes. McMichael waited, as Stiles nodded to give Ogden a go-ahead. The interrogation commenced.

"Lieutenant John Ogden, Jacksonville PD," he said, flashing his shield.

"You Timothy McMichael?"

"That's right, Officer," McMichael countered, trying not to reveal a newfound sense of urgency.

The second officer he recognized as Chief of Detectives L.J. Stiles. He had seen his picture in the paper, had heard his voice on the radio. But it wasn't Stiles who was speaking now.

"Mr. McMichael," Ogden continued, "we've located your van with the help of the Morgan County Sheriff's office and the vehicle is being processed right now by a number of criminologists from both offices and a unit out of Springfield. I expect your van will be unavailable to you for at least twenty-four more hours. In the meantime, I have a few questions for you, Mr. McMichael," careful not to intimidate his interviewee too much.

"I don't understand, Lieutenant. Someone stole my van. Was it damaged?" That was all Tim McMichael could muster, for it was apparent that Ogden was interested in questions for which he wanted answers, and not in providing answers for someone else's queries.

Stiles hung back and observed as Ogden proceeded to question the man.

"Mr. McMichael, when did you realize the van was missing?" Ogden asked, pen poised for McMichael's response.

"Friday afternoon. When I got back from camping out with a buddy and a couple of girls."

"When did you report it missing?"

"Later that afternoon. At first, I thought my brother had borrowed it. He has a set of keys, but he didn't know where the thing was. That's when I called the police."

"What time was that, Mr. McMichael?"

"I don't know. 'Round fivc, I gucss."

"Why did you not call sooner, Mr. McMichael?"

"I told you; I didn't know it was stolen till then. I finally got hold of my brother and he told me he didn't have the van."

"Where were you at the time?"

"Bahan's, uptown."

"Where did you call from? Here?"

"No. Bahan's."

"Who, if anybody, can verify your whereabouts then?"

"Look, I already told the cops all of this. I—"

"Well, Mr. McMichael, you're telling it to me now. Just answer the question, please."

Ogden's look told McMichael the detective meant business and he was quick to supply the name of his friend and anything else Ogden might ask about.

A smile crept across the face of L.J. Stiles.

"Does anyone else drive or ride in your van, Mr. McMichael?"

"Once in awhile I take on a part-time man when the job calls for it. And that van is my only transportation. So, yes, sometimes my friends ride in the van."

"Have you been sick lately, Mr. McMichael?"

He had not.

"Did you throw up in the van recently, Mr. McMichael?"

No. He hadn't.

"Has anyone else thrown up in your van, lately, that you know of?"

McMichael was puzzled, but again answered that no one, to his knowledge, had vomited in his van. He cringed at the thought of his van's present state.

"Can I have the address of the people who went camping with you, Mr. McMichael?"

When McMichael dictated the names and addresses of his fellow campers, Ogden was quick to end the conversation.

"Thank you, Mr. McMichael. If we have any further questions, we'll be contacting you. You plan on being around for the next few days, don't you?"

Ogden did not wait for a reply. He was quickly getting into his car and intending to pull away. But L.J. Stiles was at his window just as quickly and leaned over to address Ogden.

"You get up on the wrong side this morning, Lieutenant?"

Stiles was smiling again.

"Guess so, L.J."

Ogden was careful to not allow McMichael, who watched from his stoop, see his smile at Stiles.

He shrugged and put his cruiser in reverse before pulling away.

Stiles turned his attention to McMichael as Ogden finally did so. He proceeded to let McMichael know that he appreciated his answering the lieutenant's questions and that the department would return the van as soon as possible. He climbed into his Crown Vic and, his back to McMichael, waived at an upstairs window in the house across the street. An undercover police employee, an off-duty dispatcher, lived there. Stiles had assigned the young dispatcher to watch Tim McMichael for the four hours that would immediately follow Stiles' visit with McMichael. The dispatcher was hungry to serve and eager to make a more substantial contribution to the investigation.

The dispatcher had strict orders to have no contact with McMichael, or anyone else, for that matter, and to report via cell phone to headquarters if McMichael suddenly moved from his residence. He pulled the collar of his shirt up around his ears and settled into his seat, propping his feet on the table below the window through which he would "surveil" his neighbor. Had he worn a cap, he would be pulling it down over his brow, playing the role to which he had been assigned as best he could.

Stiles was not overjoyed at the thought of placing a dispatcher in the field, but was short-handed, as usual, and desperate to learn more about the young target of Ogden's latest barrage of questions in the case. He didn't know if McMichael had any knowledge of Amanda Hayes's whereabouts, but he was determined to find out.

Max Jansen sat at the counter of one of many restaurants on Morton Avenue. He hoped to satisfy his appetite for a late lunch devoid of any healthy aspect and to pick up on the mood of the town as it struggled with the fact that one of its young citizens was missing.

"What'll you have today?" the waitress asked.

"Roast beef plate and keep the coffee comin'."

"Coming right up, sir."

Suddenly Max sensed the presence of Jack McGlothen, a reporter from the Jacksonville daily newspaper. Young McGlothen was not so nearly as experienced as he thought himself to be, nor as talented. Yet he was arrogant. The intruder sat next to Max and turned toward him.

"What are you doing here, Max? You're not covering the Hayes story, are you?"

"What if I am?"

"Well, that's what I heard, Max. You're not on the story. She is," McGlothen said, pointing to an attractive young lady at a table in the corner of the restaurant.

She was Lori Bentley and she was, indeed, the reporter Max's editor had assigned to the story of the missing Jacksonville girl. She was a fine reporter, enthusiastic, capable, and hungry. Max, however, was not interested in giving McGlothen any satisfaction.

Max did not tolerate the Jack McGlothen's of the world well.

It violated his sense of superiority, for he was convinced that, although he might not be a great reporter, a Bob Woodward-in-the-making, he was vastly more talented than McGlothen. He had not yet made his mark on the profession. It was true. But, even if he never did, he could not see any justice in allowing a local newsboy like McGlothen even think they were in the same league.

Jansen spoke in a whisper.

"Oh, her? She follows me everywhere. She idolizes me, Jack. Can't write a lead sentence without my help. And you know what?" Jansen said, motioning McGlothen closer, seemingly to whisper in his ear, "she can write rings around you, Jackie-boy. Now, leave me alone. I'm working."

"Working?"

"You wouldn't know real newspaper work if the printed instructions appeared in bold print above the fold, Jack. Now go away. You bother me."

Impudent little prick, Jansen thought.

McGlothen left Max to his thoughts, confident that he was sufficiently under Max's skin. He was hopeful of breaking the story before Max could come up with an angle from which to cover the story.

Back to work, Max was listening for any piece of information that might come out of conversation in the restaurant. A name of someone who might be a source of information, some rumor that might have a hint of truth to it, something that would get him started down a road to truth was all Max wanted. If he did not find it here, that was okay. He had to eat anyway. Meg's friends, Max's temporary landlords, had split early that morning, off to work, Max presumed. At any rate, there was no food in the house. The nerve of some people.

The restaurant was full of the usual lunch crowd plus a few non-regulars, and like Max, out for the latest on the investigation of Amanda Hayes's disappearance. Max had been right in assuming it would be the topic of discussion throughout the restaurant. He winked at the waitress and told her he would return after a trip to the bathroom. Nature's call was the furthest thing from his mind. He was scouting the people who were intently discussing the story he hoped would make him famous.

Several customers were discussing Amanda within the groups of people seated at their own tables, but a greater number of people were having inter-table discussions, sharing what they knew or what they had heard someone else knew or what they thought they knew. Assumptions about the moral character of the girl could be heard, as could assurances that the girl was a nice kid, regularly seen at church on Sundays and brought up by good parents. Guesses about her whereabouts ranged from Springfield, staying with friends and afraid at the ruckus she had caused, to aboard an alien spaceship, from aside a road with her thumb extended and looking for adventure, to lying in a ditch next to the road, dead. No one wanted to admit that it was a possibility, but facts were facts.

"These are violent times we live in, you know."

"It happens all the time nowadays."

"Just thought it'd never happen here, though."

Max slowed as he encountered various conversations, taking in all he could, even joining in on one or two, agreeing with the last thing one of the speakers had offered as a theory. He hoped to ingratiate himself to the crowd, develop some rapport with anyone who might know just a little more than the next person.

Finally, he had made his way back from the restroom, his food waiting on him. He sat quietly and ate, wishing he were seated nearer one group in particular. The crowd at the table near which he wished he were seated was better dressed, more educated he guessed, perhaps more reliable in what they had to offer a hungry reporter. What they had to offer had to be more satisfying to this hungry reporter than the roast beef, which lay in front of him.

He finished his meal just as his colleague from the *Times* was exiting the restaurant. She had seen him there, he was sure. She had walked right past him, not speaking. He thought he saw her shake her head slightly as she walked toward her car. She was not the type to rub it in. But she must have been happy to be given such a great assignment at his expense. To say reporters, even reporters for the same newspaper, were competitive would be an understatement.

Enough of this, he thought. Time to go to work in earnest. A press conference, a briefing really, was twenty minutes away at City Hall. He did not want to miss anything that might be revealed there and, yet, he knew from experience that he would, perhaps, have to dig deeper into what the police were not saying to get at the truth before his colleagues. And that meant getting hold of someone in the police department who could give him a clue about what direction he needed to go. Detective Stiles, he thought with a smile.

He had not even thought of it before seeing him on the street a day earlier. He would get to work with Detective L.J. Stiles again. Or did they do battle? Max wasn't sure. He had always enjoyed their relationship, such as it was. It had not been that long ago, that Stiles and Jansen had been working in close proximity. He wondered if Stiles had missed him.

Twenty minutes later, Max Jansen stopped his car outside the Jacksonville Police Department and began collecting his notepad and pen for the upcoming press conference. He was increasingly skeptical about learning anything significant through these police briefings. Besides, the reporter assigned to the story by his editor at the *Times* would attend the event and he could get the information second-hand. Max was more intent on finding Amanda Hayes, or what had happened to her, than the fact that the Jacksonville Police did not know these things.

As he began to exit the car, Max saw the man he had seen the previous day, speaking with Lieutenant Stiles along College Avenue. The man was neatly dressed in beige Dockers, a light blue shirt and loosened tie. He moved quickly from the doorway at the west side of the police station toward his car parked along the street, just beyond the parking lot. He looked over his shoulder at the doorway he had just exited. Standing inside the door was L.J. Stiles, Chief of Detectives.

Two visits with Lieutenant Stiles in two days, Jansen thought. He'd have to find out who this bird was. Max jumped back into his car, quickly jotted down the license number of the automobile he had decided to follow and proceeded to do so at a safe distance. The object of his pursuit traveled north for a block, then turned west on Lafayette.

Several turns later, generally toward the southwest of their point of departure, Max's mark signaled one final turn. As the man pulled into a driveway and stepped out of his car, he gave no indication that he was even remotely aware that Max had followed him. Instead, he reached into the back seat of his car and pulled out a soft-sided briefcase. Two children appeared at the front door of the house and ran down the walk to greet their father. Twins, by their relative sizes.

Lisa McLean stood in the doorway and watched the scene. Having driven past the home and pulled over at the side of the road, Max Jansen observed as much through his rear-view mirror. He looked for his notepad that lay in the passenger seat across from him. 1180 Benton St., he wrote hurriedly. As he looked back to his mirror, he saw Gary McLean moving up the walk and into the house with his young family.

SIX

What resulted from Gary's second hour class on Monday and its efforts to deal with the fact that Amanda Hayes was missing for unknown, scary reasons was, for the lack of a better name, a "pep rally." It was scheduled for six-thirty that evening in the school's auditorium and was aimed at energizing and organizing a student body into action. Gary's students wanted to save a life. The JHS student body, spearheaded by Gary McLean and a junior class begging for his leadership, was committing itself to an all-out, "grassroots" effort to find Amanda Hayes.

Many students from Gary's second period class had spent the day lobbying a cooperative administration to allow students to meet that evening on school grounds. Others were collecting supplies with which they would produce posters that would soon be hanging throughout the Jacksonville community. Still others were spreading the word among the remainder of the school about the big event.

As Gary drove from his home toward the school, he pondered his role in all of this. He had prepared his administration for the pleadings of his followers. He had contacted Lieutenant Stiles in seeking guidance and support for the group's efforts and had informed Amanda's parents of the happenings. He had added his personal thoughts about Amanda and his hopes for her safe return when he spoke with Mrs. Hayes on the telephone that afternoon.

Predictably, she was appreciative of the school's actions and of Gary's prayerful thoughts.

Lieutenant Stiles had given his full support to the students' involvement where it concerned hanging posters, handing out flyers in public places, and having a prayer vigil. He even told Gary he would show up and address the group in the auditorium. But he had warned Gary about the dangers of having the students out at night looking for Amanda. The police, after all, had not eliminated the possibility that a person or persons, having taken Amanda, would not strike again. Stiles, in fact, had not eliminated any suspects in such a scenario—even Gary McLean.

Neither had, for that matter, Max Jansen. For it was Max, in his rented car, who now followed Gary to the high school. Having contacted a friend in the Secretary of State's office to learn Gary's identity from his license number, Max was curious about Gary's involvement in Amanda's life and the extent to which Gary might be involved in the girl's disappearance.

"You're too cynical," Meg had told him earlier on the telephone. "You had better watch yourself and hold your suspicions in check, before you make an accusation against an innocent man."

"Yeah? Well you don't know this guy, either," Max had reminded Meg. "And you just think he's squeaky clean because he's a school teacher."

Meg, herself a professor of modern languages at the University of Illinois at Springfield, held an affection for others in her profession not shared by Jansen. This had been the source of many discussions in the past. Max, it seemed, had not had much use for many of his teachers, either in high school or college. Although Meg had forced him to admit, on occasion, that he owed much to his schooling and that he had not, as he often opted to claim, done it on his own, Max was skeptical of most educators.

On this night, however, Max and Meg had, once again, agreed to disagree and had left it at that. Meg had found herself less effective in convincing Max that he was a curmudgeon over the phone. She was far more convincing in the flesh, when she could look into his eyes, read him like a familiar old book, and make him admit his errors before he proceeded to go about committing those errors again. In person, she had rightfully convinced herself, she could make him say just about anything, anything except, "I love you."

If Gary suspected he was being followed, he had not given any indication to Max. His eyes appeared to remain fixed on the road ahead. There were no repeated glances in the rear view mirror and his speed did not vary. Max, after all, was good at this type of thing, having followed many suspects, eyewitnesses, and their lawyers over the years. He was convinced that he could do this in his sleep and remain undetected.

Gary arrived back at Jacksonville High School at six-fifteen, disappointed that more cars were not already filling the parking lot for the rally. As he exited his car and made his way across the lot toward the front doors leading to the auditorium, he noticed Max's rental and a dozen or so other cars pull into the lot and beginning to empty themselves of their passengers. Many students carried signs, posters, and flyers with them. They had been busy, it appeared, working on various projects even before the meeting had begun.

All right, Gary thought, with a smile emerging for the first time that day. These kids are catching on. Perhaps some good might come of this whole affair. His smile disappeared and his thoughts leapt immediately to Amanda. How could he think of something like that now, he wondered. Amanda's the important thing here, he reminded himself. Gary entered the auditorium along with his many students who had come to help him organize a search for their friend. He had failed to notice Max, sitting low in the driver's seat of the rented car.

Trey Cederquist was hard at work, directing Luke and Marcus, as they moved one heavy box after another from one side of the room to another. Had they wives to direct them so, in an attempt to get the living room furniture just right, it would have been no more unnerving or frustrating. But Trey was convinced the shifting of boxes was absolutely necessary and there was no arguing with him when he got this way.

Boxes were stacked neatly on all sides of the room, which was the sum total of the entire building, a twenty-eight by sixty foot warehouse with a corrugated metal exterior at the rear of the eighty acres that was Cederquist Industries. No longer a working component of the family business, the huge shed was now vital to Trey's personal operation. He possessed the only key to several padlocks that secured the remote building. No one employed by CI, however, was likely to even come close to the warehouse. No one, that is, except the night watchman and Trey had paid to keep his eyes, ears, and mouth shut. Most other Cederquist employees had probably forgotten that the warehouse still stood there, nestled as it was in the southwest corner of the company's main property.

The view into the windows of the warehouse on all sides was blocked by boxes, which were placed in such a way that they would block light from inside the shed, as well. No one could see into the shed, even if he put his nose to the glass. Nor could one detect that someone was inside at night, which was principally when Trey and his helpers were present.

Whatever Trey was up to in the shed was not something he wished to share with the employees of his father's company. Nor did he wish the world to see the path that had been carved from the back door of the shed, through a makeshift "gate" in the back fence, and on through the woods for perhaps half a mile. Trey had purchased the property next to his father's company, which manufactured plastic containers, from a local farmer to insure privacy. He secretly rented the property to its former owner.

"Let's get a move on, girls," Trey barked. "After you get these boxes in place, you can take those five over there, move 'em out one-by-one and bring the two from the truck in on your way back. And remember; be careful with those two. They contain glass tubing like that over there."

"Right, boss," Marcus responded.

"Sure thing," Luke echoed, who mumbled something under his breath for good measure.

The wheelbarrow Luke and Marcus used for transfer along the wooded path had been modified to carry the boxes, the sides having been bent to hold the boxed product rather than dirt or sand or gravel, for which the conveyance had been designed. Trey would not accept even the possibility of a dropped box along the path. That would mean delays or possibly even lost product and neither was good business. He had quite an operation in place here. There was even, at the other end of the path, an earthen loading ramp, up to which Luke's Ford pick-up was backed. Trey had thought of everything.

Lieutenant L.J. Stiles arrived at the front door of the JHS Auditorium at precisely six thirty-five. As he made his way across the now-crowded parking lot, Max Jansen approached him, asking the predictable questions about the investigation after offering his hand to Stiles and his most business-like greeting. Stiles took Max's hand and smiled back. He trusted Max more than most members of the press, but could not figure out why exactly.

"No news, yet, Max," Stiles said slowly in answer to Max's first question. "We have no leads, whatsoever," in answer to Max's second question. "And we have eliminated no possible scenario; nor have we put anyone on or taken anyone off a list of possible suspects," in anticipation of Max's third.

Fair enough, Max thought, smiling at his own predictability. He paused to write the comments in his notepad but stopped to look up at the police lieutenant as Stiles waved over his shoulder and he marched on toward the auditorium doorway. Max was not surprised when Stiles suddenly turned on his heel, looked coolly into Max's eyes, and said, "But we will find her, Max." He paused. "You can quote me."

Once Stiles was inside the auditorium, he could see that few seats remained unfilled. At the front of the hall, standing behind a small podium, Principal Norm Singletary was addressing the crowd that Stiles could see included, not only JHS students, but also many adults. Not the least conspicuous among the crowd was his boss, the mayor. The village president of South Jacksonville was less visible, Stiles thought, if she were there.

Stiles made his way through the aisle on the left-hand side of the auditorium toward the front and stood at the steps leading up to the stage, awaiting an introduction, which Gary McLean had told him would come at about seven o'clock. He patiently stood with his back to the wall, scanning the sea of faces, wondering who, if anyone, knew anything about the case that might help him solve it. His eyes met Gary's as the latter stood opposite him at the right of the stage, waiting for the principal to turn the microphone over to him once again.

"Once again," Principal Singletary concluded, "I applaud your efforts. You have shown us once more that Jacksonville is a special community and that Jacksonville High School is a special place. We care about each other here. We've always taken care of each other here. Let's not forget to take care of each other now, as we do what we can to bring our friend home."

The principal turned awkwardly toward Gary, who took his cue and quickly ascended the steps onto the stage. The crowd, just as awkwardly, struggled to find itself. Do we applaud? Do we verbally respond in approval? It was a nervous smattering of applause that resulted, sending the principal off the stage and greeting Gary McLean, teacher, friend, leader, as he approached the mike.

"Thank you, Mr. Singletary. And I want to echo your very appropriate remarks. Let us not forget to take care of ourselves and of each other during these very difficult times. You students need to keep up with your schoolwork, keep getting plenty of rest, eat regularly, all of that. I've been speaking with our school counselors here at school today. They wanted me to be sure to tell you this tonight. You have to take care of yourselves while we try to cope with this matter."

He paused, briefly. "There's another concern, too. About taking care of each other, I mean, that we have to address. We don't want to alarm you or your parents, but there are some very real concerns that we have that I want you to listen to and think about. We don't know where Amanda is. We hope she is safe. We hope she is out of harm's way. But the very real possibility exists that someone or, perhaps more than one person, is behind her disappearance."

The crowd was now very quiet. Gary measured his words carefully.

"The possibility also exists that this person or persons are still in the Jacksonville area." Now, he got to his point. "I don't want any of you to meet up with someone like that, if that person does exist. You must be careful until we know who or what is behind Amanda's disappearance."

The hush that had fallen over the room was now gone and conversations broke out throughout the room. Gary raised his hands in an effort to quiet the crowd. He began to speak again, but found it necessary to raise his voice as well, before he could regain control.

"Now, we don't want you to panic. There is nothing that I know of to indicate that anyone is in danger, but until we know what's happened to Amanda, I don't want any of you to take any unnecessary risks. And that includes what you do in your efforts to help find Amanda."

Gary looked pleadingly at Lieutenant Stiles, who recognized that Gary needed help. He sprang up to steps of the stage and approached the podium. Gary was relieved to find he had an ally on whom he could depend, both in alleviating the crowd's fears and in heightening their awareness of the possible dangers. He introduced Stiles to the crowd and backed away as Stiles attempted to do what the two men had discussed earlier in Stiles' office, what they both had agreed would be necessary to do on this evening.

"Let me assure you, first of all," Stiles began, "that the Jacksonville Police Department, in cooperation with the Morgan

County Sheriff's Department and the South Jacksonville Police Department and a lot of other local and state agencies, are doing all we can to locate your friend. As Mr. McLean has told you, there is not at this time any evidence, first that anything tragic has happened to her or that anyone has harmed her in any way, or that, should such a person exist, he is in our city or will do anything to anyone else. All we know, at this point, is that Amanda is not where she needs to be, at home with her parents or in school with you. That's all we know."

He paused for effect.

"But," pausing again, "since we don't know where Amanda is, and we don't know what might have happened to her, we don't want to expose you to even the remotest possible danger, should that danger exist. What I am saying to you, young people, is that you should do what you should always be doing when you are out and about in our city. Be careful. This is not the world in which your grandparents or even your parents grew up. You must exercise some degree of caution when you are away from your home, away from your parents."

"I am asking that for the next few days, you not travel alone. Use a buddy system. Most of you are apt to do that anyway, so we're not asking a whole lot from you at this point. Simply, stay together as you go to and from school, your jobs or out to eat. Let your folks know where you're going."

Students responded with a collective groan, followed by some awkward laughter. They wondered if it were all right to laugh with Amanda still missing.

Stiles continued, acknowledging the crowd's desire to share a laugh even in the face of a possible tragedy.

"Let them know when you'll be back and whom you will be with. We aren't suggesting that you hide in your homes or that you barricade yourselves behind the doors of your homes. Just be a little more aware of what's going on around you, especially as you go out hanging your posters or handing out your leaflets about Amanda. And, again, stay together."

"Thank you, Mr. McLean," Stiles said, turning now to Gary. "Thank you for the opportunity to speak and thank you for your efforts in organizing the production of the materials you and your students are going to distribute."

The two men shook hands and Stiles left the stage. Max Jansen, having followed Stiles into the auditorium, had found a seat on the step in the aisle leading upward to the rear of the auditorium. He had tried feverishly to record all that was said, but was struck once again by the feeling with which Stiles always approached his job. Stiles had, with the help of Gary McLean, made the message clear and palpable to the concerned citizenry of Jacksonville who had assembled on this night out of fear and love. Max was touched by Stiles' obvious affection for the people he served. He was even finding it hard to suspect McLean of anything at the moment.

Gary was now turning the microphone over to one of several ministers in attendance. The parish priest at Amanda's Catholic Church was leading a prayer for Amanda's safe return. He included in his prayer a request for forgiveness for anyone who might now have Amanda with him and for that person to be touched by this forgiveness, so that Amanda might soon be returned to her home safely.

When the priest had concluded, Gary returned to the podium. He calmly told students that posters and flyers were placed just outside the auditorium on tables. He asked that students move toward the exits and that on their way home, in no less than pairs of students, they hang a poster somewhere between the school and their homes, so that it might be visible to passersby. Gary again emphasized that, if any student were traveling home alone, he or she should go straight home and not bother to hang posters.

The crowd moved toward the exits, led by Max Jansen who snatched up a flyer, folded it quickly, and stuffed it in his pocket. He moved outside and across the parking lot to his car. He had to stop briefly and remind himself what the rental looked like before he found it and climbed in. He decided to wait for Gary to exit the auditorium. When he finally saw Gary step out into the night with several other adults, who one after another reached for Gary's hand and apparently thanked him for his efforts, Max decided to leave ahead of Gary and return to his temporary quarters for a beer and a good night's sleep. It had been a long day.

Ben Hayes, worn and worried, had not worked at all that day, but thought it best that he stop in at his office to check up on the mail. He secretly hoped that something there might take his mind off Amanda and the concerns he felt more and more for her safety. It was nine o'clock and Cederquist Industries would be deserted, except for an inept security guard, who Ben had felt should have been cut loose long ago.

He pulled into the main gate at CI and drove slowly toward the main office building in the middle of the complex. Mercury vapor lights illuminated the parking lot and it was difficult to see beyond the lot fronting the east side and main entrance to the office building. He pulled into a parking space, on which his name was neatly stenciled, white paint on the black asphalt.

As he turned off his engine and swung his left foot out the open door, he distinctly heard a man's voice from some distance to the south. One word, and one word alone, had been yelled, apparently in pain, or disgust, or possibly in anger. Hayes could not tell which. But he knew he had heard the word clearly.

"Shit!"

Hayes looked around quickly in all directions. No sign of Bleuther, the inept guard. Probably him that had yelled, Ben thought. Scared himself when he walked around a corner and encountered his shadow. Oh, well. I'll page him when I get inside and have him investigate, his thoughts continuing. Probably nothing, anyway.

"What are you doing, Marcus?" Cederquist whispered. Trey was not at all happy. He had heard Marcus' loud outburst from inside the warehouse and had run outside to investigate.

Luke had left the wheelbarrow on the path and had already started back. Now he was running back toward the others at hearing Marcus' cry.

"What happened?"

"That seems to be the question, Luke." Trey was staring intently at Marcus, who now began brushing his knees with his hands. A box lay at his feet.

"'Twasn't nothin', Trey. I tripped on that damn fence again," he quickly added, "But I didn't spill nothin'."

"Make sure you don't, pinhead. And, for chrissakes, don't be yelling, either. You want someone to hear you?" He shook his head in disgust and mumbled something about incompetence, as he turned and re-entered the shed, leaving the two dunderheads from Kentucky outside.

Luke looked at Marcus, wishing, as he often did, that he could help his friend.

"You okay?"

"Yeah."

"Look. You leave that box and go on down the path to where I left the wheelbarrow. I gotta tell Trey something."

"Now, just a minute, Luke. It's your turn to wheel that box out there—"

"Marcus, shut up and do what I said. I seen lights out in the parking lot while I was on the path. I gotta tell Trey. You hear? I'll catch up to you with this here box in a minute. I'll carry it out by hand and you won't have to wheel any more boxes in tonight. Okay?"

"Okay."

Trey was busy unpacking one of the boxes the boys had already brought in from the truck. He was startled when he heard Luke call his name from just inside the door.

"What's up, Luke?" he said, regaining his composure. "You scared me half to death, boy."

"Trey, I seen lights, headlights, in the parking lot when I was out on the path."

Cederquist looked worried and began to pace immediately.

Luke continued, trying to calm Cederquist, "Probably ol' Bleuther, Trey. Nothin' to fret on. Just thought you oughta know."

"Yeah, you're probably right, Luke. But I'm gonna go check it out, anyway."

He moved toward the doorway. He stopped suddenly and turned.

"Luke, you gotta get Marcus to be more careful. We can't afford any screw-ups. You talk to him and tell him that I won't have him around anymore if he keeps screwing up."

"I will, Trey. I'll talk to him. Sure thing."

"You boys, get on outta here for tonight. And remember. Don't go home til I say it's safe. Better stay out at the cabin. I'm going to see what's going on up at the parking lot."

Meg answered the phone on the second ring.

"Hi, Meggy. It's me, Max."

"Well, it's about time; don't you think. It's late."

Max rolled his eyes and took another bite of a candy bar he had found in the kitchen downstairs.

Finally, Meg checked her tone and asked, "So, what have you been up to, Max? You getting any leads on the missing girl? I haven't been getting much information from what's-her-name's stories in the *Times*. So, when are you going to break the big story?"

"You're getting as bad as me, Meg. Questions, questions, questions."

"Well, you're not the only one who's curious, George."

Max laughed. She was good for him, good for him, indeed. Quickly, he returned to a reality he did not want to get used to.

"I'm getting nowhere, Meg. Nowhere. I went to a rally they had at the high school tonight. That teacher we talked about earlier organized it. I've been seeing him talking regularly for the past couple days with Stiles, the Chief of Detectives over here. Looks to me like the guy's a dweeb and is up to something, but I don't know."

"Max, you're too suspicious sometimes for your own good. I just saw that teacher on a commercial for the Channel 20 news at ten and he looks like a nice man."

"I don't believe you, Meg. You don't know the guy, do you? You see about three seconds of him on TV; you don't even hear his voice; you don't even know what he said at this meeting tonight. But you think he looks like a nice man," mocking her by sweetening the last few words.

"Well, I probably know as much about him as you do, Max, and you've got him convicted of kidnapping, murder, and who-knows-what-else," she countered.

"I know a little more about him than you do, Meg; alright?"

"Like what?"

Max was rolling his eyes again. "Gary McLean; married; two kids, boy and a girl, twins, age four; English teacher at Jacksonville High; drives a '90 Corola; wife Lisa, unemployed, drives a Dodge Caravan. He's a Jacksonville native; she's the former Lisa Olson, from Effingham. They met in college, Illinois College, here in Jacksonville. They're in debt up to their eyeballs—"

"All right, all right. That's enough." Max, as usual, had done his homework. "Sounds like the all-American couple to me. Leave them alone, Max."

"Not while there's a chance in hell that this guy's dirty."

"There you go, again, Max, with your Sam Spade-talk. The guy's not dirty, I tell you. He's a teacher—"

"And that makes him automatically clean?" Max interrupted.

"Well, no; not automatically," she fought back. "Just clean." It was all she could manage. No use fighting logically. Max wasn't into it. She caved in and changed the subject.

"You taking care of yourself, Max?"

"Yeah; I'm fine, Meg. Thanks for asking."

"You sound tired, and lonely," she ventured.

"Correct on both counts, Meg. You think you might drive over for a visit? Say, tomorrow?"

"Well, I'm off work, remember. My wonderful vacation has

had enough of Oprah and Rosie. That's for sure. When and where, cowboy?"

"There's another rally after school tomorrow. They dismiss early for spring break at eleven. Meet me at the town square at noon?"

"I'll be there, lover boy." Then, after a brief silence, "Max? I miss you."

"Me, too, Meg. Good night."

Lisa McLean had finally finished the supper dishes, the ones she had fought over doing with her mother earlier that evening. She and her mother always had the same argument. Her parents would come up to spend the week with the twins and, yet, when Lisa would tell her mother that she would do the dishes and let grandma play grandma, grandma wanted to play homemaker. When these kids have kids, Lisa reminded herself, I am doing no dishes.

She and her mother had, of course, both taken time out with Maddie and Steve, leaving the dishes for later. It had helped take Lisa's mind off of the meeting her husband had organized that evening. He was back now, downstairs telling her dad all about it. She had heard the car in the drive and Gary come in the side door.

Earlier that evening, she had watched Gary back out the drive and move away. She recalled catching a glimpse of a dark blue Ford pull away from the curb just down the street, move slowly past their house, and disappear along with Gary in the distance. Was he being followed? Ridiculous, she thought. Or was it?

Gary was at the top of the stairs, calling her name quietly, for he knew that the twins should be asleep or very nearly so.

"In here, Gary," she volunteered from their bathroom. She was removing her contacts. "How was the meeting?"

She could tell he was worried.

"I guess it went okay. Stiles showed up, as promised. Singletary did an okay job. I rambled a bit myself."

"I'm sure you did just fine, Gary. This can't be easy for you, I know." She held out her free hand, the other clinging to a towel.

Gary was undressing for bed. He allowed Lisa to stroke his face gently.

She did not know whether to bring up the blue Ford or not. She did not want to upset Gary, but wondered whether or not she should be upset, herself.

"Gary," she began, "do you think that Lieutenant Stiles would have you followed?"

Gary was surprised.

"For what?"

"I don't know, honey. I just—"

"Look here, Lisa," he said, taking her in his arms. "I haven't done anything wrong. I am in no danger. Why would Stiles have me followed?"

She knew the question was rhetorical. She nodded and received his kiss openly.

"Is Dad still downstairs?"

"Yes. He said he was going to read for awhile."

"I'll be right back. I'm going to tell him good-night."

On her way down the hall, Lisa stopped in front of the twins' bedroom. Soon they would be moving one of them across the hall into a separate room, but they slept in twin beds across the room from one another for now. She looked down on their beautiful faces, lit dimly by an Oscar the Grouch nightlight. She thought of Amanda Hayes, of the blue Ford, and she worried.

Bleuther had not answered his page. Mildly disturbed by this on any other occasion, Ben Hayes was not too concerned on this night. He had, after all, bigger things on his mind. He had struggled to work his way through his mail, finding it almost impossible to think of anything but his daughter. Somehow, he had found a way to occupy his mind for about half an hour and then found it too difficult to go any longer.

He made his way down the hall toward the exit he nearly always used when he was leaving work. It saved him a few steps taking the exit, rather than going out the main entrance to the office building. As he stepped outside the exit, he saw the figure of a man, silhouetted by the parking lot lights. The man was leaning on Ben's car, smoking a cigarette. Ben looked to his left and to his right. He saw no one else and decided to move toward his car, clutching his briefcase, intent on using it as a weapon if need be. As he approached the man and his car, Ben recognized the figure as Trey Cederquist. No sense of relief, however, came to Hayes.

"Hi, ya, Benny."

"Trey."

"What's up, Ben?"

"Perhaps I should be asking you what's up, Trey," Ben said, looking over his shoulder now in the direction of the warehouse where Ben was sure he had heard a man, not Trey Cederquist, another man, yell, "Shit."

Trey was quick to move around Ben, between where Ben stood and the warehouse, some five hundred feet away. "You just don't worry about what ol' Trey's up to, Benny. You got enough to worry about, don't you? Any sign of that little girl of yours, Ben?"

Hayes detected the hint of a smile on Trey's face. Son-of-a-bitch, Ben thought.

"I guess not," Trey said, when Hayes did not respond.

Deciding to change the subject and, therefore, the control of the conversation, Ben began, "What is it you're up to, Trey? You're not up to your old tricks, are you?"

Trey was on the defensive.

"Look, Hayes. You don't know what you think you know. You didn't see anything last year. I don't care what you think you saw. You saw nothing."

Ben had him where he wanted him.

"I saw you using cocaine last year, Trey. In July. Is that what you're talking about? And I don't think I saw it. I saw it."

"Kiss my ass, ol' man. You wouldn't know cocaine from powdered sugar. Besides, even if I did something like that, you won't tell the old man, because you know I know things about you, too."

Now, Ben was at the disadvantage. He had an idea what Trey claimed to know about. And Ben was well aware that Trey had a way of making trouble for people. Trey was convinced that Ben had diverted company funds for his own use. Cederquist would have a difficult time proving this, for Ben had done nothing wrong. But would Cederquist have to prove anything? He was a Cederquist, after all.

Ben had tried to convince himself that the boss's son did not hold all the cards, especially when he had caught Trey in his office putting white powder up his nose the previous summer. But Ben knew that saying anything to Marshall Cederquist, Jr., would prove risky, at best. He found himself where he despised being found, at the mercy of Trey Cederquist.

Seeing that he could accomplish nothing more with Trey, he turned to move toward his car. Trey was quick, again, to move this time between Ben and the car. He stood between Ben and the driver's door, paused, and ceremoniously opened the door for Ben.

"You take care, now, Benny. And I sincerely hope that little girl of yours turns up real soon."

Ben pulled the door shut, Trey's fingers just clearing the way for the door to slam shut. Trey laughed loudly enough for Ben to hear inside the car. The engine started, Ben moved away, squealing the tires on the parking lot pavement. Ben hurried toward the gates to Cederquist Industries. He slammed his open hand hard on the steering wheel, causing him to veer to the left before regaining control of his car. His emotions were another matter.

SEVEN

Margot Hayes had left her home early Tuesday morning and stopped by the Jacksonville Police Headquarters in City Hall, hoping to learn from someone there, anyone, that there was some news on her daughter's whereabouts. There Lieutenant Lawrence Jon Stiles had informed her, sadly, that there was still nothing he could tell her. He had tried unsuccessfully to reassure her that everything humanly possible was being done to locate Amanda and return her safely to her parents.

Their conversation had been brief and Margot mumbled to herself in disgust, for she had been gruff with the detective. She was ordinarily an understanding, even forgiving person. At least, she thought of herself in such terms. She recognized that she was not herself lately and tried to convince herself that anyone in her current situation would understandably experience some type of metamorphosis. She did not want to get used to it, either. She worried about how all this might end and how it might change her.

That would have to wait, however, for now she was on her way to Springfield. She dreaded the long ride. She was done, she told herself, using time to think of places where her daughter might be, of people with whom she might be staying, either of her own free will or under other, more tentative, circumstances. Now, as she merged with eastbound traffic on Interstate 72, she realized she would have to fill time with thoughts of something else, something more productive. Of what, she had known not. But now, a plan of action was taking form.

Margot had pleasant memories of Amanda's childhood with

which to play in her mind. Perhaps they would make the journey to Springfield go by more quickly. She could recall Amanda's birth down to the last detail. Amanda's first steps, her first pet, her difficult start at school, the third grade picture in which Amanda had smiled, forgetting her earlier refusal to do so because she was minus two front teeth. Happy, joyous memories, which brought a rare smile to Margot's own face. Then, an invasion of doubt and worry. Would these memories be all she might have left? And would they continue to bring smiles her way?

Even with her return to reality, Margot found herself moving past the New Berlin exit, last of only two between Jacksonville and Springfield, and approaching the Wabash Street exit, the first of six, which could take her into the state capital. She would soon reach the Sixth Street exit. Time had somehow, mysteriously, moved faster than it had since she had first become aware that Amanda was missing. Perhaps it had something to do with her destination in Springfield.

Visiting a psychic would be a first for Margot Hayes. Then, again, having a missing child was a first.

Marshall Cederquist, Jr., speed dialed Murphy, Louderback, and Wiggins and waited impatiently, first, as a receptionist answered and, then, as she connected him with his lawyer and best friend, Stu Murphy.

"Stu, I have been thinking about this all night and I have decided that I want to offer a reward in this matter concerning Ben Hayes's daughter."

"What you mean to say, Marshall, is that you want to offer a reward for Margot Hayes's daughter. Am I correct?"

"Don't be a smartass, Stu," Marshall shot back.

Had anyone else been so impertinent with Marshall Cederquist, Cederquist would have hung up. He would not have found the reminder of his affection for Margot amusing. And there was certainly nothing at all amusing about a missing teenage girl. But

Marshall knew that Stu had meant no disrespect for Amanda. Nor was he rubbing Marshall's face in an extramarital affair from long ago. He was just reminding his old friend that there were considerations that must be made before making such a move.

"Marshall, you'd better stop and think about this."

"I have, Stu, and it's going to get done," he paused, "with you or without you."

Murphy thought about the last time that he had heard Cederquist use such a tone with him. From time to time, over the many years they had known each other, Cederquist had said this very thing. Cederquist had never once had to do anything without Stu Murphy's assistance, but Murphy had always made it a point to give his client the best legal advice he could. Murphy had rarely been able to convince Cederquist to change his mind and, to his credit, Cederquist was usually correct in the end. When, on occasion a venture had proven fruitless, Murphy gave his friend the support he needed. Cederquist knew he could count on Stu Murphy. Still, it had been some time since Murphy had heard such determination in his friend's voice.

"Okay, Marsh. It's gonna happen. But, as your lawyer and as your friend, I have to tell you why you should not do this."

"I'm listening." Cederquist knew the arguments that were about to be presented to him. Out of respect for Stu, Marshall Cederquist would listen. Then, of course, he would go ahead and do what he had intended to do all along.

Both men knew that Cederquist could afford, financially, to offer a sizeable reward. But there were public relations considerations, which could not be ignored. Few people knew of the affair between Cederquist and Margot Hayes. Actually, Murphy was sure that no one besides the three of them had any knowledge of the matter. Still, Murphy reasoned, more than a few eyebrows would be raised when an announcement of a reward by Cederquist was made.

Marshall Cederquist was an important man, respected by all who knew him. The problem, as Murphy had always regretted, was that few people in Jacksonville really knew him. Cederquist was not aloof, just busy. He was not unfriendly, but content to move among a small circle of friends. He was, indeed, magnanimous, giving generously to charitable causes, but was not given to self-congratulatory show. So, few people knew he was unselfish, choosing instead to see him as just another wealthy, and therefore greedy, businessman. Some of these people would find it hard to believe that he would offer such a reward just because Amanda's father worked for Cederquist Industries.

Stu Murphy made all of this abundantly clear. When he had finished presenting his case, Cederquist had only one question, "How much do you think I ought to offer for this reward, Stu?"

Murphy, smiled as he shook his head and leaned back in his chair, the phone at his ear, "I don't know, Marsh. What'd you have in mind?"

"Ten thousand."

"Sounds reasonable." After a brief pause, for Murphy knew he need not ask if Cederquist were sure, he said, "I will take care of it." Then, another pause, for he knew he must measure his words, "I just ask one thing, Marshall. You let me handle the whole thing. I contact the bank, the press, even Ben. I don't want any of your emotions for Margot spilling out. Let me protect you from that."

Cederquist was confident that he could handle such an announcement without difficulty, but had intended for Murphy to take care of matters all along.

"Do it," he said simply.

Margot had wrestled with the notion of visiting a psychic throughout the evening before, although she had mentioned it to no one, especially not Ben. He would not approve of her visit. His objection would be swift, she was sure.

She and Amanda had often talked of one day making such a visit. Several psychics advertised regularly in the Springfield papers and they had even spotted a shingle or two hanging along

Seventh Street, as they had driven south from the Capitol. Margot thought visiting one of the establishments might make for an interesting mother-daughter outing someday and had secretly hoped it might prove enlightening, too.

Ben had always dismissed such ideas out of hand. Foolishness, he had branded them whenever the two Hayes women brought such things up. A shared wink and the two knew they would have to one day make the trip to Springfield covertly. Shopping he would approve of, one told the other, although they would have to come home with some purchases to hide their true purpose in making the trip. They laughed together more than once at the thought of such deception.

Today, however, Margot made the trip without the lighthearted festiveness she had so looked forward to when she and Amanda had planned the adventure. She was grieving, she feared, and there was no proof, yet, that grief was called for.

Perhaps, if she could consult with someone with a heightened cognition, a connected awareness, about her daughter's disappearance, she could locate her baby. She wasn't sure if she believed in the powers advertised in the papers or on the shingle hanging on the post outside the house she now found herself parked beside. What could it hurt, she told herself. She exited her car, strode the twenty paces to the front door, and entered.

A small front room or reception area, unoccupied by either receptionist or customer, was just inside the door.

Customer. Was that what she was? Or, was she a client? Not a patient. A sucker? She shook her head and reached for the doorknob.

"May I help you?" someone said from just beyond the archway over Margot's shoulder as she closed the door behind her. A woman, in her forties, stepped into the archway, following her voice.

Margot abandoned the knob, turned, and looked closely in the direction of the voice. She was surprised. But, then, she had told herself beforehand, had told Amanda on occasions before, that, no matter what she found during such a visit, she would be surprised. She simply did not know what to expect. She had not, however, expected to find such a pleasant-looking woman. The woman was dressed casually, but bore an elegance, stemming from some part of her which Margot had not yet identified. The woman smiled and immediately put Margot at ease.

No long, flowing, print gypsy dress, bodice gathered at the waist. No exotic headdress, or scarf, or dangling gypsy earrings. Just a modest, middle-aged woman, who could have been one of Margot's friends from the card club.

Margot smiled nervously and cleared her voice before speaking. "Are you the psychic?"

"Yes, I am," came the warm response. The woman moved toward her at a friendly pace. Perhaps she sensed Margot's anxiety. Perhaps she sensed anxiety in many, most, all of her customers. Clients? Suckers? What would the psychic call Margot, anyway? Margot wondered. Perhaps this anxiety would be perceptible even to a non-mystic.

"I guess I'm here for a reading," Margot volunteered, wondering if that was the correct term.

"Wonderful," the psychic said. "Won't you, please, sit down. I was just cleaning up in the kitchen in back. Let me turn off the water I'm running and I'll be right with you."

Margot sat in one of four chairs spaced neatly along two walls of the room. Opposite sat a receptionist's desk, complete with telephone, Rolodex, appointment book, and pen and paper. A computer keyboard and monitor rested atop a typewriter stand. The CPU sat upright on the floor beside the desk. Above the monitor, a sign spelled out terms and conditions for doing business with Madame Lazar, or whatever-her-name-would-turn-out-to-be. "Cash only. No personal checks without ample identification. Payment beforehand. No exceptions," the sign read.

Margot rose as the Psychic returned, drying her hands with a dishtowel. She offered a dry hand, finally, and introduced herself as, simply, Doris. She motioned for Margot to follow her through the archway and down the hall in the opposite direction from which she had emerged earlier. Margot followed closely, hoping to skip formalities and get right to her problem and learn if Doris could help her.

Doris opened a door to what had been, at one time, a bedroom in this modest two-story. Margot speculated that Doris probably lived upstairs.

The room was dark for midday, the curtains having been drawn and the room's single lamp emitting the wattage of a nightlight. Doris turned a dial on the wall that brightened things by one hundred percent, but it was still somewhat dark.

"Perhaps, I should pay you first, Doris. How much is your fee?" Margot asked.

Ben Hayes had enough of sitting around his home doing nothing. He had decided there was nothing he could accomplish at work. His mind was, understandably, on Amanda. Yet, he felt he was wasting valuable time doing nothing but sitting at home waiting for the phone to ring. Margot had left earlier that morning, saying only that she needed some time alone. Ben suspected that his wife had stolen away to church. He had to admit that it made more sense than sitting at home.

Keys in hand, he locked the door behind him, unusual for either of the Hayes's and made his way for his car at the end of the driveway. Once inside, he turned the radio off and backed out slowly. Where would he go? He decided quickly that he had not driven through Morgan County's southwestern corner and that he might as well get to it. Amanda had to be somewhere and he wasn't going to find her at home.

Margot sat herself opposite Doris, a small, square table between them. Doris placed her elbows on the table and leaned in slightly.

Margot sat upright with her hands folded in her lap. Doris smiled openly.

"What is it you've come to see me about today?"

"My daughter. She's missing."

"I'm so sorry."

"She's been gone since Friday morning. She never made it to school that day and no one's seen her since."

"How old is your daughter?"

"Seventeen." Anticipating the common assumption, Margot continued. "She did not run away. We get along fine. Amanda. That's my daughter. Amanda and her father get along fine. He's a little distant, I think. But they get along fine. She has a boyfriend. And he's at home. Looking for Amanda, actually. But it's not one of those situations where she's run off with a boy, or anything."

Margot decided that, perhaps, she was talking too much. She paused to learn what it was that Doris would want to know, rather than ramble on about things that Doris might not be interested in.

"Tell me more about Amanda," Doris said.

"She's bright. She loves school. She has lots of friends. One girlfriend in particular. Melissa. She's a good girl. And Keith, her boyfriend. I don't know a lot about him. He's new. But he seems real nice. The first real boyfriend, I think, she has ever had. She hasn't said too much about him. But she seemed to really like him."

Margot suddenly remembered that she had brought something of Amanda's with her. She pulled it out of her purse and lay it on the table.

"Here. I brought this. I didn't know if you'd want it or not. I've never done this before. Visited a psychic, I mean."

Doris picked up the necklace that now lay on the table. Y-shaped, it was a chain joining several glass amulets on either side of a larger stone, from which hung a single amulet of the same bluish color as the other smaller stones. The larger stone was an opaque white. Doris handled the necklace with great care, although there was nothing about the necklace to suggest that it was of great value. Still, Doris was respectful of Margot sensibilities and of her daughter's possession.

"It's lovely," Doris said.

"She likes to wear it sometimes. I think she may have got it from Keith. But I'm not sure." She paused. "I thought you might need something of Amanda's." Her voice trailed off into imperceptible mumbles.

"What does Amanda look like?"

"She's really very pretty. I have a picture of her," she continued, as she reached once more into her purse. "Here it is."

Doris smiled. "She is very beautiful."

Doris continued to hold the necklace in both hands and look at Amanda's picture that lay on the table now.

"Can you help me, Doris?"

"I can try," she answered sincerely, although something in her voice alarmed Margot.

"Is she alive?" Margot asked, fighting back tears.

Doris, lay the necklace down, reached across the small table, and took Margot's left hand in hers. She looked deeply into Margot's eyes, now moist with tears. Doris sought desperately to comfort Margot and struggled to find the words that might meet the other woman's needs.

"Are you a religious person?"

"I am a practicing Catholic," Margot responded. "Yes," she continued with greater certainty. "Yes, I'd say I am religious."

"Then you should pray for Amanda."

"I pray for her everyday," Margot said.

"And, yet, you come to me."

Neither woman spoke for an instant. Then Doris began again.

"And you should continue to pray for her for the rest of your life."

Margot wasn't sure how to interpret Doris' suggestion and listened for more concrete information. It did not come.

"All of our children need our prayers, our positive thoughts, vibes, whatever we want to call them, sent by whatever means, by whatever messenger, to help them through life's course. Amanda is no different. She needs your help, now, I sense. She's in trouble, I fear. Something bad has taken place, but I don't know what. But I do know that she needs you. Think of her. Pray for her. Send as much positive energy her way that you can."

"I have been. I've been trying. I talk to her, you know. Since she's been missing I think I've talked to her more than I have in years."

"Good. Keep that up. It might help her. I can tell you no more."

The two women talked for several minutes more about those things a mother can do for her daughter. Of things a mother cannot do.

Margot wanted to know more. But she wasn't sure if she was ready to hear everything. She got up to leave, followed by Doris, who placed her hand on Margot's lower back.

Together they walked down the short hallway and through the front room. Margot exited the house and stopped a few steps away from the front porch. She turned and looked deeply into Doris' eyes, just as deeply as Doris had looked into Margot's back in the room where they had visited the past twenty minutes or so.

"Pray?"

"Yes. Pray for Amanda."

Margot turned and walked toward the curb where her car was parked.

"And I will pray for you," Doris whispered to herself.

EIGHT

The school calendar called for a dismissal just before noon. Ordinarily this would result in students flitting off in a hundred different directions. Today, however, as they began their spring break, hundreds swarmed together in and around the small open-air amphitheater on the town's Central Park Plaza for a rally, planned by Gary McLean and his second hour English class. The morning newspaper had carried a story about the gathering and about three hundred people were waiting for roughly the same number of students who parked several blocks away and approached the Plaza on foot.

Students quickly set up a portable PA system and handed a microphone to Gary. Nervously he set an agenda for the afternoon. A prayer, an update on the search for Amanda and some instructions on handing out or hanging flyers from a uniformed policeman who had been sent by Lieutenant Stiles, distribution of more flyers, and some words from some of Amanda's classmates. And, if she arrived on time, perhaps Mrs. Hayes would speak.

Present in the crowd was Lisa McLean. Unable to be at the assembly at school the previous evening, she had left the twins in her mother's care for the afternoon. She and her father had walked from her home to the square, enjoying the rare time together. He was off somewhere, probably reading the names on the war monument at the center of the Plaza.

Meg Watkins was also there, looking for Max Jansen, but becoming increasingly focused on Gary and the message he was delivering to the crowd. As he became more confident, he commanded everyone's attention. Meg moved through the crowd, careful not to bump into people, but listening closely to each speaker, as Gary introduced them. When Gary returned to the microphone, Meg suddenly became aware of Lisa, intently, proudly, lovingly watching her husband.

"You're his wife, aren't you?" Meg found herself saying.

Startled at first, for Meg was a stranger, she said, "I'm sorry. What did you say?"

"I said," Meg began to reply, remembering herself. "I'm sorry. I can't believe I just did that. It's just, I mean. Oh, I feel so silly."

Sensing Meg's embarrassment, Lisa engaged her with a smile. "It's okay. Really."

"I just saw the way you looked at him and knew you were his wife." She smiled. "You are his wife, right?"

Lisa looked back across the sea of people toward her husband at the microphone.

"Yes, I am. I'm kind of embarrassed, though." She looked to her right, then her left. Leaning forward, "Does it really show?"

They both laughed. Meg introduced herself and Lisa offered her hand.

Max Jansen had seen the two speaking and approached. Before Meg could make an introduction, Max was shaking his head and asking the two what they thought of the rally, which was just concluding. "So, what do you think of McLean? Is this guy for real? I mean, come on!"

Now Meg was embarrassed again. "Well, I don't know, Max." Turning to Lisa, "What do you think, Mrs. McLean? Is your husband for real? I mean, come on," mocking Max now.

Lisa smiled at Max, giving him the opportunity to gracefully salvage the moment, if that were possible. It was not.

"Oh," Max said simply.

"I assure you, Mr.?"

"Jansen," Meg inserted, always helpful in her attempts to help Max feel the full effect of his lack of social skills.

"Mr. Jansen," Lisa continued. She noticed the wire-ringed tablet Max carried and quickly concluded that Max was a reporter of some kind. "My husband is very much for real. He cares very much for his students and they, as you can see, care about him. Do you have any questions?"

Across the plaza Gary was directing students and fielding questions from concerned parents. He was in his element and seemed confident in his dealings with all he encountered.

Awkwardly, as both Meg and Lisa had intended him to feel, Max stammered, "I should inform you, Mrs. McLean, that I am a reporter."

"I had assumed as much, Mr. Jansen," pointing to his spiral notepad.

"Well," continued Jansen, "I am covering this story for one of the Springfield papers and I –"

"Max is my," Meg interrupted again, struggling for an apt description. "What exactly are you, Max? I always have a hard time with this one. Are you my boyfriend? My lover?"

"I am a reporter," Max said, now perturbed with Meg.

"Oh, yes, of course. He's my reporter."

Meg and Lisa could not contain themselves and laughed loudly at Max's expense. He shook his head and turned to walk away, just in time to run into Gary.

"Hello. I'm Gary McLean. I see you've met my wife," he said, offering his hand.

Introductions were made all around. While Gary agreed to a short interview with Max, Lisa and Meg moved away and continued to talk. The two women exchanged phone numbers, Meg providing the Fletcher's number where Max was staying. They agreed to talk later, for the two had quickly become friends.

Gary and Max, on the other hand, were not at all sure they would like each other.

David Shireman and Matt Crawford rode their bicycles along the potholed pavement, aiming at puddles formed by the rains from the night before. Their pantlegs wetter from each new splash, the eleven-year-old friends maneuvered themselves dangerously close to one another as they wove their way to the outskirts of the city toward their favorite playground.

Noted for its championship soccer teams and its steel-town toughness, Granite City sits just across the Mississippi River from St. Louis, Missouri and within view of its famous Gateway Arch. Like most cities of its ilk, it is home to a vast industrial park, a combination of vibrant, modern manufacturing plants and the wasteland of their dilapidated, long-unused predecessors. The latter provided boys like David and Matt with plenty of space in which to live out their fantasies.

The boys entered the grounds of the now-defunct Traynor Manufacturing Company through a hole in the rusty chain-link fence that surrounded the place. They had failed to notice that the lock on the gates had been removed since their last visit. The boys were in the habit of making their way through the hole, hiding the bikes from the infrequent passer-by who might otherwise notice them, and ducking inside for the adventures that awaited them and their overactive imaginations.

Having ditched their bikes in the high grass outside the northeast corner of the building, the two ran inside. The clang of the metal door, banging against the wall as they entered, flushed several pigeons that flew in various arcs, exiting the building through either broken windows or some of the many holes in the corrugated tin roof. Sunlight streaked through these openings, slicing the darkness of the rectangular warehouse's interior. The length of the building ran north and south.

David had been the first to climb high into the building's iron framework and make his way across one of the many beams the two had found passable, from one side of the large building to the other. After some initial reluctance to traverse the beam, Matt was quick to find the task do-able and found the sense of accomplishment to his liking. That had been over two years ago and the boys made a trip out to the Traynor building at least twice a week to take part in the ritual.

Straight to the metal ladder, bolted to the wall at the opposite end of the building, the two raced, eager to ascend to the height of the building and begin the first of five or six passes across the breadth of the building's trusses.

Afterwards the two would typically descend to the floor of the building. The two friends would rattle around the discarded assemblage of machinery and uncover their stash of cigarettes and a Bic lighter, neatly wrapped in a plastic garbage bag to protect it from the elements and hidden in a drawer of an old tool chest. A quick check to see that one of them had brought some breath freshener would be followed by each boy smoking one or two cigarettes. Then they would head toward home.

As usual, David won the race and made his way up, leaving Matt standing at the foot of the ladder. He watched as David reached the top and moved carefully across a narrow gap to the beam that stretched the two-hundred-foot length of the building. Once David was off the ladder, Matt began his ascent, carefully coordinating his footsteps with the strides his hands were making. When he reached the top, he knew he had stepped upon forty-two rungs, putting him high enough to rival many circus performers. His first look down was always a tense moment, but he quickly overcame his fear and secured his grip on the beam onto which David had earlier made his way.

"Come on, slowpoke," David yelled.

"I'm comin', butthead," Matt countered.

David was now about halfway across the length of the fourth crossbeam, his favorite, for whatever reason. Matt usually crossed the second. The march across the I-beam was not a no-hands trick. The boys were foolhardy, but not crazy. The middle portion of the roof truss was always there to hang onto, criss-crossing between the upper portion, just beneath the roof, and the beam on which the boys walked. Still, the endeavor was invigorating for David and downright scary for Matt.

Matt was moving across his beam, not having to hurry to match David's pace, for David had stopped mid-way across and was sitting in the V-shaped framework of the truss, waiting. Matt secured himself in his V and looked across at David, sitting confidently with his chin in his hand, pretending to be bored.

"What's the matter, David?"

"Nothing. I'm just sittin' here."

"What are you sittin' for?"

"I don't know. Just sittin'; that's all."

"Come on. I'm going on across the rest of the way," Matt said, sure enough of himself, but still not wanting to look down past the beam. "You comin'?"

David stood and began to move forward, when he suddenly yelled, "Whoa!" He nearly fell, but tightly grabbed the ironwork rising diagonally before him.

Matt startled as he heard David yell. Still he managed somehow to turn slowly and look at David. His friend had a firm grip on the ironwork and stared intensely at something directly below him. Carefully, Matt moved back across the distance of ten or twelve feet he had just traveled and looked in the direction of the object which held his friend's attention.

There, hidden from all sides, but exposed to the two boys' view from above, lay the body of a young woman. It was some time before either of the boys looked at the other. Mouths agape, the two remained silent for what seemed like several minutes.

Finally, Matt spoke, quietly, "What we gonna do, David?"

"I dunno." David looked across at his friend. "Guess we can't just act like we never seen this, huh?"

"No way. We got to tell somebody."

They both knew whom.

Trey Cederquist sat in a recliner and twisted the top of another bottle of imported beer. The television news at six o'clock mentioned only that Amanda Hayes was still missing. No leads in the case had been discussed with the media and police appeared to be baffled. An eight-second clip was shown of the rally that afternoon on the Jacksonville uptown plaza. Gary McLean could be seen in the background, microphone in hand.

Cederquist was agitated. McLean could be trouble if he kept pushing Amanda's friends in an effort to locate her, or uncover some piece of evidence that might turn the search in Trey's direction. Then there was the matter of Luke and Marcus. He worried about loose lips and told himself again that the pea-brained Kentuckians would have to be dealt with at some point.

Marcus stumbled into the doorway of the cabin. It was the first time he and Luke had seen the cabin since they had followed Trey's orders, to the letter, and disposed of the body of Amanda Hayes. Their trip back from the St. Louis, metro-east area had been uneventful and Trey's plan had worked well enough.

The two had raced back to Jacksonville and parked themselves at a popular watering hole east of town. Upon their arrival, as instructed, they even bought the twenty-or-so patrons a round of drinks, insurance that they would be remembered. An alibi. Marcus had to be reminded several times in recent days of the word's pronunciation. He understood the concept, but he'd be "damned if he could remember the frickin' word" he had protested.

Now, Luke was shaking his head again as he followed his drunken friend back into the scene of their crime.

"Let's see if ol' Trey stocked the fridge with some beer," Marcus said, as he bowled a chair over on his way to the corner of the cabin's front room, where a stove and refrigerator constituted a kitchen.

"Ah, shit," he said, as he discovered the cupboard was bare.

"No beer?"

"No! Not a goddamn one."

"Just as well, ol' buddy. You've had enough."

"Hell, I know there was beer in this icebox when we was here the other day, Luke. Goddamn Trey musta drank it all."

"He wouldn't drink our beer, Marcus. Ain't good enough. He's gotta have his imported shit. More 'an likely, he done cleaned this place up, like they's nobody been here for ages. He's a smart one."

"We got any beer left in the truck?"

Luke, now seated on the couch, looked at Marcus in amazement.

"For chrissakes, Marcus, why don't you just give it a rest?"

"Fuck you, Luke."

Luke began to rock forward on the couch, ready to tear into Marcus like he had not done in recent memory, but like he was constantly on the verge of doing. The two had a violent history between them. But they had always somehow been able to patch things up, despite the numerous scars, chipped teeth, and even the broken bones the two had seen fit to give one another.

"Very original, Marcus," Luke shot back and then gave in to the idea. "There's probably a beer or two from that twelve-pack we bought yesterday. Go see if it's behind the seat in the cooler."

Marcus ran, stumbling out the door just as he had coming in, leaving Luke alone to contemplate his predicament.

How had he gotten involved in this? He wanted to cry. The whole mess had been one colossal mistake. He had made mistakes before. But, unlike Marcus, he had never made one that could land him in jail for more than a night or two. For all he knew, he could be put to death for his involvement with Amanda Hayes. Scared did not do justice to a description of his feelings, feelings he could not even discuss with Marcus.

"Whew, boy," Marcus said, as he reentered the cabin's front door. "It's still good an' cold. Ice's melted in that little cooler, though. I found me a sack to carry these three in. I'm puttin' 'em in the icebox."

Marcus turned to look at Luke, who seemed distant. His face looked sad.

"You want one, Luke?"

"Nah. You go ahead, Marcus."

"What's the matter?"

"Nothin'! I'm just thinkin'."

"'Bout what?"

"Nothin', I tell ya."

"Okay. Sorry."

Marcus had his feelings hurt. He didn't like it when Luke was short with him, which happened often enough. But he soon forgot his pain and his mind jumped to something else.

"Hey, look what I found, Luke."

"Some of the stuff we done made for Trey."

Luke looked to see Marcus, holding a bag of clear plastic, one of those kind that zip shut and stores the freshness of its contents.

"What are you gonna do with that?"

"I don't know," responded Marcus, not very convincingly. "Thought I might try me some. You wanna have some, Luke?"

"Hell, no. What for?"

"See what it's like, Luke. Ain't you curious?"

"No, Marcus. I seen Trey take that shit. You seen him yourself. You know how he gets."

"Shit, Luke. That sonofabitch is crazy without this stuff," Marcus said, looking over his shoulder as he did so.

"Yeah. Well, he's a damn-sight worse when he's usin'. And I don't see no point in sticking my foot in that creek."

"Yeah. Maybe you're right." He tossed the bag on the couch and opened another beer. "I'll stick with this here beer."

"That'd be the smart thing to do, Marcus."

Luke sighed with relief. He had averted another crisis.

Two Granite City Police squad cars awaited a third that carried David Shireman and Matt Crawford in the back seat. David was fascinated with the scene before him. Wire mesh separated him and his friend from the variety of police equipment, including a shotgun, nestled proudly against the dash in its upright position between driver and passenger-partner.

Matt was still trying to get used to sitting in a backseat where there were no door handles. No matter how many times he got to ride in his stepfather's patrol car, he would never become accustomed to having no door handles. This was scarier than usual. Of this he was sure, as sure as he was of the trouble he would find himself in with his mother, once she learned of his adventures in an abandoned warehouse on the outskirts of the city.

The boys had quickly climbed down off the perches from which they had seen the body about forty-five minutes earlier. They resisted the temptation to take a closer look at the body before mounting their bikes and riding into town. The boys made the trip, they were convinced, more rapidly than ever before. Gasping for air upon their arrival at the police station, they soon found the calm needed to explain what they had seen to Hal Templin, Matt's stepfather and a Granite City policeman of nineteen years.

Now outside the patrol car, Hal explained to the patrolmen who had arrived shortly before him what the boys were telling him they had seen. He gave a nod to one of the men and turned abruptly toward the back door of his vehicle, opened the door, and motioned the two outside with his thumb.

"Well, boys, show us this body," the one to whom Templin had nodded said. He motioned them toward the building with an extended arm, the other hand thumb-hooked in his gun belt.

As the five moved toward the open gate near where the three cars were parked, Hal Templin urged the boys to tell them how they had happened to be in the building. Matt's shoulders arched, as he said nothing. David, it appeared, would be the boys' spokesman.

"We rode our bikes out here," he hesitated, for he knew what this would mean to Matt, "like we always do."

David could sense Matt cringing. This would mean big trouble and probably put a halt to the boy's warehouse adventures.

"And?" Templin said, watching Matt's reaction to all of this.

"And we got into the place through that hole in the fence over there," he said, pointing to the hole, as they moved through an unlocked gate. The boys looked surprised. "We didn't know we could get in this way. These have always had a chain and a big ol' lock on 'em."

Matt was dying a slow death now. With every detail he could imagine his mother's face hardening, as the story would later be conveyed to her by Hal. Or worse, Hal might make him tell the story. She'll kill me, he thought.

David continued. "We went in this door and we just walked around and found the body over there," he said, pointing again.

"Over here?" the officer in charge asked the one to whom Templin had nodded outside. He had stripes on his shoulder that neither Templin or the other officer, a boyish-looking officer, had on their sleeves. Officer Shoulder-Stripes moved in the direction in which David had pointed.

"Yes, sir. Right over there, behind those junk machines."

All five moved toward the dead girl. She was dead. The boys had assured the policemen that she was dead. She hadn't moved in all the time they had watched her from above. The last detail, however, had been conveniently omitted from their story, thus far. The boys had not discussed the need to keep a secret of the fact that they had seen the dead girl's body from more than fifty feet above. They each just knew that this was a detail neither of their mothers needed to hear.

The policemen could see no body. She was hidden from all sides. The officer in charge walked all the way around the area where the dead girl lay, finally climbing atop one of the old machines and looking down upon her.

"Here she is," he said matter-of-factly.

Templin was the next to hop up upon another of the machines that surrounded the scene, well hidden from the view of all from floor level. He surveyed the scene quickly and hopped back down, standing close to Matt now.

"I don't understand," Templin said, stooping, trying to see the body from a low position, "how you boys could see the body from out here."

Neither boy spoke for several seconds.

"Well?" Templin spoke again, growing perturbed.

Matt lifted his head, looked Templin in the eye, and pointed first with his hand at his shoulder, then extending his arm toward the rafters above them. Templin looked directly above him, stared, and then lowered his gaze to the boys. Matt cringed again. But Templin only placed his hand on Matt's right shoulder and gently shook it.

"Boy, your momma is gonna skin you."

"I know."

David decided that this had not been so bad, after all. "You wanna see how we get up there? I'll show you." He began to move toward the ladder, but Templin called him back, sternly.

"That's okay, David. I think we've got the picture. And we will discuss this later," said Templin, looking at Matt again. "But now, we have to get to the bottom of this situation here. Did you boys touch the body, or anything around it?"

Both boys shook their heads. Matt was especially happy to be able to answer the question with what he assumed was the right answer. David further explained that they had not done anything except climb down, run to their bikes, and ride into town. The police knew the rest.

Officer Stripes was still standing atop his machine, looking at the corpse, then writing in a small spiral notepad, then looking at the corpse again. He may have been drawing a picture, Matt decided. The officer suddenly leaned his head to the side, pressed a button on a small box mounted above his shoulder, and spoke into the box. The boys could hear the voice of a dispatcher, answering the call. After four or five exchanges, the conversation was over and Stripes was jumping onto the floor next to the boys. He directed the boy-cop to look around outside for anything unusual, reminding him of the care with which he should investigate the grounds surrounding the building.

Next, he spoke in muffled voice to Templin, who nodded again and told the boys to accompany him outside where they would have to wait. Wait, that is, for the inevitable boom-lowering after

Matt's mother had been informed of his whereabouts and David's parents could also be brought up-to-date. The three began to walk toward the door through which they had entered. Matt stopped suddenly.

"Hal? She is dead, isn't she?"

"Yeah, Matt. She's dead. From the looks of things, she's been dead for a couple of days, maybe. Come on. Let's get outside. We have some calls to make and then I've got some questions for you both."

When Meg had asked Max to have supper with friends, she expected that Max would have to be dragged, kicking and screaming, to the dinner table. She was surprised at Max's response. Max could not wait to get to the home he had been staking out only hours earlier.

Instead, it was Gary who was not too keen on the idea of entertaining. His unenthusiastic response to Lisa's invitation to the couple Lisa had met that day had more to do with the idea of entertaining than with whom they would be entertaining. Gary felt like he was betraying Amanda. He shouldn't be partying, but out beating the bushes in search of Amanda along with everyone else.

Lisa, however, thought Gary could use the distraction, if only for an hour or so, then help Max write his story and, perhaps, do Amanda some good in that way. She had asked and her parents were eager to comply with her request that they take the twins for an overnight at the Amerihost. They could all swim in the motel pool and have a good time enjoying the visit. Lisa could only hope that Gary might come around to enjoying this evening at home.

When Lisa apologized for her husband's gloomy disposition to Meg early in the evening, as the two women prepared a salad, Meg was quick to respond.

"Oh, anyone would be bummed about a missing student. Just

wait till Gary gets to know Max better. Then it'll be the company that he objects to."

Lisa laughed out loud. The two women were quickly becoming friends. Perhaps they each saw in the other what each wanted most. Lisa saw in Meg an independent professional woman, intelligent, witty, self-effacing. It was an attractive lifestyle to Lisa. Meg looked at Lisa and saw family, roots, bliss. Neither woman wanted to give up what each had, but each coveted some of what the other possessed.

While the women put the finishing touches on four salads and laughed out loud in the kitchen, the men sat at the dining room table and drank beers. Their response to the laughter from behind a swinging door to the kitchen was to roll their eyes, grin at one another, and shake their heads. The unspoken truth to which they both subscribed was obvious. They would never understand what was going on just beyond the swinging door.

"So, Gary," Max started.

Here it comes, Gary thought.

"What made you decide to become a teacher?"

The way he said it was so familiar to Gary. He had heard what he was about to hear so many times before. He decided to give Max the standard answer, which he felt would lead to the predictable next question. Gary, of course, would follow up with his standard response to that query and away they would go. Gary tried hard not to sound as though he was on automatic pilot.

"I love to learn, Max. I guess I just want to pass that love of learning on to my students."

Max thought he would gag. Oh, come on, he wanted to say. But he was reminded of his awkward introduction to Lisa earlier that day and bit his tongue. "What is it about learning that turns you on so?" came out of Max's mouth unexpectedly.

"I don't know. I guess it's that moment of discovery, that sensation of enlightenment. I always thought that was neat."

Neat? Had he really said "neat"? Max thought to himself.

"Oh," started Max before he caught himself. "It's not really that simple. Is it?"

Gary thought about the question. "Yes. Yes, it is. I want to see that look on my students' faces that say they've got it. They understand. They didn't understand before. But now they do."

"Did Amanda understand?"

Gary stared into his guest's eyes. "What do you mean, Max?"

"I mean, did she understand? Was she smart? Did she get it?"

"Yeah, she got it most of the time, Max." Then he caught himself. "She gets it." He was reminding himself of how much he thought of her. "She's a bright kid. Not a straight-A student, necessarily, but a good mind."

"She's a good kid, Gary?"

"Are you interviewing me, Max? Should I ask for your press pass? Maybe you want to get your tape recorder out and tape me."

Max's hands went up, surrendering.

"We're just talking, Gary. No interview. If you aren't comfortable talking with me about Amanda Hayes, we can drop it. Talk about the weather or baseball."

Gary smiled. "So how do you think the Cardinals'll do this year? So-so start, so far, eh?"

"Least you're not a Cub fan," Max countered with a smile.

"How do you know, Max? Maybe I just wanted to change the subject."

Now the two men laughed out loud.

"That's cool," Max volunteered, and they talked baseball for the next ten minutes.

As the women joined the men with drinks of their own, Lisa was relieved to find the two discussing something other than missing children. She wanted to see Gary get away from the worries of the past few days. She knew Max Jansen was in town only because of Amanda's disappearance. But she had hoped that having Max and Meg as dinner guests would not lead to a full night of where-oh-where-could-Amanda-be.

Max, it seemed, was cooperating.

"So, Gary, it looks like you read a lot." Max pointed at the bookcase in the living room. It was stuffed with college textbooks, literary anthologies, and paperbacks. The two men talked of a shared interest in literature, particularly fiction. Gary leaned toward techno-thriller. Max liked crime stories, predictably enough.

Throughout dinner, Gary, his wife, and their guests talked of literature, of writing, and of the newspaper business. It was interesting conversation. Lisa must be loving this, Gary thought to himself at one point. She did not get enough of this, he was deciding, and he committed himself to finding more opportunities for Lisa to socialize in this fashion, once things settled down.

As the girls were clearing the table and dismissing the men, the two males retired to the living room for more conversation and drinks. Gary poured another glass of wine for each of them and Max suddenly changed subjects.

"Gary, I would like to talk about Amanda Hayes."

Gary tilted his head and looked at the ceiling. He'd known he could not escape the reporter's questioning forever.

Max continued. "I'm not even covering this story for the *Times*, Gary." He shook his head, fumbling for words. "I don't even know what I'm doing here." Max couldn't imagine why. But he was letting his guard down.

Gary turned toward Max, hoping to get a glimpse of his character. "Then, why are you so interested?"

"Why are you so interested?"

"What are you trying to say, Max? That I have some interest in this girl other than what I have told you? She's my student, Max. She matters. They all do. You can't just spend all this time with these kids and not come to care about them. And once in a while, one comes along who cares back. Not cares back for me, you understand. She just cares. About life. About what you're teaching. About," he hesitated, "about whatever it is she cares about."

"What did she care about, Gary?"

"I wish you'd quit talking about her in the past tense."

"I'm sorry." And he was.

Gary was tired. He stroked his hair with his left hand. With the fingers of his right, he nibbled at the tablecloth, collecting its borders in waves before flattening them again with a tug.

"This girl is a nice kid, Max. She is popular. She's pretty. She's a good student. She likes helping other kids learn. She'd be a good teacher one day, if that's what she decides to go into."

"Did she tell you that's what she wanted to do?"

"No. But I've told her more than once that she'd make a good one," he recalled with a smile. "She blushed whenever you gave her a compliment."

It sickened Gary to catch himself using the past tense and he quickly corrected himself. He stood and moved into the living room and leaned with one arm against the mantel over the fireplace.

"What about the boyfriend?" Max asked, fearful of losing his momentum.

"Keith? Keith's a good kid. I didn't have him in class. Saw him play on the baseball team when he was still in school here. Seems like a nice kid."

Max tried to be delicate. "Were they doing it?"

Gary wanted to throw Max out of his house and watch him bounce out to his car at the end of the drive. "Now how would I know that?"

"You got ears. Teachers hear, right?"

"Those who choose to listen for that kind of stuff hear. Right. But I don't concern myself with hallway gossip, Mr. Jansen."

The temperature of the room seemed to drop perceptibly.

"Look, Gary. I don't mean to offend you or Amanda. I'm just interested in finding out what's going on with this girl. Like I say, I'm not even covering the story for the paper. I'm probably crazy for spending my vacation this way. But here I am. Knocking myself out, working twenty-four hours a day –"

"You're workin'?" Gary responded.

"Hey, don't tell me you thought I came here tonight for the lasagna. I came here tonight to see what you were made of, to find out what you know about this girl and why she’s disappeared, and to.” He suddenly stopped.

Gary slowly looked up from the fireplace. “You thought I had something to do with her disappearance?” Gary uttered in disbelief.

“Thought crossed my mind. But just for a second,” he quickly added. “I know you’re not involved. But I thought you might know something. Something even you didn’t think you knew that might lead me to the girl.”

“Now, you sound like Lieutenant Stiles.”

“L.J.?”

“That’s the one.”

“He’s cool, Gary. You don’t need to worry about Stiles. He’s good, too. Matter of fact, I kinda look at this as a competition. Who’s gonna find the girl first? Him, or me?”

“I kinda look at it like, what a shame it is that a nice young girl like Amanda isn’t at home with her parents, or out on a date with her favorite boy.”

“Goddamn, you’re sensitive.”

Gary shook his head. What makes him tick, he pondered.

Max decided to change the subject again. But he wasn’t abandoning the investigation. He merely wanted to get away from the topic of Amanda, at present.

“What can you tell me about Marshall Cederquist, Gary?”

“Which one?”

“Which one? What do you mean?”

“Well, Max, there’s Marshall Cederquist, Junior, and there’s Marshall Cederquist, the Third.” He could not resist a smile. “They call him ‘Trey.’“

“I’m talking about the fella who put up a ten thousand dollar reward for the girl’s safe return or for evidence leading to the conviction of those responsible for her disappearance,” Max quoted from a press release.

Max gave Gary time to react. Seeing no visible reaction, he spoke again.

"Are you surprised by the reward?" Max asked Gary. "That's a lot of money."

"No, not really. Why should I be? Amanda's father works for Cederquist and the old man seems like he's the generous type."

Max looked puzzled. Gary decided to give more information without being questioned.

"One of the grade schools in our district needed computers a couple of years ago and Cederquist donated about fifteen computers from his business when they bought new ones. The school was able to put together a nice lab and update their secretary's computer."

Max did not seem to react to the news. So Gary continued. "I wish there were more men like that out there, offering to help schools."

"More men like who?" Lisa asked, as the two women joined their men in the living room.

"Marshall Cederquist," Gary responded.

"Well, I don't have to ask which one," Lisa countered.

"Why is that, Lisa?" Max asked, now interested.

Lisa shrugged. "I guess because I'd find it difficult to believe that anyone would wish there were more men out there like Trey Cederquist."

Gary leaned forward, smiling, and whispered, "Lisa has a past with Trey." He emphasized the word "past." So Max and Meg knew he was teasing his wife.

Lisa gave her husband a look of disgust and told the story.

"The little prick tried to hit on me at a party once. It was a Christmas party a couple of years ago."

Max and Meg each sat up in their seats.

"Gary was in the other room, talking sports with the other men and Trey Cederquist was in the kitchen flirting with every woman in the room. It was so weird. Well, I went down the hall to the bathroom and when I came out, there's Trey, standing in the doorway with his arm stretched out across the opening like he's going to hold me prisoner or something."

"Oh, my God, Lisa. What'd you do?" Meg asked.

"I said, 'Excuse me, Mr. Cederquist,' and I tried to duck under his arm. But he grabbed me around my waist with his other arm and slobbered something about a Christmas kiss or something. So, I hauled off and slugged him."

Meg laughed. "Oh, gosh. You slapped him?"

"Nope. Pow!" Lisa responded, as she reenacted her punch to Trey Cederquist' stomach.

"What happened then?" Max asked, laughing nervously.

"Well," Lisa said, smiling at Gary, "I helped him into the bathroom, closed the door, and went into the living room to sit on my husband's lap."

The four of them howled with delight.

"Poor little Trey took a few minutes to recover, then joined us all in the family room. He saw me sitting in Gary's lap whispering in his ear and made a hasty exit," Lisa continued.

They all laughed again.

"She never told me a thing about it until we got home that night," Gary said. "Every time I see the guy, now, I have to try so hard not to laugh that I can't get myself worked up enough to haul off and hit him myself."

More laughter.

"Let's just say," Lisa said finally, "that Trey Cederquist does not enjoy the same reputation in this town that his daddy does."

The story was a good way to end the evening and they all promised to get together again soon. Max and Meg thanked the McLean's for their hospitality and made their way to their respective cars in the driveway. Max waved warmly to the McLean's and worried only slightly that Gary would be unable to forget some of the unpleasantness from their earlier conversation.

On his way to the Fletcher's, he made mental notes of his conversation with Gary and promised himself that he would try to, at least, get a look at Trey Cederquist when he visited Cederquist Industries the next morning. He had heard the news earlier that afternoon of the reward being offered by the elder Cederquist. It was then that he had made up his mind to visit CI. Now, he thought that, while he was in the vicinity, he might as well take in the sights. He laughed out loud at the prospect of seeing Trey Cederquist, doubled over at the waist.

NINE

Early Wednesday morning Lieutenant L.J. Stiles watched carefully as a team of crime scene technicians worked in silence. Earlier they had worked the scene where the van had been abandoned and found in a farmer's field. City employees had towed the van belonging to Tim McMichael to a city garage on the city's north end and parked inside away from the elements. The wrecker crew had been careful to move the van without disturbing any evidence which might be gleaned from the vehicle, now the center of attention for Stiles and his fellow peace officers. Jacksonville police had even videotaped the hook-up and detachment from the wrecker, close ups documenting the state of the vehicle before and after the van's transport.

Parked alongside McMichael's van was a white Dodge van, Illinois State Police painted on its side, along with yellow stripes stretched across its length. The stripes widened as they arched toward the rear of the vehicle.

"What are you hoping to find, L.J.?" Nathan Bottomley, garage attendant, asked.

"Something, anything, Nate, that'll tell us that Amanda Hayes has or hasn't been in that van," Stiles responded.

"Do you think she was in the van?"

"I don't know. But these boys here," nodding toward the crime scene team, "they're going to find that out. They're good, Nate. The best I could get out of Springfield. I only wish I had been able to get 'em over here sooner. But, unfortunately, they're a busy bunch."

The state police had a man posted at Jacksonville Police Department headquarters. But he was on a well-deserved vacation and was out of the country. He would be upset when he heard that he had missed out on this case. Stiles had the experts he needed, nonetheless.

Three technicians, precise and focused, moved about the van as they obviously had done with many other vehicles, their every move well choreographed. They were dressed in dark trousers, black shoes, and blue jackets, white letters on the back. I.S.P. Even Stiles was impressed. Nate was overwhelmed. His garage had never before hosted such an elite team of investigators. Wait till Mary hears about this, he thought to himself, as he watched them work.

"Nate, get them anything they ask for. But you stay out of their way, hear?" Stiles said. "I have to go uptown. I'll just be a page away, though. So holler if you need me."

With that, Stiles quickly made his way to his car, fueled at the pump outside by another garage attendant who was supervised by Bottomley.

Stiles would be interested to hear what, if anything, the three technicians would find. He knew one thing. If anything in the van could determine if the van and Amanda Hayes's disappearance were connected, these guys would find it. He felt confident in their skills, since they had proven to him, time after time, that they were knowledgeable and thorough investigators. And he expected to hear from them soon.

He was particularly interested in the vomit that had been harvested from the rear of the van. He felt all along that this would be a key, could be a key to finding Amanda. People did not steal that many vehicles in Jacksonville. And stolen vans rarely turned up a few miles out of town in some farmer's field. They made their way to chop shops far away, their parts dispersed in myriad directions. No, the detective had a gut feeling that the van might have been used to transport a captive Amanda Hayes to a waiting vehicle. He feared that the second vehicle was long gone by now and the thoughts that swam through his mind now were quite negative.

As Stiles neared the police station's parking lot at Douglas and

West, he heard the dispatcher bark his radio call-name over the cruiser's radio.

"Ida-one, Jacksonville."

"Ida-one," Stiles confirmed his copy, acknowledging the Jacksonville Police Department's dispatcher. Her use of Stiles' call-name was reflective of his being the JPD's lead investigator.

After Stiles responded, the excited dispatcher spoke again.

"Ida-one, report just in. Unidentified body found. Granite City. Female, Caucasian, late teens, five feet-four, one hundred twelve pounds, coal black hair."

Numbness crept down his arms as he turned into the parking lot. "I copy, Jacksonville. I'll be inside in just a moment."

Please, Lord, Laurence Jon Stiles thought, don't let this be her. I want to find this girl alive. I want to bring her home to her mother and father. He shook his head, opened the door of his car slowly, bending his large frame as he stepped onto the asphalt parking lot, and lumbered toward the open door on the station's west side.

A uniformed officer named Hanner met him at the doorway, handing Stiles a phone number on an index card.

"Captain Mansfield Aldretti, Granite City Police, 555-3600," Stiles read aloud. "Has anyone talked to this Captain Aldretti?"

"No, sir. Marchman took the news off the wire about ten minutes ago and I called Granite City. Their desk gave me Aldretti's name and number. Said he'd be the man to contact if we thought the girl might be our missing person, sir."

Hanner's voice broke as he finished the sentence. He had added "sir" as much to regain control of his voice as to formally address his superior. Stiles was continually amazed at how officers in the department, big, rugged, men's men could, at times, come so close to losing the war of emotions they regularly fought. His pride in such men, men who obviously cared for the people they served, grew each time he witnessed this phenomenon.

The two men stood just inside the doorway of the station, Hanner looking over Stiles' shoulder into the parking lot. Stiles looked down at the card in his hand, finding it odd to hope that the body found in or near Granite City belonged to some other policeman, in some other town. He bit his lower lip as he flipped the end of the index card with one hand against the fingertips of the other. He leaned forward, fighting inertia, and stepped slowly toward his office where a phone awaited him.

"Hanner," Stiles stammered.

"Yes, sir?"

"Let's keep this off our radio for the time being, til we know more."

"Sure thing, Lieutenant. Whatever you say."

Stiles dialed the number on the card. He waited impatiently as the phone at Granite City Police Headquarters went unanswered for six rings. Finally, someone picked up.

"Yes, this is Lieutenant L.J. Stiles of the Jacksonville Police Department."

"No," Stiles continued, with perpetual frustration, "Jacksonville, Illinois."

"That's right, Illinois. Near Springfield. Do you know where Springfield is, Sergeant?" Stiles was surprised at his irritability. "Look, Sergeant. I don't have time to give you a geography lesson. May I speak with Captain Aldretti?"

"Yes, I know he's busy. I am busy, too." He tried to hold his tongue for he knew the desk sergeant was probably only doing his job, protecting Aldretti from nuisance callers. Still, his frustration grew.

"Look. I know that you boys have found a body down there that has everybody's attention right now. That's why I'm calling, Sergeant. It may be our body. We have a missing girl, who fits the description of your Jane Doe. Now, may I, please, speak with your captain?"

The desk sergeant finally agreed to put Aldretti on the line, providing, he had added, "that I can find him."

Stiles hated himself when he was rude to anyone, especially so when he found himself being rude to a man, or woman, in uniform. But it was so often necessary, it seemed, to behave in this way in order to get what one wanted. Information that needed to flow quickly, smoothly, was often the victim of turf wars between agencies. Different municipal police departments, local and state agencies, or state and federal bureaucrats. It didn't matter. Everyone, at times, strove to protect information it had from everyone else.

Some of the barriers, preventing the flow of information from local and state agencies to such federal agencies as the Bureau and DEA, were gone. But the walls still existed when the information was to flow in one direction or the other, at critical moments. Not always, but often. This was a great frustration for Stiles and now he was trying to decide if the desk sergeant at the other end of the line was being difficult by design or was merely incompetent.

After some time, Captain Aldretti presented himself to Stiles in a surprisingly congenial manner. Maybe he wouldn't be so difficult to deal with, after all, Stiles thought. They discussed the lack of identification on or around the body. They reviewed the physical description of Aldretti's Jane Doe and decided that this could, indeed, be Amanda Hayes. Both knew, however, that a more conclusive identification was needed and arrangements were made for a transfer of Amanda's dental records. In the meantime, plans were moving ahead for an autopsy and the discovery of a cause of death.

Aldretti told Stiles what he knew of the body. There were, apparently, some defense wounds, a broken fingernail, some bruising on the arms. Both wrists and ankles appeared to have been bound. That would be consistent with what Stiles was already deciding had been Amanda's abduction. No gunshot wounds, no stab wounds, no blow to the head. Aldretti had little more to relate, as he was leaving that in the hands of the experts. He had brought in the Major Case Squad from St. Louis, he explained. Their forensics experts were going over the body and the grounds on which it had been discovered.

Stiles concluded by saying, "Thanks for your help on this, Captain. You understand, of course, that we're hoping here in Jacksonville, that your Jane Doe is not Amanda Hayes."

"Yes, of course, Lieutenant. We'll get back to you as soon as we know anything."

Max Jansen drove his rental car onto the grounds of Cederquist Industries at nine o'clock Wednesday morning. He recalled all that Gary McLean had told him the night before about Marshall Cederquist and continued to speculate about ulterior motives Cederquist might have in offering a reward of ten thousand dollars in the Hayes disappearance. So preoccupied with his cynical speculations was Max that he had neglected to turn on his scanner when he departed his temporary Jacksonville residence a few minutes earlier. Otherwise, he might have learned of the van that turned up and of word from Granite City about a body, which had also been discovered.

The parking lot outside Cederquist Industries headquarters was expansive. He pulled into a vacant space designated for visitors and walked the short distance to the front doors beneath a huge company logo. Once inside he moved toward the desk of what appeared to be a receptionist, although Max wondered, at first, if it were an information booth or, possibly, even a security desk.

The corporate offices of Cederquist Industries were expansive, too. Its designers had built a huge capital "I" and the receptionist's station/information booth/security post was in the middle of the "I" with offices located off wide hallways extending away from the middle in both directions. They had tastefully decorated the hallways, as well. The floor was a marble-like checkerboard, brown and beige squares inside a black border. The walls were wood, cherry, Max had guessed, with a chair rail and reproductions of famous paintings. At least, Max was sure that some were famous.

He recognized a few and deduced that the others would be recognizable to those more appreciative of artistic treasures. The entire environment impressed Max. This, he concluded, was a first-rate operation.

"Good morning," a toothy young lady behind the desk said. She was smartly dressed in a blue blazer over a beige skirt and white blouse. Had Max not been enthralled with his surroundings, he would most certainly have noticed how beautiful the young lady was.

"Welcome to Cederquist Industries. May I help you?"

Max smiled back in response to her greeting and at his recollection of the son and the wonderfully entertaining story related to him the previous evening by the McLeans.

"Morning," Max replied, "I'm here to speak with Mr. Cederquist." Then, remembering himself, he added, "That's Mr. Cederquist, senior. I understand there's a son, too."

"Do you have an appointment, sir?"

"No. No, I do not."

"Well, you need to go down the hall this way," she said, pointing to her right, Max's left. When you get to the executive offices about half way down the hall, you will see Susan's desk, on your right. She's Mr. Cederquist, Jr.'s secretary. That's the one you want to see, I'm guessing. The son," she emphasized the differentiation, "is Cederquist, the third. He goes by Trey. Susan can tell you whether Mr. Cederquist is in and if he can see you."

"Thank you."

As he walked the hundred feet or so in the direction she had pointed, Max became aware of some of the names beautifully painted on the hardwood office doors in three-inch script. The third door on his left had been that of "Benjamin Hayes." He tried not to notice this fact too conspicuously and continued his march toward Cederquist's office.

Max approached a suite of offices at his right not directly connected to the expansive hallway, their points of entry grouped behind a glass wall. One entered the suite through a set of double doors that were open and inviting. Again, Max had the sensation that the offices would fit nicely in New York or Chicago.

Each office door, there were half a dozen, had a secretary stationed outside its door. Interestingly enough, not every secretary was female. This must be a very progressive company, Max thought. He was more impressed when he came to recognize that none of the office doors bore the name of either Cederquist. Instead, two smaller hallways led along the back side of the building, one to the right, the other to the left, presumably to the respective offices of Cederquist, Jr. and Cederquist, the third. This explained the presence of eight secretaries, their nameplates atop their desks.

In the far corner to the left, Max found Susan, reading from a stack of papers that lay before her. She heard him approach and reacted, causing Max to look back over his shoulder. It would have been impossible to sneak up on Susan, had she been positioned outside the wall of glass. The marble floors would have given his approach an early announcement. But once inside the confines of the executive suite, the floor was carpeted. Max hadn't noticed the change. Oh, well, Max thought, I wasn't trying to sneak up on her anyway.

"Can I help you, sir?"

"Yes, you can. I would like to see Marshall Cederquist, Jr., if I might. My name is Maxwell Jansen. I am a reporter for the *Capital City Times* and I would like to speak with Mr. Cederquist about the reward he's posted in the disappearance of Miss Amanda Hayes."

He immediately regretted having given Susan his reason for wishing to see Cederquist. Then, another thought occurred to him. Had he actually introduced himself as Maxwell Jansen? Max tried to recall. He hadn't used his given name in many years, never having liked it from the beginning, even less so after Don Adams had cleverly made his character of the same name look so foolish on his TV series, *Get Smart*, while Max was in junior high. Perhaps Max's present surroundings, so business-like, so corporate, were having some strange effect on him.

"Mr. Cederquist is meeting right now with his son. If you'll have a seat, I will let him know you are here when they are finished."

Max thought of asking how long that might be, but decided against it. Instead, he smiled and nodded to Susan and retreated to one of several comfortable seats in the center of the suite's reception area and picked up a magazine which lay atop a giant glass hockey puck which served as a coffee table.

Inside Marshall Cederquist, Jr.'s office a rather heated conversation was drawing to a close. Trey had stormed into his father's office fifteen minutes earlier, demanding to know what his father was trying to do in offering ten thousand dollars for Amanda Hayes's safe return. Naturally, he had failed to mention what he knew of the girl's disappearance and his father was puzzled about what Trey found so wrong about the reward.

Trey had argued for ten minutes against his father's involvement, at times quite logically, citing some of the very points which Stu had argued a day earlier to Cederquist, Jr. Trey, however, also raised points which lacked logical origins, emotionally arguing against family or company involvement in anything detached from the manufacture of plastic goods in which the company specialized.

"You're always giving money to charities, Dad. I just don't understand it. We've worked hard here," conveniently including himself in the list of those who had made the company what it was, "and you seem like you just want to give the whole goddamn thing away."

"Now, just hold on, Trey," his father countered. "I do what I can to help the community, especially those who are less fortunate than we are. And that hasn't hurt the company, or your life." He quickly decided to add, "one damn bit."

Before he could continue, Trey was at it again, recounting times, far in the past, when the company had donated money to charitable causes or materials to local schools or used equipment to some of the local churches.

Cederquist, Jr., wanted desperately to argue each point with his reasoning at the time. Trey, he tried to say, those materials went to the schools you were attending. Those monies were going to good causes. Those churches needed our help. But he could see that Trey was not going to be convinced. In fact, Marshall wondered what emotional stake his son could have in all of this, for Trey was obviously upset, far more upset than he had ever seen his son where it concerned business.

Finally, Trey had had his say. When he had calmed himself to the point that his father felt that he could conclude their discussion, Marshall made one last statement about Ben Hayes. He reasonably stated the fact that Ben was a long-time employee of the company, and spoke of the responsibility that Marshall felt the company had to help an employee in Ben's position.

"That sonofabitch doesn't give a shit about Cederquist Industries, Dad," Trey had shouted.

Marshall had heard enough.

"Trey, I won't sit here and listen to you talk that way, especially about one of our employees. Ben Hayes has worked hard for this company and deserves more respect than that and I won't have you speak about him that way." How ironic, Marshall thought at the time, that he should stand up so strongly for Ben and his right to respect, when he had denied him such respect so long ago. Perhaps it was hypocritical to do this now, but it felt right and he continued.

"You just calm down about this, Trey, because you're not going to change my mind. What's done is done and I won't discuss it with you anymore. Now, get out of my office. I don't want you here right now. I can't believe the way you talk, sometimes."

Trey was moving toward the door and reaching for the knob when he suddenly turned and glared at his father once more.

"I don't know about you, old man. But I'm ready for you to retire. You're gonna ruin this company one day and there won't be anything left for me. I can see it happening right before my eyes and I can't do anything about it."

With that, Trey moved through the door and tried to slam it behind him, as he had tried to do hundreds of times over the years. The door closer prevented it from happening, though. That was precisely why, several years earlier, his father had had the closer installed.

Max Jansen saw Trey Cederquist for the first time as the latter left his father's office and moved quickly across the room to the hallway opposite the one that he had just exited. Trey was obviously upset about something and Max had an immediate dislike for the younger Cederquist. He saw a spoiled, little rich boy when he looked at Trey and his contempt for people like him rose instantly.

With what Gary and Lisa McLean had told him of the two Cederquists, father and son, Max was sure he would like the elder Cederquist far more and he had not yet met the man. He would get his chance very soon, for Susan was calling him now, telling him from across the twenty feet or so which separated them that Marshall Cederquist, Jr. would see him.

He rose, laying his copy of *Entrepreneur* magazine on the glass hockey puck, and moved swiftly so he would not keep Cederquist waiting. Also, he hoped that there might be some tell-tale sign of what had transpired between father and son left on the elder's face when Max got inside.

Max followed Susan down the narrow hallway of about twenty feet, bordered by a small private restroom to the left and windows exposing the manufacturing plant to the west. Susan opened the door and they found Marshall Cederquist moving around his expansive desk and extending a hand to Jansen.

"How do you do, Mr. Cederquist. As, I am sure, your secretary informed you, I am a reporter with the *Capital City Times*," Max started.

"Hello, Mr. Jansen. What can I do for you?"

"I'm here about the reward you've offered in the Amanda Hayes disappearance, sir."

"Well, as you know, Mr. Jansen, all inquiries about the girl's disappearance and the reward my company has offered are to be directed to Mr. Stuart Murphy, my attorney."

"Yes, I know, Mr. Cederquist. But, you see, I don't exactly enjoy talking with attorneys. I thought I'd come directly to you and get the story on this reward straight from the horse's mouth."

"But, Mr. Jansen, maybe, I dislike talking to reporters in the same way you dislike speaking with attorneys," Cederquist said, winking at Max, disarmed for the moment.

"I just thought you'd like to explain –"

"Have a seat," Cederquist interrupted. "As long as you're here, we might as well talk."

Max sat hurriedly and reached in his jacket pocket to remove his notepad.

Cederquist knew he should ask the reporter to leave and instruct him to see Stu Murphy. But, he had gone this far. He decided to grant the interview but wondered what Margot's reaction would be to the printed result.

"Can you tell me why the reward was offered?" Max began.

"Quite simply, Mr. Jansen, the girl is the daughter of one of our most valuable employees, Ben Hayes. We want to do what we can to return the girl to her parents' home. We are a large company. We have the resources available to us to do this. So we did it."

"Yes, but ten thousand dollars is a lot of money, Mr. Cederquist," Max countered, knowing that Cederquist had already addressed the issue. He hoped that Cederquist would volunteer more, however.

"Mr. Jansen," Cederquist said, pausing, for his patience was waning, "as I told you, we are a large company. Ten thousand dollars is not really that much, relative to our annual budget. I don't know what else I can say."

Max imagined an annual budget with line items such as "reward," "ransom," or, perhaps, "damsels in distress."

"I see," was all Max could come up with. Once again, Max realized that he had been ill prepared. He had shown up for an interview, hoping his target would tip his hand, instead of doing the legwork necessary for Max to know what it was exactly he suspected Cederquist of and zeroing in on the target's vulnerabilities. Perhaps, he thought, I don't deserve to crack this story, or any other.

The interview was ended, as quickly as it had begun. Jansen was unable to learn of any ulterior motive Marshall Cederquist might have had in offering the reward. He was almost pleased, for a change, to confirm the positive opinion of other people about one in Cederquist's position. Gary and Lisa were correct. Cederquist seemed like he was all right. Polite, personable, apparently on the up-and-up. Yet, Cederquist had held firm and even embarrassed Max. Still, Max somehow found this far easier to swallow than when others had done the same.

Max excused himself, apologizing for his attempt to circumvent the system Cederquist and his lawyer had developed. He thanked Susan for her cooperation as he passed her, wondering, as he did so, what had prompted her to admit a reporter, in the first place. He guiltily retraced his steps down the long marble hall, exited the building, and ran straight into Trey Cederquist at the bottom of the steps in front of the building.

Ben Hayes tried to busy himself in the garage set back from the southeast corner of his two-story home on North Caldwell. He took great pride in the home he and Margot had purchased sixteen years earlier. The house was quaint. He had remodeled seventy-five percent or more of the house over the years, being careful to keep any one project modest enough that it would neither interrupt his small family's lifestyle nor do horrific damage to its finances.

As Hayes adjusted the angle at which his aluminum extension ladder rested against the wall at the back of the garage, he heard the sound of a car engine as the vehicle turned into the drive. The car stopped just his side of the sidewalk in front of his home, and ceased to run. Hayes turned slowly, anticipating news he was afraid to hear.

While his wife might have turned in anticipation of seeing Amanda alight from the car, had she been outside with him, Ben Hayes had been preparing himself for the worst and only stood with his back to the approaching car, waiting. After a moment, Ben turned slowly to see who had come with news.

Lieutenant Stiles was disembarking as Ben walked toward him through the open garage door. The face of the detective betrayed nothing to Hayes as the two men approached each other. Ben could feel his wife's eyes from behind him, as she stood inside the living room window. The two men shared a handshake and Stiles spoke first.

"Ben, we got some news, but things are sketchy and we don't know anything for sure."

"Is she dead?"

Not wanting to hesitate, Stiles responded simply, "There's a body down in Granite City. Fits your daughter's description. But it doesn't have to be her, Ben." He worried that, perhaps, he had paused too long before adding this last attempt at positive thinking.

"Their medical examiner is working right now to identify the girl and discover the cause of death. We are delivering Amanda's dental records you provided us with. Needless to say, Ben, we hope there's no match."

"Yeah, sure," was all Ben Hayes could muster.

Again, two men stood in silence. There was not much to say, it seemed. Ben Hayes finally asked, "How long will this take? The identification, I mean."

"Not long, I would guess. We'll let you know as soon as we

hear anything, of course." He hesitated. "Do you want to tell your wife or would you like me to tell her?"

"I'll take care of it," he said immediately.

Stiles didn't have to ask if Ben were sure. He took his cue and turned to leave. He wanted to say more, offer a glimmer of hope, but found it impossible. Soon he turned slowly away from his car door and back toward Hayes. The man was already on his way to the house, his wife waiting now at the open front door. Stiles stepped into his car and started the engine. As the couple disappeared into their home, Stiles backed out into the road and slowly rolled away.

"Hello," Max said to Trey Cederquist, not wishing to let him know he knew who he was or what he thought of him.

"Secretary says you're a reporter," came the response.

"That's right, sir. I work for the *Capital City Times*. My name is Max Jansen," he said, relieved that he had left Maxwell inside, and offered his hand.

Trey did not shake it. He turned instead toward the parking lot and asked, "Where are you parked?"

"Right over there. The rental."

Trey began walking the short distance in the direction of the car to which Max had gestured. He led the way with some sense of ceremony, as though Max were being led to the woodshed, or, perhaps, to the gas chamber.

"This the one?" Trey asked, when he got to the blue rental.

"That's it, sir." And he saw Trey reach for the door and open it.

Max could not resist a smile. "It appears, sir, that I am being shown the door."

Trey was not amused.

"We don't need reporters snooping around here, Mr. Jansen." He hesitated. "What is it you're snooping after, anyway?"

"I'm here in Jacksonville about the Amanda Hayes disappearance."

No response came.

"I stopped by to ask Mr. Cederquist about the ten thousand dollar reward he's offered for the girl's safe return."

Trey's face betrayed his anguish at hearing what he had already suspected as the cause for Max's presence at CI.

"That's just—nothing. You don't have to concern yourself with that or anything else around here, for that matter."

Trey seemed to be urging Max to get into the car with all his body language. Max resisted with his own, however.

Motioning back toward the building from which he had just come, Max began, "Well, Mr. Cederquist seems very concerned for the young lady. And she is the daughter of an employee here, right?"

"Yes, that's right. Old man Hayes probably came begging for that reward."

"Well, if that's the case, Mr. Cederquist didn't indicate it to be so."

"Mr. Cederquist doesn't know what he's doing," Trey said with great contempt for his father's name.

Max still had not let on that he knew who Trey was. Trey was certainly not going to introduce himself, it seemed. Instead, Trey forced the door to Max's rental open as far as it would go and, this time, very overtly motioned for Max to get in. Max moved toward the open car door, as Trey released the handle and moved around Max toward the building.

Max, however, stopped short of sliding into the seat and spoke to Trey's back. "Mr. Cederquist?"

No response.

"Mr. Cederquist?"

Trey kept walking.

"Trey!"

Cederquist, now just short of the steps to the building, stopped dead in his tracks and turned.

"Nice talking to you," Max smiled.

Max slid into the seat and started the engine. He could see Cederquist move up the steps and into the building. He shook his head. What a cold fish, he thought. The daughter of a long-time employee of his family's firm has disappeared. With each hour that passes, the likelihood of her safe return diminishes. And Trey Cederquist does not even respond to Max's mentioning the girl. Of course, Trey does not appear to have much use for the girl's father. Or his own father, for that matter. And, there is young Cederquist's dislike for reporters. Max wondered what some snooping might uncover.

TEN

Keith Utterback arrived at the Schumacher residence around noon, sooner than Melissa had expected. She scurried to gather her jacket and push her ponytail through the back of a North Carolina baseball cap. She raced to get out to Keith's pickup, parked at the entrance to the driveway.

Once Melissa was comfortably inside the pickup, they wasted little time in getting to the subject that now consumed them.

"I know it's her, Melissa. I just can't believe it."

"Don't go jumping to conclusions. We don't know that it's Amanda's body. Maybe it's someone else. We gotta keep hoping."

Keith nervously broached another subject.

"I didn't have anything to do with her disappearance, Melissa."

She was surprised that he felt it necessary to tell her this.

"I didn't say you had, Keith. Why do you say that?"

"I don't know." He searched for the right words. "Everybody else, besides my folks, seems to think I had something to do with it."

He searched Melissa's face for some trace of suspicion.

"Well, I don't think that, Keith. It never entered my mind that you'd do anything to hurt Amanda. She liked you," Melissa said and paused before adding, "a lot."

"I know that if she cared for you like that, Keith, then you aren't the kind of guy who could do anything to hurt her."

Keith suddenly became aware that Melissa's father was approaching the passenger's side of the pickup. Keith could tell by the look on Martin Schumacher's face that the man was not happy to see him there.

"I wish everybody felt the way you do, Melissa."

Now Melissa was aware of her father's approach and she rolled her window down as her father drew near.

"Melissa, I want you inside now."

"But, Daddy."

"Now, Melissa."

Tears formed in her eyes. She couldn't bear to look Keith in the eye as she climbed out of the truck. But she was gathering her own brand of courage as the scene unfolded.

Keith also got out of his truck and walked to the front of the vehicle. His hands in his jean pockets, he nervously searched again for words that would express his concerns without revealing his newest fears.

"Mr. Schumacher, did I do something wrong here?"

Melissa's father was just as uncomfortable as he was making Keith feel.

"It's just that," he began before breaking off and forcing himself to be more direct than he wanted to be, "we don't know what happened to Amanda. And, quite frankly, we don't want you around Melissa until we're sure you—"

Keith began to speak, but wasn't sure what would have come out of his mouth, had Melissa not spoken first.

"Daddy! How could you say such a thing?"

She walked slowly toward Keith, pulling away from her father's half-hearted attempt to clutch her arm.

"Keith, remember what I just told you." She motioned with her eyes toward the truck.

"Sure, Melissa."

He was not very convincing.

With a nod toward her father, she continued, "Don't be too hard on my father, Keith. He's just scared."

"Yeah, right. I guess I can't blame him for that."

Melissa turned and walked past her father, this time avoiding his embrace.

Mr. Schumacher looked blankly at Keith, who could only surrender, open palms at his shoulders before he backed away toward the pickup's driver-side door.

At his newspaper's offices late that afternoon, reporter Jack McGlothen, with whom Max had verbally dueled days earlier in a local restaurant, was among the first to see the wire that told of a young girl's body having been found in Granite City, Illinois. He immediately called Jacksonville police headquarters to learn if they had any information on the, as yet, unidentified body. They had none, he was told. Still, he thought, he'd probably bet his paycheck that it was Amanda Hayes.

McGlothen then contacted the Granite City police. Granite City police had been of no more help than those he had spoken to in Jacksonville. It took him a couple of hours to track down a friend from college who worked on the staff of the newspaper in Edwardsville, just a few miles from Granite City. This friend told McGlothen he would get right on the story. He had heard of the body's discovery, but had not known of a missing girl in Jacksonville, he explained. The two friends, anxious to learn if there was any connection between their respective local stories, were excited at the prospect of working together.

Arrangements were made for the two to speak again within the next four hours, giving the Edwardsville-half of this newly formed journalistic team time to drive the short distance to Granite City and do some snooping. Meanwhile Jack made more telephone calls to the Granite City police, tried to make a contact with a St. Louis television station, and called on another college friend in Alton who was of no help.

He was becoming frustrated. It was time for Jack to find a buddy of his who also worked at the paper. He was an older reporter, a mentor or sorts. He would inform him of the wire service piece and of his alliance with his colleague from Edwardsville. It was five-thirty.

Located a hundred paces from the backdoor of the newspaper building, Don's Place is the perfect spot for those who work at gathering and disseminating the news to the Jacksonville citizenry. Known for its Tuesday night giveaways of St. Louis Cardinal or St. Louis Blues tickets, Thursday night crab races, and its friendly, Irish-pub atmosphere, Don's attracts a diverse clientele. There's the college crowd from MacMurray and Illinois College, as well as townies who enjoy cold beer and a game of pool or good conversation at high volume.

It was here that Jack McGlothen knew he might find the older reporter. He was not disappointed. Seated on a barstool at a high, round table across from the bar was Lanny Nowak, engaged in excited conversation with another of the bar's patrons. Jack placed his hand on Nowak's shoulder to gain his attention without yelling over the music. Lanny seemed annoyed at first seeing McGlothen, but quickly altered his demeanor when Jack spoke into his cupped hands at Nowak's ear.

Lanny then leaned toward the gentleman with whom he had been talking. The man had a young lady draped across his shoulder.

"Body's been found. Granite City. No ID, yet," he said.

Everyone at the table knew what Nowak was talking about.

Nowak returned his attention to McGlothen. When had all this taken place, he asked him. With whom had he spoken, he wanted to know. Get denials in direct quotes, he told the young reporter. Stay by the phones and keep an eye on the wire. He'd be along shortly. He'd finish his Diet Coke and return to the offices.

Thanks to the young woman draped over the shoulder of Nowak's friend, everyone in Don's had heard the news within minutes, some of it inaccurately, of course. Shortly word would spread, first, from one bar to the next and, then, into the homes of bar patrons returning home following their after-work attempts at stress reduction. More accurate accounts, plus any official updates and denials, would appear in the morning papers. Until then, word of mouth would do its job.

It was getting dark and Max Jansen was anxious to contact his new friend with news of his morning encounter with Trey Cederquist. His first attempts to reach Gary earlier in the day had failed. From his cell phone he had called the McLean home. Lisa had told Max that her husband was out hanging more posters and passing out flyers with Amanda's picture on them.

Max had decided not to tell Lisa of the conversation he had that morning with the former target of her lethal right jab. He would save that, so Gary could tell her. He recalled Lisa's recollection of the story about Trey Cederquist the previous evening and smiled again at the thought of Cederquist doubled over in pain, trying to make a dignified exit from the Christmas party at which he had decided to make a pass at the wrong girl. Max would, he told himself, enjoy hearing Gary's re-telling of the story to her later. For now, though, he was impatient to find Gary.

Having pulled over to park at a hamburger place on the east end of Morton, Max waited for perhaps three-quarters of an hour, listening intently to his police scanner. But there were no further details forthcoming and it frustrated Max.

Now he continued driving about the Morton Avenue course he had set for himself in his search for Gary.

Margot Hayes had taken the news, that the body of a young girl matching her daughter's description had been discovered, rather calmly, she had decided. There was, as yet, no other evidence leading one to conclude that the body was that of her daughter and she had convinced herself from the time she had seen Stiles get into his squad car and back away from her home that hope was still in ample supply.

The next few hours, however, proved to be quite difficult and she fought to maintain her composure in front of her husband. They had said little when Ben came in with the news that Stiles had delivered. The quiet was best handled for each of them by going their separate ways and busying their hands if not their minds with tasks of little consequence, she cleaning spotless areas of the home, he continuing his garage-straightening.

Margot didn't want to be around Ben for fear she would lose her battle to remain strong for him. And she knew that Ben was doing the same. Strangely, they were each busy, being there for the other in their separateness, their distance.

If Ben were trying to be strong for her and she wasn't feeling particularly strong, or comforted by his actions, she deduced that her husband probably wasn't holding up any better for her efforts. Still, she couldn't bring herself to go to him, to talk of their daughter who might be lying dead in a strange city, to acknowledge her fears and relinquish her hold on denial.

The phone had rung repeatedly, relatives and friends wanting the latest news on Amanda's disappearance and offering support from varying distances. She had not found herself capable of informing any of the out-of-town callers of the latest possible development. She had pretended there had been no news at all and had done so convincingly, she was sure.

As the afternoon dragged on into the evening, she dried her tears perhaps a dozen times, fighting to keep it together. She tried to imagine how joyous their reunion with Amanda would be when her daughter would finally turn up with some plausible explanation of where she had been and this nightmare would turn into a dream. Others, Margot concluded, would demand an explanation from Amanda. This would not be so for Margot. She would take her daughter into her arms and never question Amanda's reasoning or motivation for whatever it was that had taken place. And she would do so under any circumstances.

Margot wondered if, perhaps, years from now she might decide differently and one day ask her daughter just what the hell she thought she was doing all that time long ago, when she put her mother on the brink of insanity with worry. Margot prayed that she would get the opportunity to one day answer the question.

In the meantime, Margot moved from room to room, occasionally pulling back a curtain to see if she could catch a glimpse of Ben. She had spotted him only once since he had left her inside after the visit from Stiles. She panicked briefly when, on one of her attempts to check on Ben, she saw a JPD squad car slowly move past the front door.

It was becoming increasingly difficult to not think the worst, to not speculate how the news might come that they had lost Amanda forever. She closed her eyes and tried to see Amanda's face and it was strangely difficult for her to do. It had been almost a week since she had seen her daughter and her mind's eye was having trouble painting a picture of her.

Images of Amanda when she was three, or seven, or ten, were more easily produced in her mind than more recent memories. Perhaps she was willing herself to return to happier times, far removed from an inevitable, ugly conclusion Margot feared was all-too-quickly approaching.

Margot rushed to the living room where a picture of Amanda, taken the previous fall, hung on the wall. There. That's how she'll look when she comes home. A bigger smile on her face, perhaps. We'll invite all her friends to welcome her home. Ben will smile, too. Perhaps he and his daughter can return to a place where they had been years earlier, when Amanda was little and tensions that had divided father and daughter would melt away.

Please, God, Margot thought. Give that a chance.

Trey Cederquist was nervous. In the darkness he proceeded to walk across the parking lot to Marcus' apartment. While at the car he had reached further into his glove compartment for the watch he had taken from Amanda Hayes's wrist. Wiped clean of his or anyone else's fingerprints, the watch was now in a sealed manila envelope.

He scanned the surrounding area for a sign of a police presence. Detecting none, he tore the envelope. Opening the door to Marcus' apartment slightly with the key he had stolen from Marcus sometime ago and wrapping the bottom of his sport coat around the doorknob, he slung the watch, untouched, from the envelope. The watch slid along the floor, just as Trey had intended and now lay beneath Marcus' old, beat-up couch.

Just like that, without even stepping foot in Marcus' place, Trey had delivered another piece of evidence tying Marcus to Amanda. If the police were not already sure that Marcus and Luke were involved in Amanda's disappearance, they soon would be.

Lisa McLean had given Max no idea of where he might find her husband. She suspected that he might be downtown on the square or at the WalMart or Big K Mart on Morton Avenue. But she could not be sure he wasn't moving from store to store, perhaps positioning himself outside the stores as the Salvation Army bell-ringers do during the Christmas season, handing out leaflets instead of collecting change.

Max made the rounds, looking for Gary's car in the traffic moving in the opposite direction as he, himself, hopped from storefront to storefront. After one or two drive-by's, he began parking his rental and going inside to inquire of the store clerks if Gary had been in. Hours had gone by. Max finally spotted Gary outside a discount store at the far-west end of Morton, just a quarter mile east and on the opposite side of Morton from Cederquist Industries.

"Hi, Max," Gary said, as the reporter approached. Gary was, indeed, passing out flyers to customers of the store as they entered or exited the store.

"Gary," Max began, out of breath from his brisk walk from the far reaches of the parking lot, for the store was quite busy. "I've been looking all over for you."

"What's up?" Gary asked, as he continued to greet customers with leaflets.

"I spoke to Trey Cederquist this morning."

Gary cocked his head, as he looked at Max.

"I went out to Cederquist Industries to talk to the old man about the reward he's put up and I got to meet Trey."

Still puzzled, Gary asked, "And what's that got to do with Amanda?"

"Well, I think I've stumbled onto something."

For the first time, Gary ceased his passing out flyers and pulled Max aside, away from the ears of passersby. He looked sternly at Max.

"Are you saying you think Trey had something to do with Amanda's disappearance?"

Max counted with fingers stretched wide.

"I'm saying, Gary, that Trey Cederquist does not like Ben Hayes one bit. He's seriously pissed off at his old man for putting up this reward. And he made no bones about being very unhappy that I was at CI, snooping around."

"Wait a minute, Max. You're making a big leap in logic here. Just because he dislikes someone doesn't mean he'd harm his daughter. A lot of people might question Marshall's putting up that reward. Lots of people don't like reporters. And you. You can be pretty irritating," Gary said.

He was recalling the angry words and unspoken tension they had experienced during much of their conversation on Amanda the night before.

"Maybe Trey just finds it difficult to get past that charm of yours and see you for what you are," Gary concluded.

Max tried unsuccessfully not to be stung by Gary's sarcasm.

"Look, asshole," Max told Gary, "you weren't there. You didn't hear the venom, the spite, when he spoke of Amanda's father or the outrage he displayed toward his old man. And here's the most important thing."

He paused for greater effect.

"He tried to be somebody else."

Gary's interest grew.

"He wasn't aware that I knew who he was. And he never let on that he was who he was. This squirrel has something to hide, I'm telling you."

The two exchanged looks of incredulity.

"Look. I'm not saying that Trey's a kidnapper. Not yet, anyway. But he knows something, I tell you. And, unless I miss my guess, he's afraid someone's going to find out what he knows."

"You're saying he's paranoid," Gary offered.

"That's right."

Nothing more was said for several seconds as both their minds raced. Then Gary spoke.

"What are you suggesting we do?"

"I don't know. We could call Stiles."

"And what do you think he'd do with this," Gary queried, searching for the right word, "this suspicion?"

Max's shoulders dropped. He knew Gary was right. Suddenly his eyes brightened.

Gary knew Max just well enough to be scared.

"Or we could stake out our little buddy ourselves until we know more, Gary."

Gary was not biting.

"Perhaps you should contact Stiles, Max. Police stake out people. Maybe newspaper reporters stake out people. I don't know. Teachers," he said, pointing to himself, "don't stake out people. I'm a teacher."

"Come on, Gary. You're not teaching now. You want to help Amanda, right."

He had gone straight for the heart.

Gary thought before responding.

"How do I know this won't be a big waste of time. I can't waste time, Max. Amanda may not have much time."

Now it was Max's turn to think before responding.

"Look, Gary. She's been gone almost a week. I haven't said anything to you yet. But I think that, with each passing day—"

He paused. He knew Gary did not want to hear what he had to say.

"She may already be out of time, Gary. You may just have to face up to that."

Gary turned away from Max. Tearfully, he began distributing more leaflets to more customers, both coming and going. He didn't want to let go of his dream of a happy ending to this saga. He couldn't.

Max watched for several seconds, as Gary struggled to regain his composure and pass out leaflets with a smile. Max admired Gary for his efforts but shook his head at Gary's inability to face reality. He moved away into the parking lot in search of his rental.

As he reached the car, he heard footsteps behind him and, then, Gary's voice.

"Where are you going, Max?"

"To find our buddy, Trey," Max responded, as he looked back over his shoulder without turning around completely. He did not want to appear too defiant to Gary, who he considered to be more and more of a friend, someone to be admired more than suspected of wrong-doing, as Max had initially done, more respected than pitied.

"Let's go," Gary said.

"You're serious?"

"Yeah. Let's go. Come on. Before I change my mind."

ELEVEN

Dental records from Amanda's dentist, by way of Lieutenant Stiles in Jacksonville, had arrived in Granite City police headquarters around seven-thirty that night. A detective had instructed a uniformed officer to hand carry the records to Edwardsville, the Madison County seat, where an autopsy was about to be performed on the body of the young girl which David Shireman and Matt Crawford had discovered the previous day.

Paul Brandenburg, Edwardsville reporter and college friend of Jack McGlothen, had succeeded in gathering some basic information involving the boys and their discovery. He knew the officer who was delivering the dental records and inquired about the contents of the large manila envelope the officer carried to his squad car.

"Envelope got anything to do with the body those boys found here, Louie?"

"Can't tell you that, Paul. You know that."

"Well, where are you taking this envelope?"

Over the open door to his squad car, the officer, now seated behind the wheel, winked at Brandenburg and said, "Just follow me, Paul."

The fifteen-minute ride ended in a parking lot next to the county medical examiner's offices. As Brandenberg had suspected, the envelope and its contents were connected to the body. As the reporter began to exit his car, the officer emerged from his own and gestured for the other to stay put. It was a friendly gesture that carried with it a notion that, after the officer had made his delivery, he would be back, perhaps to discuss the envelope's contents.

The officer went inside, was absent from the parking lot for only a brief time, and walked straight toward Brandenburg's car upon exiting the building.

"Dental records from Jacksonville, Paul. Seems they got 'em a missing girl up there and they want to know if this is her."

With that the officer moved back, away from Brandenburg, who was still seated in his car. The reporter began to ask about results, knowing that the officer had not been gone long enough to answer his question with any certainty.

But the officer was walking away, shrugging, as if to say, "Who knows?"

The officer got into his car and drove off in the direction from which the two had come only minutes earlier. Brandenburg was quick to flip open his cellular phone and call Jack McGlothen in Jacksonville. After he told Jack what he'd learned, Brandenburg positioned himself in front of the medical examiner's office, waiting for any news that might be forthcoming. He slouched down into his car's seat and tried to get comfortable. It might be some time before he could contact McGlothen again with an update.

Trey loosened his tie as he pulled to a stop outside a bar just off Jacksonville's Morton Avenue. He had accomplished little in his day at the office, except arguing with his father and arousing the suspicions of a journalist. He knew this. He was sure of it and was having a tough time of brushing it all off. He had thought of little else since Max Jansen had left him standing at the steps to the CI entrance earlier that morning. His troubles were mounting.

Typically, Trey sought comfort in women and drink. When neither proved sufficient to take his edge off, there was one other remedy to which he could always turn. It never let him down and he always had it at the ready. Yet, something inside him had prevented Trey from going there often. He sensed a danger inherent in his use of the product he had been producing in the abandoned warehouse at the back of the CI plant. Still, there were times when nothing else worked.

Once inside the bar, Trey was disappointed that Laurie, his favorite barmaid in the establishment, was not working. Two other girls, sporting the obligatory bikini top and short pants over nylon-stockings, anklets, and cross-trainers, were working the bar's two rooms. The older girl he knew well, having frequently hit on her to no avail. But he couldn't stand to look at her. Bitch, he thought.

The girl was very attractive, but to Trey a bitch, nonetheless.

At least Laurie had been receptive to his overtures, even if she hadn't succumbed to him on the many occasions he'd asked her to. But, Trey knew, she liked the tips that came with playfully going along with his verbal come-ons and had even allowed him to touch, so long as he was discrete in his handiness.

But instead of Laurie, the Bitch was working with a newcomer. Trey was disappointed. The newcomer was not half so alluring as her co-worker. She lacked the roundness in her breasts that Trey had, at one time, found so attractive in the Bitch. And this new girl's hair was all wrong, pulled back tightly at the back of her head in a ponytail, a turn-off for Trey. He liked big hair. Perhaps her disposition would be better. In Trey's opinion, it could not possibly be any worse than that of the Bitch's.

Trey had walked the length of the bar and settled onto a stool near the far end, near the pay phone and the short hallway leading to the men's room. He loosened his tie some more and ordered a beer and whiskey without a smile for his server, for it was the Bitch. She had bumped past the Newcomer to take his order. She gave her friend an I'll-tell-you-later look as she turned her back to Trey and reached into the cooler for the Rolling Rock he had ordered.

For the first time, Trey scanned the room to see its patrons. He could see that nearly all the tables across from the bar had at least two people seated at them. Four or five other men were at the bar, perched upon their stools. Other patrons played pool in the next room, into which one could see through three openings in the wall. The Newcomer now served drinks to an unseen customer through the middle opening.

Trey drank his beer quickly, ordered a second and downed a shot of Southern Comfort. He drank the second Rolling Rock much more slowly, anticipating the buzz that ordinarily followed this ritual.

After three beers, he sat solemnly, disappointed in the scenery. One barmaid, attractive beyond description but cold as ice, the other, judged by Trey as unworthy his minimal effort at sexual dalliance. He was disappointed, too, in the lack of an intense rush from the liquor he'd passed by his palate. Now he was becoming agitated by the music playing loudly on the jukebox. What a lousy night this had turned out to be.

It was time for a hit, he decided. But he wasn't thinking of turning to the music machine and sliding money into its mouth. He pointed a finger in the air, signaling for another beer. But the beer would have to wait for his return, for he was moving quickly down the short hall toward the back of the establishment and turning right into the men's room.

He closed the door, securing the small lock behind him.

As the Bitch filled the Newcomer in on Trey and his rep, Trey pulled a Baggie out of his blazer's inside, right hand pocket and set it on top of the hand-dryer. Next he reached into the opposite inside breast pocket and pulled out an electronic organizer, which he lay on one side of the sink. From the Baggie he poured a chalky, off-white powder onto the organizer's closed lid. He licked his right index finger, inserted the tip of the finger into the powder, and put the finger, the tip now covered with a small portion of the powder, to his tongue. He winced, the bitterness attacking his taste buds.

He used the edge of a matchbook to push the remaining powder into a straight line on the surface of the organizer and pulled his pen from his shirt pocket. He unscrewed the pen, removed the ink cartridge from the bottom barrel of the pen and proceeded to inhale half of the line into one nostril, using the pen's barrel as a straw. He finished off the line with the other nostril and quickly inhaled the stagnant air of the men's room.

Trey sealed the Baggie and tucked it into his coat pocket. The residue of the powder on the surface of the organizer he quickly blew away with the rush of air from the hand-dryer. Trey struggled to reassemble his ink pen and pocket his organizer. His balance was already deteriorating. But Trey's fire was lit.

Two pool players in the room adjacent to the bar were struggling to see if Trey Cederquist had returned to his seat, while trying to stay out of sight from the target of their surveillance. They had followed their mark into the bar and quickly ducked into the adjoining poolroom. Each had shot a colored ball in the direction of the cue ball on at least one occasion, so they could stay out of Trey's view while playing their game of pool. Had anyone been watching them play, he'd have suspected they were either already drunk or really bad pool players.

For his part, Gary McLean was nervous. As an employee of the local school district, he was on forbidden ground. How had he let himself be talked into this, he wondered. Meanwhile, Max was enjoying the moment, but growing anxious at Trey's failure to quickly return. Cederquist had had plenty of time in which to relieve himself. What could be keeping him, Max wondered. He was beginning to fear that Trey had spotted him and ducked out a back door.

Suddenly, Trey reappeared at his barstool and began drinking what Max was counting as his fourth beer. That's right, Trey. Drink those troubles away. Max had grown sure with each hour that passed since he'd spoken with Cederquist that morning, that Trey was into trouble of some kind and Max suspected, or hoped, that it had something to do with the disappearance of Ben Hayes's daughter. Max didn't have time to question himself regarding his hunch. If this were all he was operating on, at least he would not be wasting his time totally. For the show was about to start.

"What the hell are you looking at?" Trey yelled.

The man seated next to him was perplexed. Max could not hear the man's response. But the patron had obviously been caught off guard. He didn't appear to have a clue about whatever it was Trey had taken issue with. He raised his hands, his beer bottle in one hand, and backed away from Trey, taking a seat several removed from his former place next to Trey.

Max saw the barmaids react with a knowing look to each other. He had seen them huddle briefly when Trey made his exit to the men's room earlier. They had shared some muffled laughter, as the older girl seemed to be letting the younger in on the facts concerning something, most likely their angry customer in the dark blazer, Max guessed.

The pool game continued, Gary coming up with four more quarters, when all the balls finally disappeared. Bad players, he discovered, sink a shot or two, even when absorbed in spying and not concentrating on the game they are using only as guise. While Gary found the barmaids, cleavage proudly displayed, distracting on a couple of occasions, Max was clearly focused on Trey Cederquist.

In the periphery, Max became aware that the barmaids had turned on a light just over Cederquist's head, in order to see better. The girls were changing a keg at a nearby tap. The light remained on for about a minute. During that minute, Max was amazed at what he saw.

Cederquist was all over the bar with his hands. First he attempted to spin cardboard coasters on edge. Next he was shuffling perhaps ten coasters, as one does a deck of cards. Finally he began flipping them one-by-one like coins. He appeared to be checking to see if heads, a Budweiser logo, had come up, or tails, the bare backside of the coaster. Trey was noticeably jittery, and this was observable from a distance of perhaps twenty-five feet.

The barmaids, too, had apparently noticed, for the older one approached Cederquist and Max heard her ask if Trey were okay. Max moved closer to better hear the exchange. He could not hear Trey's initial response. But he heard the girl ask again if Trey were all right.

Without warning, Trey backhanded her across her face with his right hand. The blow rocked her back on her heels and, frightened, she reached frantically with both hands for something to grab hold of, so she could break her fall. The counter behind her caught her at the small of her back and she regained her balance. But she was obviously hurt.

Trey was off the barstool quickly and approached the opening in the bar through which the girls entered and exited to wait tables. The younger of the girls was outside the bar at a table near the front door of the establishment and was struck with fear, unable to move.

As Trey began to move, rather awkwardly, through the bar-gate, a hand caught him at the nape of his neck. The patron who had earlier just backed off, when Trey had jumped him about some imagined and undisclosed indiscretion, now had Cederquist by the neck with one hand and was about to smash Trey's face with his other. The man seemed bigger than before somehow and acted with confidence. He had seen enough and obviously knew what he was doing. He stopped, however, when the barmaid Trey had struck shouted, "No! Just get him out of here."

Trey was in no condition to stop the man from switching his grip to the back of Trey's collar with one hand and the back of Trey's belt with the other. Trey's feet rarely touched the floor as the two made their way past the still-stunned younger barmaid, out the door and onto the parking lot.

Gary moved immediately behind Max and asked the older barmaid if she were okay. Max was on his way to the front window of the bar to observe Trey picking himself up off the pavement, dust himself off, awkwardly hoist a middle finger at the patron who had just tossed him from the doorway, and move toward his car.

"What got into him," was Gary's question, once the barmaid had assured him she was all right.

"Something," she said. "Did you see his eyes?"

"Not from over there. No."

"When I turned on the light before, I looked at him, keeping my eye on him. And his eyes were, like, dancing. Jittery, you know? It was scary. Should have been nice and wide, ya know, as dark as it is in here? But not his. No. Something got into him, all right. I think when he went in the bathroom 'while ago, he got him some go-fast."

Gary didn't know what she meant, his naivete showing through. She recognized the look.

"Methamphetamines," she offered, as she stroked her face, red from Trey's slap. "That's bad shit."

"Gary, come on. He's leaving," Max said, as he approached and grabbed Gary's sleeve.

Gary looked first at Max, then back at his new friend, as he pulled his elbow away from Max.

"No, Max. Listen. She says she thinks that he's using some kind of drug. What'd you call it?"

"Methamphetamines. And I don't think," she corrected Gary, "I know he's using."

"Meth?" Max asked, now interested in what was being said, but torn between listening to more and wanting to keep up with Cederquist.

"You got it. Meth, ice, crank. Whatever you wanna call it. It's bad shit. I've seen it before. I mean, it's effect. I wouldn't want to use it."

"Watch him, Gary." Max was looking out the front window as he made the run around the horseshoe and raced to the men's room. Gary was standing at the window, watching Trey, who sat in his car but hadn't yet started its engine.

The barmaids were now offering their thanks to the patron who had removed Trey. They checked the older girl's jaw and pointed in Trey's direction, laughing and smiling at one another, as they set the patron up with a drink on the house. Gary heard the older girl's rejection of the patron's making a call to the police. She assured the man that she would tell the owner when he arrived later, as Max returned from the men's room and approached Gary.

"Still there?"

"Yes," Gary said. "I can see him move every once in awhile. Looked like he slammed his hand on the steering wheel a couple of times, but he's still there."

"All I found in the bathroom was this," Max said, holding up an ink pen cartridge, filled with ink.

If Gary were still putting two and two together, Max had already come up with four, based partly on what the barmaid had told them.

"I'd bet a month's salary that Trey Cederquist has an ink pen in his pocket without any ink. What do you say, Gary?"

Gary leaned back and waved his arms in front of him, rejecting the bet.

Chief Medical Examiner Carletta Burman waited patiently as her assistants maneuvered the gurney through the swinging doors to the autopsy room in her Madison County headquarters. The body of the unidentified girl found in an abandoned warehouse outside Granite City lay on the gurney, covered only with a blue sheet. The body had now been in her office's possession for eighteen hours. Burman had been notified while at a conference in Springfield, Missouri, by phone and had driven several hours to get back, only to learn that she could not begin the autopsy until others, who had also traveled some distance, were done with their work on the case. Finally, she could be getting on with the task of discovering how the girl had died.

Later, she would take measures to see that the delays they had experienced that day would never happen again in her office. The relative distances from Edwardsville of key members of her forensic team would somehow have to come under her control, making the team more readily available. It would not be a popular move. But it was one she would make, nevertheless.

Technically, discovery of the girl's identity was part of the puzzle with which her office was charged. Burman had overseen the taking of hundreds of pictures and the retrieval of trace evidence. She had, within the past hour, allowed an expert in identification access to dental records. Specifically, Burman saw her own role in this investigation more simply, finding the cause of death. If the girl's identity were now known, no one had informed Burman. It wasn't that she didn't care about the girl's identity. It simply was not her area of expertise. She chose not to concern herself with it.

In an office down the hall from the autopsy room, the ID expert was concluding the composition of his final report to a member of Burman's clerical staff. He quickly read the report to himself, his lips moving slightly as he scanned its contents, once the staffer had printed out a copy for his signature.

"Looks good, Lois," he said, as he reached for his pen and signed his name at the bottom. "Let's let Car hear the news."

The staffer declined, as always, and chose instead to return to her filing. The expert walked the short distance down the hall to where Carletta Burman was about to enter the autopsy room where the girl's body lay.

"Dr. Burman?"

"Yes, Henry," she replied, without looking up.

"My report is complete, Dr. Burman. I've matched the subject with dental records from Jacksonville. Your subject is Amanda Hayes, seventeen-year-old daughter of Benjamin and Margot Hayes of Jacksonville."

No one spoke for several seconds, perhaps out of respect for the young girl, whose body lay before them, stripped of its dignity, subject soon to more systematic probing.

"Thank you, Henry. Your help, as always, is very much appreciated."

After briefly returning to her work, Burman turned her head in the direction of one of her two assistants. “Call Captain Aldretti in Granite City. Tell him he can release a statement to Jacksonville authorities so the parents can be informed. Tell him not to, under any circumstances, release the girl’s identity to anyone else until the parents have been informed and have had a chance to inform any other members of their family. If Aldretti needs to speak with me, you can put him on the speaker phone here.”

She looked down into the face of Amanda Hayes. Burman’s own daughter was sixteen years old. She would do her job tonight, as always. But it would not be easy.

“Knowing your name just makes this harder for me, dear,” she said softly to the corpse. “But we now have you a little closer to home. One more piece to the puzzle,” she paused, “and you can rest.”

“Keith, I want to thank you for coming in tonight to talk to me, again. You’ve been very cooperative and I want you to know that tomorrow’s polygraph test is just a formality. I have to be sure we can rule you out as a suspect in Amanda’s disappearance.”

“Sure, Lieutenant. I just want to help you find her. That’s all. Let’s just find her,” he concluded awkwardly.

Stiles looked down at the young man seated before him. He wanted desperately to believe him. He was reminding Keith that the polygraph expert would be arriving tomorrow, when he noticed one of his uniformed officers standing outside his office, beckoning him to come outside. He had noticed moments before as his phone line lit up with a call, but per his instructions, it had not been allowed to ring.

“Excuse me, Keith,” he said, as he stuck his head outside the door. Back inside the office, he excused himself once again. “Right now, Keith, I have to take a call down the hall. Just hang tight, okay?”

Several minutes passed before the uniformed officer who had

beckoned Stiles to take the telephone call in another office stepped into Stiles' office.

"Where's Lieutenant Stiles?" Keith asked.

"He had some urgent business come up, Keith. You can go on home, now."

Keith looked around the office nervously, as the officer led him from the office and to his parents who waited outside.

The body of Amanda Hayes lay atop the autopsy table, a body block beneath her shoulders. Her arms and neck pulled back toward the table's shiny surface, forcing her chest to pitch upward, inviting the y-incision that was to come soon.

Trace evidence had been collected, including her clothing, jewelry, and scrapings from beneath each of her fingernails. Preparing the body for autopsy had been the job of Frank Riggs, who now was ready for Car Burman's re-entrance.

The door opened automatically as Burman hit the large, round button on the wall adjacent to the door's framing with her knee. She wore scrubs, two pairs of latex gloves, shoe covers, and a clear plastic face shield. She was Frank's twin now.

She crossed her arms and listened as her assistant enumerated his observations. Frank had no need of a reminder to prepare the recording devices, its microphone dangling above Amanda's navel. He had already placed a new tape, already coded and fast-forwarded for a full five seconds. He spoke to Burman without having pressed "Record."

"Dr. Burman, I am noting some obvious decomposition of the body. I've already taken measures to determine time of death with routine samples. Marks on both wrists and ankles, consistent with rope burns. I also note what appear to be defense wounds on the palm of each hand, as well as the left forearm. Additionally, the subject is bruised, three-quarters-of-an-inch by two inches above the right eyebrow. None of these injuries would appear to be fatal, however. I'm also noting some residue of an adhesive about the mouth of the victim, doctor. My guess is duct tape."

"I concur, Mr. Riggs."

Burman looked up at the microphone, unnecessarily verifying its position. She had done this procedure hundreds of times in this very room and the mike's position never varied.

Frank Riggs pressed the record button and the procedure began in earnest.

"Dr. Carletta Burman, assisted by Frank Riggs. Autopsy number 2001-0039," continued Burman, as she checked the only written record in the room, a form now lying beneath the eye of a VisualTek atop a counter to her left and beyond the head of the corpse.

She used the closed circuit TV like a microscope at times, enlarging almost anything she might want to get a better glimpse of initially. But at the start of every autopsy, she had Riggs place the autopsy form beneath the CCTV's lense so that she might verify the number while reading its number onto the taped record of the procedure. It saved her steps and, in her mind, built efficiency into the process.

Burman read the date and the starting time into her oral record and scanned the body before her. Rigor had come and gone.

"As Mr. Riggs has noted previous to this recording," she began again and recounted for the record all that Riggs had told her before the recording equipment had been activated. She added that trace evidence had already been collected. Cheryl Moore, the county's expert at such renderings, had collected that evidence and was tagging it for the requisite lab work.

"Preparing for gross exam," Burman continued.

Riggs made the Y with a large scalpel, curving the arms of the Y beneath Amanda's breasts and extending the tail toward the pubic bone, diverting only slightly to miss the navel. From beneath the abdominal wall, a stench engulfed Riggs and Burman.

"Looks like we've got an anomaly of some kind here, Mr. Riggs."

"Yes, doctor."

Riggs continued to open their subject for further examination. After he had pulled the chest flap over Amanda's face, he tested the electric saw he would use to open the rib cage.

Once the chest plate had been removed, Riggs watched as Burman cut open the pericardial sac and severed the pulmonary artery. She stuck her finger into a hole in the artery.

"No thromboembolus present."

Next Burman opened the abdomen further, dissecting the abdominal muscle away from the bottom of the rib cage. At the same time, Riggs began cutting the larynx and esophagus from the pharynx. The remainder of the chest organs was cut free from the spine and pulled downward. Burman was intently examining the mess inside the abdominal wall.

"We've got a perforated appendix, Mr. Riggs."

"That would have been my guess, doctor," Riggs said, as he waited for Burman to remove the complete organ bloc from the hull of the body and lay it on the dissecting table, suspended above Amanda's legs by a swinging arm.

Each component of the organ bloc would be separated from the rest, weighed, sliced, and prepared for further, more complete examination. The process would continue for another hour and a half.

But Burman had made her discovery. Amanda Hayes, denied the medical treatment that would have saved her life, died of poisoning. And her own body had been her killer.

Had she experienced the onset of pain before she was taken captive? Had the pain not already grown so intense that she would have sought medical care before she had been taken? Or had she passed the pain off, perhaps thinking it was part of her menstrual cycle? Had she called her captors for help, perhaps begged for the care she was growing more and more sure she needed? Or had she been too concerned about what type of treatment her captors might give her if she asked for help?

Lots of questions, Burman thought, again frustrated that she could not answer them all.

"Some questions," she said aloud, "don't get answered."

Riggs looked up from his work, confused.

"But at least I'm alive. Can't say the same for my subject here, Riggs. Never can."

L.J. Stiles pulled away from the Hayes residence at nine, thirty. In his line of work, Stiles had, on many occasions, delivered news to parents about the deaths of their children. Young people were dying all the time. Automobiles were often involved. In many cases, alcohol had played a role. In most cases, however, the news came surprisingly suddenly. Fate had intervened.

This time, it was different. Someone, someone other than Fate, was responsible for the death of this young girl. Stiles was sure of it. This time it had been Stiles' job to tell parents, who, he was convinced, were expecting the news. It was as though they had prepared the way for him to break the news to them.

Was it conceivable that one or both the parents were responsible for their daughter's disappearance and death? Certainly. Stiles had considered this possibility from the start. But the Hayes couple did not fit the profile. He had talked extensively with them both, with their extended family, with neighbors, with both their employers. While he had not completely ruled out the possibility of their complicity, he thought the likelihood of either of them being guilty of anything was remote. And not just because of the manner in which they had reacted to his news.

Predictably, Ben and Margot Hayes had been tearful. Indeed, they were both swept away with quiet emotion, emotion Stiles could only imagine and hoped he would never experience first-hand. But they had not been surprised, as parents were when their children were killed in an automobile accident. They were not caught unawares. Their daughter had been missing since the previous Friday and, with each passing day, they had been preparing themselves, though they never spoke of it, for the news that Amanda would not be coming back to them.

Stiles could see no evidence, however, that this time for preparation had helped either Ben or Margot as he broke the news to them. The small glimmer of hope to which each had clung the past few days had been snatched from them, perhaps with the same suddenness experienced by those parents of children taken by accidental death.

Stiles had left these parents with nothing for which to hope, except the eternal salvation of their daughter. For that, Stiles had beckoned Father Schmidt, from Our Saviors Church. The good Father was better prepared to comfort these people in their grief. Besides, Stiles had a job to do, a job for which he was prepared. There was more to learn and pass on to Ben and Margot Hayes, Stiles reminded himself. How did Amanda die? And who was responsible? Now, as always, it was time for everyone to do his job.

Trey Cederquist had finally managed to start his car and drive away, leaving Max and Gary in the bar where they had witnessed the results of Trey's drinking and drug use. Over a beer the two attempted to conclude what they could from Cederquist's behavior and the possible connection it might have to the disappearance of Amanda Hayes.

Max had been convinced that Trey was trying to cover something up earlier that day at Cederquist Industries. To conceal something from Max or anyone else who might be interested in Amanda Hayes, to hide from what his father's reward might shed light on, or possibly another side of the relationship existing between Trey and Amanda's father. Now, it appeared to Max that Trey was even trying to hide the truth from himself. Could it be that simple?

Gary, on the other hand, was still finding it hard to believe that Trey Cederquist was somehow involved with Amanda's disappearance. He was a jerk, of the first order, no doubt. But abducting or kidnapping a young girl? Or concealing information he might have about her whereabouts? It was inconceivable to him. Gary found it difficult to admit to himself that he knew people capable of such behavior. And his thoughts kept returning to

Amanda. She was out there somewhere. Did it matter, at this point, who might be responsible? Getting her home was the thing.

"You guys hear the news?" one of the barmaids asked.

"What news?" Max asked, whose interest corresponded with that of Gary's.

"That guy who just came in over there just told us the police are saying they found a body of a young girl in Granite City. They think it could be the Hayes girl from here in Jacksonville."

Max did not want to look Gary in the eye. Gary sat numbly, staring at his beer bottle, now half empty, a condition that would go unchanged. Now it was Max's turn at being optimistic.

"Look, Gary," Max said, finally. "It doesn't have to be Amanda. Kids are missing all over the place. Don't give up," Max heard himself saying.

"Let's get outta here, Max."

"Sure, Gary."

And they left.

The phone call for which Stiles had waited so impatiently finally came at eleven, thirty-five.

"I've got your cause of death, Lieutenant Stiles," Car Burman, Chief Medical Examiner, Madison County, Illinois said.

"Yeah?"

"Peritonitis, due to appendicitis."

"Appendicitis?"

"That's right, detective. She was dehydrated from vomiting so much. And the appendix was perforated."

"I didn't think people died from appendicitis these days, doctor."

"They don't. If they get prompt medical attention," she cautioned.

"Could a doctor have missed this if she'd seen one?"

"A rookie MD might miss a diagnosis. Doctors have often mistaken appendicitis for menstrual pain. But this girl could just as easily have sealed her fate by passing the pain off initially. She could have thought it was part of her menstrual cycle. By the time this girl realized she was experiencing something more significant, she may already have been nabbed. It's very possible that she may have even had some sense of relief when the appendix burst. Then, she really starts hurting. Before you know it, she's dead. Poisoned by her own body."

"Let's say she gets this medical treatment. What happens?"

"Under ordinary circumstances," Burman paused, "the girl presents abdominal pain on the lower right quadrant. Maybe she runs a fever. She vomits. And somebody gets her to a doctor or a hospital. Maybe she even drives herself."

"She told her boyfriend she didn't feel well on Thursday night."

"Not surprising. I'm sure she was hurting."

"So, then what happens?"

"Doctor asks a few questions. Lays her on her back and probes the abdomen. She probably tells him it hurts when he pressures the inflamed appendix. He takes some blood, maybe an x-ray. He watches her for awhile and puts her under. Exploratory laparotomy."

"To do what?"

"To find out exactly what's wrong. Given an ideal time frame, the MD finds an inflamed appendix and the laparotomy becomes an appendectomy. Appendix out. Antibiotics are prescribed. She's out of the hospital in a few days. Back to school in another week."

"But that didn't happen. Did it?"

"No way. This girl was detained. As you were told earlier, we found rope ligatures on her wrists and her ankles. She had been gagged, too. We found adhesives residue about her mouth. We're guessing at this point. But I'll bet it's duct tape. And there were defense wounds."

"Would whoever took her necessarily know she was dying?"

"Hard to say, Lieutenant. Those are questions I've been asking myself. I didn't know Amanda. Would she have told them she was sick? Would they have known she was running a fever? They had to see her vomit, I would think. But I wasn't there. Who's to say?"

"Is that murder?"

"Murder? Manslaughter? I don't know, Lieutenant. You'd have to talk to a lawyer about that."

"Do I have to?"

She allowed herself a laugh, the first one since she came in contact with Amanda Hayes.

"I know what you mean. I hate 'em, too."

He didn't really. But they were an easy target. He reminded himself that Shakespeare, or rather a character from one of his plays, had suggested killing them all. It was too easy, though, to make such remarks and he had to admit, he genuinely liked many of the attorneys with whom he regularly worked in Jacksonville.

Stiles and Burman didn't seem to know what else to say at that point.

"Well, thanks, Dr. Burman."

"You'll get your written report soon by fax. Letter to follow."

Stiles found it hard to believe. But the lawyers could untangle that web later. His focus still had to remain on finding the person or people responsible for holding Amanda against her will, and denying her medical attention which could have saved her life. Another thought suddenly crossed Stiles' mind.

"Doctor? One more question if you don't mind. Are you sure there was no indication of drug use on this girl's part? Specifically, methamphetamines?"

"None, Lieutenant. This is a slam dunk. Toxicology's done and the girl's clean."

She paused.

"You almost sound like you wanted a different answer, Lieutenant."

"Perhaps. It's just that I've got more than one problem here in Jacksonville. I thought I might be able to kill two birds if I could find the jerk responsible for taking this girl."

TWELVE

Ben Hayes had called the last of his and his wife's extended family. His only brother had taken the news hardest. Amanda had always been a favorite of her Uncle David's. David and his wife, Martha, lived in East Lansing. They would be leaving for Jacksonville in the morning, as soon as arrangements could be made with their respective employers and the bags were packed.

Likewise, Margot's sister would be coming in from Danville. Her brother was already on the road from Indianapolis. Each had spoken words of comfort from the heart to both Ben and Margot. It had helped to hear that they were loved, but not enough.

Now, alone, Ben and Margot faced the longest evening of their lives. He held her close, stroked her back, and fought to remain strong for her. It was a battle he would lose several times that night.

Max and Gary pulled into Gary's drive at one a.m. to find the squad car of Lieutenant Stiles already parked along side the road just ahead of the drive's entrance. Gary's heart raced as they climbed hurriedly from Max's rental and Gary walked briskly to the front door. He began to enter.

"Gary," Max began, as he snatched Gary's sleeve in his hand. "Stiles could be here to tell you it wasn't her, just as easily."

Gary swallowed hard. He had not had enough time in which to prepare for this moment. Still, he allowed himself to feel grateful for Max's presence. Gary was beginning to know and appreciate Max as a friend.

"Thanks, Max."

Gary went on inside the house, leaving Max to greet the approaching detective. Hearing the news would be unpleasant. Taking the news inside later would be unbearable.

Max sat down on the front steps and Stiles joined him a moment later. Max looked up at the thousands of stars shining brightly above them and the two spoke softly of a body, an autopsy, and a family's grief.

When Max had finally come inside to tell Gary and Lisa what Gary already knew, the two men stood awkwardly at the kitchen table at the rear of the McLean home. Lisa was upstairs, tending to the children. Max could hear her talking with her parents.

"He said," Max began.

"I know."

Max was at a loss for words, an uncomfortable feeling for a writer under any circumstances. It was more painful now, somehow.

Gary clutched the back of a chair and stared blankly at the centerpiece on the table.

"Stiles says she died of natural causes, Gary." After awhile, Max continued. "Can you believe that?"

Max could see that his friend was confused. He went on to explain what Stiles had told him moments earlier on the steps outside Gary's home.

Gary was numb. After awhile, it became apparent that Max did not seem to know what more to say. So Gary said it for him, fighting to maintain his composure.

"Look, I know you want to help, Max. And I wish there were something you could say or do that would help. But this is—"

Gary was, himself, struggling for words.

"This is probably as tough a thing as I have ever had to deal with," Gary said.

Gary choked on the words. He was finding it difficult to breathe.

"I know, Gary." It seemed so futile, so useless to tell Gary what he was thinking, what he wanted Gary to know. But he wanted Gary to know it and he wanted Gary to know he meant it.

"I wish this had ended differently, Gary."

A simple thought. Perhaps an obvious one. But it was all Max could offer. Having said it, he left without another word.

Gary collapsed into a chair and sat alone at the table for perhaps ten minutes. His mind raced over visions of Amanda at her desk in school, eyes bright and smile firmly fixed. She's dead. The sight of her working feverishly over her mid-term, one pencil behind her ear, another clenched in her teeth, a third dancing across her paper. She's dead. Amanda laughing with friends in the school cafeteria, poking fun at one another in mock indignation. She's dead.

There was no escaping it. Amanda Hayes is dead, he thought. He actually phrased it to himself that way. She's dead.

He still could not believe it. He did not want to believe it.

Lisa was upstairs, having said good night to her parents. She desperately wanted to go to her husband's side, but held herself back. He needs some time alone, she thought. Or is it just my way of avoiding the inevitable that Gary is already facing up to in the kitchen, she wondered.

She had seen Stiles come and go. She knew that Max had talked with him outside their home. She had watched them from her children's bedroom window. She had heard Max come into their home. She had heard the silence that Max and her husband had danced to downstairs. Amanda was dead. But her thoughts were of Gary. How could she help him?

As she turned and started toward the top of the stairs, she saw his shadow against the wall before her as he completed the turn at the first landing and ascended the stairs. She held her breath as he neared her and opened her arms wide to him. They stood together at the top of the stairs for several minutes, holding tightly to one another and speaking not a word.

As Lisa felt his embrace weaken, she allowed him to slip past her and into their children's bedroom. Gary stood in the middle of the room, looking first at Maddie, then Steve. Lisa's face rested against the doorjamb, as she lovingly watched her spouse bend over each bed to kiss the cheeks of their sleeping babes.

For the next several hours they lay in bed, talking of Amanda. Gary had spoken of her, just as he had several of his students. Prior to Amanda's disappearance, Lisa had not noticed any special affection for Amanda on Gary's part. Amanda, it had seemed to Lisa, was just one among perhaps a dozen students Gary spoke of more often than the other hundred and ten or so in Gary's classes.

Hearing her husband speak now made it seem like Amanda Hayes had been his only student. He knew of her college plans, who her boyfriends had been, how she had done on her PSAT's. He had talked to her about becoming a teacher. She would be a good one, he was sure. She had been flattered, but wasn't giving it serious thought. She had made up her mind. She wanted to write.

"Did she?"

"What?" Gary asked.

"Did Amanda write?"

Reflecting, Gary said, "Yes. She wrote very well."

"What'd she write about?"

"Oh, I don't know. Lots of things, I guess."

Gary thought of several writing assignments he had offered up to Amanda's class both first semester, during the American Lit class he had taught, and the novels course he was currently teaching.

"We wrote about a paper a week during the first semester, mostly paragraph assignments. Once or twice a quarter I would have them write a five-to-seven paragraph essay. We've done a couple of those this semester and the kids are writing a research paper now. Then there are the journals they write every Tuesday and Thursday for ten minutes or so at the end of the class."

"She was writing a journal?"

"Yeah. They all were. Why?"

Lisa was trying not to appear too anxious.

"Could I read it, Gary?"

Gary thought for a second.

"Yes. I suppose so, Lisa. I may want to take a look at those myself. But I don't know when I might be ready for that."

He paused.

"I'll drive over to school in the morning and get them. I need to stop by and see her parents anyway."

She knew he was ready, finally, to try to get some sleep. She kissed him warmly and told him to lay his head on her chest. She'd stroke his hair and shoulders and promised to love him forever. To her surprise, he was asleep in minutes. Her eyes, moist with tears, were wide open. She wondered if it were abnormal for her to be so anxious to read a dead girl's journal entries.

At around two a.m., Max arrived at his Jacksonville lodging. "Chateau de Barney" he had begun to call it, in honor of owner, Arney Fletcher. He found Meg not only awake, but at least partially informed, as well. Stiles, he learned, had called to ask Max how it had gone with Gary McLean and had given Meg the news from Granite City. Meg had the same question about Gary's reaction to the news and listened as Max returned Stiles's call and told him about Max's conversation with Gary.

When Max hung up, Meg was anxious to learn more about Amanda's death. Max, who previously had only thought of Gary's reaction to the turn of events, was reminded by Meg of the plight of her parents and friends at school. The sense of loss, compounded by the confusion surrounding the girl's death, would take its toll on many in the community, Meg had said.

"There's a big human interest story here, Max, if you're interested in writing it," she hinted.

"That's right, Meg. But that's for someone else to write." He thought of the young reporter the *Times* had assigned to the story. "Maybe Lori Bentley would be interested in it."

Meg was sorry that Max could not see himself becoming more

involved in that type of story. People, it occurred to Meg, didn't seem to matter to Max as much as events did. Getting a scoop had become more important to him than providing readers with the level of understanding and human interest that Meg recognized as important to people in the saga of Amanda Hayes. For all the love she felt for Max, Meg felt sad for him at this moment.

"Well," she said, "someone should write it."

Max was ten blocks away. His mind was on Gary.

"He sure took it hard, Meg."

"That surprise you?" Meg asked, surprised herself that Max's thoughts had, after all, been on someone else, another human being. If Max had not been thinking of all the girl's friends, at least he had been thinking of one.

"No, I guess not." He reflected on how much he had come to admire Gary, quite a lot for only having met him thirty-six hours earlier. It felt good to have a friend so committed to his profession, so loyal to his charges.

"So, what do you think happened to the girl?" Meg asked, concluding that Max was further removed in his thoughts than he was.

"Stiles says she was definitely abducted. She may have died of a ruptured appendix, but it was a direct result of her being held against her will. They found abrasions on her wrists and ankles, even her shoulders. They had duct taped her mouth so she couldn't yell for help, I guess. Forensics couldn't fix the time of death too accurately, but she may have been dead before anyone even missed her."

"So sad," Meg interjected.

"She had defense wounds, too. She may have put up quite a struggle, even for a kid who was probably pretty sick at the time."

"Someone snatched her up and took her God-knows-where and held her there? And she died?"

"That's the way it looks, Meggy. Stiles says they were able to tie the girl to a stolen van they found outside of town on Sunday evening. Someone had vomited in the back of this van."

"Do they have any idea of who else might have been in the van?"

"Lots of fingerprints, mostly matching the owner of the van, of course. But they got another print or two of someone the owner can't ID."

Max's eyes widened. "Shit!" he said suddenly.

"What's wrong?"

"I forgot to do something," he responded, thinking hard about something Meg could tell was significant.

"I wanted to tell Stiles about Trey Cederquist?" Max said, finally.

"Who?"

"Trey Cederquist. Remember the Bozo Gary and Lisa were telling us about last night?"

"You mean the one Lisa socked at the Christmas party?"

"That's the one." Max seemed to be gaining steam for some reason.

Meg looked Max over carefully. "Why? What about him?"

"Met him today. This morning," Max continued. "He's one cocky son-of-a-bitch, Meg. With a whole lot to hide, unless I miss my guess."

"Like what?"

"I wouldn't be surprised if he's got something to do with Amanda Hayes's death, Meg."

"Based on what, Max?" She did not like where Max was going.

"Well, he sure didn't like it when I showed up at Cederquist Industries, his daddy's business, inquiring about the reward the old man put up for Amanda's return."

"Lots of people don't like reporters, Max."

Max didn't give her enough time to add the "especially you" to the statement.

Meg wouldn't have done so. Not this evening.

"Well, he sure went out of his way to let me know he didn't want me snooping around CI and then Gary and I followed him tonight and—"

"You what?"

Max startled, then restated his announcement.

"We followed him. Trey Cederquist," he said, matter-of-factly.

"You took Gary with you? To follow somebody. Are you crazy?"

"What?" he asked. After awhile, he continued. "He's a big boy, Meg. He can take care of himself."

"Max, sometimes I just don't understand you. And Lisa? Lisa's gonna kill you."

"Whatever, Meg. Anyway, you should have seen this guy. We follow him into this bar. He has a couple of drinks. He's Dr. Jekyl. Goes to the bathroom? Boom! Mr. Hyde shows up."

"What are you saying? He changed somehow?"

"Goes berserk, Meg. Slaps a barmaid silly."

"You two didn't get involved. Did you?"

"Nah. Some guy tossed him." He smiled. "Gotta admit; I enjoyed seeing it, though."

"What happened to him? Why the change?"

"Meth."

"Methamphetamines? This guy is using methamphetamines?"

"So it would appear. At least that's what the barmaid thinks."

Max propped his feet on the bed and leaned back, raising the front legs of the chair in which he sat off the carpeted floor.

Meg thought for several minutes, still unable to link Trey Cederquist with Amanda Hayes from what Max had told her thus far.

Max could tell she was not making the leap of logic he had made, what seemed like, so long ago.

"Girl's dad works for Trey's old man. Trey doesn't like him one bit, by the way. Bad blood there, over something. I'm telling you, this guy knows something or is afraid of something. I just don't know what. Yet."

"But you're gonna find out," she said in chorus with his, "But I'm gonna find out."

"So, what's this got to do with Stiles, Max? You aren't going to tell him you suspect Trey Cederquist of involvement with Amanda's death with no more evidence than what you've told me about?"

"No. Well, yes. Not so much an involvement with her death as that the guy's dirty. And there is a connection to the girl, Meg, through her father and his employment at CI. We only talked for a few seconds at Gary's. I gave Stiles the number here and then went inside to tell Gary the news. I meant to tell him what we'd seen in bar."

"So, what do you think Stiles will say?"

"Just that he'll check into the drug use, probably. He'll say he knows Trey can be a jerk. But that doesn't make him a criminal. He's just wrapped up in the Hayes girl. He won't want to see my point. And he won't see how there could be a connection—not until I can provide him with a lot more evidence. But he'll say there's not enough to go on."

Max failed to tell Meg that Stiles, in all likelihood would give him a stern order to cease and desist on the Trey Cederquist front.

Max looked at Meg as she crawled into bed.

"Apparently you don't see a connection, huh?" he asked her.

"Little far-fetched, don't you think? You have to be sure, Max, that you're not basing this suspicion on what Lisa and Gary told you about the guy. Or on his kind. You know? The son of the rich businessman. The kind of guy you usually don't trust for any other reason than he's rich, has advantages?"

Max had to admit that it could, in fact, be his desire to see Trey take a fall for something that was ruling Max's judgment. But he trusted his instincts, too.

"Plain and simple, Meg," he said, as he sat on the bed beside her. "I don't like the guy."

THIRTEEN

The Thursday morning paper alerted the citizens of Jacksonville to the fact that the body of Amanda Hayes had been positively identified the previous evening in Edwardsville. Dental records had provided experts with the information needed to confirm the girl's identity. The media said little about the circumstances surrounding the death for few facts had been released by the Chief Medical Examiner's office there.

By nine o'clock that morning every church in town was opening its doors to welcome a throng of worshipers. Friends and neighbors began to call on the parents of Amanda Hayes, some bringing covered dishes, cakes and pies, and flowers. Curiosity seekers drove by slowly, seeking to get a glimpse of Amanda's parents and the home in which the poor girl had grown up. The street on which the home stood had never before seen such traffic.

Funeral services were hastily scheduled for Saturday morning. Amanda's body was transported from Granite City late that afternoon. She had already been dead for nearly a week.

School District 117's Crisis Response Team had met by phone throughout much of the day and would again on Friday morning, they agreed, to more thoroughly develop a plan at the home of Principal Singletary. Elsewhere, stunned classmates of the dead girl huddled, some deciding by midday to avail themselves of the opportunity to speak with counselors at the high school, which had been listed in the newspaper and was announced hourly on the local radio stations. Other students just wept openly and clung to each other mightily.

By mid-afternoon, Thursday, a group of students assembled

at the home of Principal Singletary to ask that he order the flag at school be lowered to half staff. The principal explained that this honor was accorded only high-ranking officials or those who died serving our nation in the military. He shared their despair, he explained. He eloquently detailed for the students that there were other ways for them to show their feelings for Amanda. They listened politely and left immediately for the high school, where they proceeded to lower the flag themselves.

Jacksonville was a town in mourning.

"You don't have to do this, Keith. Not now, anyway," Stiles continued.

"I want to get this over with, Lieutenant." Keith Utterback was beyond tears. He had cried them all during the previous night, it seemed to him.

Stiles had called late the evening before, explaining to Keith's parents that Amanda's body had been positively identified in Madison County. He had explained, further, that he did not expect Keith to come in for a polygraph as he had previously arranged.

Nevertheless, Keith had shown up at police headquarters with his father and was demanding to take on the lie detector. Keith told Stiles he did not want anyone thinking that he had killed Amanda. Keith's father told Stiles that he had given Keith all the information that Stiles had shared with him and his wife earlier.

"Amanda died of natural causes, Keith," his father reminded him.

"I know, dad. But Lieutenant Stiles thinks I may have had something to do with her disappearance and death. Right, Lieutenant?"

Keith waited to hear the detective explain again that he merely wanted to rule Keith out as a suspect, so he could move on to other leads. Keith had heard this before. It did not lessen the sting of suspicion, however.

"I don't want anyone thinking I'm in any way responsible for whatever happened to her," Keith continued, now consumed again in grief at the thought of his dead girlfriend.

After some time Keith broke the silence.

"I don't know what happened to her and I want someone to find out. I want to know how this could've happened and, if someone is responsible, I want them to pay."

"Look," Stiles interjected, "I understand. And we'll find whoever's responsible for holding Amanda against her will and not seeing that she got the medical help she needed. But I don't think you're up to this right now, Keith. Let's wait until after you've calmed down."

He looked at Mr. Utterback and practically pleaded for support with a look of despair. At times Stiles hated his job, he'd have to admit.

Keith's father naturally had concerns about his son's participation in a polygraph test. He had consulted his lawyer, who would be joining them shortly. Mr. Utterback had assured Stiles that they had thoroughly discussed the situation, particularly as it involved the timing of such an examination and in light of the previous night's horrid news.

Results of the test would be inadmissible in court, he knew, and this provided both Utterback and his wife with some small comfort. And, of course, they believed their son when he said he had done nothing wrong. Keith's involvement was unthinkable.

Their lawyer had advised against Keith's taking the test. But Keith was insistent and here they were. On L.J. Stiles' doorstep, waiting for their lawyer and demanding that the test be administered.

Gary dried his tears, not willing at this point to display his grief to anyone, not even to Lisa, as she entered their living room.

"What are you doing, hon?" Lisa asked, climbing next to him on the couch, her closer knee bent between them. She sensed he did not want to be bothered. But she had watched him mope around the house for several hours and felt he needed a nudge toward something, although toward what she was unsure.

"Nothing," he said quietly. "Just thinking about Amanda—and her parents. This has to be devastating to them. Their only child."

She agreed. It was wrecking their lives. Somehow Lisa wondered for how long it might also wreck life in the McLean home.

"So, what are you gonna do?" she asked.

He lifted his chin from his chest and turned toward her.

"Do? What do you mean?"

"What are you going to do," she repeated, emphasizing the final word.

"There's nothing to do, Lisa. Amanda is dead."

"Oh, I disagree, Gary. There's always something to do."

Lisa did not quite know where she was going with this. She did not know what it was exactly she expected her husband to do. But she knew that no good would come from her husband's sitting around in a funk over a dead teenager, no matter how bright she had been, no matter how great Gary's expectations had been for her, no matter how tragic her death had been.

And Lisa knew Gary. She could see him sitting there a week from now, wallowing in some sort of self-indulgent anguish. He probably thinks I'm a hard ass, she speculated. But he's got to move ahead.

Lisa's face evidently had betrayed her thoughts. For she could see the disappointment in Gary's face.

How cold his wife could seem, at times, Gary thought. Couldn't she see he was grieving the loss of one he had come to care about in some special way, for one who had shown such promise? Did she suspect that there was more to his relationship with Amanda? That he was feeling more than he actually felt? Max Jansen had, a couple of days earlier, put the question to him. But this was Lisa, for Christ sakes. She had to know how much he loved her and that he would be grief stricken at the loss of any of his students, certainly those whom he had taught for some length of time.

"What exactly do you think I should be doing, Lisa," he finally asked rather angrily.

She, too, was defensive.

"I don't know, Gary. Something. Anything."

She hesitated, trying to find a way to reveal her concern for him, for his sanity, his well being.

"Do something. Don't sit around moping, analyzing, studying. Do something. You've got other students. Don't forget them. Find—what is it you call it?—the teaching moment that you always talk about. What can your students learn from this? What can you teach them from all this?"

Gary shook his head as he stood and walked to the far end of the room, away from Lisa.

"Life is fragile, Gary. Teach your students that. Teach them not to squander the time they have here."

Gary had his back to her and thought her words sounded harsh and unfeeling. Their meaning made sense, of course. But there was time to grieve, too, he was about to complain.

As he turned toward Lisa, he could see she was crying. He rushed toward her, stopped immediately in front of her, paused ever so briefly, and took her into his arms. He held his wife as though he might never let go.

"Damn it."

Trey Cederquist learned, like everyone else, that Amanda's body had been discovered in Granite City and, to make matters worse, it had been identified. He tossed the newspaper down on the kitchen counter and fought to clear his blurred vision and escape the pounding in his head. He had held on to the slimmest hope that Amanda's body would go undetected until some day in the very distant future. How could he have placed so much confidence in Luke and Marcus?

"Those idiots," Cederquist continued, aloud.

As he had feared, Luke and Marcus were becoming more of a

liability than Trey could tolerate. They would have to be removed from the equation, he knew. Their screw-ups could bring him down if he allowed them to hang around any longer. Perhaps they had already delivered a fatal blow to Trey's chances of getting away with whatever he was guilty of concerning the death of Amanda Hayes. He would have to give this matter some careful thought, he determined.

He was in his car, now, replaying the events of the past few days in his mind and he was wishing he had employed smarter gophers. He was wishing he had held off on his plan to nab the girl for a later time, so she could die on her own time and not inconvenience him. Hell, wishing he had never heard of Amanda Hayes or her father.

As the afternoon sun sent bright rays across her lap, Lisa McLean sat on the bed. Her back against the headboard, knees bent and serving as a desk, she thumbed a spiral notebook containing the musings of a dead writer she was just now getting to know.

Gary had driven to JHS late that morning and retrieved Amanda's journals, two wire-spine booklets. Both were very nearly filled with the girl's thoughts on a variety of subjects. She had made dozens of entries throughout the past few months, beginning when school had started the previous August.

Lisa's mother had been great about looking after the twins, especially so since news of the death of one of Gary's prize students had come. A mother must still look in on how things are going, however, between the children and their grandparents. And Lisa had already put aside her reading a couple of times for this purpose. Now, she had settled in to continue her reading.

Amanda's handwriting was, at times, difficult to decipher. Perhaps she had rushed to finish some of her thoughts as the clock ticked away toward the end of a class period, Lisa thought. This might be contributing to some rather sloppy penmanship, almost always occurring at the end of a dated entry. Still, Lisa mused, her penmanship had character.

Lisa had encountered some remarks that her husband had placed in Amanda's journal, dated September 6. She wondered if she were now reading material that her husband had not seen, or if she would encounter still more remarks from Gary down the road.

For the most part, Amanda's entries were pretty unremarkable. They offered a picture of an ordinary high school junior, Lisa would venture to guess. At war with herself, at times, Amanda's emotions varied greatly. She was a happy, witty, and carefree teen in one instance and a sullen soul in the next. Her tone was often angry, even confrontational.

A summary analysis of Amanda's writing style would be up to Gary. Upon closer examination, however, Lisa found herself making a personal appraisal of Amanda and her writing. For a time Lisa was struck more by the form than the content of Amanda's writing. Gary had been right. Amanda was a gifted writer. She employed simile and metaphor liberally. She used analogy and irony, as well. Gary had told Lisa as much when he had handed the journals over to her. But seeing it with her own eyes was rewarding for Lisa, as she struggled to introduce herself to a student who had come to be very special to her husband.

As she turned the page to reveal yet another entry from the middle of October, Lisa's eye was drawn to a single word near the bottom of the page. "Rape" was written, printed rather, amidst the cursive remainder of the page, with a strong hand. Lisa rushed to the top of the page, aching to consume the page's contents leading to the bottom.

The discovery of Amanda's having been raped in May the previous year was hard for Lisa to bear. She wretched as she read Amanda's description of the events, lacking detail but long on the resulting emotions which, in Amanda's own words, "sent me spiraling out of control and into depression." Lisa forgave the cliché and forged ahead.

Amanda wrote of how her parents and some of her friends

kept pushing for her to share what she had thought she never could. For months she had put them off, never bothering to make up some phony excuse for her depression, but never offering the true reason for her behaviors. She realized that those who questioned her, unceasingly, it seemed, cared for her. They were only trying to help. But they would just have to deal with it, she explained. She wasn't ready to share the pain or the shame of having been raped.

Nor was she prepared to name her attacker. She was only then, in an October entry, ready to write any of this down. And her final words to her entry were a warning to Mr. McLean, not to bring up the subject at all. That would be her choice and right now, she explained, "I'm not ready; so, leave it alone!"

For the first time since beginning her reading, Lisa realized she had been crying. She wondered if Gary had read this yet. She could not imagine that he had, without having said something to Lisa, especially given the past week's events.

Gary had explained to Lisa, earlier in the day, that he occasionally gave the students' journals a cursory reading. He looked really only for dates as he thumbed the pages, merely checking the frequency and lengths of the entries. He had explained this to his students and assured them that, for the most part, their journals were personal.

Of course, he warned them often that anything they wrote could one day become public. He locked the notebooks in a cabinet after each writing session and removed them only at the start of the subsequent session, and this for only the journals of students who wished to keep the journals in his classroom. Some had opted to retain possession of their journals and Gary respected their wishes. He had admonished students to respect the privacy of each other's journals and to stay out of other students' work. Still, they were to keep in mind that he could not control others who might somehow get their hands on their writing. They were not to write down anything that they would not want their friends—or enemies—to read, he told them.

Lisa surmised that Amanda had been confident that no one would read her writing, with the possible exception of Gary McLean. Apparently, Amanda trusted Lisa's husband enough to risk his reading this entry. Then, there was the possibility that Amanda had hoped Gary would read the entry. Perhaps, despite her protests, she was crying out to Gary for help. Or, maybe it was all fiction. Lisa could see how a young girl might have a crush on her handsome husband-teacher and make up a story that might get her some attention.

A psychologist might know what had possessed Amanda to write what she had written. All Lisa knew was that she wanted to read more.

But, first, she must check again on her children and their grandmother.

"Marcus Dale," said the fingerprint expert.

Expert, in this case, was a relative term. Joe Cummins was the best that the Jacksonville Police Department had to offer in the way of a fingerprint specialist. Cummins had taken two courses at the FBI lab in Quantico, Virginia, and was familiar with the automated data systems used to match fingerprints. And he had proven to be on the mark in six of seven earlier ID's since returning from Virginia the previous April.

"Are you sure, Joe?" L.J. Stiles asked.

"Almost a perfect match, Lieutenant. Got the print from the stolen van here on this slide," pointing to the image on the left of a projection screen in the police station's conference room.

"The one on the right?" Stiles asked.

"That one's the print of Marcus Dale, arrested last year at the Morgan County Fair. Drunk and disorderly," he recited from the rap sheet before him.

Now he looked at Stiles.

"We matched him in our own files, sir."

Cummins began to get technical in his comparison of the two

prints, enlarged by some two hundred percent. Stiles cut him off, gently waving his hand. Later, when there was more time, Stiles would congratulate Cummins, reinforce the fact that he had increasing confidence in his abilities as the department's fingerprint man. But, first, Marcus Dale.

Stiles yelled down the hall for another officer to contact Tim McMichael.

"Ask McMichael if he knows a guy named Marcus Dale."

Then, he returned his attention to Joe Cummins.

"Do we have an address?"

"Right here, sir," Cummins said, holding an index card for Stiles.

Cummins knew the lieutenant was rushed. "Last known address is East State Street. MacMurray Apartments," Cummins said to no one, for Stiles was out the door, information in hand.

Marshall Cederquist, Jr., hesitated before he dialed the number of Ben and Margot Hayes. He was prepared to speak to either of them, but wasn't entirely sure which of the two he hoped would answer. Such an awkward, complex set of circumstances. Amanda Hayes was dead. Her father an employee of Cederquist Industries. Her mother at one-time an employee of the company herself and a former lover of the company president. The company president poised now to call and offer his heartfelt condolences.

Pretty bizarre, Cederquist thought. He wasn't proud of his past involvement with Margot Hayes, or of the deception perpetrated upon her husband all those years ago. Ben was a good man, a loyal employee who deserved better. If he hadn't known that then, so many years ago, Marshall most certainly had come to know it since.

Something else ate away at Marshall, too. He'd have to admit it. Marshall still wondered, at times if, seventeen years earlier, Margot had told him the truth concerning Amanda's parentage. Had she somehow been able to forge documents, produce bogus results from blood tests to prove to Marshall that Ben, and not Marshall, was indeed Amanda's father, despite their many trysts and Ben's countless business trips on behalf of Marshall's company?

None of that mattered now. Not at present, anyway. Amanda was dead. Ben and Margot were hurting beyond Marshall's comprehension, he was sure. He sought not to add to their burden, but to offer some solace. He had almost decided not to call, not to send flowers from the company. He then considered "appearances" and chose instead to send a beautiful floral arrangement. And he decided to make this call. It was the right thing to do.

He dialed the number.

He hung up before it rang. When was the last time he had spoken to Margot?

Had it really been three years? Yes. On the street, around Christmas, he remembered. They had startled each other. It was surprising, really, that, in a town the size of Jacksonville, they did not cross paths more frequently.

Margot had become a master long ago at finding excuses for not attending company Christmas parties, retirement dinners, other social events. Ben was hurt, at first, when she continually begged off each time an invitation came. He had tried in vain to convince her that her attendance at such affairs was mandatory, that her absence would hurt his chances for advancement at CI. Margot was finally able to convince him that she had chosen to leave all that behind when she got pregnant and quit her job, devoting herself to raising a family. Ben didn't like it, but suspected nothing, and left it alone.

Marshall, too, had taken Margot's absences at these events personally in some respects. After she had made her choice to stay with Ben, she simply stopped being anywhere Marshall might be. When Amanda was a toddler, Margot had surprised Marshall one day with a phone call. She had simply called him one day, quite unexpectedly, and reminded Marshall that she had made her choice to raise her daughter and devote herself to Ben. She was not angry or bitter toward Marshall; and she wanted him to know that. But she would not be around and wanted Marshall to know that, too.

Margot had even elected not to attend Gwen Cederquist' funeral, feigning the flu for Ben and sending Marshall a note instead. Guilt had obviously played a role in Margot's decision to remain at home. But Margot had other reasons to stay away. While saying or doing something that might arouse suspicion would have been unthinkable, particularly at Gwen's funeral, she had also determined in the end that she loved Ben. She would not hurt him.

Margot and Marshall had run into each other only a few times over the years between that unexpected phone call and their Christmas-time encounter a dozen years later. On that occasion, they nervously stood yards apart outside a clothing store, nervously apologized to each other for being there, and finally wished each other, and their families, a Merry Christmas and moved on.

Twenty seconds, perhaps, shared between people who, several years earlier, had experienced an almost insatiable appetite for one another.

Now, Marshall dialed again. This time he let it ring.

"Hello," a weary voice said at the other end of the line. It was Margot.

"Margot," he began.

"Marshall?" she found herself asking.

"Yes, Margot. It's me."

Nothing.

"Margot, I'm sorry."

"Yes. I know."

"If there's anything I can do," he mumbled, hating himself for sounding so predictable, so routine.

"That's very nice. Thank you."

She, too, sounded rehearsed. She had, indeed, said these very words a dozen times already that morning to others that had called.

After a lengthy pause, "I just wanted you to know how sorry I was to hear of your loss, Margot." This was even worse, he thought. But he continued, "Please, tell Ben that I called. Good-bye."

"Marshall?"

"Yes."

"The reward," she began. "Thank you."

"That's okay. It was the least we could do."

"Good-bye."

And, again, she was gone.

Having learned, via the scanner, that morning of the police's interest in finding one Marcus Dale, Max set about his own search. He consulted the phone book before succeeding in finding a neighbor who seemed willing to speak to him about the man whose fingerprint had been removed from Tim McMichael's stolen van.

"Sure. I know Marcus. What'd he do, anyway? Police been here already."

"Well, Mr. Denny. I'm curious about that, too. I'd like to know why the police are so interested in finding your friend."

"Didn't say he was my friend," Denny said, obviously distancing himself from Dale. Denny didn't know if he should venture onto ground he had not broken in his discussions with the police. They had left only thirty minutes earlier. But he couldn't resist the temptation. "Got something to do with that dead girl?"

Max shook his head, not a denial, but a look of surprise.

"You got any reason to believe that Mr. Dale is involved with the Hayes girl's death, Mr. Denny?"

"No," Denny replied. "It's just that that's what's got everybody talkin' and then the police show up here, looking for Marcus. Now, you. Kinda strange. That's all."

"You ever know Mr. Dale to be involved in anything illegal, Mr. Denny?"

Marcus had tried to give Todd Denny some methamphetamines once and had bragged to him that he could score some marijuana. But Max would never hear this from Denny. "Nah," Denny began. "I mean, not nothin' I know of."

"Does Mr. Dale live here alone?"

"Yes."

"Ever have a girlfriend over?"

"Not that I recall."

"Does Dale hang around with anyone at all? A buddy, perhaps?"

Denny thought hard. He guessed that there might be one fella he could think of. Another fella from Kentucky.

"Marcus is from Kentucky; ya know?"

"No, I didn't know that," Max responded, and he wrote this down.

"Yes. Don't know where in Kentucky. But I stood out here last summer one day and had a beer with them. Marcus and his buddy."

"This buddy have a name, Mr. Denny?"

"Luke, I think. Kinda quiet. Quieter than Marcus, anyway. Said he worked out at Cederquist Industries," Denny continued.

Bingo, Max thought. All roads lead to Trey. Max's mind raced.

Max could hardly contain himself as he jotted down Denny's description of Luke. He had already taken down the vitals on Marcus.

The interview concluded, Max had to decide what to do first. He needed to let Gary in on the possibility of a very meaningful connection between fingerprints found in a stolen van, the fingerprint's hillbilly-homey who works or had worked at Cederquist Industries, a spoiled little rich kid who's doing some serious drugs, and a dead teenager. Max also needed to find Marcus Dale and a tall fellow from Kentucky he knew only as Luke. And he needed to do it before anyone else did. And anyone else included the Jacksonville Police Department.

At times, it all sounded like a stretch, even to Max. But he had a feeling he was on to something. He decided Gary would have to wait until after he had spoken to at least one other person who might know either Marcus or Luke. He'd march into Cederquist Industries and ask to see Luke. What'd he have to lose? Then he'd hit every bar in town to get the skinny on the two bluegrass boys. Maybe he'd get lucky and find them sipping on mint juleps and in a mood to talk.

Trey had, on occasion, used a phony police badge before. It had been easy to procure the bogus badge through a mail-order supplier of police equipment. The badge even spelled out "Jacksonville P.D.," although it was much different from the official shields worn by Jacksonville policemen and policewomen.

He dug through his glove compartment and, having found it, slipped the badge into the inside breast pocket of his sport coat.

This would be fun, he thought. In the past he had only used the badge to impress some girls.

There had been one other instance, when he used the badge to scare the living hell out of some poor kid who was trying to buy beer with a bogus ID at a liquor store Trey frequented.

This would be the first time Trey had stepped over the line into a situation where he'd actually try to obtain information from someone under the guise of a policeman.

But, then, Trey was stepping over lots of lines these days.

"Say, there, partner," Trey began, flashing his badge at the neighbor of Marcus Dale. It was the same neighbor with whom Max Jansen had just spoken. "I saw you talking to that reporter as I drove by a few minutes ago. Thought I'd drive back by and find out what he was talking to you about."

The man looked puzzled.

"I'd heard that fella's been snooping around town and I want to know if he was bothering you," Trey stammered.

"He was asking about one of the fellas that lives over in them apartments there. Fella name of Marcus Dale."

Damn, Trey thought.

"And what'd he want to know about Marcus Dale?" Trey asked, recovering from his surprise that Max was checking up on Marcus so quickly.

"Said the police were looking for him."

Neither spoke, as the fellow looked Trey up and down, growing more suspicious now.

"Are ya?" Denny asked.

"Am I what?"

"Are you looking for him? You're the police; ain't you?"

Trey was, again, caught somewhat off guard.

"Look here, mister. I'll ask the questions here."

"You and that reporter are. Sure. And your cop buddies before him."

The older man was reflecting now and growing more confident as he did so. And he was sure that Cederquist was no cop.

"Only problem is, I'm getting tired of answering your damn questions, if you want to know the truth. So, you just take your questions and shove 'em up your ass."

Denny turned his back on Cederquist and walked away.

Cederquist knew that Marcus' neighbor was, indeed, tired of answering questions and probably no longer believed, if he ever had, that Trey was legitimate. While he was incensed at the man's disrespect, Trey had bigger problems.

Somehow, the police and Max Jansen had discovered a link between Amanda Hayes and Marcus, Trey surmised. Perhaps a link to Luke, as well, and maybe even to Trey. It was time to implement a contingency plan he had been formulating for some time. He now felt a sense of urgency about it and was deciding to act.

Trey made a hasty getaway on foot before the neighbor grew even more belligerent and decided to return. He rehearsed his call to Luke and Marcus in his head as he stepped toward his car. For now, Marcus and Luke were safe. Out of the immediate area on Trey's orders, the two were delivering product to some of Trey's customers in Champaign and Decatur. He would call them soon and provide them with more instructions. Instructions that would guarantee Trey that neither Marcus or Luke could ever pose a threat to him again.

FOURTEEN

Throughout the day Friday, Gary McLean served his students, living and dead. Gary had become involved with the counseling efforts offered by the school district for students. Many were experiencing the death of a classmate for the first time and Gary wanted to help if he could. He was also writing a eulogy for Amanda's funeral. The Hayes's had called and asked him to speak at the funeral. He was honored. But this would be truly difficult for him.

Lisa's parents had hated to leave in the middle of Gary's crisis. But they had promised Lisa's aunt, her mother's sister, that they would drive through Highland and check on a sick relative. And Lisa's father was due back in Effingham on Saturday for a Lions Club function of some kind.

Between Gary's trips to the high school to assist counselors, the phone ringing non-stop, the care of the twins, and Gary's efforts to pen some appropriate remarks for the funeral service on Saturday, it was a hectic time in the McLean home.

Gary had been vaguely aware that his wife was reading intermittently from Amanda's journals. He and his wife had yet to speak of what, if anything, Lisa was finding of interest in Amanda's writing. He longed for some distance in time, after which he could find his own way to the spiral notebooks.

Amanda's wake on Friday night would be a marathon for all involved. Ben and Margot arrived at the funeral home and entered the rear door at three-forty on Friday afternoon. A large crowd had assembled outside. Most were classmates, some with their parents, all with long faces. Those who were not crying had either just stopped for a brief moment or were about to begin. The ordeal was about to commence.

Around four o'clock an employee of the funeral home opened the doors and a flood of well-wishers, resigned to the fact that they could do nothing for Amanda, descended upon her parents. A funeral director had cautioned the Hayes against standing next to the closed coffin. It will be a long night, he had explained.

"You'll need your strength."

"For what?" Margot Hayes sobbed. And they stood. The entire evening, except for when they knelt in prayer. They would do this several times during the evening, sometimes with the entire crowd assembled and led in prayer by one of the parish priests. At other times, when either was so moved, Ben or Margot would simply assume a position at a kneeler in front of the bronze coffin bearing their daughter's remains, a picture framed and set atop the coffin's closed lid.

The flow of people was unceasing. People came in groups of all sizes, identifying themselves when introductions were necessary. Each tried to say something of comfort to Amanda's parents, struggling not to sound like every other person who had already filed by. Some, especially some of Amanda's closer friends, were unable to say anything. It was just as well. Ben and Margot Hayes understood.

The police presence at the wake was relatively inconspicuous. Lieutenant Stiles had called on the Hayes's earlier in the day, in part to pay his own respects, but also to let them know that some of his people would be attending the wake. Plain clothes, of course.

Sometimes, he explained, those responsible for a person's death desire to witness the result of their deeds. The sight of their victim's body or of a grieving parent provides them with some form of gratification. While Stiles had no reason to believe that whoever had held Amanda against her will, ultimately causing her death, fit this profile, he didn't know that this was not the case. He would have watchers at the funeral home.

One such watcher was Officer Jamie Winningham, Springfield Police Department. He had volunteered to be at the wake, supplementing a cadre of plainclothes Jacksonville policemen, but less recognizable to the Jacksonville citizenry. Winningham took great pain to dress down, in an effort to appear anything but police-like. Only twenty-six, he had the body of an athlete and the haircut of a policeman. But he managed somehow to look like any other mourner. He consciously slumped, allowing himself to relax his normally erect torso, in an effort to blend in as he sat in a rickety chair near the rear of the room where Amanda's coffin had been set.

Only one other among the half-dozen law enforcement personnel on hand knew Winningham was a cop. Dan Sexton had gone through a training course with Winningham. They had become good friends over the two weeks they spent in Champaign together. Tonight, however, they did not speak. Upon seeing his friend, Sexton knew immediately why Winningham was present. Not wanting to tip anyone who knew Sexton was a police officer to the fact that Winningham was working the wake, the two friends made no effort to communicate.

Winningham was all eyes and ears without appearing to be interested in anything but Amanda Hayes, poor girl. He had passed by the coffin, spoke briefly with the parents of the dead girl and felt no guilt at his performance. He had meant it, after all, when he told Ben and Margot Hayes that he was sorry they were suffering. It was one of the reasons he had been eager to serve when Stiles had called Winningham's commander and asked for a volunteer.

Another reason was his fascination with criminal profiling. He had set as a professional goal his swift advancement through the ranks of the Springfield PD as far as he could climb until his twenty-eighth birthday. On that day, he had promised himself, he would apply to the FBI Academy, hoping to join their ranks first as a field agent, then distinguishing himself as a profiler.

Winningham had read extensively. He felt he knew what to look for in the moving mosaic he now witnessed. He had arrived early, taken a seat in the chair he felt offered him a best view of the proceedings, and settled in for the evening. He wondered if Stiles were covertly videotaping the event.

Mourner after mourner filed by, most pausing very briefly to speak with Ben and Margot Hayes. A long line trailed down the hall and out the door onto a parking lot. It snaked to the east past the courthouse and toward the plaza for almost a block. No one wanted to hold up the line. They each knew what it was like to wait. They had just waited themselves to get where they were. Besides, the end of the line was not a happy one and most were glad, once they arrived, to escape and move on quickly.

One who did linger a bit longer at the head of the line was Amanda's best friend. When Melissa Schumacher appeared around the corner some twelve feet short of where the Hayes couple stood, Margot went to her immediately. The girl and her friend's mother spoke quietly for several minutes, walked to and away from the coffin more than once, and hugged each other tightly. Finally, Melissa and her own mother took a seat nearby at the insistence of Margot Hayes.

It was well after nine when the line finally diminished and the doors were closed behind the last of the mourners. Church would be packed tomorrow, thought one of the funeral directors as he closed the door at the eastside of the building. He was beat. He strode the few steps back toward the visitation room wearily. Once inside the room, he spotted Amanda's parents.

How do these people do it, he asked himself silently. Instantly, he told himself that he had nothing to complain about. He would quite happily return to his home, march straight upstairs to see his three children tucked safely in bed, and fall to his knees and give thanks.

Max pulled into Gary and Lisa McLean's driveway at nine-thirty. He was between bars, he explained to Gary who, with his wife, was just returning home from the wake. Max was jazzed. He was confident that someone, somewhere in this town, knew Marcus Dale and his mystery friend, Luke.

"Where you been?" he asked Gary.

"Amanda's wake, asshole."

He really didn't understand Max Jansen. Liked him instinctively, but couldn't for the life of him, tell anyone why.

"Oh, yeah," Max apologized. "I forgot."

The two shuffled their feet on the asphalt driveway, Lisa having left the pair to count the stars.

"How's the eulogy coming? Lisa told me earlier today the girl's folks asked you to speak at the funeral tomorrow."

Max was anxious to change the subject, so he could tell Gary what all he had learned from talking to Todd Denny the day before. And what he had not learned from a trip out to Cederquist Industries.

"I don't know," Gary replied. "I'm not sure I'm up to this."

"Sure you are," Max reassured Gary. "You'll do fine."

"I spent most of the day at the school, Max. Those kids are hurting. I can't imagine what they must be feeling."

He shook his head and nearly cried.

Max grew quiet.

"I do," he said.

Gary was puzzled for a moment.

"What?"

"I know how they feel."

Gary remained silent, allowing Max some time to muster up

whatever it was going to take to share something from his past that Gary wanted desperately to hear.

"My best friend in high school died. Drowned," he continued. "It's a bitch."

And that was all he said. Max didn't even offer a when, how, or a why to this lead sentence. Just who. His best friend. And what. Drowned. Max was ready to change subjects.

Because it hurt, Gary suspected. But, damn it, man. Why don't you open up?

"What are you made of, Max?"

"What do you mean?"

"That's it? Your best friend drowned; it's a bitch?"

Max could not imagine what else Gary would want to hear about something that happened over twenty-five years ago. He looked at Gary who looked back, arms spread wide, an anguished look on his face.

"What? You want me to cry or something? Blubber on and on about my good friend who bought it all those years ago? Come on, Gary. That's not me. And it doesn't do him any good. Just like it doesn't do Amanda any good for you to –"

Max stopped. He knew he had gone too far.

"Go to hell, Max." Gary turned and started for the door to his home.

"Wait, Gary."

Gary stopped, turned half way around, and looked sadly at Max.

"I'm sorry, Gary," he began. "I gotta tell you about this."

"What?"

"There's a connection to Cederquist Industries, Gary. Trey. He is involved."

Gary was unconvinced. He had heard of Max's dislike for Trey Cederquist. He had seen with his own eyes what Max had also witnessed in the bar two nights earlier. Trey was doing drugs. "Meth" the waitress had called it. And there was no doubt that Trey was a weasel. Gary and Lisa had known that for some time.

But Max was obsessing about Cederquist and Gary was in no mood to hear Max's creative theories.

But Max had his notepad out and flipped through pages of scribbling as he read. "Police found on a stolen van—in which they know Amanda Hayes had spent time—a fingerprint of a guy named Marcus Dale of Kentucky. The guy lives in the MacMurray Apartments on East State. Dale hangs around with another Kentucky boy named Luke. No last name yet. But, Luke works, or did, at one time, work for Cederquist Industries. So, I gotta believe that our boy Trey knows Luke, and, by extension, Marcus. And they probably all three know something about Amanda Hayes."

Gary was still unimpressed. And he was tired. And he was going to say good-bye, in a matter of hours, to a wonderful young lady who died much, much too soon. He didn't have time for this, but took the time to ask one question.

"Motive?"

Max didn't have an answer. "I don't have that yet," he conceded.

"That's what I figured, Max."

That stung. And Max stepped away from Gary without turning, arms slightly raised from his side, wanting to plead his case but finally dropping his arms and his case for the present.

"Good night, Max. I'm going in."

"Sure, Gary. I'll see you tomorrow."

Gary wheeled on his heel. "You coming to the funeral?"

Max's shoulders raised as his arms extended outward once again and his steps quickened toward the car at the end of the drive.

Lisa had heard Gary enter the side door after talking at length with Max. She had retired to their bedroom, positioning herself on the bed to once again begin reading journal entries.

She had yet to talk to Gary about what she had read thus far and was debating with herself about whether to tell him about

Amanda's rape before tomorrow's funeral. She had decided to wait until after the funeral, so she didn't complicate Gary's efforts at writing a eulogy. Still, she wondered if she could keep the pact, which she had made with herself.

Gary ascended the steps to the upper level of their home and stopped in the doorway to their bedroom. Lisa looked up to meet her husband's gaze.

"You coming to bed, hon?"

"Nah. I've got to do some work on this eulogy. I'm going back downstairs for awhile."

"Gary, don't be too long. You need to get some sleep."

"Yeah. Like I'm going to sleep tonight."

She knew her husband was hurting even more than he let on, but that he needed to mope a bit before she moved in to comfort him. She would leave him be for perhaps an hour and then go downstairs to bring him to bed.

In the meantime, she found her bookmark once again and returned to her reading of the journal entry Amanda Hayes had dated December fifth. "I wish my dad worked elsewhere," it began. Amanda went on to say that Amanda and her classmates had discussed careers in Mr. McLean's class earlier that morning, beginning with the wide variety of careers chosen by parents of students in McLean's class. The teacher wanted to show students, he had explained, that there were a number of options students should consider and that the list of opportunities they had developed on the chalkboard at the front of the room was only the beginning.

For one thing, he reminded them, many jobs "for the 21st century" had not even been thought of yet. This was a recurring theme in Gary's classes. Lisa knew this from being married to the teacher. But she also had read it in Amanda's journal. She had commented on it previously and was, for the most part, in agreement with her mentor. On December fifth, however, she was more inclined to think of her father's career choice rather than one she would have to make in the near future.

"I used to think it was cool to have my dad working at

Cederquist Industries, the largest employer in Jacksonville. But not anymore," she had written. It was unclear at first just what it was that had turned Amanda off about her father's working at CI. Nothing of Cederquist Industries had been mentioned in the entries Lisa had read thus far. And little mention had been made of her father. Lisa couldn't tell if Amanda's dissatisfaction stemmed from CI or from disappointment in her father.

Lisa read on. Slowly she came to the realization that it was not Amanda's father that was upsetting the girl. Amanda loved her father, had fought to protect him, she had written. From what exactly was unclear. But there was something. Strangely, the tone of Amanda's writing had become that of someone being very careful not to divulge too much. She wrote as though someone were looking over her shoulder. Still, she wrote.

"I cannot believe that Daddy works for such people. He works hard for a company that doesn't care about him at all. Daddy talks about being loyal to the company like it were family. And Cederquist threatens to take it all away."

Does she mean Cederquist Industries? Or Cederquist, the man? Lisa thought for a second and decided that it probably didn't matter. Marshall Cederquist was Cederquist Industries, Lisa had concluded, just as Amanda apparently had.

Lisa's mind jumped to her own father. At seventeen, had she thought at such length about her father and his career choices? Had she been inclined, when given the chance to write about anything she wanted, to write about her dad and the fact that he worked in a Fedders' factory in Effingham? Such thinking, Lisa determined, would not have found its way onto her journal page at seventeen.

But, then, Lisa Olson, later to become Lisa McLean, had not spent any time in Amanda Hayes's shoes. Lisa had not been raped. And she had not been given any reason to resent her father's employers, as had, apparently, Amanda Hayes. Whatever Cederquist or Cederquist Industries had done or might do to her father, Amanda was not at all forgiving.

"Bad people work at CI," Amanda wrote near the end of her entry.

Lisa thought of Trey Cederquist. "Now, that I can agree on," Lisa whispered, as she closed the journal and swung her bare feet from the bed to the floor. It was time to get Gary to bed.

The wake, now an hour into the past, had been an ordeal for Ben Hayes. He and Margot had driven home in silence. He had tried, throughout the evening, to focus his attention on his wife and her needs. While he could not remain totally immune to the pain and anguish he knew existed in his wife and witnessed in his daughter's classmates as they filed past her coffin, he found it impossible not to think of himself and his own sadness.

He had, for the most part, remained "there" for Margot and tried to relate to his daughter's young friends, at least in appearances. Beneath the facade, however, was a lonely man, thinking at once of his daughter and of his own pain.

He had also grown angrier with every tear he saw shed that night at the funeral home. He and his wife had been robbed of the only thing that should have mattered to them. Amanda had been robbed of life, of a future bright with promise, of love and family, of so much potential. It wasn't fair.

Ben could also not escape his thoughts of revenge. Revenge against whomever was responsible for his daughter's death. And, increasingly, he was convincing himself that he knew somehow who that person was. At least, who that person might be. Several times during the evening, he found himself actually shaking his head, trying to convince himself that it couldn't be true. But something very basic, something quite real told him that his suspicions were right on.

He had to be sure, he told himself, now. Standing at the top of the steps to the basement of his home, his wife now preparing for a restless night in bed before their daughter's funeral the next morning, Ben told himself that he must be sure. Schemes to get to the truth seemed too silly and would take too long. Time might be on the side of one he had suspected all along of involvement in his daughter's disappearance. He would simply beat it out of him. But he would need leverage, he told himself.

Ben stepped down each step with greater confidence. Courage, indeed, was at his disposal. He simply had to take it in his hands, have it at the ready. He would bury his daughter tomorrow, then go about the business of satisfying any lingering doubts about the man's guilt. And, when Ben was sure, make him pay.

Ben moved quickly to the opposite corner of the basement. At his workbench, Ben paused, took a key from the nail on which it hung, and reached up to the shelf, which stretched across the top of his workbench. He pulled a fireproof box from atop the shelf and lay it on the bench before him. He turned the key and unlocked the box effortlessly. Inside the box lay a handgun, a .38. A box of cartridges lay beside it.

Here was his courage, Ben thought. Here was the leverage he would need to get the man to admit the truth. Here was the instrument of truth and the revenge that would follow.

FIFTEEN

Saturday morning brought sunshine but cooler temperatures as much of Jacksonville prepared to gather at Our Saviors' Church on East State Street. As mourners neared the entrances to the Catholic church where Amanda Hayes's funeral Mass would be offered, the phone rang at Jacksonville Police Department headquarters.

"He's home," a scratchy voice at the other end of the line reported.

"Who's home?" the dispatcher, James Dodd asked.

"Marcus Dale. He's home."

"Who is this?" Dodd asked.

"This is a neighbor. You guys said, if we see Marcus or anyone else at his apartment, we should call you. He's home. I saw him."

"Fine, sir. Hang on."

The dispatcher looked desperately for another officer but was unsuccessful.

"This is about that dead girl. Ain't it?" the voice at the other end of the line asked.

"Sir, I can't really talk about that. We just want to talk with him. I would advise you to keep your distance, though."

Dodd waited curiously for a response, while he finally got another officer's attention as he approached in the hall. "What did you say your name is, sir?"

"Gotta go, officer. Bye."

The line was dead.

The dispatcher finished writing the last of his note on a pad of paper as Lieutenant John Odgen stood at his side.

"I have to get hold of Lieutenant Stiles right away, Lieutenant. He's gonna want to know this."

"He's at the funeral, Dodd."

"Sir, I think he'd want to be interrupted."

Amanda's funeral began that morning at eleven o'clock. A slate gray hearse bore her body in a rosewood coffin from the funeral home to Our Saviors' Catholic Church. The hearse crept the seven short blocks at a quiet, reverent speed. In tow was a small group of cars, the first bearing six pallbearers, chosen from Amanda's friends. The next car contained Ben and Margot Hayes, along with Margot's sister, Judith. Following were cars containing other members of Ben's and Margot's respective families.

Most of Amanda's mourners awaited the hearse's arrival at the church, where Amanda had been baptized, made her first confession, received First Communion, and been confirmed. Margot had so looked forward to the day when she would see Ben and their beautiful daughter march from the back of this church, Amanda in a long white gown, toward a handsome young man nervously waiting for them to meet him at the altar.

Instead, Margot now watched as Amanda was lifted from the back of a hearse. Six classmates carried her coffin the few paces to a carriage onto which, at the funeral director's instruction, the boys nervously placed the coffin. The pallbearers were further instructed to fall into line ahead of the coffin and proceed through the church's open doors. A few late arriving mourners stood outside and watched this ritual, performed with an almost military precision. Once inside, Margot got her first glimpse of the large group assembled for Amanda's funeral.

Father Patrick Maynard, assistant pastor at Our Savior's stood at the back of church, just inside the doorway, three acolytes at his side. To Margot, the good Father, prayer book clutched at his chest, looked tired and strangely older than his fifty-four years. A large man, with huge hands and a shock of red but graying hair, Father Maynard smiled comfortingly and nodded a welcome to her and her husband. Then he quickly turned and began his business, blessing the coffin before leading the procession toward the front of the church.

To the left, stained-glass windows loomed above her. Four huge windows depicted Maximillian Kolbe who perished in a Nazi concentration camp, Therese of Lisieux, Pope John the Twenty-third, and others, emblematic of the North American martyrs. To the right, four more windows honoring Mother Teresa of Calcutta, Mother Elizabeth Seton, Mary, the Mother of Sorrows, and Thomas More.

But it was the mural at the front of the church that spoke to Margot Hayes most clearly. The mural was not unlike a giant television screen, the kind they have in sports stadiums. The picture seemed to just be coming into focus. Long, pastel cloth banners billowed in the wind. And in the distance, Jesus himself approached, arms outstretched, welcoming all into his embrace. Welcoming Amanda into His kingdom, Margot surmised. Perhaps He also welcomed Margot, this day, as she searched for an end to her sorrow, for her return to His comforting embrace.

As she stepped so very carefully down the aisle toward their pew beside the coffin, Margot's thoughts leaped forward again to events that would never take place here. Amanda would never take those steps toward that handsome young man. She would never present a child at the baptismal fount. She would never attend her mother's funeral.

There it was.

The thought had not previously occurred to her. But it was this thought, this savage irony, which most troubled Margot. This revolting reversal of events would haunt Margot, she had no doubt, for the rest of her life. How would she bear the injustice of outliving her child?

The funeral Mass had come too quickly for Margot. She was unprepared. She had been unable to find the spiritual comfort that had alluded her since she had first learned Amanda was missing. The prayers, when she had been able to pray, had not helped. Father Schmidt's visits to her home had failed to restore her faith in Faith. She had even gone so far as to visit a psychic in Springfield. Doris had been very nice, understanding and caring. But the void in Margot's heart was still there.

Margot passed, it seemed to her, in and out of consciousness, alternately attending to Father Maynard, as he prayed over her daughter, and time-tripping through Amanda's life. She regained her composure in time to hear her sister Judith, who had moved undetected to the lectern next to the altar to present the first reading.

Margot fought to leave the scene, to escape the present, to travel once again, this time back in time to happier points in Amanda's life. She recalled spending hours teaching a seven-year-old Amanda her prayers. Amanda, like so many children, had begrudgingly entered into the pact with her mother to learn the prayers Margot's mother had taught to Margot. But before long, Amanda had warmed to the idea and came to enjoy the time she spent reciting prayers again and again with Margot. Repetition had been a good teacher and it had also served to bring mother and daughter closer together.

Margot prayed "The Memorare." It was one of the many prayers Margot had learned as a young girl. She had often relied upon its simple plea when she most needed help.

She had said this prayer often during those times, years earlier, when she struggled to put a broken marriage back together, a marriage that her husband was too busy to even realize had been falling apart.

She had recited the verse when she doubted whether anyone could forgive her or provide her with unconditional love, even though her infidelity was totally unknown to all but a few.

She had always somehow found comfort in the prayer. It had helped her before. Would it come to her rescue now?

Margot wove her way through a tapestry of memories between

Amanda's birth, seventeen years ago, and the present in a matter of minutes. Amanda's birth had been the happiest day of Margot's life. Her daughter's arrival had culminated a return to a state of remarkable happiness in her marriage which Margot had worried might be unattainable. The labor had been difficult. But Margot relished the memory of giving birth and shared in her husband's pride in both mother and child.

Amanda's first steps had been a joyous occasion. When she lost her first tooth, the whole neighborhood learned all about it from a very proud little girl. The same was true when Amanda learned to ride a bike. Starting school had been traumatic, but the evening following her first day there had ended with the pronouncement by Amanda that she would be willing to give it one more try.

More and more memories of Amanda's childhood flooded Margot's senses. She could recall such detail. She prayed she might remember it all forever and never lose touch with Amanda.

Margot rejoined the assemblage in time to hear Melissa Schumacher as she struggled to complete the second reading. Melissa, Margot concluded, is too young to have to go through this. Margot worried about Melissa. She felt a little better though when she heard the eulogy, delivered by one of Amanda's teachers, Gary McLean. McLean spoke eloquently of how Amanda Hayes would be remembered. Of how Amanda had made a difference in the many lives she had touched.

Margot recognized in Gary what Amanda must also have seen in the classroom. Here was a man who cared about his charges. His every word spoke to his commitment to his students. She saw in Gary that Melissa and Amanda's other friends and classmates were in good hands. She did not have to worry about them.

She looked upward, seeking again her own comfort from above. It seemed a natural thing to do, given the circumstances. A crisis of faith had very nearly left her without resolve, without purpose, without hope. Sunlight streamed mercifully through the stained-glass skylight above, producing a warmth in Margot she wanted to grab hold of and never to let go.

She had dressed that morning, consciously hoping that Father Maynard's homily might contain something that would restore her faith, allow her somehow to go on. And she had not heard a word he had said. Her faith, however, was intact. It had returned to her as a precious gift in the form of a prayer she had not recited in years and the knowledge that her daughter had mattered, had made a difference in the lives of others.

She was not "okay." Far from okay. But with every step she would take, one step in front of the other, with every second that snapped forward on the virtual clock in her brain, she moved one step, one second, closer to okay.

Quickly, Margot turned her attention to Ben. He needed her, she knew. Somehow they would have to make a life for themselves. She did not know how this might be done. She only knew that it would be done. She wrapped her left arm around his right, placing her hand inside his. No response. Perhaps Ben was elsewhere, as she had been moments earlier. That was all right. She would allow Ben that. She would concede that she was merely ahead of him in a voyage toward self-renewal.

"Nice work, Butch."

"My name's Harold," the homeless man responded.

"Whatever," Trey Cederquist replied, very much a vision in contrast to Harold. Trey, in his five-hundred-dollar suit, would not be mistaken for an intimate of Harold's. In fact, he worried about being seen with his new acquaintance. People would wonder what the two, so mismatched, could possibly be talking about, standing near the pay phone just in front of the Morgan County Courthouse. Trey decided it would be best to conclude their business quickly.

"Here, take this for your trouble, Harold," Trey said, handing over a fifty dollar bill.

Harold was half expecting to get brushed off without his promised payoff. He eyed the bill lovingly. It was a windfall of gigantic proportions.

"You're sure there's nothing else I could do for you, mister?"

"Nah."

"Say, now. I did just like you asked me to. That cop took the whole message down. I told him everything you told me to. And when he asked for my name, I hung up on him, just like you said."

"Good. Now, get lost. And remember. You don't know me. And I don't know you. Understand?"

"Sure," Harold said, as he smiled, turned away, and instantly became, once again, invisible.

Lieutenant John Ogden paced the circle around a table at which sat his brain trust at JPD. He had called a meeting in a conference room next to his office. He conferred with two other investigators and the uniformed policemen he felt he could trust, to go over what they knew of Amanda Hayes's disappearance and death. Stiles was at the girl's funeral.

"We know she was in the stolen van belonging to this guy McMichael. We know there was a fingerprint on the van belonging to Marcus Dale. Dale lives in the MacMurray Apartments and was seen there about thirty minutes ago for the first time since we began our search for him. We don't know if he's still there right now or not. But the place has been watched now for about twenty minutes and he hasn't shown himself. So he might be inside."

"But his car was there last night already, John. No one we know has seen him come or go since we ID'ed him as someone who might have been in that van with Amanda Hayes. We began our surveillance at nine p.m. when you told us you were going to Judge Strickland for a search warrant."

"And we're still waiting for the goddamn search warrant, as you know," said Ogden feigning great frustration. "Who knew the Judge was going to take off for Springfield last night for a goddamn rock concert and then spend the night in a hotel with his daughter and a bunch of friends over there?"

"His thirteen-year-old daughter?" one of the circled peace officers ventured, regretting the joke almost immediately.

Ogden managed a slight smile and continued. Jamison, let us know when His Honor gives the okay."

Jamison nodded obediently and collected his notes of the meeting from the table. The others followed suit and dispersed to their waiting black and whites for the short trip to the apartment of Marcus Dale. They would waste no time and be rolling when the news came of the judge's signature.

L.J. Stiles watched from a distance of one hundred yards as they lowered Amanda Hayes's coffin into the ground. He scanned the crowd methodically, just as he had all through the funeral mass. Nothing of note had occurred at the wake the previous evening. His contact from Springfield had come up empty. Likewise, he was finding nothing unusual as he observed the funeral and burial today. Unlike his watcher from Springfield PD, Stiles was not trying to hide his presence, although he was in plain clothes. It would have been unusual for him to be in uniform.

He fought off the urge to let his mind wander away from the central event and the focus of everyone else in the cemetery, Amanda's burial. But he could not allow himself to grieve with Ben and Margot Hayes. Not now. He had a job to do. The grieving family and the city he had adopted at his home were depending on him to get the job done. He had to find the bastard responsible for Amanda's death and bring him or them to justice.

Get back to work, he thought. Stiles crawled into his squad car and waited for the large group of mourners to disassemble and move toward their vehicles that surrounded the burial plot and stretched outside the cemetery grounds and down the road for perhaps half a mile.

Stiles continued to watch the crowd intently until most were in their cars and moving away from the cemetery. He did not wait to see the dead girl's parents and closest friends and relatives move away from the grave side before he, too, moved slowly down the lane and off the cemetery grounds.

He wondered how things were going back at headquarters. Had Judge Strickland or Judge Flynn been located and had either signed the warrant that would enable him to search Marcus Dale's apartment? Had any sign of Dale been registered with his cohorts at JPD?

He reached for the radio's hand-held mike. He was in for a shock.

Gary and Lisa McLean returned to their home from the funeral in silence. Max evidently had not gone to the gravesite. At least the McLean's had not seen him there. Gary had commented about Max's absence to Lisa as they drove home, but not in an accusatory way. Gary had decided not to expect Max to grieve for Amanda to the degree that he had himself. Perhaps Max was incapable of grieving for Amanda at all, Gary thought.

Max, Gary soon learned, was waiting for him. Max had parked on the street and followed their car into the drive on foot. As Gary stepped onto the driveway's surface, Max was waiting with a handshake.

"That was a beautiful eulogy, Gary."

Max had attended the funeral.

"Thanks," Gary replied, smiling. If Max were attempting to atone for his thoughtlessness of the prior evening, Gary appreciated the effort.

The two men spoke quietly as Lisa entered the house to check on the children and pay a babysitter from down the street. She was paying the sitter and thanking her when Gary stuck his head in the back door. He told her he was going for a ride with Max. Lisa thought the ride might do her husband some good. Besides, she had some reading she wanted to get back to.

The twins were doing fine in the family room, playing with Maddie's dolls at the moment. Lisa decided that Gary's ban on dolls for Steve did not have to be enforced on this afternoon. She was not as concerned about such things as Gary anyway.

Lisa curled up on the love seat with Amanda's journal and turned quickly to the page where she had left off reading the evening before. Lisa found nothing of particular interest in the pages Amanda had filled during the recent pre-Christmas season. She wrote of typical high school concerns, worried about her looks, dreamed of college which lay ahead, and speculated about what kind of date she might end up with for a Christmas dance. She mentioned Keith Utterback for the first time. Nothing specific. Just that she had got to know him better and thought he was nice.

Then, after the holiday, Amanda's writing turned serious again. She wrote of a general unhappiness and despite more specific references to Utterback, including the fact that he had asked her out for the first time around mid-January, she projected a sense of defeat. She liked Keith. But she feared the relationship, perhaps any relationship with a boy or a man, might be doomed, she had mused. The rape, apparently, continued to haunt Amanda. How could it not, Lisa wondered.

But Lisa was saddened by Amanda's negative outlook. She had read enough of Amanda's words to get a glimpse of her as she might have looked through Gary's eyes. As someone who had tremendous potential. Yet, here she was, giving in to defeat, as it were, and the game was just beginning. Then again, Lisa thought, the game hadn't lasted all that long. Was it possible that Amanda was somehow attuned to her imminent demise?

An entry from early February had mentioned a call from someone. "He called," the entry began. At first Lisa thought Amanda was writing about Keith. She quickly learned that it was not Keith to whom Amanda referred. The caller was never identified by name. She only referred to him as "the creep." And nothing specific was written either about who the creep might be or what he had had to say to Amanda.

Lisa was quick to speculate that the caller might be the "creep" who had raped Amanda. But she could not be sure. Not until she had read the following entry, that is.

Amanda's entry, dated February 10, began by recounting the discussion Lisa's husband had led that morning in class. The subject was again writing and Gary had referenced an article he had read in some thick volume on writing published in the sixties. In the article some writer, no one Amanda or her classmates had heard of, proposed using what she called "the magic of three" to provide "balance" to her stories.

Gary had gone to great lengths to provide example after example of sets of three in literature, folklore, nursery rhymes, even religion. "Three little kittens, the three little pigs, Goldilocks and the three bears, blood, sweat and tears, red, white and blue, of the people, by the people, and for the people, morning, noon and night, tall, dark and handsome, even gold, frankincense and myrrh." The list had gone on and on. The class had even volunteered a few, once they knew what Gary was getting at.

"Why is it three strikes and you're out?" Gary had asked his plebes. "The human mind is geared to expect things that come in three's. A third time is a charm, after all. Some people even believe that deaths come in three's."

Amanda had heard Gary speak of the logic of all of this and there certainly were enough examples to lead one to believe that there must be something to it. Amanda had to admit that, perhaps, Gary was on to something. Still, Amanda had concluded that she would never employ this "power of three."

"It's not for me," she wrote. "I'll never consciously use it in my writing. I like Mr. McLean and I usually try to follow his advice. But not this time. Not me. I hate the name 'three'."

"The name three," Lisa spoke. That's odd, she thought. Perhaps she means the "word three" or the "number three."

Then, it hit her. Lisa sat upright, her breathing becoming more rapid as she reread the passage from its beginning.

She went to call her husband.

Ogden got his call at eleven, thirty-nine. An officer had the search warrant in hand, signed by Judge Julius Flynn.

"Okay. Let's move out," Ogden said quietly.

"What do you mean, he's about to move in on the apartment?" L.J. Stiles shouted into his hand-held mike.

"Like I said, Lieutenant. Ogden has a group rolling. Warrant's in hand. I got a call just before ten, saying Dale's in his apartment and Ogden's rolling."

"Now?"

"Yes, Lieutenant Stiles. He's requested radio silence. Code word's to be the first word spoken on his frequency. Signaling a 'go' or a 'stand down.'"

"Lieutenant?"

"I'm here, Dodd."

Stiles had not imagined the scenario, taking place without him.

"I understand, Dodd." He swallowed hard. "Guess I'll go watch the fun, Dodd. Tell the Chief I'm on the way. Out."

Lisa reached Gary and Max via Max's cellular telephone and sounded quite desperate in her plea for them to return home immediately. Max sensed Gary's urgency and cut corners dangerously to get his friend home as soon as possible.

"You gonna tell me what's wrong, Gary?" Max asked, as he slowed down for a stop sign.

"I don't know, for sure. Lisa's upset about something, though. She sounded like it's a five-alarm fire."

"It's not the twins, is it?"

"No, they're fine. But something's got her worked up. She

said she asked Meg to come over when she called her to get your cell phone number.

Max sped through intersections and Gary thought of asking him to slow down. This was not an emergency. Just urgent. But Gary, too, was dying to know what Lisa was so worked up about. She had refused to tell him over the phone.

"Just get your ass home, Gary. You've got to see this," was all she had said.

Meg had already arrived and Lisa stopped telling her friend the news, to begin anew when Gary and Max rushed through the door.

"What's up, hon?"

"Gary, sit down. You've got to hear this."

The two men shot into their seats around the dining room table and listened as Lisa began to explain.

"You know how I've been reading Amanda's journals?"

Gary nodded. He now realized that Lisa must have discovered something in the journals that might shed some light on her sad ending. He prepared himself to be amazed.

Max looked first at Gary and then at Lisa, hearing of the journals for the first time. His elbows rested on the table and his open palms pleaded for an explanation. But he spoke not a word, as he did not wish to delay the obvious payoff he knew Lisa must have.

Lisa continued, but not until she had closed her eyes for a moment and caught her breath. She was not physically winded. But she thought she might lose her breath when Gary heard what she was about to divulge to him.

"Gary, Amanda was raped."

The response was predictable. Only Meg was not surprised, for Lisa had gone this far into her narrative before the men had arrived.

"Not recently," Lisa added. "Last year. And she didn't write about it till sometime late last fall."

Gary wrung his hands on the dining room table as Lisa let the story unfold. Amanda hadn't identified her assailant. And she hadn't told a soul about the rape. Not her parents. Not even her best friend.

After a few seconds, Gary asked, "Is there more?"

"Well, she didn't like her father working at Cederquist Industries. That's for sure."

Gary was not alone in wondering what that had to do with Amanda's having been raped. Lisa answered three puzzled looks with news of a third significant entry in the girl's journal.

"Do you remember talking to your students a few months ago about some author who advocated using 'threes' in writing to achieve balance in a story, Gary?"

"Sure, Lisa. I do that lecture every year," he answered, growing more perplexed by the minute.

"Well, listen to this." And Lisa began reading the February tenth entry.

"It's not for me. I'll never consciously use it in my writing. I like Mr. McLean and I usually try to follow his advice. But not this time. Not me. I hate the name 'three'."

Lisa paused to let what was, to her, the obvious, sink in to the others. No one spoke.

"Don't you get it, Gary? Doesn't she mean 'number'?"

"I guess so," he responded blankly.

"Was she not exact? Don't you teach your students to say what they mean or mean what they say, Gary?" repeating the line he so often had poured into his students' ears.

"What are you getting at, Lisa?"

"Gary, she wrote 'name.' She meant 'name.' 'I hate the name three.' The name three, Gary."

It was Max who spoke next.

"Trey."

SIXTEEN

Four policemen secured the area, stopping all foot and automobile traffic in a four-block radius. Three other officers of the Jacksonville Police Department, one a woman, quickly tightened the noose around the MacMurray Apartments, just as they had discussed earlier that morning.

The floor plans were committed to memory over a light lunch and the unit was talked through the whole operation once more before they loaded themselves into vehicles. Each one inventoried his or her gear for Lieutenants Ogden and Grearson. Next, he or she stepped into the van or squad cars to which they'd been assigned. Radio silence would be maintained, until a coded command would begin their assault on the living quarters of Marcus Dale. Lieutenant John Ogden would give the command from a plain wrapper Crown Vic, parked across the street.

Prior to the operation's onset, two young men in white shirts and ties had descended on seven of the eight apartments in the cinder block-constructed complex. The building faced south and Dale's apartment sat lower left, as seen from East State Street. The men carried black books, presumably Bibles, and were neatly groomed.

One man went up the steps on the building's south face to ring the doorbells of the two upstairs apartments on the east side. No one answered at either door. The other, at ground level, found no one at home in either apartment downstairs. As he ascended the stairs at the building's west side, above Dale's apartment, he was joined by the man who had checked the upstairs apartments to the east. Together they called on the apartment directly opposite Marcus Dale's.

This time, the Bible-toting officers got an answer. One of the officers handed a written message to the young woman who had opened the door and motioned for her to read it in silence. The other officer flashed his shield at the young woman, careful to keep his back to Dale's door, should he prove to be home and curious about the sudden onslaught of religious doorbell ringers.

The two policemen made their way inside the young woman's apartment, securing her apartment and insuring her safety. Ogden who watched intently gave the command.

"Disturbance at the ferris wheel," a reference to the metal icon in Community Park at Morton and Main, which served as the city's symbol.

In an instant two new friends appeared seemingly out of nowhere, preparing to approach the apartment from the rear. Another moved in from the east. They, too, would approach from the rear, initially, then hurry off to the building's west face and provide backup. Meanwhile, two vans converged on State Street, one from the west and another, from the east. Ogden and Grearson watched from a distance of three hundred feet, parked directly across East State Street to the south, along the curb on Spaulding Place.

Twenty-five seconds after three officers had secured the apartment across from Dale's, the place was surrounded. Dale's one bedroom apartment had only a small window at the rear, no side windows, and a larger window at the front of the apartment. One other small window at the front over the sink in a closet-sized kitchen peeked out from beneath the iron exterior stairway. This small apartment was about to explode with excitement.

Its lone inhabitant was startled, but soon appeared to become quite oblivious to all the commotion once the door had been kicked open. Rabbits don't get all that excited. After all, Marcus had left it plenty of food and the door to the cage had been left open. The rabbit happened to be in its cage when officers had burst in. It cowered in the corner of the cage initially, while the uniforms went about their business.

Three members of the tactical team had entered the apartment, leaving five others to surround the building outside, not counting the two van drivers or three policemen in plain clothes protecting a frightened young woman in the apartment next door. And, of course, Ogden and his small entourage watched from across the street. The three who had entered the apartment made quick work of a complete search of Dale's place.

"Nothin' here but a rabbit, Lieutenant," Littleton barked into his shoulder-mounted microphone.

Ogden threw a glance at Grearson, seated beside him. "Good job, nonetheless, Littleton. Stand down."

The full assault force began to breathe more normally and allowed themselves to become a recognizable presence as he or she moved in to congratulate each other on their assault of a rabbit. A few smiles were shared, but each one knew that some other outcome might just as easily have played itself out. There was no reason to feel embarrassed at the precautions they had taken or the training they had implemented.

L.J. Stiles contented himself with the fact that no one had been hurt in the raid, which he, too, had watched from a distance through a set of binoculars. He had arrived just in time to see four members of the team attack from the front. Stiles had literally been looking over Ogden's shoulders the whole time.

It was overkill, yes. But Ogden's team had performed well. At least what Stiles was able to see from his vantagepoint had been done very competently. Stiles had reason to feel pride in what he had witnessed. The team itself was obeying orders and had performed admirably. Stiles told himself he would not give in to the temptation to ask Ogden if he were planning on interrogating the rabbit.

Trey Cederquist dialed the cell phone number to contact Luke and Marcus once again. He had spoken to them twice since planting Amanda's wristwatch at Marcus' place and paying Harold to make the bogus call to the Jacksonville Police Department. Now, however, the "boys" were out of the cell phone's service area.

Earlier that morning, he had sat in his car and watched Amanda's funeral procession move past on its way to the cemetery. Later, he had enjoyed listening in on what he could hear of Ogden's bold maneuver over his police scanner. He had laughed when the report was made that a well-fed rabbit was all police had found when they burst in on Marcus' apartment. He wondered how long it would take them to find the watch and make the connection he'd wanted them to make.

He dialed the cell phone again and, this time, Luke picked up.

"Hi, ya boys. Did you make all your deliveries?"

"Done and done, Trey."

"How many times do I have to remind you not to use my name?" Trey screamed at the phone.

"Goddamn. I forgot. Sorry."

"For Pete's sake, anybody could be listening in, you idiot."

"I said I'm sorry."

Luke found himself more and more tired of Trey's bitter tongue and endless orders. But he was smart enough to know that he wasn't smart enough to get past this Hayes investigation without Trey's help. So he'd have to put up with Trey's excessive verbal abuse, he figured. At least for awhile longer. But it was getting more difficult each time he spoke with Trey. He knew that soon he would light out for parts unknown. Perhaps Montana.

"Listen up, cockroach. Stay off the main roads. You hear? Back roads all the way home. I'll meet you where we always meet. Try to be there by eight-thirty or nine. Got that?"

"Gotcha. Nine, at the latest."

"Alright. You boys stay outta trouble now."

"What'd Trey say, Luke?"

"Said to meet him on the road in Scott County around eight-thirty or nine. And stay on the back roads, like we haven't been told that before."

"Yeah," uttered Marcus, "does he think we're stupid or something?"

Luke looked back at Marcus who drove on toward the sun, smile on his face, as though he and his friend hadn't a care. Luke found it hard to stay angry at Marcus for very long. The two had been through a lot together, particularly in the past week. Marcus had said some terrible things to Luke over the course of that time. But all had been forgiven. He punched his friend in the arm and smiled back.

Meg was still trying to absorb all that Lisa had told her about Amanda's journal entries. Max and Gary's reaction had been to get into Max's car and leave the women there to rehash the whole scenario.

"Let's go over this again. The little twerp you punched in the stomach at the party, the guy who hit on you, is the guy responsible for this girl's death?"

"I think so, Meg," Lisa said, her own eyes wide with amazement.

"And you think he's a rapist?"

"It would appear so."

"Why would he kidnap Amanda, Lisa?"

Lisa had no immediate answer.

"I mean, why would he take that kind of risk? If he's already raped her—"

"Maybe he wanted to do it again," Lisa suggested, suddenly.

"Maybe. Lisa, can I see the journals?"

"Sure. They're in the other room."

The two women moved quickly from the kitchen, through the dining room and down a short hallway and into the living room, where Amanda Hayes's journal entries lay across a coffee table. Lisa had been scrutinizing them once again since Gary and Max had left them there nearly an hour earlier.

Meg took the first entry handed her by Lisa and, as she began to look at the page, suddenly became very nervous.

"Where did Max and Gary go, Lisa?"

"To find Lieutenant Stiles. They said if they weren't able to find Stiles, they'd go looking for Trey Cederquist themselves."

Meg's spirits obviously sagged. She lay back against the cushions of the sofa on which she sat. With that, Lisa began to experience her own nervous anxiety.

"What if they find him?" Meg asked.

"I know. That worries me, too."

Trey Cederquist pulled to a stop in front of his ex-wife's apartment building. He was not in a good mood. A frown dominated his face and he dragged his feet as he moved across the asphalt parking lot to the rear of his car.

Before entering Vicki's building, Trey opened the trunk of his '95 Lexus and rummaged around, pushing aside a suitcase and a small satchel. He reached inside the satchel as he peered over the open trunk lid. Seeing no one, he quickly extracted first one pistol, a .357 Magnum, and then a second gun. Smaller in size, this second pistol was inside a small holster, designed to be concealed on one's lower leg just above the cuff of one's pant leg.

He checked both weapons. They were loaded. Safeties on. The smaller weapon, a .380 semi-automatic, was re-holstered. Trey placed each gun behind the spare tire on the right side of the trunk. With that, he glanced to first his left, then his right and slammed the lid of the trunk with both hands.

He moved with greater confidence now and was quickly up

the steps and reaching for his key to Vicki's apartment as he entered the building.

L.J. Stiles worried that Marcus Dale might no longer be in the Jacksonville area. Even if he were still in the vicinity, Stiles was at a loss as to where to look for him. The department had discovered through a computer search that Marcus had stolen a truck back in Kentucky and served a two-year term in the Blackburn Correctional Complex in Lexington. He had been a model prisoner, been released early as part of a massive release to purge the overcrowded prisons, and had avoided any trouble with the law since then. A picture had been obtained and Stiles looked at it intently.

"Lieutenant? Phone call," Dispatcher Dodd said.

"Who is it?"

"Max Jansen?"

Stiles picked up with some indifference.

"Hello, Max. What can I do for you?"

Ben Hayes often went for long drives through the Morgan County countryside. He would cruise for hours, contemplating problems at work, weighing the advantages of one mutual fund over another, or simply trying to figure out what to buy Margot for her birthday or their anniversary.

He usually took these rides alone, of course, enjoying the peace and quiet. Occasionally, he would take a six-pack of Budweiser along for company. Today, he had a different passenger as he wrestled with the weightiest of decisions. A .38 caliber handgun lay on the seat beside him. The gun was loaded and Ben's decision had already been made.

Stiles rolled his eyes as he exited the west door of the police station at around eight, forty-five. It seemed he'd just finished a phone conversation with Max Jansen and here Max stood in the parking lot next to Stiles' car. Along side was Gary McLean who suddenly had some mysterious link to Jansen.

Before either of the men awaiting him could speak, Stiles began, "Look, fellas, I appreciate what you're trying to do. But I'm really busy right now."

"Look, L.J.," Max started.

"Max, I told you on the phone that I don't have time for this. You've got nothing to tie Trey Cederquist to this thing other than your mutual dislike for the man."

Stiles sneaked a look at his wristwatch.

"Lieutenant Stiles," said McLean, "I think you should at least listen to what we have."

"I have listened," Stiles snapped. Then he turned toward Jansen. "You tell me Cederquist doesn't like reporters snooping around. Well, Max, lots of people don't like reporters. Period. Know what I mean?"

Max was getting tired of hearing this.

"You tell me Cederquist is a jerk. I know that. I've busted his chops myself," Stiles continued, recalling to himself a drunk and disorderly complaint against Trey from two years ago. "But I can't arrest the man for being a jerk. I can't even question him for being a jerk."

Stiles' patience was growing thin.

"You tell me Cederquist is doing methamphetamines. You got any proof?" He paused. "Oh, yeah. A barmaid told you." He paused again. "Sorry, fellas, she's not an expert witness in the strictest sense."

He knew not to interrupt. But Max sometimes didn't listen to the smart voice in his head. "L.J." he tried again.

"So, now, you guys tell me the Hayes girl wrote something in a journal about someone you think might have been Trey Cederquist. Well, you know, if I had more time, I'd go over those journals myself, one-by-one. Matter of fact, why don't you bring those journals in, Mr. McLean, so my people can start going through them. Meanwhile, I'm trying to find a guy we've tied to the van that Amanda Hayes spent some time in and I can't play these games. And, oh, this guy wasn't Trey Cederquist."

"No, it was Marcus Dale," Max interjected.

Now he had Stiles' attention.

"How'd you know that?"

"Never mind, L. J.," Max said, as he turned and started toward his blue rental. He motioned for Gary to follow, leaving him to wonder if the conversation with Stiles was, indeed, over.

"You're not interested in anything we have," Max yelled over his shoulder.

"Max," Stiles shouted, "what else do you know?"

A smiling Max turned and said with satisfaction, "He hangs with a buddy from Kentucky. Name's Luke. And Luke, Lieutenant Stiles, used to work at Cederquist Industries."

Intrigued, Stiles allowed Max to retain control of the conversation. This was information he wanted, needed.

"What's this Luke's last name, Max?"

"Don't know that yet. But I'm telling you, L. J. These guys are connected to Trey and Trey is behind the death of Amanda Hayes."

"Did this Luke know Ben Hayes?"

"Now, that would be interesting to know, I suppose. But what you really should be asking is, 'Did he know Trey Cederquist?'" Max had crossed a line with that comment.

"Don't tell me how to do my job, Jansen."

The two sparred visually for a moment. Neither wanted the conversation to end. Each suspected there might be information he might want to flow in one direction or the other. But the tension was building between two strong-willed professionals who often, it seemed, were on opposing sides, when this was not really the case at all.

"Did he?" Gary asked, attempting to break the tension and continue the flow of information. "Did this Luke know Trey Cederquist?"

"We don't know for sure," Max had to admit.

"Cederquist Industries employs five, maybe six hundred people, Max. It would be wrong to assume that Trey Cederquist knew Luke. At the same time, it would not be surprising to learn that he did know him, or of him," Stiles concluded.

"But, L. J.," Max continued, "put it all together, the meth, the Hayes-Cederquist relationship through CI, the fact that Trey Cederquist is an ill-mannered, mean-spirited son-of-a-bitch, the journal entries I told you about over the phone, and now Marcus and Luke being tied to Trey—"

"That's a stretch, at best, Max."

"But it's worth checking out. Isn't it?"

Stiles shrugged, not wishing to admit that he was growing interested in following up on this information. The conversation was over, except for one last question Stiles wanted an answer to.

"Max, how'd you find out Dale's buddy had worked at CI when my people failed to learn this?"

"Why, L. J., I can be quite charming, at times. You should know that."

"Yeah, right."

The two investigators traded smiles and parted.

Gary was perplexed when the conversation ended without another word. He followed Max a short distance to the rental car, leaving Stiles standing alone in the parking lot. Gary rushed to open the passenger's side door.

"Is that it?"

"What do you mean?"

"Is that it? Is he going to investigate Trey or not? Aren't we going with him?"

"Gary, did you think he was going to swear us in as deputies? Make us part of his posse? Tell us the horses were out back?"

"Don't be a smart ass, Max."

"Look, Gary. Stiles and his policeman buddies, they work alone.

I'm a reporter. I usually work alone, too. They do their thing and I do mine."

"So, where do I fit in?"

"Good question." Max thought for a moment. "Until we get that figured out, why don't you just stick with me and we'll see if Stiles can get his job done, so I can do mine."

"You're confusing me, Max."

"We just gave Stiles a little help, so he can do his job, catch Cederquist. That will enable me to do my job, be there when Stiles does his and report it to the world. You? You get the satisfaction of seeing Trey pay for what he did to your friend."

"You've got it all figured out. Don't you, Max?"

"It's all real simple, Gary. It just gets complicated sometimes."

Gary decided not to ask what Max meant by this oxymoron. Actually, he was pretty sure he understood what Max was saying.

"Max, how did you find out that Luke used to work at Cederquist Industries. Stiles didn't know that. His people had asked, probably the same people you talked to, and they didn't discover that Luke even existed."

Max frowned. He hated admitting it had just been luck which got him most of his information at times.

"Oh, so you're gonna stick with that bit about being charming, huh?" Gary teased.

Max allowed a smile to break through.

"Just lucky, I guess. I probably asked a question or said something to a neighbor of Marcus' that sparked a memory. That apparently didn't happen when the police interviewed him. Or maybe the guy just doesn't like policemen. Hell, maybe this particular neighbor wasn't home when JPD came calling. It's a lot of luck sometimes."

Stiles continued to stand in the parking lot, making mental notes about what Max and Gary had left with him.

"What's up, Lieutenant?" Sergeant Dave Tolar asked, as he approached.

"Nothing, Dave. Couple of amateur detectives. That's all."

Just then Lloyd Becker rounded the corner and was obviously delighted to run into Stiles.

"L.J., you're not going to believe this."

"What's that, Becker?"

Becker handed Stiles a pad of paper, on which Becker had written an important piece of information. He repeated the message as he handed it over.

"That apartment on East State Street that Odgen raided this morning?"

"Right, the rabbit hutch," Tolar said with a smile. He was standing at Stiles' side but was too courteous to read over his supervisor's shoulder.

"Yeah, well, they found more than a rabbit inside, sergeant," Becker continued. "Girl's watch," he said, pausing for effect, "and it matches the description of the watch Amanda Hayes's parents gave us. Has her initials etched on back—AMH."

Stiles was deep in thought. "Dave, let's go for a ride."

"Where we going?"

"Cederquist Industries."

Trey Cederquist sat on the back bumper of his Lexus, waiting for Luke and Marcus to arrive. He had arranged the meeting on the pretext of planning the trio's next move in distancing themselves from the Hayes investigation. As usual, the two were late, probably a result of an argument over which was better, the Big Mac or the Whopper. Their endless, mindless conversations on the trivial aspects of their meaningless lives had always irritated Trey. He thought of several other disturbing characteristics they each had or, more frequently, shared with one another.

He had always thought of them as a pair. He struggled to

recall more than three or four occasions when he had encountered either of them without the other. They had drifted into town together from some small town in Kentucky. Trey had heard them speak of it often, but had not bothered to listen closely enough to even guess the first letter of the town's name. He simply hadn't cared enough to listen.

For perhaps three years the two had served Trey Cederquist well, not always as legitimate employees of Cederquist Industries, but as dependable, tight-lipped gophers with unquestioning loyalty. He had counted on the two often and was now banking on their service in one more, final role.

Headlights, beams directed at divergent angles, appeared at the crest of the hill just to the south of Trey's position on the deserted road. It was them, alright. Trey recognized the dilapidated Chevy pick-up from the crossed beams and the chainy sound of the truck's engine. He gasped for air as the two men approached, Marcus behind the wheel and struggling to gain control of the wheel as he broke in the loose gravel.

Good, Trey thought, they have already been drinking.

Once the truck came to a stop about fifteen feet beyond Trey's car on the opposite side of the road and facing north, Trey grabbed the sack containing a twelve pack of beer that he had placed on the ground behind his car. He had opened a beer himself, had taken perhaps two sips, and decided scotch would have served him more readily had he thought to bring some.

"Well, how you boys doing, tonight?"

They smiled at Trey and each mumbled their greetings. Marcus finally was able to put the truck in park, shaking his head and laughing at his own folly. Luke was opposite Marcus with his right arm propped in the open window and one leg hoisted upward, bent at the knee, his foot on the dash. The radio was playing Dwight Yocum. The two had obviously been enjoying their ride. Each was finishing another can of Miller Lite and neither hesitated when offered a fresh can by Cederquist.

Empties, or very nearly empties, were chucked backwards into the truck's bed and tabs were opened on the new cans, almost simultaneously.

"Always in sync, aren't you boys?"

They laughed. "We always in sync, Trey," Marcus slurred. "Beer drinkin', burpin', pickin' out the prettiest girl at the dance. It don't matter. We're there. In sync."

His head rested against the back window and Marcus was very nearly out.

"He's a goner, sure fire, Trey," Luke volunteered. "Been drinkin' since noon. I told him I should drive, but he won't listen. Will ya, Marcus?"

At that, Trey reached into the cab, left hand poised. Luke looked back toward Trey just in time to see the gun. A loud blast filled the truck cab and, in an instant, Luke was dead. Marcus had no time to react, his ears ringing with the concussion from the shot that killed his friend. He never heard the next shot that came from the same weapon, its barrel pressed against his cheek.

Blood was everywhere. The back window was a mass of flesh and bone. Marcus's legs were violently shaking involuntarily as Trey surveyed the scene and stepped back from the truck. He, too, was stained with the blood of either or both of his victims. He carefully looked first south, then north, and saw no sign of approaching traffic. He hadn't expected to see anything for he had chosen this spot long ago for its desolation.

Trey carefully wiped the handle of the pistol with a rag he had ready at his hip pocket, placed the gun in Marcus's left hand, pressed the hand firmly around the gun, making sure Marcus's index finger made contact with the trigger, and dropped the gun into his lap. Neither of the victims had noticed the latex gloves Trey then removed from his hands. He next peeled what turned out to be his outer clothing off his body, revealing another layer of tee shirt and slacks.

He carefully checked the outer portion of the truck. Reassuring himself that he had not touched any part of the door or fender, Trey took one last look inside the cab.

Finally, Cederquist donned a second pair of latex gloves, tossed what was left of the twelve pack without the bag into the cab of the truck, and filled the bag with his outer clothing, both pairs of gloves, and the rag. The bag he threw into his car's trunk hastily. He would dispose of it all later. Trey was in his car and driving away from the scene in a matter of seconds.

Now, that wasn't so bad, he thought to himself. Gets easier every time.

SEVENTEEN

The trip L.J. Stiles had made to Cederquist Industries had proven fruitless. Marshall Cederquist had been in his office even though it was a Saturday night. But he was not happy to hear of the suspicions people had about a possible connection between his son and others that may have been involved in the disappearance of Amanda Hayes. That had been as far as Stiles had taken it with the elder Cederquist, choosing not to alert him of other assumptions that Max Jansen and Gary McLean had made about the younger Cederquist.

Stiles had stayed up until around eleven, trying unsuccessfully to find some comfort in the fact that Amanda had died of natural causes. Someone was responsible for the girl's death, nevertheless, and Stiles was determined to discover that person or persons' identity and bring them to justice.

He had slept fitfully for awhile. Finally, around three a.m., Stiles was finally able to move into a deeper sleep, only to be awakened at four, fifteen by the telephone.

"What is it?"

"Lieutenant Stiles? Jacksonville PD?"

"Yes! Who is this?"

"Sir, this is the Scott County police. My name is Randall. We got us two dead bodies out here in the country and Sheriff Jessup thought you'd like to come take a look, sir."

Stiles hesitated, but only for an instant.

"And why, Randall, would I be interested in your two dead bodies?"

"Well, sir, I don't rightly know. Sheriff told me to call you and tell you we got what looks like a murder-suicide here. Thinks you might be interested about who it is, I guess."

"And who is it, Randall?"

"Two fellas name of Hayden and Dale. Luke Hayden and Marcus Dale, sir."

"Where the hell are you, Randall? And how do I get there?"

Early Sunday morning Gary sat in the driver's seat, trying again to find a comfortable position, a job made more difficult by the presence of the steering wheel of Max's rental car. Max was just waking from a catnap, one of many between bouts of conversation which had punctuated the evening the two had spent together in front of Trey Cederquist's apartment.

"So, you didn't even have time to attend the burial, eh, Max?"

Max looked impatiently at the bottom of the bill of a baseball cap he had donned to provide shade from the streetlight's glow. He decided he wouldn't apologize again for skipping the girl's burial in favor of trying to find some incriminating evidence with which to nail young Cederquist. He had been over this ground before.

"Gary, I told you last night. I thought the best I could do for Amanda was to find out just how responsible Trey Cederquist is for her death. I wasn't gonna do that at the cemetery."

"It only took about half an hour, Max."

"Gary, I know how long a funeral lasts. Okay?"

"It's just that it wouldn't have hurt you to at least show your face."

"No. You're right, Gary. It wouldn't have hurt me. But it wouldn't have helped Amanda. That's my point. That's all I'm saying."

Both knew that, in all likelihood, this was not the last conversation they would have on the subject. Gary, it seemed, could be as pigheaded as Max. Bad mix, that.

Suddenly, Max caught sight of Trey's car arriving at his apartment. It was five o'clock in the morning and they could only guess from where he had come. They had failed to locate him in their search the night before, after the two had struck out with Lieutenant Stiles.

Trey was behind the disappearance and, apparently, the death of Amanda Hayes. He had raped her the previous year, causing the depression her friends and family had seen in Amanda for a time. Her family had reacted to her altered behavior, not knowing in the slightest what it was they were responding to. Her classmates had chalked it up to teen angst, common to each of her friends at one time or another. But no one had suspected the depth to which her troubled mind had plunged.

Then Trey had somehow become involved with Amanda's disappearance.

His motives were not clear to either Max or Gary. But Max was beginning to suspect that it may have had something to do with Trey's drug use.

Now, Trey emerged from his car outside his garage and looked over his shoulder anxiously. He walked quickly to the front door of the building, a duplex with ornate hedges and ivy growing up one side of the building. He picked up Saturday's paper and hurried himself as he unlocked the door and disappeared.

Neither Max nor Gary had spoken since Max had placed a single digit in the air to shush the world. Finally, Max spoke quietly, as though Trey, now inside the building, sixty yards away, might hear.

"Well, there's our boy."

"Yeah," Gary countered, "I wonder where he's been all night."

"Hard telling."

"He does look like he has something to hide. Doesn't he?" Gary asked, looking for Max's confirming nod.

"Damn right he does. I've always thought so. Since I first laid eyes on the S-O-B out at Cederquist Industries."

"Yes. You did, Max. I have to give you credit. You called it."

He looked across at Max who was reaching for the scanner's power button.

"We'll just sit tight here for awhile. Let's see what Jacksonville's finest are up to this morning."

They each listened intently as amazing news came across the air. Murder-suicide in Scott County. Two men. Middle-to-late twenties. Names, Marcus Dale, the man wanted for questioning by Jacksonville PD in the disappearance of Amanda Hayes. And Luke Hayden, Kentucky driver's license.

"Sonofabitch," was all Max could say.

It was more than Gary could come up with.

Stiles and another Jacksonville detective, Lloyd Becker, arrived in Lynnville, west of Jacksonville, and followed a Scott County deputy, as directed. They followed the deputy onto Heaton Road and spotted the crime scene on the rise several miles south of Old Route 36 and southeast of Riggston. Whirling flashes of red and blue beams of light painted the trees on either side of the road. Ten to twelve men, two in uniform, the others not, stood about pointing, scratching the ground with their toes and looking off nervously in a variety of directions.

As the two Jacksonville policemen approached in Stiles' unmarked Crown Vic, Stiles laid out a plan for the two once they reached the scene.

"Lloyd, you look the inside of the truck over real good, while I visit with our Scott County friends. Okay?"

"Sure, L. J.," Becker said.

"We're gonna compare notes after a bit, so keep a sharp eye out." And Stiles winked at Becker.

The two foreign policemen disembarked and were greeted almost immediately by a Scott County officer. Not Randall. Another.

"That's Randall down there, Officer. He's the one that called you," the other volunteered.

"Thank you, deputy. What do we have here?"

"Hell if I know," was the terse comeback.

"What's his problem?" Becker asked, as he moved alongside Stiles for the walk down the hill toward Randall.

"Knows we're on his turf, I guess. You take the truck. Now."

"Ten-four."

Becker broke off to the left directly toward the truck, parked on the east side of the road, facing north. Stiles kept walking, but slowly, south along the road toward Randall. He hadn't recognized the name, or the voice over the phone. But he had met Randall several times over the past seven or eight years. Nice fellow, Stiles recalled. Very conscientious, but hadn't had a lot of training.

The two shook hands and Randall began to fill Stiles in. The Sheriff, he explained once again, was sure that Stiles would want to see the crime scene before it was disturbed. Someone had recognized the name of Marcus Dale, almost immediately, as the suspect in the Jacksonville girl's disappearance and death. It had been simple to get his wallet out of his hip pocket due to his position inside the truck. Luke Hayden's name was on the registration hanging from the sun visor over the steering wheel.

"Looks like we've got a crowd here, Deputy."

"They're just curious, Lieutenant."

"Anyone come and gone?"

"No, sir. If they came, we told them to stay til we're all done with them."

Stiles nodded his approval. He didn't need a contaminated crime scene, where car tracks or footprints could not be accounted for.

"So, Randall, where is Sheriff Jessup?"

"He's on his way, Lieutenant. Been down in Belleville for meetings all week. Wasn't due back till this evening. We called him right away. Sheriff keeps up on what's going on and when he heard the names of these boys and that you've been looking for one of 'em, said to call you real quick. That's what I did."

"Thank you, Randall. I am grateful beyond words to you and Sheriff Jessup." His smile was genuine. But Stiles couldn't wait to have a look inside the cab of the red and white pickup. "Shall we?"

The two moved back up the incline toward the pickup and Stiles exchanged glances with Becker. Becker gave Stiles his best "you-have-a-look-for-yourself" posture and stood aside. He didn't want to influence the lieutenant. They had agreed that they would each look the situation over individually and then compare notes.

Stiles looked into the bed of the truck. He saw a blue tarp, not too neatly folded, lying in the front of the bed, behind the passenger's seat. There was also some type of chain lying in the rear of the truck bed.

He moved toward the front of the truck, stopping to look for several minutes inside the open window on the driver's side. He looked at the inside from every conceivable angle, then moved around the front of the truck and approached the passenger's side. From the ditch below, he stood on his toes to see inside the truck.

What Stiles saw was horrific.

Luke lay against the open passenger's side door. He had been shot in the left temple. A mass of blood had flowed from the left side of his head, while an equal amount of blood could be seen above him on the interior of the vehicle's roof and door. His hands lay in his lap, elbows extended, like he were hanging on to a ski rope. His expressionless face was a pasty white, except where blood red turned now to black had invaded. A large entry wound behind the left eye was crusted over with the dried blood.

Marcus lay on the driver's side, his brains splayed out across the back window. His legs cocked to the left, bent at the knee and allowed his torso to lean to the right. A single bullet had entered his left cheek at point blank, leaving a gaping wound. His head was leaning to his right and toward the back window, vividly displaying the trauma caused by the bullet. A pistol was in the grip of his left hand. It appeared, to the uninitiated, that Marcus had murdered Luke and then turned the gun upon himself.

"Mind if we take some pictures, Randall?"

"No, sir. Not at all," Randall replied, a bit self-consciously. He hadn't done so, yet. And he'd been on the scene for almost an hour.

Stiles moved out of the ditch and approached Becker in the middle of the road, Polaroid in hand. The two spoke in whispers, as Randall and the other assembled deputies and civilian onlookers wondered what was being said.

Becker nodded his agreement and went about taking several pictures of the truck's interior, stopping to reload the camera several times. Stiles took pictures from Becker as the camera ejected each print. He was careful not to let prints touch each other, holding them at arms length, waving them slightly in the cool morning air. This did nothing to hasten or enhance the development of the picture. But it was a habit Stiles shared with many people.

Ten or fifteen minutes went by before Stiles was done, planting each photo on the hood of his car, while Becker returned the Polaroid to the Crown Vic's rear seat. Now Stiles was again approaching the pickup truck containing the remains of Luke and Marcus.

"Well, Lieutenant. What do you think?"

"Well, Randall. I think you got yourself a double murder, here."

Randall scratched his head. "How ya figure?" shaking his head in amazement. "Shit, Lieutenant, we got us one ol'boy splattered all over hell. Shot point blank in the face from the left, where the other fella's sitting. That one's swallowed a bullet. His brains are all over the back window and the goddamn gun's in his hand. Looks to me like the fella sitting in the driver's seat done drove his buddy there, and then himself, straight to hell."

"Randall, this is no murder-suicide." He paused. "Been made to look like one," he conceded.

"And, how's that?"

"Look at the blood, Randall. All that blood."

Randall looked. He'd seen it all before. Sickened him to look again. But he did. Looked for something about the blood that meant that what he'd concluded before could be mistaken. Didn't see anything different about the blood this time.

"Everything in the cab is covered with the blood of these two men, Randall. Isn't it?"

Randall guessed that it was, yes.

"Not everything, Randall."

Randall looked again.

"Well, Stiles," he muttered, "ain't everything covered with blood. There ain't blood on everything."

"No, but there is blood everywhere around that beer can lying on the floorboard. Right?"

Randall looked. Right. There was blood all around it.

"But there's no blood on it, at least not on top of it."

"What the hell are you getting at, Stiles?"

"Someone else was here, Randall. Threw the can in after the blood had been spilt. After these two men were murdered."

Now, Randall could see that the can had been thrown into the cab. Yes. After the gunfire. After the bloodletting. Several cans, in fact, looked like they might have been placed in the truck's cab after the gunfire. It appeared that one can had even rolled in the blood about a quarter of a rotation. It had blood on one side, but not where it should have had blood. Not if it had been lying on the floor when the blood splattered from the head of either of the two dead men.

Randall was convinced. He reflected quietly for a moment, until he became agitated.

"Shit! That means we got us a murderer on the loose. Doesn't it?"

Others, standing about and surveying the scene but not part of the conversation suddenly began to listen more intently.

"Yes, Randall, you do. Someone who wants us to think that this one," pointing at Marcus, "killed that one and then himself."

"Shit," Randall said, this time more quietly.

Stiles felt a tug at his sleeve. It was Becker, with whom he had conferred moments before. Moving away from Randall and the others, the two Jacksonville policemen conferred again. They were in agreement on how the deaths had occurred. But Becker had concerns about how the crime scene and the rest of the investigation would be handled. Stiles was aware of his colleague's lack of confidence in their Scott County neighbors and addressed it head on. They spoke in muffled tones.

"Permission to speak openly?" Becker asked.

"I know," Stiles said calmly, "you want to make sure these guys don't fuck up. Right?"

"That's right, Lieutenant."

"How many murder scenes you been to, Lloyd?"

"Three," Becker said instantly. He recalled each vividly.

"Three, huh? Well, I've done about twenty-five. And I probably just made sixteen mistakes I'm not even smart enough or trained well enough to recognize, Lloyd."

Stiles drew in a breath.

"I'm tired of this we're-better-than-them attitude we sometimes have in our ranks. Maybe these Scott County boys are smarter than you give 'em credit for. Lighten up on these guys. I think they'll do okay. But we do need to get the State Police involved."

Becker nodded his agreement.

"Give them a call and then you stay with Randall till they get here. Kinda watch over things. I'm more concerned that they won't sequester some of the evidence than that they'll miss something, though, Lloyd. Besides Jessup's on the way. He's a good man. You make contact with him as soon as he arrives. Do what you can diplomatically to make sure he doesn't give out too much information to the press. Remember, we want to know more than the murderer knows or what any friends he has might know."

"Roger that." Then, after a thought, "And where will you be?"

"Back in Jacksonville. See if you can get a ride back into town from one of these fellas when you're done here. Or we can send a car out for you."

Becker shook his head, as he looked the scene over once again.

"What is it, Becker? You look like you got something else on your mind."

"I do, L.J."

"Look, Lloyd. I'm sorry if I jumped on you. It's just that I think we get a little full of ourselves."

"It's not that, L.J.," Becker responded, nodding toward the rear of the truck.

"I checked out the truck bed, under the tarp."

"What'd you find?"

"Whole case of lithium batteries, L.J."

"No shit."

"Yeah. And a small propane bottle. I'm guessing it's got anhydrous in it, Lieutenant."

Stiles let the facts sink in, silently surveying the scene.

"Meth," Stiles finally said, almost in a whisper.

"Looks that way," Becker said.

Stiles now nodded and placed a hand on Becker's shoulder. They had been waiting for a break like this for sometime. But neither man was having any success pulling up a smile at their good fortune.

"Make sure ISP gets that bit of information and help them tear the truck apart right here if they can find evidence of the meth labs we've been scratching around for all this time.

"Gonna be a long goddamn day, L. J."

"Yes. But I'm glad you're here, Lloyd. I know the scene's in good hands. But remember, Lloyd, you're in their house. You're a guest. Behave yourself. I don't want any reports that you came in here and big-timed these folks."

"Alright, L. J. I hear ya. Good luck. Wherever you're headed."

Stiles gave Becker a wink and was in his car without responding to Randall who had more questions about the murders.

Marshall Cederquist, Jr., listened as the news broke over one of the local radio stations. Details were sketchy but the reports spoke of two dead men, southwest of Jacksonville in Scott County. Reporters were on their way to the scene. Names were being withheld, pending notification of relatives. More news would be relayed to an anxious west central Illinois population when it became available.

What the devil is going on, Cederquist thought. First Amanda Hayes is discovered dead in Granite City. Next, reports are that she had, indeed, been kidnapped and detained, indirectly or directly causing her death. Now two men were dead. Could there be a connection? And, if so, what did it say about life in Jacksonville?

Cederquist had lived his whole life there, except when he'd gone away to college at Northwestern. He'd returned here to lead the company business into prosperity beyond his father's imagination. He loved his town and hated to see its image tarnished with news of such tragic ilk.

Thoughts of yesterday's visit from that reporter and Gary McLean from the high school returned. They seemed to think that some former CI employee was linked to Amanda Hayes's disappearance and hinted that his son, Trey, was somehow involved. They were cautious not to go too far with their accusations. But the implications were obvious.

Trey had screwed up before. That was certain. Hundreds of times, it seemed. But Cederquist thought his son incapable of having anything to do with such events and summarily dismissed Trey's accusers. He had told the two visitors to get off CI property. He'd been much more direct with them than he'd been with any non-CI employee in some time. It wasn't his nature to raise his voice. But no one was going to libel Trey's good name like that.

And then Lieutenant Stiles had come calling, making veiled references to accusations and reports from others about Trey. Marshall had deduced that the others were Jansen and McLean. But it was inconceivable that Trey could be involved in Amanda's death. He had been polite to Stiles, but had insisted that he knew of no Luke at Cederquist Industries. He had told Stiles he would look into it when business opened on Monday. Stiles had told him he would return with a warrant for CI employment records if that became necessary.

It had been difficult to face such questioning. He feared that there might be more such questions to follow. It was the answers to these questions, however, that Marshall Cederquist most feared.

Now, Cederquist sat at his kitchen table, pondering the unthinkable. No. No, he thought. Trey wouldn't. Couldn't.

Stiles exceeded the speed limit as he reentered Jacksonville, approaching Cederquist Industries and recalling the accusations Max Jansen and Gary McLean had voiced against the heir to the CI throne the previous afternoon and evening. He had decided it was time to look more closely into the chance that Luke Hayden had, indeed, been an employee at Cederquist Industries and the possibility that Luke, and perhaps, Marcus, had known Trey Cederquist. He would insist on seeing Marshall's employment files, immediately if need be.

He tried to shake off the notion that the son of one of the most influential men in Jacksonville could be connected to men who may have victimized a young girl and then been blown away by some third person. This third person, thought Stiles, must be one mean son-of-a-bitch.

He glanced in the direction of the parking lot at CI as he entered the west end of Jacksonville. He didn't expect to see any cars there and didn't. He made his way east on Morton until he reached Westgate and turned left. North on Westgate to Mound and then a right. He was headed to Marshall Cederquist' home. He rehearsed his presentation of certain facts that would be difficult to introduce to the gentleman he had always considered an upright citizen and a man to be respected.

He turned right again and wound his way up a hill and into a cul-de-sac where Marshall Cederquist had built a beautiful home many years ago and, with his wife, had raised their son. Cederquist's car was in the driveway. This would not be easy.

Marshall Cederquist, Jr., answered the telephone, half worried that it might be someone confirming his worst fears. Someone connecting his son with two dead bodies on a country road outside Jacksonville. He was, at first, relieved to learn that the caller was a stranger, asking about his daughter-in-law.

"Mr. Cederquist. My name is Teresa Martinez. I baby sit for Melinda. Vicki asked me to watch Melinda last night. She hasn't been by to pick Melinda up yet. And I haven't been able to reach her."

"Do you have Melinda with you now, Ms. Martinez?"

"Yes, sir. I have been trying to reach Vicki since about ten o'clock last night. This is not like her, Mr. Cederquist."

"Let me get this straight. You have had Melinda with you since last night. And Vicki hasn't phoned or anything."

"That's right."

"Did Vicki give you any indication that she'd be staying out overnight, or that she would not be picking Melinda up last night?"

"No, sir. She told me she'd be picking her up at nine or nine-thirty. She was going to a movie with a friend at seven o'clock."

"And what would you like me to do, Ms. Martinez?"

"Mr. Cederquist, I have a little girl of my own and we want to go to church this morning. I can take Melinda to church with us. But I don't want to walk to church with the girls and have Vicki show up, looking for us. Could you try to locate Vicki? I'd go over to Vicki's myself. But I don't have a car."

"I don't know what to do, Ms. Martinez."

"Mr. Cederquist, I have a key to Vicki's apartment. Could you take Melinda home and wait for Vicki. I'll give you her key."

"Yes. I can. Where do you live? I'll come right over."

Cederquist took down the address and pulled on a sport coat, grabbing his keys as he marched toward the door.

The doorbell began to ring as Cederquist was turning the knob.

Gary could not believe he had allowed Max to leave the car. For nearly ten minutes, Max had been gone, stumbling through the yard adjacent to Trey Cederquist's duplex, scrambling low along the ground toward Trey's home. Gary had watched nervously as Max made his way to a window the two had decided would probably provide a view of Trey's bedroom.

As Max was about to stand erect beside the window and peer inside, Trey exited the front door. Max was around the corner from Trey's position first at the front door and then in the driveway. Trey would not see Max, Gary thought. Unless, when Trey backed out of his driveway, he backed far enough into the street to bring him in line with the side of his building or he backed up the street in the opposite direction, drove south, and looked quickly to his left.

Max, initially unaware that Trey was no longer in the building, went about his task breathlessly. He had not heard the door slam. But when he heard Trey's car start up, he scurried to the front corner of the building and peeked around to see Trey backing out and driving away to the north. He waited until Trey was several houses down the street and approaching the only turn he could take to exit the subdivision.

Gary had the car running by the time Max reached the car and jumped inside. The two exchanged a brief look in the other's direction.

"What are you waiting for, Gary? Follow him."

Gary shook his head and listened to his heart race, his pulse thumping at his temples. Finally the teacher raced ahead. Several blocks later, the two were discouraged to realize that they had lost Trey in traffic.

"Just what is it you want to talk to me about, Lieutenant?"

"Marshall, I don't want to get into it with you now. I know you're concerned about your granddaughter and your daughter-in-law."

"Ex-daughter-in-law, actually. But you're right. I am a bit worried. This Ms. Martinez sounded alarmed. Said it's not like Vicki to leave Melinda with her and not pick her up when she said she would."

Neither man spoke for a moment.

"I do appreciate your helping me to check this out, Lieutenant."

Stiles drove on, his eyes darting from the road to his nervous passenger, toward the home of Vicki Cederquist and her daughter, Melinda.

"Don't mention it."

"But I want to know now. What is it you came to see me about?"

Stiles could put it off no longer.

"It's Trey, Marshall."

They both had known that Marshall, while he couldn't have possibly guessed at the details, knew that his son would be the topic of conversation when Stiles got round to talking.

"Does it involve those men I heard about on the radio this morning?"

"Yes. Yes, it does," Stiles responded, surprised, one, that Marshall had already heard news of the murders and, two, that he had connected these men with his son somehow.

Stiles had asked the question the night before. Now, he was asking again.

"Did Luke Hayden work for Cederquist Industries, Marshall?"

"I didn't know last night. We employ hundreds of men and women, as I told you, Lieutenant. But, after you left, I checked the records. He worked for us briefly last year."

Stiles hesitated. "I'm afraid that I have someone telling me that he suspects Trey of having some connection with this man and another man, Marcus Dale. Dale, we've concluded, is connected with the disappearance, and perhaps the death, of Amanda Hayes."

"That's what they said on the radio. That the one fellow had been wanted in connection with Amanda's death."

Cederquist held his breath for several seconds.

"My god," Cederquist said.

What must it be like, thought Stiles, to fathom for the first time the enormity of some tragic event with which your only son may be involved. He pressed on, despite his sympathy for Marshall Cederquist.

"We'd been looking for Dale for about twenty-four hours. Found his fingerprint on the van we think was used to abduct Amanda. And we have found a watch belonging to Amanda in the guy's apartment."

"And, now, he's turned up dead," Cederquist said, stealing the exact words from Stiles' mouth.

"That's right. Along with Luke Hayden."

"And you think Trey knew these men?"

"I guess, Marshall, that's what I'd like to find out."

"Have you asked Trey?"

"No, sir. No. I haven't."

Stiles started to explain that he had only recently begun to believe that Trey Cederquist could possibly be involved in this whole mess. Stiles had what he had always considered to be an excitable, mediocre newspaper man and a well-intentioned, but naive high school English teacher feeding him their theories about some sort of conspiracy. They had some flimsy evidence that, somehow, was starting to look like something Stiles felt compelled to investigate. Very compelled to investigate when two alleged co-conspirators had turned up dead that morning.

Stiles' squad car came to a stop in front of Vicki Cederquist's apartment. They had decided not to stop at Teresa Martinez's for a key. Neither man moved for an instant. Each, it seemed, was trying to figure out what to say next.

"Well, Marshall, here we are. Let's see if your daughter-in-law is okay. Then, we can go have a talk with Trey together."

They each climbed out of the car and made their way up the driveway. Vicki's car was in the drive. Both men looked inside the vehicle as they walked past it on opposite sides. Stiles led the way up a few steps to the landing at the front door. The policeman pushed the doorbell button.

After the chimes had played several times, Cederquist reached for the doorknob. Locked. Cederquist looked impatiently at Stiles.

"Ms. Martinez told me she has a key. But there's no time to go over there now. Break it in, Lieutenant."

"Perhaps she's out for a walk, Marshall."

"Break it in."

Stiles leaned forward as he extended his raised right foot quickly. The door swung open with a violence that Cederquist had not expected. They each leaned into the doorway.

"Vicki?"

"Ms. Cederquist?"

"Vicki. Are you home?"

The two shrugged in unison. Stiles moved into the apartment first. Cederquist followed close behind, but moved into the rear of the kitchen, past the island, as Stiles stepped into the middle of the living room and looked down the hallway toward the bedrooms.

Stiles heard Cederquist's gasp and looked quickly to his right to see Cederquist stepping backward, staring down at the body of Vicki Cederquist.

Stiles moved around the island to see her lifeless form, legs outstretched, her torso leaning against the corner formed by the dishwasher front and base cabinet. Her clothes were torn. She had been beaten savagely. While there was not an excess of blood, she did bleed from her mouth and from one ear. It appeared that she had been dead for several hours.

Stiles looked over his shoulder at Marshall Cederquist, who stood motionless, except for shaking his head in disbelief.

"What has he done?" Cederquist asked.

Stiles did not have to guess whom Cederquist meant.

Meg had arrived at Lisa and Gary's home around nine Sunday

morning. Lisa welcomed Meg and told her she knew nothing more of the two men's quest to convince Lieutenant Stiles of Trey Cederquist's culpability in Amanda's disappearance or to confront Trey Cederquist himself. This quest had kept the two men out overnight and both women were growing more concerned.

Meg was again skimming Amanda's journal entries as Lisa explained. Her empathy for Amanda and keener understanding of what the young girl had endured for the past year was quickly replaced with concern for Max and Gary, when Lisa told her she hadn't heard from the pair since the preceding evening. That last call had come from Gary after Meg had returned to the room where Max was supposed to be staying with her friends. Now, Lisa and Meg were more scared than concerned.

The two women began to embrace, sensing an urgency that neither wished to succumb to. Meg pulled away at the last moment.

"Cell phone. Max has a cellular telephone."

"What's the number?" Lisa asked, new hope coming easily to her.

"Let me think. Let me think," Meg said frantically, waving her hands in the air near her face.

She calmed herself, stretching her arms, as though she sought the numbers from a shelf above her.

"Okay, I got it. Where's your phone?"

And she dialed. There was a brief delay before she heard an all too familiar response.

"Your LCI customer has moved out of the service area. Thank you for using LCI."

"Shit!" Lisa said.

"What?"

"He's out of the service area."

"Shit."

"I already said that, Lisa."

They looked at each other and smiled.

"Look, Lisa. They're fine. We'll keep trying and we'll get hold of them soon. Don't worry. Max knows what he's doing."

"I was feeling better till you said that," Lisa dead panned.

"Yeah. Me, too."

Upstairs, one of the twins began to cry.

"Oh, no," Lisa said, "that's just what I need."

"Don't worry. I'll go check on the kids. You stay here. Relax. Try to get hold of Max and Gary again. Here's the number." She wrote the number on a piece of paper. "It'll be okay," she reassured Lisa.

Meg ran up the stairs at the rear of the house, leaving Lisa sitting at the kitchen table. She drummed her fingers on the table's top, finally reaching for a pen that lay at the opposite end of the table. The idea struck her quite suddenly and she rose from her chair in search of another piece of paper on which she could write a note to Meg. She looked over her shoulder, listening for an approaching Meg, but heard no such approach. She could hear Meg and the twins laughing with great enthusiasm.

Hurriedly she scratched out her message, something about staying with the kids. More about going to find Gary and Max, and a reminder to tell Stiles of her search if he were to call. She placed the note and pen on the table near where Meg had sat only moments earlier and grabbed her car keys and purse on the way out the back door.

As she pulled the wooden door after her and backed out, pushing the screen door with her backside, she turned to see an imposing figure on the top step of the landing outside her doorway.

"What are you doing here?" Lisa asked.

EIGHTEEN

Gary and Max had finally stumbled upon Trey Cederquist late Sunday afternoon, driving rather recklessly along Morton Avenue in front of the WalMart store. For the most part the two had driven aimlessly from CI to Trey's home, from one bar to the next, seeking some sign of Cederquist. Now they followed him as he turned south on Massey Lane and continued south before turning onto a Leach Farm Road. Soon they encountered the entrance to a dirt road, heading north.

It was more of a path really that ended or began at Leach Farm Road, directly south of the Cederquist Industries property in the southwest corner of Jacksonville. When Trey turned in at the entrance to the path, Gary parked the blue rental under a tree some fifty yards east of the entrance and on the opposite side of the road. The two decided on Max's going in on foot. Gary was to stay behind with the car.

Once again, Gary could not believe the lengths to which he found himself willing to go in pursuit of Trey Cederquist. Had he allowed himself to be sucked into staking out, tailing, now stalking someone who had kidnapped a young student of his and, who now, evidence strongly suggested, had committed murder? Had he allowed Max's enthusiasm or, Gary was thinking, Max's stupidity to put them both in peril? Then he thought of Lisa. If Trey Cederquist didn't kill Max, Gary concluded, Lisa McLean would.

He watched as Max made his way across the road and down the path. Max wouldn't like it, but Gary was not about to sit there and let Max go in by himself. It might risk losing Trey, should he suddenly exit from the path in his vehicle. But Gary was out of the car and hotfooting it to catch up with Max.

For his part, Max's engine was revving as never before. He could not recall ever having felt so alive. The excitement was new and, he was now convinced, he had been missing out on something important. Never again would he sit behind a desk, waiting for a story to come to him. From now on, he thought, I will go out and break the story. If I live through this, he added as an afterthought to himself.

The reporter and teacher-turned-amateur-sleuth moved silently in tandem, a couple hundred feet or so apart, through the afternoon warmth northward up the path. Each stayed close to the brush on either side, in case Cederquist might suddenly appear. Gary was not trying to hide his efforts from Max. But the prospect of Trey coming back down the path was a concern. Still, Gary wasn't too skilled in this area and Max suddenly became aware of Gary's presence.

After they had moved about a quarter of a mile down the path. He looked back at Gary and shook his head. Oh, well, he thought. I wouldn't have waited back there, either. Again he moved ahead.

Gary followed, closing the gap between them by perhaps twenty-five or thirty yards at every turn. Soon, the two were coming upon Trey's car and moved quickly into the brush. Gary caught up with Max as he moved through the brush alongside the car. Together they saw the gaping hole in the chain-link fence, marking the southern boundary of Cederquist Industries. They each wondered what reason Trey would have for sneaking onto CI property, even though they had speculated all along that Trey had been headed toward the family business.

A pungent odor hung in the air. Something, perhaps chemicals inside the building, gave off a foul smell that brought tears to Gary's eyes. Max, too, was aware of the smell, although he had a muted reaction to it. He, after all, was used to living with the smell of gym socks.

"What do you think he's up to?" Gary whispered.

"I don't know, Gary. But I'm gonna find out."

The two began to move toward the fence. First Max, then Gary slipped through the hole. Max moved past the doorway at the southeast corner and along the south wall of the shed that lay just inside the fence line. Gary moved north, along the shorter east wall. As Gary moved slowly toward a lone window on the east face of the building, Max was moving more quickly past several windows on the south face, fearing that Trey might emerge from the door on that side, near the fence hole.

Gary stretched to get a look through the window, finding his view blocked by cardboard boxes stacked just inside the window. He moved toward the northeast corner of the building. Before him to the north, lay the massive parking lot that separated CI proper from this older, largely deserted outbuilding. He looked along the north side of the building and he saw a figure disappear behind the other end of the building.

As Gary turned back toward the south, he found himself in the presence of Trey Cederquist, gun held firmly between Trey's two hands.

"Just what the fuck do you think you're doing here?" Trey asked, motioning now with his left hand to answer quietly.

Gary could think of nothing to say. He stared back blankly at Trey.

Trey moved toward Gary, traversing the thirty feet between them with only, it seemed to Gary, two or three steps. Gary turned his back to the warehouse and slid down the corrugated tin until his rear end rested on his right heel. Trey reached down to take Gary's collar in his left hand and pointed the pistol he held in his right hand at Gary's head.

"Let's go," Trey said, as he pulled Gary up to a standing position. "We're gonna take a ride."

Before they got to the corner of the building, Trey suddenly stopped short and put his mouth close to Gary's ear.

"Are you alone?"

"Yes," Gary said quietly.

"Then why are we whispering, dipshit?" Trey said, as he clutched Gary's collar tighter and shoved him in the direction of the hole in the fence.

Peeking around the southwest corner of the building from the western end, Max had caught a glimpse of Trey and Gary moving through the hole in the fence toward Trey's car. Trey had obviously gotten the drop on his friend and Max whispered, "Shit," as he rose to his feet. At the moment he had risen to his full stature, he felt the muzzle of a gun at the back of his neck.

"And just who might you be?" the holder of the gun said.

Max didn't answer.

"I asked you who you were, asshole." And his assailant spun Max around to face him.

Ben Hayes held the gun at Max's chin.

Max wanted to calm himself. But the look in Hayes's eyes would not allow Max such relief.

"One more time. Who are you?"

"Max Jansen. I'm a reporter, Mr. Hayes." Max led with his eyes in the direction of Trey and Gary. "Trey Cederquist has got my friend. Gary McLean. Your daughter's teacher."

Max could see that Hayes was having a rough time comprehending all that Max was telling him. With a sense of urgency he'd never before experienced, Max pleaded with Hayes to trust him and to follow Cederquist before he could hurt Gary.

Suddenly, Max and Ben heard Cederquist starting his car.

"Come on," Hayes snapped.

The two ran a hundred yards or so to Hayes's automobile, which they jumped into hurriedly. Ben, behind the steering wheel, started the car quickly and sped north toward the front gate with Max gasping for breath and looking frantically toward the south. As Ben exited the front entrance of Cederquist Industries and turned left, on a hunch, the two looked southward once more, trying desperately to see between buildings on the CI property for a sign of Trey's vehicle.

The topography fell away as one looked south from Route 36 toward the parallel country road heading west. Suddenly, in the afternoon sun, they caught sight of dust rising from the country road, dust rising behind a car moving fast. It was headed west. Ben and Max moved west along Old Route 36, watching the dust continue to rise on the path parallel to their own, one mile south of them.

Meg stopped at the bottom of the rear stairs of the McLean home, listening for some indication of Lisa's presence somewhere on the home's first floor. She'd been laughing and playing with the McLean twins for almost an hour. It appeared that Lisa was nowhere in the home.

"Great!"

Then she saw the note Lisa had left for her.

Ben Hayes drove fast, but under control, and contemplated just how he could get on the same road as Cederquist without losing distance and, therefore, contact with Cederquist. If Cederquist turned south, Hayes had to be in a position to do the same without having to backtrack. That would risk losing him, too. If Cederquist turned north, perhaps Hayes would have him. Head on. That might work, Hayes was thinking.

Max begged Hayes to be careful. Gary's life was in Trey's hands. And theirs, he added. Max couldn't tell if Hayes were even hearing what he was saying. Max kept talking, hoping that Hayes would regain the control he had obviously lost at some point before he'd encountered Max back at the warehouse.

A mile west of town on Route 36, just past the Route 67 Corridor annex, Hayes found that he had lost sight of Cederquist's car, forcing Hayes to slow to a near stop. Both men looked expectedly in all directions, anticipating, hoping for a glimpse of the car with Cederquist at the wheel.

Trey Cederquist continued westward toward Scott County until it took a right at Potter Road. Northward toward Route 36 and then left Trey and Gary traveled, slowing their speed at Trey's instruction. He did not want to alarm a state trooper or county deputy. Trey was smarter than that, he told himself.

Gary was not so sure. He stole a glance in Trey's direction whenever he could and could see that Trey was, again, under the influence of something powerful. The same stuff, Gary presumed, Trey had been high on at the bar on Wednesday night.

Gary recalled the violent tendencies Trey had displayed that night and it scared him. Trey hadn't had a gun then. He had simply backhanded that waitress viciously. Had Trey had a gun then, he no doubt would have shot her and, in all probability, the young patron who had come to her aid. What a cluster that would have been, Gary concluded.

Trey did have a gun now and Gary was the one in his sights. Gary had never been so frightened. He thought of Lisa and the twins. He fought to remain focused, but found it difficult to maintain his composure. Trey made the task harder by periodically shoving the gun into Gary's ribs or at his right temple, whenever there was a break in oncoming traffic. This made it nearly impossible for Gary to drive.

They turned left onto Route 36 but only traveled a hundred yards before turning right onto Vasey Lane. Vasey immediately veered westward until they turned right onto Markham Road. Suddenly Trey ordered Gary to pull over. Would this be the end for which Gary was destined? A cemetery lay ahead as the road again crested at its intersection with Liberty Road. His mind raced.

Trey ordered Gary from the driver's seat, as the car slowed at the right of the desolate lane, perhaps a mile to the south of its rendezvous with the busier Route 67 which looped westward before its arching back northward miles later. Gary still sat behind the steering wheel and waited for more instructions, hoping as he stalled for a chance to make a getaway. With the vehicle now at a complete stop, Trey rounded the car's front end, his gun pointed at Gary's head.

The thought of pushing the accelerator to the floor flashed through Gary's mind quickly. But Trey had been careful to put the car in park before exiting the passenger's side. A move to engage the car's transmission, necessary for an attempt to run Trey over, would give Trey ample opportunity to pull the trigger of the gun he pointed at Gary through the windshield.

Gary did not think he could depend on Trey's being a poor marksman under the circumstances. The stakes were too high. Gary disembarked numbly when ordered to do so by Trey, now having completed his trek around the front of the Lexus.

Trey pushed Gary over the hood of the car and mumbled something to Gary about not trying anything funny. As Gary tried to think of what funny maneuver he might possibly effect that would extricate him from his present circumstances, Trey busied himself with opening the trunk of his car. He extracted rope and duct tape and scurried toward the front of the vehicle, where he proceeded to tie Gary's hands behind him. He positioned Gary's hands, backs to one another, so that his palms were turned out, elbows arching outward, and pulling the shoulders together.

It was apparent to Gary that Trey was practiced in this procedure. Having never had his hands bound before, Gary could only guess at Trey's effectiveness. At least, initially, it appeared that Trey Cederquist knew what he was doing. He had done this before.

Next, Trey spun Gary around to face him, being careful to keep Gary teetering off balance and, all the while, being protective of his gun hand and his personal space. No head for Gary to butt, no genitals for him to knee, not even a shin to kick. Without hesitation, he peeled a two-foot length of duct tape and wrapped Gary's mouth, completely encircling Gary's head and pressing the tape's adhesive to each cheek. The tape snatched at the hair on the back of Gary's neck. This would hurt when it was removed. At least, Gary hoped it would.

His hands bound behind him and unable to speak now, Gary stumbled when led by Trey to the rear of the car. Trey again opened the trunk lid, jerking at Gary's elbow when they turned the corner at the rear of the car. It was apparent that Trey was intending to put Gary inside the trunk, a prospect that Gary found frightening. Suddenly, Trey punched Gary's chin, not with his fist, but with the base of the pistol's handle. As soon as Gary's knees buckled and his head and shoulder slammed the rocky surface of the road's shoulder, Trey was pulling Gary up again, this time with both hands.

Trey turned Gary away from the car to face him as he tossed Gary headlong into the trunk, which became dark instantly with the slam of the trunk's lid. Gary was disoriented and struggled to regain his equilibrium in spite of his restrained upper extremities and the cramped darkness of the trunk's interior.

He could feel the car's movements soon and could detect the turn onto the hard road, a turn made at high speed. Soon Gary was also aware in the forward recesses of the trunk of the presence of someone or something else.

Gary, it turned out, was not alone.

NINETEEN

Gary McLean choked on the increasingly potent exhaust fumes of Trey's vehicle. Intellectually he knew that what he could smell was of lesser concern than what he could not. Nevertheless, his lungs burned and his heart rate quickened. He tried not to worry about dying in the trunk of the '99 Lexus. His attention turned again to the other presence in the trunk. Gary listened for any sound that wasn't part of the drone of the car's engine or the hum of its tires on the pavement. But beyond the movement of the car there was silence.

Whatever he or it was that was lying in the trunk with Trey, it had not moved. It did not speak. Perhaps its mouth was duct taped, as was Gary's. Gary had not seen it during his sudden arrival to the trunk's interior and the lid had been closed quickly, too quickly for Gary to perceive his companion by any other means but feeling it now with his hands, hands which were still tied behind his back.

After an initial groping, Gary had removed his hands from the location of what Gary perceived to be a human body. Or could it be a corpse? He was aware of its relative position in the trunk and began to grope again in the hopes of obtaining more information about his fellow passenger. Still, it did not move, although Gary thought he detected a trembling as his hands clumsily contoured its figure.

He maneuvered his own body, altering its position to allow his hands greater access to whoever lay beside him. Soon his hands arrived at what very obviously was a woman's breast. For a flickering moment he felt the violent beating of a heart behind the ample breast of a mature female, who quite suddenly kicked Gary in the back of his leg, just below the knee. It's a she and she's alive, Gary concluded.

Gary quickly removed his hand, having discovered that his companion, in addition to being alive, was also quite protective of her virtue, regardless of their predicament. Gary could only assume that, whoever this woman was, she had not volunteered to ride in Trey Cederquist's trunk. He could not begin to guess the woman's identity. For now, he was too busy protecting his own personal space from another invading foot, which intentionally delivered another jolt to his lower extremities.

Whoever this woman was, she was not happy with Gary's unexpected company. He had no reason to believe that, despite their common crisis, she was interested in joining forces in an effort to extricate the pair. Perhaps she will come around, Gary reasoned, if the ride continues for any length of time. For now, at least, she had stopped kicking him. He could feel her squirming toward the side of the trunk at which both their heads lay.

Gary for an instant thought of rolling over to face his fellow passenger. But it was too dark in the closed trunk to see. He decided that keeping his back to her, whoever she was, would be safer and stayed in his present fetal position, facing the back of the trunk.

This returned Gary's attention to more urgent matters. What did Trey intend to do with them? It was difficult to imagine that Trey's plans would amount to anything good. He was driving the Lexus wildly, cresting hills at speeds that caused the car to leave the road's surface on several occasions.

"Oh," Gary mumbled suddenly beneath his duct tape muzzle. Without warning, she had kneed him very hard in the small of his back. His kidney ached now and he was glad he had abandoned the notion of turning over to face his nemesis, just as quickly as the notion had occurred to him. No sense exposing himself to the lady's knee anymore than he already was.

Having turned yet another murder scene over to, in this instance, Jacksonville Police Department investigators, including John Ogden, Stiles now made his way to Cederquist Industries. He had ordered a squad car to the home of Teresa Martinez and had another take Marshall Cederquist to the Martinez home, so he could see for himself that his granddaughter was safe. Marshall would have to leave Melinda with the policewoman who met him there and tell her later of her mother's death. Stiles had given him strict orders to get to CI headquarters as soon as he was sure the girl was safe.

Stiles had waited until crime scene staff had secured the apartment of Vicki Cederquist and then moved quickly to Trey Cederquist's home. No one was there and Stiles hurried now to meet the elder Cederquist at his company's main offices. Stiles had only to wait a few minutes before Cederquist arrived with Lloyd Becker, just back from a full day in Scott County. Lloyd wanted to tell him of the State Police's arrival and that of Scott County Sheriff Wayne Jessup. But Stiles cut him off abruptly.

"I think I know who killed those two already, Lloyd."

"You're shittin' me, L. J."

"No. He's not, Officer," Marshall Cederquist, Jr. interrupted, as he approached on foot from his car. "He knows that my son killed those two men. Just as he knows that my son has also killed his ex-wife."

Becker stood between them, completely dumbfounded. He looked to Stiles for confirmation. He got it.

"That's about the size of it, Lloyd," Stiles said, his hand upon Cederquist's shoulder.

The three made their way up the steps toward the front door of the main office building. Cederquist was reaching for his keys and had them at the ready when they arrived at the doors. He was doing everything he could to assist Stiles in stopping his son from hurting anyone else. But that didn't mean it was going to be easy.

The plan that Stiles laid out was to search Trey's office for any clue that might speak to his whereabouts. Perhaps they would find a note, phone logs, something, anything that would give them a clue about what Trey would be doing next. All the appropriate authorities were already on the lookout for Trey's late model sports car, as well as the Lexus. His physical description was being committed to memory by each of Jacksonville's peace officers and transmitted across the entire state to thousands of others at that moment.

As they entered the building and hurriedly turned left toward the more important offices in the company's headquarters, they passed an open office door, the only open door of perhaps twenty that lined the hallway leading to Marshall and Trey's office suite. The open door was access to the office of Ben Hayes.

Cederquist stopped. It was odd, that any door be left open on a Sunday afternoon. No other car besides those of Stiles, Becker and the elder Cederquist occupied the parking lot at present and the one office door left open was Ben's, he explained.

"Perhaps we had better look inside," Stiles suggested.

Cederquist led the others into Ben Hayes's office. A potted plant lay on the carpeted floor, the result of a hurried exit, it appeared. Perhaps Ben had been in to look over some paperwork that morning. He often did so, Cederquist explained.

"On the day after his daughter's funeral?" Becker asked.

"I suppose that's possible," Stiles suggested.

"If he knocked this plant over, I guess I can understand him not taking the time to clean up the mess on the floor," Cederquist offered.

"But would he leave the door open?" Stiles countered.

"Not ordinarily," Cederquist answered. "But, he would be distracted. Lord knows he has enough on his mind these days."

"What's that?" Becker asked, as he pointed toward Hayes's desk.

Stiles and Cederquist both looked at the envelope sitting atop the desk, the only thing on the desk, save a penholder and a desk pad.

"It's addressed to you, Marshall," Stiles offered.

"Should I open it?"

"Please."

The note, addressed to Marshall Cederquist, hinted at the fact that Hayes had known for sometime that Trey had been involved with drugs. At first Hayes had suspected only recreational drug use, because he had caught Trey snorting what Hayes thought to be cocaine nearly two years earlier. Within the past few hours, the note explained, Hayes had discovered that Trey was manufacturing some kind of drug in the warehouse on the south end of Cederquist Industries property. Hayes had discovered a crude lab of some kind and was convinced that Trey was heavily involved in the production of something.

Hayes's note rambled on about how he was convinced that Trey was behind Amanda's abduction and, therefore, was responsible for the girl's death. Trey had made comments about Amanda while she was missing, the note said. Ben was convinced Trey knew something.

Still more information followed. Trey was wrongly convinced, Hayes had written, that Ben had appropriated company funds for himself. Hayes denied these allegations and stated that he could prove them false.

Finally, the note had concluded with Hayes's promise to kill Trey Cederquist if he could get Trey to confess to what Ben suspected or if he could find proof enough on his own.

How much more could Marshall Cederquist bear? He stood transfixed by the note. Stiles removed the note from Marshall's grasp and read it intently with Becker standing over Stiles' shoulder, doing the same.

"We must stop him, Lieutenant," came Cederquist's words, finally.

"Stop whom?"

"Stop them both, I suppose," Cederquist answered. "I don't

want Trey to hurt anybody else. But I don't want Ben to kill him. I don't want my son dead, Lieutenant. And I don't want Ben to take Trey's life and pay for it the rest of his own, either."

Becker may not have known it to be true. But Chief of Detectives L. J. Stiles doubted not a word as he returned to the task of locating Trey Cederquist.

"Where could your son be, Marshall?"

"I wish I knew. Believe me."

"We know he's not at his home. We've got people there already. And he's obviously not here. Is there another home? Is there Cederquist property besides this plant that Trey might run to?"

"The only other property we own, besides my house in Florida, is a lake lot out west of Meredosia."

Stiles shot a glance at Becker, who returned the look.

"I'll contact all the airports in the area and the police in Florida," Becker said. Then he turned to Cederquist. "Where is the home in Florida?"

"West Palm Beach. 23 Cecilia."

"Where is this lake lot?" Stiles questioned.

"It's just a little pond, really. We have a cabin up there. The company has picnics up there once in awhile. Trey used to spend a lot of time there when he was a boy."

"Do you think he'd go there, now?"

"Who knows, Lieutenant? I've given up trying to figure Trey out. I do know this, though."

"What's that?"

"I'm damn tired of cleaning up the boy's messes."

TWENTY

Marshall Cederquist, Jr., had spent perhaps ten minutes alone in his office, calming himself, trying to come to grips with the realization that his son was a murderer. He called the policewoman with whom he had left his granddaughter to check up on the child once more. It still remained to tell Melinda that her mother was dead. It somehow did not seem important for Cederquist to think of what he would someday have to tell her about her father.

Next, he unlocked a drawer at the base of his desk, a drawer he had not opened for several months. The gun was still there. Pristine. Right-out-of-the-box-new. Just as it had been for over ten years. He had purchased the .38 for protection, although he could not have said from what or whom. On the advice of friends he had made the purchase. He traveled a lot on business, but rarely had he taken the gun along. For the most part the weapon had remained in the drawer, except for one or two practice shots right after Cederquist had acquired the gun.

Finally, Cederquist wrote a note.

In another room, Lloyd Becker had continued to tighten the ring around Trey Cederquist, confirming search efforts at area airports, the Amtrak station in Springfield, and car rental outlets by passing along Stiles' orders through JPD. Roadblocks were even put into place at several Jacksonville exit points. Area police departments were being notified of Trey's suspected crimes and were given his physical description by phone and fax. Photographs would follow soon.

Meanwhile, Stiles had walked the short distance to the southern edge of the Cederquist Industries property. He desperately wanted to see for himself what he knew he would find there, a meth lab. From the note he and the elder Cederquist had found on Ben Hayes's desk, Stiles had concluded that he was about to find the source of the methamphetamines he and his fellow Jacksonville officers had been trying to uncover for almost three years. Trey Cederquist, Stiles now reasoned, had been the producer of the easily made, high profit drug. That case would soon be closed, Stiles thought, but at what a horrific cost.

The smell presented itself to Stiles as he approached the back door at the building's southeast corner. He recognized it easily, for he had taken more than forty hours of training in meth production. He expected to find what he had been trained to find, right down to the two separate sets of directions, or recipes, one a check list. This was often necessary, for the "cook" often became disoriented during meth production. Inhaling the fumes made it difficult to remember where he was in the recipe's many steps.

Stiles pushed an unlocked door open and stepped inside slowly, gun drawn. There were no cars in proximity to the warehouse. But he had looked through a hole in the chain link fence behind the warehouse before entering the corrugated steel building. Although he had seen nothing but a narrow path leading nowhere, one could not be too careful. Once inside the warehouse, Stiles made a quick survey of the building's interior, finding little that was not boxed up and ready for shipment or newly arrived glassware and metal pots and skillets.

Boxes were stacked high throughout the building, blocking the windows and huge sliding door at the east end. The maze created by the rows of boxes stacked too high for a tall man to see over them was intricate. It seemed as thought the twists and turns of the labyrinth had been designed so. The only open space inside the building, located at the northeast corner was set up like a high school chemistry lab, albeit with second-rate equipment. Beakers and other glass containers were neatly arranged around a stove, several bins and glass jars, containing over-the-counter cold medications, rat killer, lye, and other chemicals which might be used to produce the volatile compounds. It really was quite well organized, an efficient factory for the production of methamphetamines.

By the time Stiles had concluded a cursory journey throughout the building, he returned to its only entry point and found Becker explaining methamphetamines to Marshall Cederquist. Becker, too, had figured out what Trey's little lab was producing, it appeared. If he hadn't figured it out when they were all back inside CI's corporate office, Becker quickly recognized the smell as he and Cederquist approached on foot across the wide expanse of parking lot.

"Very cost effective, Mr. Cederquist," he continued. "There would be no need to ship illegal substances in to this point from some foreign country. Practically no risk. It's all right here. A couple of trips to any of a number of stores we all shop at, drop a few hundred dollars for ingredients and your son had what it would take to make several thousand dollars worth of illegal drugs. Cheaper for him to make. Cheaper for his customers to buy than cocaine. And the buzz lasts far longer. You can smoke it, snort it, eat it, or inject it. Whatever you want."

Cederquist could only shake his head, as he held a handkerchief to his face, protection against the foul smell. This was all too much to comprehend. Too much for him to bear. And right under his nose.

"But how would Trey learn how to make this stuff?" he asked in disbelief.

"I could take you back to your office and get the recipe off the Internet like that," Becker said, snapping his fingers.

Marshall suddenly recalled his insistence years earlier on Trey's taking chemistry courses in college to better prepare him for a career in plastics production at the company he would one day head. In all likelihood Trey would have no need of an Internet recipe, Cederquist surmised.

But Cederquist continued to look for some sense in all this. His son had been producing illegal drugs on CI property. Ben Hayes had evidently known something of Trey's drug involvement.

Perhaps Ben had tried to blackmail Trey, although the likelihood of that was remote, Cederquist concluded. Perhaps he just had threatened to expose Trey, prompting Trey to kidnap Hayes's daughter. It was hard to explain.

Still, Cederquist wanted it to make sense. If a person has to lose everything he stood to lose today, at least, Cederquist figured, it could all make some kind of sense.

"Let's get out of here," Stiles commanded. "This is over our heads. DEA can handle this evidence. It's too dangerous."

Max watched Ben Hayes intently as the latter sped on. They had spotted Trey as he crossed Route 36 at Potter Road and Vasey Lane. They had traveled west, then taken a right onto, first Markham Road, then a left into an S-turn on Perbix Road. Next came a hard right up and over the railroad tracks at Thomason Road, before making a mad dash north, until they turned left onto Route 67.

Max suddenly sensed that Hayes now knew where they and the two they followed were heading. Hayes no longer emoted the same sense of urgency he had earlier in the chase. Max could no longer see the Cederquist vehicle in front of them. It had moved on ahead and out of sight. But Ben made every turn with confidence. He knew he was on the right path, a path that would lead them to Trey Cederquist. Max thought he even detected a hint of a smile on Hayes's face.

Ben had seemed, also, to relax in his attitude toward Max. He had not held the gun on Max since they had jumped into Ben's car and Ben now looked over at Max with less frequency with each passing mile. The gun lay on the seat between them and Max grew, for the moment, less stressful as the pair entered the small river town of Meredosia.

"Where are we going, Hayes?"

"Don't worry, Mr. Jansen. We're almost there."

Max's internal barometer was again on the rise, as he concluded that "there" was where they would find Trey Cederquist, with a gun, and Gary. There was ample reason to worry about catching up to Trey and Gary. At least, Max thought, the guy I'm with has a gun he intends to use on someone else. Max could only guess that Gary could not say the same for Trey Cederquist.

In fact, Max had to force himself to think of Gary as still alive at the very moment.

When Max reached inside his coat for his cellular telephone, Hayes reacted predictably, clutching his pistol and aiming it at Max's head. He did not fully trust Max and, Max assumed now, had been watching him more closely than Max had thought.

"What are you doing?"

"Relax, Mr. Hayes. I'm getting my cell phone. You've got to let me call for help. You don't want to do this on your own. Let the police handle Cederquist. Let's just make sure my friend is all right and then wait for the police. Please, let me call."

Ben was not at all sure he wanted the police to be anywhere near them when he caught up with Trey. He had determined that he would kill Trey himself. He had said so when the two had first begun to follow Cederquist and his latest captive. He waved off the notion of Max's calling anyone initially.

"Mr. Hayes," Max said. "Ben." Max made an attempt at familiarity. "At least let me call Gary's wife. She can contact anyone we decide needs to know about this. I know you want Cederquist. But, right now, I want to do whatever it takes to get Gary out of this mess."

Hayes looked over at Jansen and nodded his approval.

"Soon as we get to the top of this hill here, we're gonna make a turn into that wooded area up ahead. You can make your call then, while I go in after Trey."

"No, Ben. We need to wait for the police to come and handle this."

"Look, you. I'm not gonna do anything that'll get your friend killed if I can help it. If he's still alive," he added. "But I am going to kill that sonofabitch Trey Cederquist myself. I'm gonna look him right in the eye and he's gonna look me in the eye and know it's me killing him."

Max could see tears forming at the corners of Hayes's eyes. Max tried to think of all the arguments one is supposed to use in a situation like this. Don't do it. Think of your wife. She needs you. Don't throw your life away. Let the authorities take care of this.

He did not think any of them would sway Ben and, besides, there was no time to make his case. Hayes was turning right up an inclined gravel drive to a locked gate forty yards off the hard road. Hayes was quickly outside the car and packing his pistol in his belt.

"Make your call now if you want to. I'm going on ahead. Stay here if you want. Follow me if you want. I don't care."

Max decided not to argue the point and went ahead with his call. He had to stop and think of Gary's number before dialing. For the first time, he felt guilty about having involved Gary in this investigation. But he fought off the temptation to wallow in his guilt and placed the call instead.

Three quarters of a mile ahead of Ben Hayes, at the end of the grown-over lane, was Trey Cederquist. As Cederquist had stepped from his car, he surveyed the scene slowly. Desolate, except for a pond and the cabin where days earlier Amanda Hayes had died. Just the way Trey wanted it. He moved to the rear of the car. Nothing stirred perceptibly inside the closed trunk of the car. Trey opened the trunk with his automatic key and had in the other hand the .357 Magnum he had removed from his jacket pocket.

Light flooded the now open trunk and, although no direct sunlight greeted Gary McLean, he squinted as he leaned up on an elbow to see Trey standing outside. Gary could see instantly that Trey had his gun pointed in Gary's direction. Soon he felt its short barrel on his cheek.

"Get out, asshole."

Trey was grabbing Gary by the nape of his neck and pressing

the gun into Gary's face during Gary's clumsy exit. He pushed Gary to the ground, even as Gary's foot first touched the rock-hard ground behind the Lexus.

Inside the trunk a second passenger sat upright in disbelief. Her eyes widened in terror as she looked beyond the trunk's opening to see her husband, bound and gagged, as was she, with rope and duct tape. Gary was lying face down in the dirt. Lisa McLean was shaken with fear that Trey might pull the trigger of the gun he now pointed at the back of Gary's head.

Instead, Cederquist kicked Gary in his left ribs, exposed by Gary's having his arms bound behind his back.

"Sit up, asshole, and get a look at your little lady."

Now, Gary, despite his pain, was sitting up with some unwanted assistance from Cederquist. Trey had a handful of Gary's hair and was directing Gary's attention to the trunk of the car. Sitting inside the trunk was Lisa and the ghastly recognition of his wife and the danger they both now faced was more than Gary could bear. He struggled mightily to stand and free himself from Trey's grasp. He was rewarded for his efforts with a solid blow to the chin with Trey's gun hand.

Gary was barely conscious as his body slammed into the gravel path leading to the cabin. He scratched at the ground with his toes and lost the battle to regain his equilibrium.

"Okay, Mrs. McLean. Out of the trunk," Cederquist commanded.

Lisa tried to kneel inside the trunk. But the lid and her cramped legs made it impossible. Trey moved closer and reached inside the trunk to effect her exit. He would not be gentle. This she had known.

"Come on, goddammit. Hurry."

Trey was worried about Gary's next attempt at escape. But Gary was not yet up to the task. He lay prone on the ground, moving slightly and trying desperately to reorient himself to his surroundings.

Once he had Lisa out of the car's trunk, Trey pushed her to the ground, but away from where Gary lay and was now beginning to roll over. The couple had perhaps ten feet of space between them. Lisa recovered from her spill onto the ground enough to begin to move toward Gary.

"No, no!" Cederquist yelled, moving between them, just enough to force Lisa to retreat from Gary's location and sit quietly on the ground now perhaps fifteen feet from her husband.

Trey had the gun pointing alternately at each of them.

Lisa noticed a second pistol, a smaller one she guessed, strapped to the ankle of their captor. It did not look as menacing as the gun Trey held in his hand. But she worried that either gun would end up doing damage to either or both of them.

Gary was collecting himself now and had assumed a sitting position, his legs outstretched in front of him. He shot a glance in Lisa's direction between checks on Trey and his actions. His eyes were also scanning the lake in front of him, the cabin set atop a hill, to Lisa's right overlooking the lake and the woods in all directions. The trio appeared to be isolated from any immediate assistance. There were no neighboring farmhouses. And the ride in from the hard road Gary had estimated at perhaps a mile or more. If any help were coming, Gary could not have guessed from where it might come.

"Come on, McLean. You're the one who wanted to be so goddamn nosey. Snooping around in my business," Cederquist said, hoisting Gary to his feet. "Well, come on. I'll show you where it all happened."

Cederquist grabbed Gary by his left elbow, pulling him to his feet.

Gary did not know what Cederquist was talking about. But he was in no position to argue. And, so long as Trey talked, he wasn't using the gun. So Gary did what he was told and looked over his shoulder, praying for help, as they moved toward the cabin.

"You, too, missy. Let's go."

Lisa resisted his assistance, but was glad to finally be on her feet. She shot Gary a glance to tell him she was okay and the three of them moved up the hill together.

"Max? Where the hell have you been?"

"Meg? Is that you, babe?"

"Yes. It's me. Now, where are you? Is Gary with you? Is Lisa? I've been worried sick here. Lisa's gone, looking for you guys, I guess. At least, I hope she is. What I don't understand is her car is in the driveway. But she's gone."

"I'm okay, Meg." He hesitated just enough for Meg to guess that there was bad news concerning Gary. When she didn't speak, Max continued.

"Trey's got Gary, Meg."

"What?"

"You gotta call Stiles. Lieutenant Stiles at Jacksonville PD. You call him right now. We're at some wooded area outside Meredosia. We just crossed the Illinois River going south, I think. We took a right onto Route 99 and pulled off the road at the top of the hill on the way to Versailles. Ben Hayes seemed to know this is where we'd be going somehow."

"Ben Hayes? He's with you?"

"Yeah. You might say that. Meg, he says he's going to kill Trey and he has a gun."

"What about Trey?"

"I don't know. I can't imagine Gary'd just go off with that asshole Cederquist if he didn't have some kind of weapon. But I don't know. Just call Stiles and tell him to get his ass out here. And tell him to bring his friends."

"I will. Max, be careful."

Meg looked at her own image in the mirror hanging on the wall of the small bathroom just off the McLean kitchen. She tried to comprehend the enormity of the danger Max and Gary were in. It seemed surreal. Lisa was gone, God-knows-where. Gary had been taken by Trey Cederquist. Max and Ben Hayes were in pursuit.

She did not have time to think of much else. She had to contact Lieutenant Stiles immediately.

Stiles was wrapping the door to the warehouse with yellow crime scene tape when word came over his wireless that he had an urgent phone call from a Meg Watkins. He walked the short distance to his squad car, which had been brought down to the warehouse by one of the many policemen now on the scene at Cederquist Industries.

"What's up," he said tersely when he picked up his car radio.

Meg went into as much detail about the location Max had described for her moments before. She hoped she was remembering it all. But she could not be sure. Stiles listened carefully and wrote down the important details on a small pad of paper.

"Marshall," he yelled while he still had Meg on the line. "Where was that piece of land you were telling me about before? The lake lot you said the company owns?"

"Outside Meredosia."

"Bingo. Ms. Watkins. I think we know where this place is. You sit tight and wait to see if you hear from Mrs. McLean. We'll be in touch."

Turning to Marshall, who approached with a confused look, Stiles commanded, "Get in."

Cederquist was around the front of the squad car quickly and the two sped away, not bothering to tell anyone where they were going. They could do that by radio. In the meantime, lives were hanging in the balance. Stiles wished he knew for sure just how many. This was not a situation over which he had much control. At least he knew that Cederquist could get him to the place where chips were going to fall. Perhaps he would be able to catch a few.

Trey Cederquist removed the duct tape from the mouths of both Gary and Lisa McLean. But he had not been touched by their expression of concern from one another or their assurance to one another that each was all right, despite their plight.

"Go on, McLean," Cederquist said. "Back on down the hall there. The room on the right."

Trey pushed him down the hall, but less violently than before.

"That's it."

Gary looked through an open door to a small room. No bed. Just a chair, carelessly tossed into a corner. What is it he wants me to see, the prisoner wondered.

"That's where your girl died, McLean."

It all sunk in rather quickly with that.

"Yep. Right here. She just dropped dead. The little bitch."

Gary reminded himself that Trey had a gun. He nearly lunged at Trey despite his disadvantage. Had Lisa not been sitting in the other room, her hands still bound like his own, Gary might have done it. Trey had brought him here for no other reason than to show Gary where his friend had perished due to Trey's negligence, his lack of compassion, his careless attitude toward life.

There was some emotion on Trey's part, however. Trey held the gun up, pointed more or less in the direction of Gary. His eyes were moist and his voice broke as he tried to explain Amanda's death. Still, he was not quite in touch with these feelings, as yet. He fluctuated between trying to convince Gary that her death had been an accident and blaming Amanda for her thoughtlessness at being sick when he had plans for her.

"She wasn't supposed to die, goddamnit. Hell, she wasn't even gonna get hurt. Not a scratch, I tell you."

"Then why'd she die?"

Gary had spoken to Trey for the first time.

"How the hell was I supposed to know her goddamn appendix would burst? Isn't that what the police are saying? I didn't make her sick. Shit. I didn't even see her till she was already dead."

Gary looked at him, perplexed.

"Yeah. That's right. She was dead before I even got out here. It wasn't me that grabbed her. It was them," Cederquist ranted. "Hell,

I don't know. Maybe those boys hit her or something. Made her appendix hurt. I'm no doctor. But I didn't lay a hand on her, McLean. You hear me?"

"It's still your fault though. Isn't it?"

"Who the hell are you to say anything's anybody's fault?"

Trey backhanded Gary across the face with his right hand, the hand that held the gun. Gary was hurting from the previous punch. Now, he was really in pain. Blood ran from his nose and lip.

"You just keep your mouth shut, McLean. You don't know anything. You just shut up."

Gary decided he would try not to pass out blame, but felt it was imperative to keep Cederquist talking. He would choose his words carefully. But he would talk. Time was on his side, wasn't it? If he could just keep Trey talking.

"Rawlings? Get the toxicology from the D. E. A. out to Cederquist Industries right away. Ask that they inspect the grounds surrounding the warehouse at the southern edge of the CI property," Stiles said into the mouthpiece of his car's radio unit.

"Ten-four, Lieutenant. I'll get right on it."

Marshall Cederquist was intent on providing directions to Stiles as they sped west in the unmarked Crown Vic.

Stiles could tell that Marshall, Jr. had heard his commands to dispatch and he could see that Cederquist was curious about the need for toxicologists at the warehouse.

"Your son's operation involved some pretty nasty stuff. Chemicals," Stiles began, his concentration divided between road and speedometer. "That whole area will have to be inspected, including the creek that runs past your plant to the south. And any wells in the area."

Cederquist shook his head slightly, his eyes remaining focused on the road ahead of them. The full significance of Trey's actions was quickly sinking in.

"There could be some contamination," Stiles concluded.

Cederquist nodded his understanding.

"There," he blurted out, "you turn left up here, and go through Meredosia."

Max had begun his search for Ben Hayes even before he had hung up the phone, ending his brief conversation with Meg. He saw no sign of Hayes on the path ahead. Max did not believe, however, that Hayes could have advanced too far at his age.

Hayes had, indeed, moved far ahead, oblivious to Max Jansen or the rest of the world, for that matter. His only interest was in pinning Trey down at the cabin and taking his revenge. Perhaps his motivation was winning out over his age and the extra few pounds Ben was carrying.

Ben knew the grounds well enough, he reasoned. He had been there many times over the years. Cederquist employees were often entertained there and were given the chance to fish the waters of the small lake upon request. He could not recall the last time he had been there, perhaps a couple of years or longer. But that was not important. What was important was that he knew where Trey was and was familiar with the layout of the cabin, a definite advantage, he concluded confidently.

His heart raced as he briskly walked the mile and a quarter to the lake. He would have no trouble getting to the cabin undetected, even though the trees were bare of leaves. There would be enough foliage to conceal his approach. Ben also speculated that Trey was too busy to worry about Ben's arrival. To the best of Ben's knowledge, Trey had been unaware of Ben's pursuit and Trey had a hostage to worry about, too.

Ben must have checked his .38 pistol a dozen times as he hustled along the path. Across the water's eastern-most edge Ben could see the cabin. A two-bedroom, log structure, it had a large porch across the entire width of the building's front. Beside the door in the middle of the building's face on either side was a window.

Ben struggled to recall how many windows the sides and back of the structure had. He believed there were more windows on the south side of the cabin, facing him, than on the back of the cabin. Because of the lake's location, Ben would be approaching the cabin from the front-left. He would decide when he got closer if he'd need to change the angle from which he might best attack the cabin.

Max Jansen had climbed the same fence and had covered the same ground over which Ben Hayes had stridden moments earlier. As he followed the pathway leading back to the lake and the cabin, Max struggled with his decision to leave the cellular telephone in the car. Perhaps he would need it later, when he got to wherever Ben was leading him. Wherever Trey was holding Gary.

But Max had not brought the telephone along, fearing that he might be trying to conceal his whereabouts and have the phone suddenly ring. He wondered now if it were possible to turn the ringer off. He had not checked. Turning the thing off might have posed a problem. Then again, turning it on would bring attention to him under circumstances when this might prove disastrous. But it was too late. He was not going to turn back to retrieve the phone now. He had to re-locate Ben Hayes. Max hoped they could survey Gary's predicament and, together, wait for Stiles to arrive.

He was walking very fast, he thought, but could not seem to catch up with the older Hayes. Max was unfamiliar with the location and was hesitant to make up too much ground. He did not want to encounter Trey unless he were somehow put in more control of matters.

Max did not see how that might happen. But one can always hope, he thought. When you're used to only reporting on events, after the fact, and when you're suddenly thrust into a situation involving people you've come to care about and other people have weapons, well . . . well, you just wish you could somehow gain the upper hand in these situations. Of this he was convinced.

Max marveled at his thought processes. The things a man thinks about at a time like this. Max had never before experienced a time like this. All these thoughts going on in his head while his heart raced as never before.

And there was the physical load to which he was subjecting himself. He had known he was out of shape. But this was alarming. Max thought himself foolish to worry about a cell phone betraying his whereabouts. Hell, he reasoned, his pounding heart would give him away.

Suddenly, Max saw Ben Hayes, about a hundred yards ahead and crouched behind some cattails along the side of the lake. Max watched as Ben made his way across the path that Trey had used to drive toward the cabin. They were perhaps five hundred yards short of the cabin's front door and Max watched as Ben began looking to the left and right. He was apparently making decisions about how to approach the cabin with stealth.

Max decided he would maneuver himself in Hayes-like fashion, following the course Ben laid out before him. At the same time, Max knew that he would not be able to follow Ben to the end of this course. Max had no gun and, for that reason, would have to use even more caution in approaching Trey than Ben had been using. Still, Max would have to be in position to do something, whatever that might be, when the time came to act. Now was no time to be wondering if he would have what it would take for him to act. The bets were already down.

"I can't believe how stupid I've been," Stiles ranted. "All this time we've been looking in the country. Farm rental property, places like that."

Cederquist heard Stiles, but was deep in his own thoughts.

"And all this time, Trey is stinking up the area south of your plastics factory with a back yard meth lab."

Cederquist could only shake his head at his own stupidity.

"The little shit was probably calling all the shots. Those two boys from Kentucky that he blew away out in the country," Stiles rambled on, vaguely aware that he was saying things that hurt his passenger deeply. "He had them stealing anhydrous ammonia tanks while he's out buying lithium batteries here and there. All the glass beakers and rubber hoses back in the warehouse?"

"Yes," Cederquist said, on cue.

"All part of his operation. Make it. Ship it. And count the money."

"You forgot using," Marshall added.

"You think?"

"I know it, Stiles. I know it now," Cederquist said. "I see all the signs now."

"That's no excuse."

Marshall looked sternly at the policeman.

"I'm not making excuses, Lieutenant."

The look they exchanged lasted for a moment, Stiles breaking it, for fear he might lose control of his car. When Cederquist was sure Stiles was in the proper lane, he continued.

"I'm just saying that my son's decision making might well be somehow explainable."

"Paranoia?"

"Yes."

"Irritability."

"Yes, I guess so," Cederquist asserted. "He's a user, then."

"A tweaker."

"What?"

"A tweaker. Meth user, operating on no sleep, sometimes for several days at a time. That's when he can really get cranky. Violent."

Stiles let it sink in.

"He's dangerous, Marshall. I know that much."

Soon the pair arrived at the gate defending the lakeside cabin from civilization.

Stiles pulled into the lane, parking directly behind Ben Hayes's auto and looked across the front seat at Marshall Cederquist, Jr.

"So, this is it?"

"That's right, Lieutenant. Beyond the gate the road leads through those trees down to a lake and around the water on its eastern finger, up a hill to the cabin I mentioned. That must be where Trey is."

"And he has Gary McLean with him."

"Yes. And it would appear that Ben is here, too."

Stiles emerged from the cruiser and ambled toward Hayes's empty vehicle. He glanced inside and saw several loose cartridges lying on the seat between the driver and passenger. He shook his head and became increasingly aware of just how out of control the situation had become.

Stiles surveyed the setting before returning to the car. He rounded the car and went to the trunk. From the trunk he extracted a rifle and shells, which he stuffed into his lightweight jacket. He checked the Velcro on his bulletproof vest and reached inside the car for another vest.

"Here, Marshall. Put this on."

Stiles tossed the vest to Cederquist, who struggled to put it on and catch up with Stiles. Stiles was already across the fence and backing away.

"Is there a back way out of here, Marshall?"

"The whole four hundred, eighty acres is fenced in. But you could drive through the fence. Still, the back edge of the property is thickly wooded. I don't think anyone's going out except back this way."

"Remember, Marshall. You're showing me the way in and then you're staying out of sight. I may even ask you to return to the car. And, Marshall, if I tell you to, do it."

Cederquist did not respond. But, as Stiles again checked his weapons, Cederquist checked the inside pocket of his blazer, which he had pulled back over the kevlar vest Stiles had given him. The gun he had taken from his desk drawer was there. As Stiles scoured the immediate surroundings for a sign of anything, Cederquist switched the gun's position, tucking it inside his belt at the small of his back. He wondered, as he did so, if he could actually use it if the time came. He was determined to stop his son. But if it came to doing so with a gun, could he?

TWENTY-ONE

Inside the cabin, Trey forced Gary McLean into a chair in the middle of the front room. Gary's hands were still bound tightly behind him, palms outward. His shoulders ached and his face, having by now taken several blows from Trey, was swollen badly. He could not see clearly from his left eye.

Cederquist next led McLean's wife down the hall, pushing her inside the bedroom at the northwest corner of the cabin. Inside the room in which Amanda Hayes had been held captive and died, Trey pushed Lisa hard against the wall and suddenly spun a chair, the room's lone piece of furniture, toward Lisa and demanded she sit in it.

Gary listened intently from the front room, weighing his options as he tried desperately to hear what was taking place down the hall. Soon, too soon Gary convinced himself for Trey to have hurt Lisa, Trey returned and took inventory of the room. Gary was now confident that, for the time being, his wife was safe and he was free to take stock of his surroundings.

On one wall of the cabin's front room, Gary could see a picture. A young Trey Cederquist, smiling proudly as he held a fish aloft for the camera to capture and record. A younger Marshall Cederquist than Gary ever remembered seeing stood to the side, barely in the frame but beaming his own pride at the sight. Such a contrast thought Gary, between then and now.

"What are you looking at?" Trey asked, suddenly aware that the picture held some interest for Gary.

Gary did not respond.

"That's me and the old man, there. I was probably," he thought for a second, standing directly in front of the picture, "ten years old. Caught that fish right down the hill there."

"What happened to that kid in the picture?" Gary asked, wondering if he should be so bold. He thought constantly of his wife at the rear of the cabin.

"What do you mean? That's me, dipshit. It's me. I'm here. I'm what happened."

"You don't look anything like that kid in the picture."

Trey was puzzled, at first. He wasn't thinking on the same level as Gary until, finally, he looked Gary square in the eye.

"Oh, I get it. You're being cute, huh?"

"That kid's happy. You don't strike me as being all that happy, Trey."

"Look, McLean. Don't try that psychobabble bullshit with me. I don't give a shit what you think. About me or my old man. Anything."

"Your dad seems alright to me, Trey."

Trey looked at McLean in disbelief.

"What do you know about my old man? You don't know shit."

Trey's eyes were wide and bloodshot. His hair, usually neatly trimmed and always combed, was shaggy and in need of a good washing. Trey's clothes, too, were wrinkled and stained. And Trey lacked the bravado that he normally displayed.

He was pacing now. Back and forth in front of a seated Gary McLean he crossed. Trey had been reflecting on Gary and others like him who had thought they knew him. He had encountered them for as long as he could remember. Jealous people. Small-minded people, who gave Trey an excuse to hate them.

"You think because my old man has money that everything was perfect, huh? Well, you don't know shit."

"You keep saying that."

"You think because we have money we're snobs. Or maybe you think you're better than me. Is that it? You ain't any better than me, McLean. You and your college degree. So what? I didn't finish college. So what?"

Neither man spoke for several seconds.

Trey's gun, always a presence, was a pistol. Gary did not know what kind. He knew little about guns. Only that they scared him. He found it difficult to look at the one pointing at him now.

Gary, sensing the end of their conversation, took the initiative and began to once again busy Cederquist with talk. Trey, Gary thought, isn't capable of logical thought right now or of meaningful dialogue. But that didn't matter in the least. He just needed to keep Trey talking.

"Why are you doing this, Trey?"

"Doing what?"

"Why do you have me here? Why did you abduct Amanda?"

"Amanda? What do you care about Amanda?"

He pronounced her name with such hatred. Gary could not imagine what Amanda had done to Trey that caused this hatred. But it was real. Gary countered with his own view of Amanda.

"I liked her. She was a great kid," Gary said.

"You have a thing for her, McLean? Is that it? I bet your wife there would love to hear about that. Did you have a thing with her?"

"Of course not."

"I did," Trey said, a wicked smile across his face.

Gary could not believe Trey had put it to him that way. He was sure he did not want to hear anymore about Trey's conquest of Amanda. He had all the facts he wanted about that episode from Lisa's rendition of Amanda's journal entries. But he was not exactly in a position to demand that they change the subject. Just keep him talking, Gary continued to tell himself. Maybe Lisa could escape if Gary bought some time. Maybe they could both survive somehow.

"You didn't know that. Did you?"

Trey was enjoying the exchange now. He circled Gary, who watched pensively.

"Nope," Trey continued. "She didn't tell anybody about ol' Trey. She knew better."

"You're sick."

"Shut up!" Trey shouted and again he flashed the gun in Gary's face.

Trey was breathing heavily, consumed by the memory of exercising such power, such dominance over the young girl.

"She came to the plant one day, looking for her daddy. Well, he wasn't there that day. But I told her he was. She came right on into the office there, and I sat her down on the couch in her daddy's office and we did it."

Gary bit his tongue, the gun Trey held in his hand and Lisa's presence in the other room the only things preventing Gary from attacking, bound hands or no.

"Well," Trey continued with an evil grin, "I did it."

"I don't want to hear this."

"Well, now, McLean. I thought I had already established the fact here that I don't give a shit what you want." Cederquist angrily emphasized the final words.

Trey stood over Gary, now, jamming the muzzle of his gun in Gary's neck.

"You just shut up and listen."

"I refuse to listen to this."

"McLean, you are in no position to refuse anything," Trey said, as he waved the gun wildly in the air and backed away from Gary.

Trey smiled at remembering the details. He would enjoyed recounting them for his audience of one.

"I kept her panties when I was done. I'd ripped them off her and did my thing. But I wouldn't let her have 'em back," he said, reflecting. "I think that hurt her as much as me screwing her."

Gary imagined how Amanda must have felt at Trey's violation of her body, his subjugation of her.

"I loved it," Trey added, shaking his head as he smiled the smile Gary recognized from the picture on the wall.

"You sonofabitch," Gary responded.

The back of Trey's hand, the one which firmly gripped one of his two pistols inside it, came quickly across Gary's face. Gary fell hard to the floor, blood flowing again from his nose and a new, gaping cut on his cheek now spilling forth.

Just outside, below an open window, Ben Hayes crouched with his shoulder and hip against the cabin's south wall. He clutched his pistol more tightly, as he bit his lip hard and prepared to act.

Her hands still bound behind her back and mouth again duct taped to prevent her cries for help, Lisa sat in the chair Trey had demanded she sit in. It was the same chair in which Amanda had been bound, in which she had died. She was very happy that Trey had not decided to bind her to the chair. But she did not wish to remain in the chair any longer than necessary. Trey had departed for the front room, leaving her alone to contemplate a means for her escape.

Lisa worried about Gary in the front room with Trey, who could actually be a killer. She knew that Gary would want her to do everything she could to get out of the cabin and away from Trey. Her husband had told her so in the glance he had shot in her direction when they were still outside the rustic cabin. She had to get out and go for help.

There was a window, locked she could see, on the north wall, opposite the room's only door. When she stood, she could look out the window at trees, perhaps a hundred yards away in each direction. It appeared to Lisa that the ground outside the window fell away toward the west, just as she had noticed it sloped away toward the lake on the south side of the cabin. The lower ground to the west, however, was dry and she suspected that there might be a dam somewhere in that general direction backing up water to form the lake on the cabin's opposite side.

Overall, Lisa got the impression that the cabin's window was quite high above the ground outside it. A jump or a fall from the window from such a height, of perhaps eight feet or more, could hurt. But no other option existed. She had to go out this window for help and sooner was better than later. If Gary could manage to keep Trey occupied, perhaps she would have time. First, she must unlock the window.

She pulled the chair across the hardwood floor with her foot, dragging the chair as quietly as possible. She turned the chair, so that the back rested against the windowsill. She was able to climb atop the seat. It had been easier than she had imagined it might be to place one foot in the middle of the seat to prevent its tipping and hopping up quickly with the other foot. The chair creaked under her weight and she stopped for an instant, careful not to make more noise and risk alerting her captor.

She carefully turned her back to the window and reached upwards for the lock, an older, ear-shaped mechanism atop the lower window casement, that pivoted beneath a phalange attached to the upper window piece to lock the two in the closed position. The lock was tight. But she was finally able to move the metal handle counterclockwise after a couple of tries. She stepped off the chair, again careful to remain as close to silent as possible.

She removed the chair, this time grasping the round wooden back with her fingers and pulling it across the floor. She backed herself to the window's jamb and clasped the cutout on the bottom of the window's frame with her fingertips. She pulled upward with all her strength. But the window would not budge.

"Damn it," Lisa whispered.

It's painted shut, she thought to herself, as she turned around to inspect the window's casing.

Max Jansen watched from a short distance, perhaps thirty yards, as Ben Hayes had crept around the corner, stepped up onto the front porch and made his way to the front door of the cabin. Max was unable to speak or otherwise call for Ben's attention, not that it would have mattered. Max had not heard Trey's boasting. But he sensed from watching Ben's approach to the door that no one could have stopped Ben from walking into the cabin.

All Max could do was continue to follow Ben's move. Just as he had done a dozen times over the past several minutes, replacing Ben's former position each time Ben moved ahead to a new one. This meant Max had to sprint toward the cabin and position himself in front of the east, front wall, where he could better observe the events that were intensifying with each passing second.

Max was again coming to realize that, with each new location, each recurrence of Ben departing and Max filling Ben's newly created void, Max was becoming more a part of the story he knew was about to unfold. It was closer than he had been to a story before and closer than he had ever intended. But a friend had never before been held hostage at gunpoint, either.

Ben Hayes entered the open door to the cabin to see Trey Cederquist standing over Gary, taunting him and yelling for Gary to get to his feet. Trey's back was to the door and to Ben. As Trey raised his hand again, preparing to slam the butt of the pistol's handle onto Gary's skull, Ben shouted for Trey to stop.

Trey turned awkwardly to find Ben standing in the doorway, pistol aimed at Trey's heart.

"Throw down the gun, Trey."

Trey glared at Hayes defiantly.

"Throw down the gun," Ben said, enunciating each word numbly.

Still Trey held the gun, aiming at the ceiling.

"I'll do it, Trey. I swear I will. I'll shoot," Ben said, his confidence growing.

Finally, Trey slowly lowered the pistol and, bending slightly at the waist, dropped the pistol onto the floor. He stood erect and raised both hands to shoulder level.

Gary was finally becoming aware of Ben's presence and struggled to regain his feet. His eyes were watery and he could feel the thick blood caked about his face. His vision was blurred but becoming clearer.

"Mr. Hayes. What are you doing here?"

"I've come to claim what's mine, what belongs to me."

"Yours?" Gary asked.

"The life of this scum," he said, pointing at Trey Cederquist with his pistol. "I've come to kill Trey."

"You don't have the guts, Hayes," Trey said.

"Ben, you can't. You can't take the law—" Gary began to say.

"Take the law into my own hands," Ben interrupted. "Yeah, I know all about that. But this is something I have to do, McLean."

"Ben, you can't. Think of your wife. She needs you. You'd be of no good to her in jail. It's not worth it, Ben. Let the law deal with him."

As Ben Hayes shook his head and continued to keep Cederquist in his sights, Gary stood finally and positioned himself very nearly directly between the adversaries. He could fully understand what Hayes was feeling. Indeed, he was feeling his own rage. But he was convinced that Trey should be handled by the authorities and not by Ben Hayes.

At the moment Gary stepped between the two men, Trey reached down to the ankle of his right leg, pulled his cuff up and retrieved a second weapon, this one a smaller pistol but large enough to do the damage Trey intended. Over Gary's right shoulder, Trey fired a single shot, striking Ben Hayes in his right shoulder.

Ben's gun fell to the floor as Ben stumbled backward, slamming against the open door, pushing it further open. He slid down the door's length to the floor. Blood ran down his chest beneath his shirt and a burning pain radiated down his arm and across his back.

The concussion from the blast pounded in Gary's head. No other sound registered in his right ear. His teeth hurt. Once again McLean was struggling to regain his equilibrium. When he realized that Ben had been shot, he rushed to his side.

"Hold it. Right there."

Trey again hit Gary, this time on the back of his head with the butt of the smaller pistol's handle.

Trey was again in control.

The blast from inside the cabin came just as Max Jansen was preparing to move toward a corner at the front of the building. He was considering a step up onto the porch when the shot altered his plans.

Max found himself, instead, beneath the front porch of the cabin, having dove under the two-by-six framing of the porch's structure. He scrambled to see through the cracks between the floorboards of the porch. Lying on his stomach, twisting his torso, straining to look, first, above, then to the left and the right, Max was helpless. He had trapped himself.

That is, if Trey had fired the shot.

Could it have been Gary, or Ben Hayes, who had fired at Trey? Had there been more than one shot? Max could not be sure.

Lisa had spent the past several minutes pushing on the window's casing, trying to separate the casing from the frame. When she heard the shot, she fought the inclination to panic. It was time to pull this window from its seat and effect her escape. If Trey had shot Gary, he'd need help fast. And Trey might be coming for her. If something else had happened, a little noise couldn't hurt.

She pulled mightily, praying the window would free itself without report, just in case. Her fingertips, clutching the carved out handle, slipped a few times as she pulled upward. But, finally, the window dislodged and slid with some reluctance toward the header. Lisa swung one leg over the open window's sill, bowed at the waist to swing her head and shoulders beneath the window. She took a deep breath and pushed herself out the window toward the ground below.

Lisa hit the ground and rolled. Her shoulders ached as she

tried quickly to recover and hustle back toward the cabin's western face. She was afraid Trey might look out a window and see her. She moved uphill along the back of the structure, around the corner and toward the front of the building and another window, the one she had noticed earlier at the south end of the living room.

The ground rose to a point that allowed her to peek through the corner of the window. Over the shoulder of Trey Cederquist she could see her husband. He was alive. He stood and had apparently not been Trey's target. She was overjoyed at the sight of Gary, alive and well.

She was also quite sure Gary had seen her through the window. She saw it in his expression, the glimmer of recognition in her husband's face. There was only one problem. Trey Cederquist, too, had seen the recognition in Gary's expression.

Lisa ran toward the back of the cabin again, as fast as possible. Trey had turned quickly and ran to the window. Lisa could hear him struggling with the window as she rounded the corner at the back edge of the cabin, imagining that Trey now had his head and shoulders outside the window, looking for whatever had caught Gary's eye.

He saw nothing.

The sound of the gunshot from the cabin's interior had quickened the pace of L.J. Stiles and his guide, Marshall Cederquist, Jr. The two had stayed on the road until the cabin came into view, when both men had begun to use the natural cover of the landscape to conceal their approach.

When they heard the blast, neither man spoke. Nor did they take the time to look at one another. They simply double-timed it across the ground between where they were when the gun fired and the cabin, which lay ahead and to their left, as they circumnavigated the eastern tip of the lake's finger. Stiles moved ahead of the older man and motioned with his free arm to stay back. But Marshall kept coming.

Cederquist had moved to the opposite side of the overgrown road, to the outside of the arc created by the curve of the road around the lake. Stiles was on the inner arc, among the reeds and cattails at the lake's edge. Both men fixed their gazes on the cabin as they approached, wondering who may have suffered injury or worse as a result of the gunshot.

Stiles checked his vest and hoped that Cederquist was doing the same. Better yet, he hoped that Marshall had heeded his command to stay far behind, safe. He knew better, however. Marshall was moving now, fanning across the path of and to the left of Stiles. He was moving ahead.

Ben Hayes had rolled onto his left side with some assistance from Gary McLean, while Trey retrieved his discarded pistol and Ben's gun from the floor of the cabin. Suddenly Trey became aware that something had moved outside the cabin's door. He again hammered the back of Gary's head with the pistol's handle. Next he stepped into the doorway and looked in each direction. When he stepped out onto the porch, he stood directly above Max Jansen, who still lay on the ground beneath the porch.

Max lay still, believing himself to be, as yet, undetected. He tried to look out across the open space he had followed Ben Hayes through moments earlier. Beneath Trey Cederquist's Lexus, twenty to twenty-five feet from the front edge of the porch, he saw two feet, one planted firmly on the ground, the other toed into the ground behind a bent knee.

Max surveyed the rest of the area, this time looking toward the lake, moving only his eyes within their orbits. He did not wish to move, to even rotate his neck, for fear of alerting Trey to his presence.

Trey Cederquist saw nothing alarming as he looked out across the open yard, flanked on his left by woods and the right by the lake. From his elevated position on the porch, he did not see his father crouching behind the Lexus, in which he had driven the McLeans to the secluded lakeside. He turned to reenter the cabin, looking for signs of life from Ben Hayes and consciousness from Gary.

"Trey."

The younger Cederquist heard the unmistakable voice of his father and turned the one hundred, eighty degrees and pointed the pistol in his left hand toward the direction of the voice.

Marshall Cederquist, Jr., stood now a few steps away from the vehicle behind which he had initially hidden himself. He was in plain view of his son on the porch, of Max Jansen who lay beneath that porch and of Lieutenant L.J. Stiles from his covert position in the plant life at the shore of the lake.

"Dad. What the hell are you doing here?"

"Trey, who fired the gun?"

Still pointing the gun in his left hand at his father, he looked at the gun in his right. It was the one he had fired into Ben Hayes's shoulder moments before.

"I did, Dad. I fired the gun. I shot your international sales director, Dad."

The older Cederquist grimaced, imagining the additional pain his son was inflicting on the Hayes family.

"That's right. Ben's in here."

Without looking away from his father, Trey addressed Ben who lay motionless inside the doorway, "What do you say, Ben? You alive?"

There was no answer.

Trey, shrugging, continued, "Well, I guess not, Dad. Guess you'll have to find yourself another man."

"Trey, stop this. Stop it now."

"Just what the hell is your problem?" Trey asked, dropping both hands to waist level, his arms extended. "I asked you before. What are you doing here, anyway?"

"Just trying to clean up another one of your messes, son. Just one more mess."

Lisa now moved slowly away along the south side of the cabin, the lake's side, toward the front of the cabin, ducking below window openings at the rear and at the midpoint in the structure.

Stiles, hidden to all, entered the water at the lake's edge. Standing in thigh-deep water, he had seen Lisa as she turned the corner at the cabin's rear and began slinking her way toward the confrontation out front. He could only hope that she might return to the back of the cabin and stay safely out of the way.

Stiles searched his mind, concentrating on how he might gain more control of this entire situation. He watched a confusing scene grow more troublesome with each new development. Trey Cederquist stood on the porch a gun in each hand. Beneath him lay Max Jansen, prone and obviously frightened. Before the younger Cederquist stood his father, dangerously exposed to his son's whim and wrath. Moving closer to the volatile situation was Lisa McLean. And then there was Gary McLean and Ben Hayes, inside the cabin, exact whereabouts unknown, conditions also a mystery.

A single shot had been fired inside the cabin. Who had been shot? Not Trey. Gary? Ben Hayes? Stiles had to concentrate, he told himself, on what he did know. He could not move his position relative to Trey without giving it away. But, as Lisa McLean moved toward the front of the cabin, she got dangerously close to the line of fire between Stiles and the younger Cederquist on the porch.

Stop! he wanted to scream.

"Yeah. Well, I didn't ask you to clean up any of my messes," Trey replied, sarcastically. "So, just get the hell on outta here. Mr. McLean and I got some business to settle."

"I'm not going to let you kill anyone else, Trey. Do you even know that Vicki is dead? And the police say you killed those two men out on some country road."

The father struggled to convince the son to let him check on Ben Hayes's condition, hoping to stop the flow of blood he imagined might be running away with Ben's life.

"Ben may still be alive, Trey. Let him go and the other young man, too."

"You just shut up, old man," Trey yelled.

Trey stepped closer to the edge of the porch, pointing his gun once again at his father. The two men stood now fifteen feet apart, as the older Cederquist had been taking several small steps toward his son as they spoke.

Suddenly the barn-like siding against which Lisa leaned on the cabin's south outer wall cracked. She was sure that Trey Cederquist had heard the noise. Lisa bolted, running toward the lake and directly into the path down which Stiles was intending to send two bullets from his .38 toward Trey Cederquist.

But Stiles couldn't shoot, for fear of hitting Lisa.

"Stop! Stop, right there."

It was Trey's voice. Lisa knew she had been spotted and she stopped as Trey had commanded. She stood there, facing the lake, her hands bound behind her and sure that Trey Cederquist was about to shoot her in the back. She fought for the composure to pray and lost.

Trey, indeed, was looking down the barrel of his .357 Magnum at Lisa's back.

Stiles had no choice. Hoping to shock Trey into moving, perhaps exposing himself to a shot to either the right or the left of Lisa McLean, Stiles yelled as loudly and clearly as he could.

"Police!"

Trey responded, pointing his other pistol in the general direction of the voice. He could not see Stiles, however. Stiles, hidden waist deep in the lake water, prepared to aim his gun at Trey Cederquist's heart.

"Throw down your weapons, now," came the second command from Stiles.

"Do as he says, Trey," the elder Cederquist pleaded.

Stiles repeated his second command.

Trey's mouth tightened, as he quickly raised his pistol in the right hand and fired a single shot in the direction of Stiles' voice. Lisa dove headlong down the hill and rolled on the ground toward the lake.

Simultaneously a bullet entered Trey's upper torso at the left side. Trey dropped the weapon and collapsed, first, to his knees, then heaving forward to the point where he flipped over the edge of the porch and crashed to the ground below.

Standing directly in front of the cabin, Marshall Cederquist held his gun, arm fully extended, smoke wafting from the gun's barrel.

Stiles had not fired his weapon. He marched up the hill, gun constantly aimed at the younger Cederquist, who now barely moved. Lisa regained her feet and ran behind him, looking to the front door of the cabin, where her husband emerged. Gary looked relieved and told her before she reached the porch that Ben Hayes was in need of medical attention.

Max Jansen, meanwhile, lay on the ground beneath the porch, face to face with Trey Cederquist. He looked into Trey's eyes. Max could see that Trey still clutched a pistol in his left hand. Max could not tell nor did he particularly care if Trey Cederquist were surprised to see him there. When Trey began to move slightly, Max reached out and clutched the left hand. The resistance caused by Max's reach was enough to prevent Trey from pulling the gun away and using it.

Stiles was wet up to his ribs now and he dripped water as he approached the pair. Max was by now somewhat exposed from beneath the porch. Stiles stepped on Trey's left wrist and told Max to disarm Cederquist.

"You okay?" Stiles asked.

"How the hell would I know?" Max replied.

TWENTY-TWO

Max moved quickly between two separate dramas now unfolding, one inside the cabin, the other near the edge of the porch under which he had found safety only twenty minutes earlier. Lisa, with some assistance from her dazed husband, attended to Ben Hayes's wound. Ben, surprisingly, was conscious, even alert.

Max cautioned Gary, urging him to sit down. He could see that Gary had been badly beaten by Trey Cederquist before the shooting had started and Gary was reporting that his ears were ringing. He could hear nothing in his right ear. Gary, however, was not to be swayed and insisted on helping Lisa tend to a bleeding Ben Hayes.

As Max returned to the scene outside, he heard Stiles who knelt beside the wounded Trey Cederquist.

"You have the right to remain silent," Stiles began, after alerting authorities, both state and local.

Understandably, Stiles did not want anything Trey might say now to be thrown out of court, should he live to stand trial for his crimes. And Trey, it appeared, was trying to speak. His father, as Stiles had instructed, held a compress on Trey's wound, slowing the flow of blood from his son's chest.

Max's initial reaction to hearing Stiles "Mirandize" the younger Cederquist was harsh. You have the right to just go ahead and die, you sonofabitch, Max thought. A new Max, altered somehow forever by what he had witnessed, what he had become a part of on this day, smiled at the prospect of the old Max, who, it seemed, would continue to make an occasional cameo.

Perhaps Max would never completely change. But, on this

day, Max was quick to re-think his attitude toward Trey Cederquist and suppress his old tendencies. He would leave unsaid what previously would have been allowed to gush forth at the expense of any and all. Certainly the old Max would not have held back from verbally pancaking a drug-trafficking, murdering slug like Trey Cederquist.

Perhaps it was the respect he felt for the elder Cederquist that contributed to Max's reassessment of the situation. What does it say about a man who can care enough about right and wrong that he is able to put a bullet into his own son and then, minutes later, tend to his wounds with such compassion? Max reflected on this as he surveyed the scene.

Stiles had finished reviewing Trey's rights. Next he used the cellular phone inside Trey's Lexus to call for medical assistance and to notify authorities back in Jacksonville of the shootings. He handed Max the phone.

"Dial 911 and ask the dispatcher to hook you up with the paramedics on their way to this location," Stiles told Max. "Then take the phone inside so Mrs. McLean can report to them on Ben's condition."

All but Gary, and perhaps Trey, could hear approaching sirens. Policemen and paramedics from the surrounding area were finding a logjam at the gate to the property. Ben's Lincoln Towncar and Stiles' Crown Victoria were parked in front of a locked gate. A state trooper had decided to cut the fence to the left of the gates and simply re-route two ambulances and several police units around the obstacles.

As Lisa spoke via the phone with paramedics she would soon see face-to-face, Max again watched Marshall Cederquist. Max would probably never go so far as to suggest he felt sorry for Trey Cederquist. But he most certainly recognized a true sadness in Marshall. He saw clearly the regret with which Marshall was overwhelmed and not just regret over the day's events. No, this was, Max suspected, regret for a lifetime—Trey's lifetime.

Who's to say, Max thought, that if I really put my mind to it,

I couldn't capture that emotion in words, write a story of a father, a son and the flood of emotions that Marshall Cederquist must certainly be experiencing right now?

Max was suddenly aware that policemen and emergency medical technicians were everywhere. Working in teams, paramedics tended to both Trey Cederquist and Ben Hayes. Lisa had done a good job of caring for Ben until help arrived, slowing the flow of blood from Ben's shoulder and preventing the onset of shock. Max had overheard one of the techs say so. He was proud of Lisa and was sure Gary would be, too, had it not been for his own injuries. Lisa was now looking for another EMT to care for her husband as he watched the team load Ben into the back of one of the two ambulances. Soon the McLean's made their way toward the same ambulance and joined Ben for the ride into Jacksonville and Passavant Area Hospital.

As they did so, Max retrieved the phone. In seconds, Max had Meg on the other end and waved good-bye to Lisa as the ambulance moved away. Max explained to Meg all that had taken place. He watched closely as the second emergency team continued working on Trey Cederquist. Soon Max was telling Meg that the team had Cederquist on a gurney and was strapping him in tightly. Next Max was asking Meg to wait while he told Stiles that he would see that Marshall got to the hospital. They'd take Ben's car, he explained. Max had taken Ben's keys as they pulled him across the porch toward the ambulance. He concluded his call to Meg when he told her he would see her soon at Passavant.

Stiles was inside the back of the ambulance quickly. He wasn't about to let Trey Cederquist out of his sight at this point. A paramedic told Trey's father that they had been able to stabilize Trey and surgery was anticipated. Then the ambulance arced its way back around to the southern shore of the small lake and Max was left to walk back toward the road to Ben's car.

Marshall said he would walk along with Max, but suddenly balked for an instant. He looked questioningly at Max. Perhaps Cederquist had suddenly remembered that Max Jansen was a reporter. Did he suspect Max's intentions were less that honorable, Max wondered? Cederquist was probably worried that Max might simply be working on a story, angling for a comment from a father who'd just shot his son and watched an emergency crew take him to the hospital and an uncertain fate.

"Don't worry, Mr. Cederquist. There's a story here and I'm sure I'm going to write it. But you don't have to worry about saying something on the record. I'll only do this story with your assistance, if you're game. And we won't begin working on it today."

Marshall nodded.

"You got anyone you want to call?" Max asked, offering the phone.

"Yes, I do. Thanks."

As the two walked back toward the road, Marshall contacted Stu Murphy and gave his old friend the story in an abridged form. In the end, Stu got two assignments, in addition to meeting Marshall at the hospital.

"If Trey survives, he's going to need legal counsel, Stu. Make your contacts and get the best man you can find. I trust your judgement on this. Next, get started right away on getting me custody of Melinda. Vicki's gone now. Her parents are both deceased, so I don't think this should be a problem. But I need you to take care of that, Stu. I want a second chance here. I won't make the same mistakes I made with Trey."

The first ambulance, carrying Ben Hayes and the McLean's, arrived to not only emergency room personnel but also Margot Hayes and Meg Watkins. Once the ambulance had hit the road with the EMT's and Trey Cederquist, Stiles made sure an officer was on his way to the Hayes home and to chauffeur Margot to the hospital.

Meg, too, arrived at the hospital with the twins in tow. She immediately contacted a social worker's office, asking for help with the kids while they all waited for their parents' arrival. She watched

Margot Hayes anxiously and said a silent prayer that Margot would not lose her husband to Trey Cederquist as she had her daughter.

Max could see doctors tending to Gary in one emergency room, Lisa at his bedside, and across the hall the Hayes couple, Ben on his back with Margot now at his side. His hand was firmly surrounded by her own prayerful hands.

News came first that Trey was going right into surgery with an uncertain prognosis. Meg looked for some visible reaction from Max and was surprised at his lack of expression. Max finally smiled broadly, however, when they were told that Ben was also on his way to surgery, but with a much brighter outlook on the part of doctors attending to him.

"He'll be fine," a nurse said with a wink.

"Good. Thank you," Max Jansen responded.

Margot Hayes followed Ben's gurney to the operating room corridor and stood silently as the doors closed thirty feet ahead of her. Stiles appeared suddenly at the intersection of hallways, having followed Trey Cederquist into surgery behind another door. Max and Meg, too, stood in the hallway, near the door to a waiting room for family and friends of surgical patients. All eventually entered the waiting room and filled the next hour or so, alternately with anxious conversation and nervous silence.

Word finally came that Ben Hayes would, indeed, survive and probably make a full recovery. The bullet he had taken had missed all vital organs and two doctors had removed it without difficulty. They now explained to Margot that they would have to watch carefully for signs of infection, but were very optimistic. Meg could sense the relief in everyone assembled, including Max Jansen.

Marshall Cederquist had arrived with Stu Murphy just when doctors were giving Margot the good news. He approached Margot as soon as the doctors had left and the two spoke softly, Marshall taking Margot's hand briefly as he told her how terribly sorry he was. Sorry that Ben had been injured. Sorry that Amanda had died. Sorry that his own son had played a role in each event.

Margot listened politely before gently pulling her hand away. She was careful not to give Marshall the impression that she was angry. She wanted Marshall to know that she was truly grateful that her husband was going to be alright and that she had come to learn of Marshall's role in stopping Trey before he could continue hurting Ben and the others. She imagined, rightly, that this had not been an easy thing for Marshall to do.

"Thank you, Marshall. Thank you for giving me my husband back."

Margot left the waiting room and moved toward the recovery rooms down the hall and to the left.

Twenty minutes later a third doctor arrived and informed Marshall Cederquist, his lawyer, and Chief of Detectives L.J. Stiles that Trey, too, would very likely live. His surgery had gone well enough. But there would be a long road to recovery. All three men thanked the doctor and stood awkwardly in a huddle before Stiles excused himself. He walked slowly out of the waiting room and approached a pay phone near the nurses' station. He fumbled briefly with change in his pocket before giving up the cause and reaching instead for his calling card.

Marshall Cederquist, Jr. and Stu Murphy were left to stare blankly out a window at the parking lot below. Stu placed a hand on Marshall's shoulder, as Cederquist finally gave in to the tears which came quietly, but abundantly.

Watching all of this were Max Jansen and Meg Watkins. Arm in arm the two crept away, leaving Cederquist and Murphy with their privacy. The two lovers moved down the hall past Stiles, who could be heard speaking on the phone with one or both daughters, hundreds of miles away.

"I'm fine, girls. I just wanted to hear your voices."

Stiles smiled as Max and Meg moved past him.

"Maybe I can come down there and see you in a couple of days. What do you think?"

As Max and Meg walked past the nurses' station, they had only to look to their left to see Margot Hayes, standing outside her husband's recovery room, or to their right, where Lisa McLean awaited Gary's arrival from an examination.

Margot stood, transfixed on the door to Ben's recovery room, waiting to hear that it was okay to enter. Max watched her with a mixture of happiness and sadness that Meg had not tuned in to. She was looking at Lisa. Meg tugged at Max's arm, pulling him round to see Gary emerge from the examination room and fall into Lisa's arms. It was as though Gary was placing his good ear next to Lisa's beating heart, finding comfort in what he heard there. Max was the first to speak.

"At least Gary and Lisa have each other," he said. With more reflection, he continued. "And Marshall's going to be there for his little granddaughter, huh?"

"Sounds like a happy ending to me, Max."

But Max was looking back down the hallway toward Margot Hayes, who stood twenty-five paces away, her hands over her heart. A nurse had finally appeared in the doorway and, together, nurse and wife entered Ben's recovery room.

"I don't know, Meg. Let's not forget Amanda. Anyway you cut it, three minus one is still only two."

"Yeah, I guess that's what it comes down to, huh?"

"Oh, I don't know," Max countered. "I guess you could also say that one plus one is two."

Maybe there's hope for you yet, Max Jansen, a contented Meg thought. Maybe there's hope for you yet.